"A *fine* book, beautifully written, with marvelously drawn characters, and historically accurate in its main events. A poignant tale."
—ROBERTA GELLIS
Author of A *Shimmering Splendor*

Bridget—Both earthly and goddesslike, her destiny is to continue her sacred bloodline. . . .

Raoul—War takes him through the gates of hell, pushing him to betray the bloody cause of the Cross and become an exile. . . .

Simon—Strong, proud, fierce, and unbreakable, he is a born warrior who will stop at nothing to ensure victory. . . .

Magda—As Bridget's daughter, she accepts her special gifts, aware that her heritage has made her dangerously vulnerable to persecution. . . .

"Stunning stuff—this is what historical novels are about."
—DR. COLIN GROVES

Also by Elizabeth Chadwick
Published by Ballantine Books:

THE WILD HUNT
THE RUNNING VIXEN
SHIELDS OF PRIDE

DAUGHTERS
OF THE GRAIL

Elizabeth Chadwick

BALLANTINE BOOKS • NEW YORK

Copyright © 1993 by Elizabeth Chadwick

All rights reserved under International and Pan-American Copyright Conventions. Published in the United States by Ballantine Books, a division of Random House, Inc., New York. Originally published in Great Britain by Michael Joseph, an imprint of Penguin Books Ltd. in 1993.

Library of Congress Catalog Card Number: 95–94039

ISBN 0-345-38840-2

Based on an idea by Tony Sutcliffe

Manufactured in the United States of America

First American Edition: August 1995

10 9 8 7 6 5 4 3 2 1

ACKNOWLEDGMENTS

On this page I want to say thank you to all the people who helped me in writing *Daughters of the Grail*. Indeed, without them, *Daughters* would not have been written at all. Tony Sutcliffe first set me the challenge and introduced me to the triumph and tragedy of the Cathars. My research was aided by my good friend Alison King, and our discussions over numerous cups of coffee provided me with valuable insights into my characters.

I would like to thank my husband, Roger, for standing over mountains of ironing without complaint whenever the need has arisen. Greater love hath no man. I have also appreciated the support of my parents who have come to the rescue with child-care services and freshly baked cakes when there have been more tasks in the day than I have hands.

I owe many thanks to my agent, Carole Blake, who has been with me every step of the way—usually ahead, smoothing the ground. A special thank you goes to Pamela Strickler and Lesley Malin Helm at Ballantine. *Daughters* is as much their project as mine. Together we have planted, nurtured, and pruned. I am proud to have them as editors, and humble, too.

CHAPTER ONE

The Black Mountains of the High Languedoc, Summer 1207

BRIDGET KNEW THAT her mother was dying. The golden life force that should have shone steadily within and around Magda's body was only a weak, guttering spark, and when Bridget placed her hands upon her mother's injuries, there was no response to the surge of her healing energy.

Outside the mountain cave in which they were sheltering, a summer storm raged across the High Languedoc. Bridget felt the lightning tearing through her body, saw it through her hot, tired lids. She had been born during just such a storm, and the power of the lightning was in her veins. It was a sacred life-gift, a manifestation of the forces of the One Light. But tonight it came to take her mother.

"Don't leave me," Bridget whispered in a tear-choked voice. "Please don't go; I'm so afraid." She bent her cheek to her mother's hand. The fingertips were crusted with blood, only raw flesh where trimmed pink nails had once existed. The slender wrists wore weeping red bracelets where manacles had abraded the skin. Those wounds would have healed in time, but upon Magda's forehead was the terrible, mortal injury where the priests had branded her to the bone with the sign of the cross she had refused to kiss. *Witch and heretic,* they had called her; *foul devil's whore.* Her poor mother, who had never done or wished anyone harm in her entire life.

Her mother's smudged eyelids fluttered and lifted. "You have many years to live," she whispered, "and a duty to fulfill; you are the last of my line." Her throat moved as she struggled

1

to swallow. Bridget quickly helped her to sip from a small horn cup containing an herbal tisane.

Magda drank a little and relaxed. Her gray eyes were wider now and brighter, all her remaining life force concentrated in their gaze. "You must find a consort when the moon time is right to seed your womb. That is the way it has been since the great stone circles were raised, before the holy thorn was planted."

"But Uncle Chretien . . ." Bridget started to say, and cast an involuntary glance over her shoulder toward the dark cave mouth.

"Your uncle will not stand in your way on that matter. He is a Cathar, and for him it is necessary to be celibate; but he knows that it can never be that way for you." Magda's eyelids drooped and her breathing grew shallow and rapid.

Bridget listened for the sound of footsteps outside, but there was only wind hissing through the stunted trees on the mountainside and rain lashing the ground. Her uncle Chretien and his companion Matthias had gone to find decent shelter for the horses against the violence of the storm. There was not enough room in the cave, but Matthias had seen a derelict goat shed lower down the slope. Although it was closer to the village, no one was likely to be abroad to see them in this weather.

The fire she had kindled earlier was dying, and her mother's hand resting in hers was as cold as ice. Bridget set more firewood on the embers. Closing her eyes, she reached down inside herself and drew forth her life energy in a lightning-bright thread. Flames surged beneath the outspread hand she passed over the fire, leaping as if on strings to her command. The strange animal paintings on the cave walls were given the illusion of life by the clambering flare of light and contrast of shadow. Bridget knew that if she sank deeper into her trance, she would see small, olive-skinned men marking the walls with fire-blackened sticks, painting pictures of their prey to invoke success in the hunt. She would hear their sacred chant and taste the smoke of their fire, burning where hers now burned.

Flame to flame, she felt the connection before she withdrew her hand and turned once more to her mother. "It is very hard," she said softly, and heard her own voice echo off the walls with the forlorn note of a lost child.

Magda lay more motionless than the paintings. Although her mother's lips did not move, words entered Bridget's mind with precise clarity. "The path of our bloodline has never been otherwise. Always you will find stones cast in your path, but if you turn them over, you will find the love and courage to endure."

A tremendous flash of lightning sundered the night, shaking stones loose and rattling them down the mountainside. Thunder crashed deafeningly overhead, and as the echoes surged around the cave, Bridget felt the warmth of a kiss upon her cheek and then on her brow in tender blessing.

"Mother!" Bridget's anguished cry mingled with the tail of the thunder and outlasted it, but Magda did not respond. Her abused, exhausted body lolled in the slackness of death—an abandoned shell. Bridget whimpered softly, then stifled the sound behind compressed lips. Her mother was with the One Light now, was free of pain and persecution. The only reason to weep was for herself.

She kissed the bruised, gaunt cheek and gently removed a silver amulet from around her mother's neck. She hung it around her own neck where it clinked softly against an identical token—an incised design of a six-pointed star within which a dove rose out of a chalice. On the obverse, a spear stood upright in a cauldron, the weapon's tip rippled with lightning.

At the cave entrance she heard the sound of masculine voices raised against the storm. One was a rich baritone, full of depth and confidence. The other, lighter voice had a slightly exotic, Eastern accent. The two men pushed through the bushes concealing the cave entrance and entered within. Their conversation ceased as their eyes fell upon Bridget. Her uncle Chretien drew his breath softly through his teeth, and his gaze went from her to the still form on the pallet by the fire.

"May she walk in the light," he said compassionately. "She had a perfect spirit."

His smaller, gray-bearded companion approached Magda's body and crouched on his heels. His right hand was badly mutilated, missing two fingers and a thumb, the stumps a puckered, angry red. He touched Magda's glossy black braid with his remaining fingers.

"She was still so young," he said in a voice that was close to breaking. "They should have taken me instead."

"They would take us all if given the opportunity." A deep weariness in his fine, dark eyes, Chretien shook rain from his old cloak. Then he opened his arms to Bridget, and with a small, wounded cry, she ran into them, pressing herself against the smoky wool smell of his garments, seeking the illusion of sanctuary. She had always known that the path she trod was lonely and dangerous, but never had she felt it so keenly as now.

Later, after she had washed and prepared her mother's body for burial, Bridget sat before the fire, a cup of fortified wine between her hands, and looked through the smoke at the two men who were now her only family—Matthias the scholar and Chretien, her father's younger brother. For six years she and her mother had been traveling with them, visiting the villages to preach the Cathar way and offer healing and comfort to the sick. As their fame had grown, so had the hostility of the Roman church, to whom Catharism was a cancerous heresy that must be cut from existence at all costs.

Her father had been of the Cathar persuasion in his last years—a searcher, never able to find what he was seeking, even when he dwelt in the shadow of the Cornish stone circles with her mother. When Bridget was ten years old, he had fallen over the side of a merchant ship and drowned. She and her mother had set out to take the news to his family. They traveled in the footsteps of the Goddess to Brigantium, which was now called Compostela and dedicated to a male saint, and on through the high mountain ranges into the land of Oc. Finally they came to the town of Béziers where Chretien lived. The Cathars had been able to move openly then, without fear of persecution from the Church of Rome. Now it was a different matter. Her gaze, somber slate-gray, flickered to the body of her mother, enshrouded in a threadbare blanket. If the songbird was killed, there was nothing left but an empty cage.

"When the storm has passed we must leave," she announced to the two men. "There is nothing for us here."

Chretien shook his head. "Where will we go? Only the remote high places like Roquefixade and Montségur are safe these days."

As he spoke the name of Montségur, a fleeting vision of a castle engulfed by fire flickered across Bridget's inner eye. She saw a night sky crowned in lightning and heard the cries of hundreds of people raised in suffering. "No, not Montségur," she said quickly. "Not yet. We still have many friends who will give us shelter and protection."

"And I must obtain fresh parchment and quills," Matthias said. Unconsciously he rubbed his mutilated right hand with the fingertips of his left.

Chretien nodded, but his lips were pursed. Turning to Bridget, he said, "I would be happier if you stayed in the mountains. There are too many prying eyes in the towns of the plain."

"No," Bridget answered resolutely. "It was my mother's dying wish that I continue our bloodline. I know that if I retreat from the world now, I will not find the father of my child."

Chretien looked into the fire without speaking. Bridget sighed softly. Long ago, after much heart-searching and discussion, her mother and Chretien had agreed to differ in their views on procreation. To the Cathars, begetting a child was the trapping of an immortal spirit in sullied flesh. To her mother's more ancient religion, it was a sacrament. She knew that Chretien would not press her, and in equal respect she would not seek to persuade him of the necessity of her cause.

In the lingering silence, another image blinked across her mind. This time it was of a vigorous, sturdy woman in her middle years, red-cheeked with heavy braids of iron-gray hair coiled above her ears, and a huge, toothy smile. "We will go to the lady Geralda at Lavaur!" she said decisively. "She's a staunch Cathar and she was very kind to us last time we visited."

Chretien raised his eyes from the fire and, after a moment, nodded approval. "Matthias?"

Bridget heard Matthias's hesitant agreement, and knew that with or without the men's approval, she had to go to Lavaur. The town itself was not important, for she could grasp nothing of its essence in her vision, but the road leading there was. Something tugged at her core, twisting and tightening her soft inner organs as if the child her mother desired her to bear were already kicking in her womb. She pressed her hands to her flat stomach and the feeling vanished, but not the certainty that the road she chose now was all-important to the future.

CHAPTER TWO

DISPLAYING A PRUDENCE beyond his twenty-one years, Raoul de Montvallant covered the Venetian goblet with his palm and shook his head at the squire who leaned to replenish it. It was not that he disliked the wine (which was superb); indeed, on a different occasion he would have drunk as deeply as every other young man present, but tonight he had good reason for remaining sober.

He slid a restless glance at that reason—his bride, Claire, to whom he had been betrothed since childhood. He had last seen her when she had a gappy smile and mud upon the hem of her gown from playing in the bailey puddles after a summer rainstorm. Her smile today displayed nearly perfect white teeth, a slight overlap of the front two being the only flaw. The hem of her gown was embroidered not with mud, but with lozenges of gold thread glittering against a background of sumptuous green velvet.

Her hair, brushed down to proclaim her virginity, glowed like silk on fire, and Raoul wanted to run his fingers through its ripples to discover if it was as soft as it looked. For the briefest instant she returned his glance, her eyes the bright brown of new chestnuts, then her lashes swept down, leaving him the unrevealing half-moon of creamy eyelid and smooth brow.

He tried to think of something to say that would not seem trite or banal, but found himself tongue-tied by the beautiful young woman who bore no resemblance at all to the skinny girl he remembered. The knowledge that they would soon be alone together, in bed and naked, made his throat dry up.

6

Although he had no vast experience of women, Raoul was by no means innocent. Occasionally he had visited the *maisons lupanardes* of Toulouse, where one of the whores had taken a fancy to teach him that there was more to pleasure than the brief, rough simplicity of his first encounters. Claire, however, *was* innocent, a virgin, unlikely to help him if he fumbled. She was also very desirable, and he was hot for her to the point where he doubted his own control. He reached for his cup, remembered that it was empty for that very reason, and rested his hand flat on the table instead.

"Champing at the bit, eh?" laughed Father Otho, the priest who had officiated at their marriage in the castle's dusty, neglected chapel. "I don't blame you—I wouldn't mind taking her for a ride myself!" He bit down on an apple comfit, his face stout-cheeked and bloated like the stuffed boar's head that had been presented during an earlier course of the feast.

Raoul clenched his fist and thought about punching it into the priest's overfed face. Father Otho was a lying, lecherous glutton, caring for his own pocket and pleasure above the needs of his flock, who, through his slovenly mismanagement, were few and indifferent. "What a pity you are sworn to celibacy," Raoul said acidly, his blue eyes hard and bright.

"Yes, isn't it?" The priest's chuckle was interrupted by a loud belch. Pouched in the flesh of easy living, his expression was distinctly salacious as he smacked his lips. "Still, we all have to make some sacrifices in life, don't we? That's it, boy, fill it up, fill it up!" He gestured imperatively to the wooden-faced squire, then raised the brimming goblet and leaned toward Raoul's father. "A magnificent cellar you keep, my lord!"

Berenger de Montvallant afforded Otho a tepid smile, but his eyes were cold with disgust.

"And he'll drink it dry before the night is out," Raoul muttered as the cleric's attention settled on one of the younger, prettier maidservants attending the bride.

"If he weren't my second cousin and I hadn't promised his father I'd give him a living here, I'd have turned him off long ago." Berenger rubbed his palm across his freshly trimmed beard and paused to tug fiercely at the hairs salting the point of his chin. "Is it any cause for wonder that the Cathars flour-

ish among us when lard-tubs like him rule the clergy? Jesu,
just look at him, stuffing his face again."

Raoul's eyes flickered to the pudgy hand crawling over a
dish of sugared almonds, watched it convey them to the wet
lips and cram them in the greedy mouth. His gorge rose. He
looked away down the hall and saw that more guests had
arrived—three pilgrims, their cloaks and broad-brimmed hats
worn and dusty. He watched Alein, his father's understeward,
find them a place to sit among the crowded trestles at the
lower end of the hall. There were two men, one in his forties,
the other about ten years older. Seating herself between them
and thanking Alein with a smile was a young woman. Framed
by wimple and veil, her face was one of sculptured beauty—
not flawless, but totally arresting, as if lit by an inner glow.
Raoul studied her curiously, wondering where she had come
from and where she was going. Pilgrims occasionally stopped
at Montvallant on their way to Toulouse, but usually they
claimed hospitality at the church in Villemur.

The young woman was hidden from his sight as a serving
maid leaned across the trestle to dish out bread and wine. He
craned and ducked his neck, trying to keep her in view. The
musicians who had been playing softly through the various
courses of the feast changed their tempo, and the lively strains
of a traditional jig filled the hall. Berenger nudged him.

"Are you not going to dance with your bride?" he teased.
"People are waiting for you to lead her out."

Raoul was immediately aware of the expectant stares of the
wedding guests and could see that they were wondering why he
was remaining in his place when it was traditional for the newly
married couple to take the floor first. Quickly he rose and, turning to Claire, extended his hand to assist her to her feet.

She blushed delicately and placed her slender fingers in his.
The new gold of her wedding ring shone like a promise. Raoul
forgot the pilgrim woman as he led his bride onto the floor
where a space had been cleared for those who wished to
dance, forgot everything but the feel of her lissome body
lightly touching and leaving his as they stepped and turned
in the age-old patterns of celebration.

"More bread, Bridget?" asked Chretien, offering his niece
the brimming basket of small loaves.

"I couldn't eat another morsel!" Leaning her elbows upon the trestle, she watched the dancers with wistful eyes. Theirs was another world, one that she could glimpse but never belong to. Part of her longed for the colors, the revelry and carefree exuberance that cared for nothing beyond the moment. Sometimes it was very hard to be who and what she was.

The dancers swirled toward her, the young bridegroom trapped in a group of other young men. He was laughing as he tried without any great effort to escape their clutches. Bridget's breath caught at his proud, masculine beauty, at the magnetism of his vigorous young body and the joy she could feel surging through him. Her body responded like a plucked harp string. She dropped her gaze to the board and stared at a dark wine stain on the wood, her heart thumping painfully, her nerve endings raw. His eyes were bluer than the barring on a jay's wing.

The entire hall suddenly erupted with cheers and shouts, approving whistles, and cries of encouragement. She saw the bridegroom being borne away toward the tower stairs, still snared by his comrades.

"What's happening?" Bridget asked her neighbor on the trestle.

Her gaze not leaving the jostling bunch near the stairs for one moment, the woman half-turned. "What's going to happen, you mean!" she chuckled. " 'Tis the bedding ceremony. Time for Lord Raoul and his bride to become better acquainted."

"Oh." Bridget nodded. That was why she had felt his vigor just now, but of course, tonight it already had its focus. The new wife, surrounded by other women, was being led from the dais to a different set of stairs. She had the graceful gait and coloring of a doe, and the same startled, shy expression.

Silently, with determination, Bridget wished the couple well. Envy was no part of her upbringing or of the Cathar creed by which her guardians lived, but tonight she felt its sting.

"What's the matter?" Chretien leaned toward her, concerned.

Bridget forced a smile and shook her head. How could she say that her body was tingling with the desire to be in the bride's place tonight? "I am overfaced by all this bounty," she said, "and very tired. It's past time I sought my pallet. . . . No, finish your wine. I'd like a little space alone first."

Chretien subsided, but there was a frown between his heavy brows. "You would tell us if there was anything wrong?"

"Of course I would," she said a little too brightly, and hurried away from his shrewd scrutiny.

Outside, the warm evening air was scented with hot charcoal and cooking smells from the extra braziers burning in the courtyard. Moths blundered to their deaths in the flames of wall torches. The sound of lute and pipe, the thrusting beat of tabors, followed Bridget relentlessly, pounding through her groin in dull waves of longing. She stopped to lean her forehead against the cool stone of the castle wall, and breathed deeply.

"Bridget? Bridget my dear?"

She turned quickly to see a tall woman hurrying toward her, tripping over her blue silk gown in her haste, her headdress slightly askew. "Geralda?" Bridget took a step forward and was engulfed in an overpowering, matronly hug.

"I have just seen Chretien and Matthias in the hall, and they said I would find you out here. Let me look at you!" Still holding Bridget by the shoulders, Geralda of Lavaur examined her thoroughly. "So much like your mother," Geralda said, and tears brightened in her dark hazel eyes. "Chretien told me she had been killed. I'm so sorry."

"She is one with the Light." Bridget's own vision was suddenly blurred. "She was caught healing a sick woman in one of the hill villages by two traveling friars and put to the torture." Her voice faltered as she whispered, "I miss her so much."

Geralda's embrace closed around her again, maternal and comforting. Bridget shuddered, and gave vent to a brief storm of tears while Geralda held and soothed her like a child. Sniffing, drawing herself together, Bridget made a determined effort and pulled away.

"Did my uncle tell you that we were on our way to you at Lavaur?"

"Indeed he did, and you will be most welcome. I have some new manuscripts I want Matthias to look at, and the people will want to hear Chretien preach and to come to you for healing. The friars will not dare to interfere with me!" Her eyes glittered with a warhorse ferocity that was emphasized by her prominent teeth.

Bridget knew that Geralda had every right to be confident, for she had a brother, Aimery, who was one of the foremost warriors in the South. Every right, and yet the flickering torchlight made dark hollows in Geralda's cheekbones, turning her face into a skull. Shivering, Bridget started to walk toward the small shelter that she and her guardians had pitched against the bailey wall near the main gates. Her feeling of foreboding increased as she and Geralda walked past the well housing. In a moment the vision would come in all its dreadful clarity. She did not want to see Geralda's end, and slammed shut those particular doors in her mind. As a distraction, she asked about the wedding.

Geralda was only too pleased to hold forth. "I've known Raoul since he was a babe in arms," she crooned. "Such blue eyes and fair hair. Back in the Montvallant lineage there was Norse blood, and every now and again it surfaces. He's my godson, you know . . . or he was when I was a Catholic. He and Claire have been betrothed almost since birth, but they seem delighted with each other, don't you think?"

Bridget murmured agreement. The closed doors in her mind reflected the image of Raoul de Montvallant's golden virility and the doe-eyed beauty of his bride. Entwined limbs upon cool linen sheets. Feverish body heat. As Geralda gossiped merrily on, Bridget watched the moon rise above the castle walls, illuminating the sky in a wide halo of silver, and in its glow, saw a man and a woman, light and darkness and fire.

CHAPTER THREE

SHIVERING WITH NERVES, Claire looked around the bedchamber where she was to spend her wedding night. The room was opulent with comfort and color. Tapestries of scarlet, blue, and gold adorned the walls and kept the drafts at bay, and where there were no tapestries, the walls were painted with tableaux of everyday life, pastoral scenes of sheep husbandry and vine cultivation.

The great bed of walnut wood—a platform for the rituals of conception, birth, and death—brutally dominated her awareness. It was magnificently adorned for its various purposes. Hangings of blue and scarlet brocade, stiff with embroidery upon the theme of the Virgin and Unicorn, were draped at each corner. Claire found her gaze becoming fixated upon the coverlet of dark blue sarcenet worked with stars of thread-of-silver to represent the night sky. The maids folded it back to reveal a bolster and sheets of crisp, white linen awaiting the inscription of her virgin blood. If her legs had not turned to water, she would have run from the room.

Over the hearth, a maid had set an infusion of wine and spices to simmer. Beatrice, Raoul's mother, drew Claire to the fire and bade her stand on a mouflon rug while she was undressed by the women wedding guests.

"This is a happy day for me." Beatrice hugged Claire and kissed her warmly. "I am more than proud to call you daughter."

Claire returned the embrace, her stomach clenching into a hundred knots. She liked Beatrice, but she was no substitute for her own mother, Alianor, who was going to ride away tomorrow. Claire's anchor was now supposed to be her new family, but she felt terrified, as if she had been cast adrift and no one had noticed.

The thought of Raoul made Claire so queasy that she had to compress her lips. What were they going to say to each other? Or were they going to talk at all? She heard the maids giggling as they scattered the bed with herbs to promote fertility. Claire was not ignorant. Alianor had taken her aside several weeks before the wedding to explain all about the joys and duties of being a wife. Besides, she had often seen animals mating in the yard and in the fields. Once, in the stables, she had caught a groom with his chausses round his knees about to enter a kitchen maid, so she was aware that men were no different from dogs or bulls when aroused. Her mother said that the act was supposed to be a pleasure, but Claire could not imagine how. And if there was supposed to be blood on the sheet in the morning, surely there would be pain?

The gauze veil and chaplet of stiff, gold flowers were unpinned from her hair, and her mother took a boar's-bristle brush to the chestnut-gold tresses to burnish them to an even more glorious shine. "Child, you are beautiful," said Alianor mistily. "I'm so proud of you. I wish your father had been alive to see your wedding day."

Claire swallowed, unable to respond. Usually she remembered her father, dead these past five years, with a warm, sad affection, but tonight she had room in her mind for little but her own fear. Obediently she raised and lowered her arms to the commands of the women, and watched the garments gather upon the clothing pole until she was naked. Near the fire it was not cold, but her skin was covered in small goose bumps, and her rosy-brown nipples rose ruched and stiff to crown her breasts.

Softly in the background, two musicians played a duet upon lute and harp. Cool silk slithered over her shoulders as she was urged into a loose bed-robe, and her hair was rearranged over it in a sheaf of glowing color.

Her teeth chattered and her body was numb with fear. People spoke to her, but her heart thundered in her ears, and she could not hear what they said. And then the door burst open. With the dull resignation of a trapped animal, she watched the bridegroom's party push rowdily into the room. Raoul, naked beneath his furred green mantle, was jostled in their midst. There was much noisy laughter and good-humored jesting. Raising her lids, Claire saw that Raoul's color was high, and that the smile on his face was as fixed and nervous as her own. Their eyes met across the room, and he made a small, rueful gesture. For an instant, Claire responded. Then her courage failed and she lowered her gaze.

Beatrice pressed a gilded cup of hot wine into her hands. "Drink and take heart," she whispered, giving another reassuring hug.

Claire set her lips to the cup and sipped mechanically. The taste of cinnamon and hot red grape flowed over her tongue. Then Raoul was beside her. Taking the cup from her hands, he set his lips to the place where she had drunk, his arm lightly upon her waist.

Cheers and calls of encouragement, bawdily good-natured,

were hurled by the young men. Claire's face burned even as Raoul's palm seemed to be burning through the thin silk robe into her spine. He turned her on his arm to face the gathering.

Father Otho elbowed his way forward to perform the benediction that would free the couple from public scrutiny, that would cleanse and purify their marriage bed and bless any fruit that came of it. He was drunk, his black eyes moistly glittering and unfocused.

"Well, well," he said, leering at Claire, "it hardly seems a moment since you were a tight bud on the stem, and now behold the open rose, ready to be well and truly plucked!" He pressed the side of his nose with an unsteady forefinger.

Anger and shame welled up in Claire's breast. Light jesting, she could accept; it was all part of nuptial tradition. Every bride and groom were teased on their wedding eve, but not by the priest, his face congested with drink and lust. Raoul started to lunge, but was restrained by his mother's grip on his arm.

Berenger de Montvallant, his swarthy complexion dull red, said through his teeth, "I suggest you confine yourself to the words of the benediction."

Except for the continuing harmony of the musicians in the background, the room was suddenly very quiet. The priest tried to draw himself up, but his feet were unsteady and he lurched sideways into one of the guests. "No sense of humor," he muttered, pushing himself precariously upright. "Can't take a jest."

Otho thrust out his lower lip like a sulky child, but prudently approached the bed and started to mutter the blessing. His speech was slurred and the Latin words not in their correct order or form. He flicked holy water indiscriminately around and presented Claire and Raoul with a cross to kiss.

Claire felt sick. Father Otho was breathing as stertorously as a mastiff, and the rank stench of his sweat was overpowering. She would not have been surprised to see the tip of a forked tail twitching beneath the skirts of his habit. Unable to bring herself to touch the cross with her lips, she kissed the air above it. Raoul, too, kissed the air, his face taut with leashed temper. The gold clasp on his cloak flashed and flashed with his rapid breathing.

Father Otho hiccuped to a stop. A belch erupted. "You can get to work now, lad," he chuckled. "Let's have a good bloody sheet to display in the morning, eh?" His lewd amusement terminated abruptly in a horrified squawk as Raoul seized him by the throat of his food-stained habit, and twisted him off his feet.

"A pity you won't live to see it!" he snarled, tightening his grip.

Otho's complexion darkened alarmingly. A rasping noise emerged from his throat, and the veins in his forehead bulged. After an interval, Berenger reluctantly intervened, trying to prize his son's fist from the priest's windpipe. "Let him go, Raoul; you don't want to sully your wedding night with murder."

"Don't I?" Raoul said furiously, but relaxed his grip. Flexing and clenching his hand, he stared at the semiconscious man puddled at his feet.

Berenger gestured peremptorily to two gaping servants. "Take Father Otho outside and leave him there to sober up," he commanded. "As near to the midden heap as his behavior dictates."

"Yes, my lord." Grim satisfaction on their faces, the two men lifted the priest and lumbered him out of the bedchamber, carelessly bumping his head against the wall.

Berenger made apologies all around, his color still high. "Time, I think, and well past time to leave bride and groom in peace," he said gruffly, embracing first Raoul and then Claire with anxious tenderness. "You must not let him spoil tonight for you."

"No, Papa." Raoul's smile was wooden and contrived. Claire shivered. Her bones seemed to be made of ice.

One by one the guests wished them well and departed. Raoul went to the musicians still softly playing in the background, and with a quiet word and a handful of silver, paid and dismissed them. The silence after they had gone terrified Claire. She sipped at her now cold wine.

To keep herself from panicking, she went to the flagon the maid had left warming on the hearth, and tossing the cold dregs on the fire, refilled the goblet. The hiss and splutter of evaporating liquid shocked the silence. Half-hypnotized, Claire stared into the jagged turrets of flame. Heat scorched her face, and when she tasted the wine it was like drinking the heart of the fire. She tried to move her feet, but discovered that she had no control over them. Nor could she tear her eyes from the gashes of light and the prowling darkness behind.

Raoul returned from barring the door and was horrified to see her so close to the flames. Crying a warning that she would set her robe alight, he hastened to draw her away. Claire blinked up at him through a hundred mirrored tongues of flame and put her hand to her dizzy forehead.

"Claire?" He held her shoulders and looked anxiously into her face.

"I'm sorry." She lowered her hand. Her head felt light, and yet at the same time it seemed far too heavy for her neck to support. "It has been such a long day, that is all."

"In more ways than one." Raoul grimaced. "I swear I would have felt no remorse at strangling Father Otho."

The memory of the way the priest had defiled her wedding chamber when he should have been blessing it added to her tension and weariness. An aching lump swelled in her throat, impossible to swallow down. She bit back a sob, but the effort jerked her shoulders and gave her away.

"Claire, don't, I cannot bear to see you weep," he said, his own throat working. He pulled her against him, offering the comfort of his strong, warm body. Claire hid her face within his cloak and stifled her sobs against its prickly softness.

"I had a feeling of dread when I looked into the fire just now," she whispered against the steady thud of his heart, "as if the whole world was burning and I could do nothing to prevent it. I used to have nightmares about fire when I was little. Once a priest came to our castle and preached a sermon about the flames of hell that awaited all heretics. My mother said that I did not sleep properly for months afterward."

"Priests!" Raoul snarled the word softly. "I know for certain that hell must be full of them!" He pressed his lips to her herb-scented hair and nuzzled lightly down to her fire-hot temple. Cupping her face in his hands like a chalice, he kissed her salty cheek, the corner of her mouth, and finally the softness of her lips. "Jesu," he said with a catch in his voice, "you're so beautiful."

His eyes were bright and narrow, his breathing very fast. Claire felt as if she were about to be devoured. The taut hunger in his expression frightened her, but at the same time a strange new excitement began to tingle in her breasts and loins.

As he murmured reassurances, his trembling hands moved upon her body. He continued to kiss her, lightly exploring her eyelids, cheeks, and chin, nibbling her throat, pausing to suck upon the pulsing vein beneath her ear until she shivered and threw her head back. Stealthily he reached to the tie on her bed-robe, and then his hands were inside, gliding upon her naked skin, drawing her hip to hip against him.

Claire gasped as she felt the thrust of his manhood, hot as a branding iron against her belly. She wriggled, trying to escape, but he held her still, one hand upon her buttocks, the other soothingly stroking her hair and the valley of her spine.

"Don't struggle," he pleaded. "Dear Jesu, I'm as frightened as you are."

Some of Claire's tension abated at his admission. Wide-eyed, she stared up at him, holding her breath.

"I promise, I swear to God, I'll try not to hurt you," he said hoarsely. "Please, I want tonight to be pleasurable for you."

Claire swallowed. "I want that, too," she answered, her voice barely audible.

They stayed as they were for a moment longer, locked together in nervous uncertainty. Then Raoul swept her up in his arms and carried her to the bed.

CHAPTER FOUR

ON THE HIGH, silent walls of Montvallant's battlements, Bridget filled her lungs with air that was still night-cold and, facing the place where the sun would soon rise, sat down cross-legged. The sky beyond the merlons gleamed like the pearly interior of an oyster shell. Softly, under her breath, she began to chant the sacred words taught to her by her mother and by her mother before that, the legacy of an unbroken female lineage more than a thousand years old.

As her voice rose and fell, the surrounding walls dissolved away. Light pulsed around her, changing hue, flowing into and filling her until her whole being was like a cup, brimming with the emanation of the power. A single spear of sunlight burst through the gap in the merlon where she sat waiting. The pain was intense. Liquid fire consumed her body until she was brighter than the light itself. She became a burning disk suspended above it, circling like a wheel, her eyesight that of a cruising eagle looking down on the tiny figures below.

The sky was black and a man was being nailed upon a cross. Bridget felt excruciating pain as the nails drove through his feet and wrists. At the foot of the cross she saw two weeping women, one young and dark-haired, the other older but with a bone structure that defied her years. A child clung to the rumpled skirts of the younger one, a little girl with eyes the crystal color of Bridget's own. Her name was Magda, daughter of Mary Magdalene, granddaughter of Mary, and tiny niece of the man hung in suffering on the Romans' tree. Even if Bridget had not known this through the ancient traditions of her bloodline, passed down from mother to daughter, she would have felt her belonging in the very marrow of her bones.

The wheel spun, gathering momentum and brightness. There was fire, harsh with smoke, and within it the cries of men and the bitter wailing of women and children. The flames fed upon blood. Instinctively Bridget recoiled, for the heat was so fierce that it seemed to singe her brows and hair. She was no longer one with the sky, but one with the fire—with all the people burning in the fire. A soundless scream burst from her lips as she fought to tear free.

Through the flames the young bridegroom strode toward her, a sword in his hand, his expression torn with a terrible grief. He was so close that she could see the black chevronels on his gold surcoat, the tawny stubble grizzling his jaw, and the tears blinding his vivid blue eyes.

Behind him, weeping, reaching out to him, was his wife, her long, chestnut-red hair straggling free of its braid, her face smudged with bruises. The fire roared up, sundering them completely, and he came on toward Bridget until he was kneeling before her. Their eyes met and she felt the shock pierce her body like a thrust of burning steel. He laid his sword across her palms and she closed her hands over it until the twin edges cut her flesh and her blood trickled down the engraved fuller in a thin, scarlet thread. As the sun blazed in full glory over the horizon, she saw what was to be, and her high, wild cry soared from the battlements to strike the dawn and shatter into a hundred echoes.

In the bridal chamber, Raoul tossed and moaned, beset by a vivid dream. Images of fire and the glitter of weapons flashed across his mind. He heard screams of men in triumph and agony, the terrified squealing of horses, and knew that he was fighting for his life. His sword arm was aching so fiercely that he could scarcely parry the blows raining down on him, and that in itself was strange. He had never tasted battle, let alone fought in one to the point of exhaustion.

A knight was riding him down. White horse, white surcoat splashed by a blood-bright cross, white light glaring from the edge of the sword as the horseman swung it to cut. The blade sliced through Raoul's shield like a knife slicing a loaf. The world darkened, and through that darkness a woman's voice sought him, calling, calling, pulling him toward the light. He saw her in the distance, black hair flowing, and hands outstretched. He answered her beckoning, compelled from the root of his soul, and suddenly she was facing him, her eyes like gray crystals, cutting him until he bled.

"Raoul, in God's name, wake up! Raoul!"

His scream of terror echoed in his skull as he tore himself away from the dream woman and surfaced wide-eyed into the sun-flooded brightness of his marriage chamber. A voice still called to him, but it was soft with anxiety. Chestnut hair trailed over and tickled his naked chest. Claire's worried face hung over him.

"You were dreaming, my lord."

"Dreaming!" He shuddered. "God's wounds, I've never

been so frightened in my life!" He covered his eyes with the palm of one hand. He was soaked with sweat, the sheet clinging to his body like a shroud. Sunlight filtered through the waxed linen across the window arch, and he could hear his mother's doves cooing on the ledge outside. Claire was tousled and beautiful beside him, but he felt like a cat that has had its fur ruffled the wrong way by a careless hand.

"What was your dream about?"

"I don't remember, only that there was a battle and a woman with long, dark hair." A shiver rippled through him. "Jesu, I feel as though my veins are filled with ice."

"Perhaps it is because of what happened last night?" she suggested.

He turned his head on the pillow and frowned. "Last night?"

Claire blushed beneath his scrutiny. There were many aspects to last night, not all of them unpleasant. "The priest, I mean, Father Otho. Perhaps you dreamed about fighting because of that."

"Perhaps," he said doubtfully. "There was a woman in pilgrim robes at one of the lower trestles who looked like the one in my dream."

The rumbling of wain wheels and the cheerful shout of a guard drifted up to the window as the castle gates were opened to the morning. He threw off the damp sheet and sat up. The linen beneath him bore brownish smears of dried blood, and his shoulders were sore where she had clawed him at the moment of defloration. Struck by a pang of guilt, he looked at Claire. She returned his scrutiny, full underlip caught in her teeth.

"I did not mean to be clumsy with you," he said awkwardly. "You might not see it as such, but it was a compliment to your beauty. I couldn't wait any longer."

The lip came free and tentatively curved. "It didn't hurt that much, only at first, then I forgot the pain." She blushed again.

"Then you are not upset?" Tempting his eye, the blush descended to the cleavage of her creamy breasts.

"No, I'm not upset . . ." and then as he leaned eagerly toward her, "a little sore, but I was assured by your mother and mine yesterday that it will quickly pass."

Although there was no distress in her voice or attitude, he

felt the slight tensing of her body, and immediately checked himself. Perhaps this morning it would be better to confine his admiration to gentle words and caresses rather than engaging in another bout of lovemaking. Time alone was what she required now, and then time with other women. And he needed to recover from the vivid violence of his dream.

He kissed her nose and the corner of her mouth in light affection, and left the bed to put on his clothes. "I'll send in your maid," he said over his shoulder as he went to the door.

Claire smiled gratefully and burrowed back down beneath the covers.

When Bridget descended from the battlements, Chretien was at the outer well, filling the water flasks for the journey to Lavaur, and Geralda was giving him directions and saying her farewells.

"I would travel with you myself," she said, her voice full of regret, "but I have promised Berenger and Beatrice to stay awhile at Montvallant. Besides," she added with a small, rueful smile, "the less attention you draw to yourselves, the better. Journeying in my company would hardly make you anonymous." Her bright gaze lit on Bridget, who had silently begun to help Matthias load their few belongings onto the horses.

"Perhaps you should stay here and rest for another day," she suggested. "The Montvallants are sympathetic toward Cathars, and Bridget looks exhausted."

Chretien opened his mouth.

"No," said Bridget quickly before he could speak. "It would not be wise. Two traveling friars are on their way to Montvallant." She strapped a pack efficiently to her mount's crupper. "I saw them in the sunrise." She could have added that the time was not yet ripe for herself and Raoul de Montvallant to meet in the flesh. There was moon-blood between her thighs, and the groom had his new bride to sow with seed. Mindful, however, of her uncle Chretien's Cathar morals, she kept that particular information to herself.

"You have had a vision?" Chretien's voice was sharp with concern.

Bridget sighed. "Several," she said, and gathering the reins, lifted herself into the saddle. "Are we ready?" Her mount circled, mouthing his bit. She stroked his neck and turned him toward the castle gates.

Chretien considered her thoughtfully as he mounted his own horse. Making the sign of the Cathar blessing over Geralda, he followed Bridget across the courtyard.

Matthias, bringing up the rear, paused as they came to a midden heap beside the gates. A priest lay snoring on his stomach, sodden as a joint of marinated meat. He shook his head sadly, but with no great surprise. "I doubt we'll ever be ready," he said heavily.

CHAPTER FIVE

IT WAS PEACEFUL beside the river. In the midday heat, the trees lining the banks of the Tarn provided welcome shade for the picnickers who rode down from the castle to take their ease by the water.

Most of the guests had departed Montvallant after the wedding breakfast and the traditional parading of the bloody bedsheet, but a few still remained. Geralda of Lavaur and her brother Aimery, as friends of long standing, had been invited by Raoul's parents to stay awhile longer. Aimery and Berenger shared a passion for hawking and were keen to fly and compare their birds, while Geralda and Beatrice had at least a year's worth of gossip to exchange.

A little apart from the older people, shielded from their scrutiny by a screen of willow and ash saplings, Claire shifted Raoul's head to pillow it more comfortably in her lap as he dozed in the heat. Her eyes dwelt upon the natural upward curve of his lips, his dense gold lashes, and the darker feathering of eyebrow. Pleasure and fear knotted her belly. Dear Jesu, how handsome he was, and all hers. It was as though her arms were being piled full of treasure and she fretted that one day she was going to lose her hold and see it break on the ground at her feet.

Her mother had left yesterday amid hugs and tears and promises of an early reunion. The parting had been desperately painful for Claire. She was only just seventeen, and although her new family had been nothing to her but patient and kind, everything was different, and there was so much to learn. It was very difficult not to be overwhelmed, and she welcomed this moment of solitude.

She leaned back against the tree supporting her spine and watched the sunlight weaving through the willow leaves, fashioning a trellis of green and gold; a fairy arbor for the lady and her knight. She heard Geralda's deep laugh, the splash of two squires horsing about in the river shallows, the high, joyous warble of a skylark.

Stealthily she reached toward a tall cluster of meadow foxtail growing near her tree and nipped off a stem between her sharp fingernails. Stifling a giggle, she dangled the plump tip of the seed-head over Raoul's nose. He twitched and raised a languid hand to brush away what he obviously thought was a hovering midge. Claire waited a moment and repeated the move, almost laughing as Raoul swept his palm across empty air. She clamped her lips tightly together, but not before a small sound had escaped. When Raoul appeared not to notice, she dangled her bait again, tickling, teasing.

With the speed of a striking snake, Raoul grabbed her arm, pulled her down and sideways, and rolled her beneath him, hands braceleting her wrists. A grin flashed. "What are you going to do now?"

Claire wriggled beneath him and angled her head, inviting a kiss. "Bargain for mercy?" she suggested breathlessly.

"Show me." He released her arms so that he could brace his weight and at the same time caress her body.

They kissed. Her hands slipped beneath his tunic and she spread her fingers upon the damp curve of his ribs. Warmth flooded her body and centered in her loins.

"You drive a hard bargain, my lord," she whispered against his mouth.

"I trust you to eventually soften my resolve." He nuzzled aside her wimple to nip a line from chin to throat, and reached within her surcoat to fondle her breast. In the midst of the embrace, Aimery's inquisitive Pyrenean hound—one hundred pounds of canine muscle and bone padded lavishly in white fur, its pink tongue dripping—wagged up to investigate the undulating tall grass. Raoul strove to shove the dog away, but it only jumped boisterously from side to side and barked loudly, desiring to play.

Aimery whistled sharply and the hound gamboled to heel, but the damage was done. Raoul sat up and squinted through the brilliant sunlight at his father's friend. Claire sat up, too, her face on fire as she smoothed her rumpled garments.

"I'm sorry, did I interrupt something?" Amusement glinted in Aimery's eyes. He ruffled the exuberant hound's coat.

Raoul glared. "You're not sorry at all. In fact, I'd not be surprised if you did it on purpose!" Reluctant humor edged the irritation in his voice.

Aimery grinned. "I can't stop Blanc from sniffing out game in the bushes when that is what he is trained to do." He tugged a folded hawking gauntlet out of his belt and drew it onto his fist. "You can do that all night if you've a mind. Let your poor wife alone awhile and come and look at the paces of my new hawk." He glanced over his shoulder. "Your father's waiting."

As the women watched the men ride away, hawks on their fists, the lady Geralda clucked her tongue and laughed. "Aimery's been desperate to show off that hawk to Berenger and Raoul. Never has such a bird existed before if you're to believe his praise! I tell you, he has driven me half-insane with all his talk of it!"

"So now you are wholly mad," said Beatrice mischievously. The remark made Claire widen her eyes and appraise her mother-in-law afresh.

Geralda's laugh this time was as full-throated and deep as a drum roll. "Beatrice de Montvallant, as the Good God is my witness, you should be ashamed of yourself, teasing an old woman!"

"I thought that Cathars did not lie," Beatrice retorted, eyes dancing. "You have but ten years advantage over me, and I have no intention of admitting dotage yet!"

"You've got Berenger to keep you on your toes and a new wife to tutor." She gave a quick smile to Claire. "All I've got is Aimery and his molting hawks!"

"You have your faith."

Geralda subsided at that, but her smile remained, deepening the seams at her eye corners. She glanced round at their attendants, but only Claire's maid Isabelle was within earshot. Geralda assessed the girl for a moment, then decisively produced a small, leather-bound book from the pouch on her belt. "Now that the men have gone, let me show you something," she said eagerly, her fingertips tracing the interlaced circles tooled in gold on the cover. "It's not that I'm hiding anything; Aimery's heard me read from this several times, but he's about as interested in it as I am in his hawks."

"So what is it?" Beatrice looked both curious and apprehensive.

"A book of ancient wisdom. A man in the town brought some manuscripts back from a pilgrimage to the Holy Land and bequeathed them to me when he died. I'm having them translated little by little into our own tongue by a Cathar scribe in my household. Here, listen." Opening the book at random, she read aloud in a clear, firm voice.

" 'To know oneself at the deepest level is to know God. Look for God by taking yourself as the starting point. Learn who it is within you who makes everything his own and says, "My God, my mind, my thought, my soul, my body." Learn the sources of sorrow, joy, love, and hate. If you investigate carefully these matters, you will find Him in yourself.'

"Is that not wonderful? And yet the church would deny us." Geralda's face grew hard and her voice angry. "If they could, they would burn every book not written in Latin and every book that disagrees with their narrow image of God." She snapped her fingers. "You don't need that useless priest of yours in order for your cry to reach God, Beatrice. Stand before Him as you are and He will hear you!"

"I have never tried to find God through Father Otho."

Beatrice shuddered. "That would be like drinking wine out of a filthy cup."

"Precisely!" Geralda struck the ground to emphasize her point, her eyes so bright that they looked almost feverish. "The priests serve the God of their own worldliness, not the one of simple truth! They tell us to believe in blood-guilt, in hell. If Jesus was sacrificed on the cross to take away our sins, why is there any need for a church? And if we are still sin-burdened, why was there a sacrifice at all? Such cruelty is not the conception of the God of Light." She shook her head from side to side. "Oh, I tell you, our consciences are ruled with fear and oppression, and when we try to free ourselves, we are punished."

"You are lecturing to those who sympathize." Beatrice laid a calming hand over Geralda's. "I have long been a believer in the Cathar faith, and I know that Claire comes from a family who welcome the Good Men into their home."

Claire murmured shy assent. Her mother often gave food and lodging to traveling Cathar priests, although she wondered why they should be called Good Men when there were so many women among them. From these itinerant preachers she had learned that the Cathar way to the truth was to live a pure and simple life—prayer, celibacy, and plain, meatless fare. The teachings of Christ were followed, but with the bare minimum of ritual. There was no Son of God, only the one bright light of the deity. His counterpart, the dark Rex Mundi, ruled the world and all its lusts, and was to be shunned.

Only the intensely committed took the final, austere vows, but there were other levels for those who believed in the Cathar way and were not yet prepared to subject themselves to the rigorous discipline required. Some only came to it on their deathbeds, others after they had raised families and outgrown the passions of youth.

Claire had often toyed with the thought of becoming one of the Cathar Perfecti. She had dreamed of it the way other young women mooned over the images of knights in burnished armor and troubadours with smouldering eyes. A dream, but close enough to reality that here, beside Geralda and Beatrice, she could feel its very breath.

"Would you read some more," she requested softly, "before the men return?"

The lady of Lavaur eyed her thoughtfully. "Nothing would give me greater pleasure, my dear." Geralda's own voice softened and Claire saw in her expression that she had recognized a kindred spirit.

On their return from the picnic, the women retired to the bower to freshen their hot faces and change their garments. The men, when finally they tore themselves away from the hawk mews, made do with stripping to their braies and swilling themselves at the trough in the yard. Claire stood on tiptoe in the window embrasure and peeked out on Raoul, admiring his loose-knit grace, and the play of his muscles beneath the diamond-sparkle of water droplets. There was a jug of marigolds near her arm, and plucking a flower, she tossed it down toward him. It missed, but the bright movement caught his eye, and glancing up, he smiled and blew her a kiss.

Humming softly to herself, still binding her chestnut plait with a length of gold braid, Claire descended the tower stairs to the hall. At their foot, she was startled to see her father-in-law in the company of two black-clad friars and a sour-faced Father Otho.

Claire gasped and took a step backward. Then she gathered herself sufficiently to dip a curtsy, cross herself, and lower her eyes.

"Daughter," greeted the older of the two friars in a cool, thin voice. A knotted scourge hung from his belt beside a set of wooden rosary beads. One of his thumbs was almost obliterated by a chunky gold seal ring inlaid with a gray cameo. She fastened her eyes on the ring, too frightened to look up lest he read the guilt of heresy in her face.

Berenger's tone was formal and slightly strained. "Claire, my dear, will you tell Lady Beatrice that we have guests at the high table tonight—Friar Dominic and Friar Bernard."

"Yes, of course." She was turning to make her escape when Raoul walked nonchalantly through the tower doorway. His shirt and tunic were slung over his shoulder, his bare chest was beaded with water droplets, and a marigold was tucked behind his ear. He, too, stopped short when he saw the two friars and

Otho. The curve of his lips straightened and a look of irritation flickered across his face before he schooled it to polite neutrality. The moment the necessary introductions had been performed, he excused himself, sliding Claire a 'heaven help us' look on his way.

She knew that he had been on his way to see her, that without the presence of those dour black robes, he would have swept her into his arms and paid her for the marigold in kisses and love-play. Biting her lip, dismayed and anxious, she hurried back to the bower to warn Beatrice and especially Geralda about the unwelcome guests.

The meal that followed in the hall should have continued the afternoon's golden mood, but the presence of the two friars and Father Otho blackened it beyond redemption. The Montvallants put a polite veneer on their resentment and unease, and uniformly wished the daylight hours away, the sooner to retire.

Friar Dominic dipped a piece of bread in the salt dish and gazed around his audience. "Have you heard that a crusade is to be called to put a stop to the Cathars if Count Raymond of Toulouse does not curtail their activities himself?" he queried.

Berenger rubbed his palm across his beard. "There has been talk of a crusade since I was my son's age." He glanced at Raoul, who was holding Claire's hand. "And that is further back than I care to recall. I doubt that it will come to anything." His gaze continued along the high table to Father Otho, who was ogling the bosom of Claire's maid Isabelle. "The church would do better to set its own house in order before it casts stones elsewhere."

The friar's face darkened. "Men are weak reeds. There will always be a need for reform, but the disgrace of the Cathar heresy cannot be permitted to survive."

Berenger strove to keep his voice even. "Count Raymond would never stand for a French army on his soil."

The younger friar, who had been pushing a sliver of chicken around on his trencher, raised obsidian-black eyes to Berenger. "With all due respect, my lord," he said primly. "Your overlord is so lazy, he seldom bothers with anything if it is beyond arm's reach and demands making an effort."

"He would make an effort for that!"

"But not for ridding himself of the heretics," retorted the young friar, his knuckles showing a glaze of white where they clenched upon his knife handle.

Berenger forced himself to remember that the friars were guests beneath his roof and could only thank God, whichever one, that Geralda and Aimery had opted to keep to their rooms, or by now the arguments would have ignited the hall like a barrel of hot pitch.

Friar Dominic laid a warning hand upon his companion's. "Although I made mention of a crusade by way of a gentle warning," he said to Berenger, "we are not here to preach at you. Truly, all we wish is a night's lodging, and perhaps a little information if it be in your power to give it." Smiling at the squire serving at the high table, he accepted another cup of watered wine, and indicated that the glowering Brother Bernard would have the same.

"Oh?" said Berenger warily.

"We are seeking some heretics, whom we have heard are in the vicinity."

There was silence. Beatrice's face drained of color and Claire pressed herself against Raoul, her brown eyes huge.

"You mean the horse-faced bitch, Geralda of Lavaur, and her brother Aimery?" said Otho, wiping his sleeve across his mouth. "Yes, they're here. I saw them this very afternoon riding back from a day of dalliance by the river. More than half this town's poisoned by the Cathars and their vile practices, and they're openly encouraged at the castle!" He glowered maliciously at Berenger.

"My guests are no business of yours, and I will not have them harassed in my house," Berenger retorted, calm but furious. "Their beliefs are their own concern. And if there are Cathars in this town, you are more to blame than anyone, Otho. Who would want you for a confessor?"

Friar Dominic raised his right hand. The light gleamed on the cameo ring. "Please," he said coldly. "Lord Berenger, as you say, your guests are your own affair, although I would counsel you most seriously to have a care for your immortal soul."

Berenger tightened his lips on his temper and did not speak.

He promised himself that Otho's career as Montvallant's priest was finished.

"We are seeking two men and a woman traveling together," continued the friar. "One is known to be a senior Cathar Perfect, Chretien de Béziers; the other goes by the name of Matthias. He's a scribe from Antioch, two fingers and the thumb missing from his right hand. The woman is young, and some would say beautiful." His lip curled on the final word. "She claims to be descended from Mary Magdalene and the blessed Virgin herself, and by their blood to own miraculous healing powers."

The younger friar leaned earnestly toward Berenger. "They are known to preach abominations that go even beyond what the ordinary Cathars would dare. They are Devil worshipers!"

Berenger shook his head and was relieved to say with a clear conscience, "I have neither seen nor heard of anyone fitting your description."

Friar Dominic eyed him with pursed lips, then took his stare along the high trestle, hunting.

Berenger saw him stop at Raoul. His son blinked for an instant and then stared directly back at the friar. Berenger knew that expression of old. When Raoul had been caught playing pranks as a boy, he had always tried to brazen it out with one of those looks.

"I saw two men and a woman," offered Father Otho. "I do not know if they are the ones you are seeking, but the woman was indeed lovely, and the men were dressed like Cathars." He hooked his thumbs in his belt, folded his fat hands over them, and smirked at Berenger and Raoul.

"When was this?" The friar leaned forward like a fisherman seeking the gleam of a silver belly in the shallows.

"At the young lord's wedding. They had a shelter in the bailey near the main gates."

Raoul said quickly, "If you mean the ones who arrived late to the feasting, they were respectable pilgrims on their way to Compostela. I spoke to one of the men, and he was certainly a better Catholic than yourself. His name was Thomas and he came from Anjou."

Otho began to splutter.

Berenger interrupted him. "Would you like to explain to the

good friars how you were so drunk at the wedding feast that you could not perform the words of the benediction at the bedding ceremony and had to be removed to sleep off your excesses? I doubt that night you could even remember your own name. Raoul, I know, was stone-sober." He turned once more to the friars. "Seek elsewhere for your heretics; you will not find them here."

"Were those three people truly at Montvallant?" Claire asked Raoul later as they lay in bed, their limbs entwined in the aftermath of vigorous lovemaking. It had been an outlet for all the tensions of the day, a brief escape into the purity of physical sensation.

Raoul nuzzled the top of her head. "I saw them, yes."

"Was the man really from Anjou?"

"I don't know. I never spoke to him. We were bedded not long after they arrived." He was silent for a while, his hand trailing lightly over her damp body. Then he added softly, "I would rather be damned for lying to those friars than I would for letting them set their claws into innocent people . . . and they know it."

The night was warm. Between herself and Raoul there was a slippery layer of love-sweat, but instead of seeking the cool of the sheets, Claire moved closer to him, fear shivering down her spine. "What if there is a crusade?" she whispered, her hand balled into a fist upon his chest. "What if the pope does send soldiers to crush the Cathars?"

"What if the sky fell on our heads tomorrow?" Raoul took her bunched fingers and kissed them open. His tongue tickled her palm. "My father said that there has been talk of a crusade since time began and it has always amounted to naught. Stop worrying; the darkness always makes fear so much bigger than it is—among other things," he teased, licking and nipping his way up her arm before transferring his attention to the tender swell of her breast. His other hand smoothed down over her belly, forefinger lazily exploring, until she gasped and arched.

But later, when she descended from the shattering heights of pleasure, the fear was patiently waiting for her, like a wolf, its jaws wide open.

CHAPTER SIX

SUMMER'S CLIMAX BURST in a glorious, burnished harvest. Ripe, dark grapes and succulent olives were trodden and pressed to extract their juices under a sky so blue that it cut the eyes to look up. Peasant men, sweating and half-naked, toiled from dawn to dusk, scything in white fields, picking orchard fruits and nuts, driving their animals to a final fattening on the glut, and gathering in winter faggots.

Geralda and Aimery returned to Lavaur, but itinerant Cathars came frequently to Montvallant, sent by Geralda in the knowledge that they would receive a warm welcome. Extra hands were always needed at harvesttime, and the Cathars, in exchange for food and lodging and a listening audience, were hard workers.

Sometimes Cathar Good Men spent the night at the castle itself and held prayer meetings in the courtyard. On other occasions, Claire and Beatrice attended gatherings in the town and the villages of the surrounding countryside. Raoul and Berenger usually declined to go with them, being tolerant of the faith, but not as interested as their wives. Indeed, Raoul even went so far as to grumble half-teasingly to Claire that she was neglecting him in favor of their two most recent Cathar guests, two leathery old men who stank of goats.

Contrite, she abandoned her plans to attend the next meeting and went with Raoul instead to inspect the harvesting. Her maid, Isabelle, was disappointed—of all the women, she was the one most taken with Cathar ideals. Torn both ways by guilt, Claire gave the girl leave to go and hear the Good Men preach.

"You wanted to go with her, didn't you?" Raoul probed as they paused to water their horses at a stream meandering through the orchards.

Claire looked at him through her lashes. There was humor in his expression; indeed, she could see the faint lines that would one day be permanently graven between nostril and mouth. "Not as much as I wanted to be with my husband," she said diplomatically.

"Sometimes I wonder," he murmured.

Claire was shocked by the underlying discontent in his voice. Dear Jesu, was her desire to be away with Isabelle and the other women so obvious? "You must not think like that!" she cried, and leaning across her mount, laid her hand over his.

He glanced down at her gesture and the lines deepened, although not in the direction of a smile. "Perhaps I don't want to share you with the Cathars," he said. "Perhaps I fear you will become one of them and I won't be able to touch you anymore."

"Oh, Raoul!" A lump in her throat, she tightened her grip, but he pressed Fauvel forward and she had to let go. Biting her lip, she urged the mare to follow and tried to think of something to say that would mollify him without compromising her own position. Apart from reassuring him of her love, there was little else she could do, for she was not prepared to give up her meetings.

Perhaps on their return to the castle, she could soothe him in their bed, prove to him that however much she admired the Cathars, she admired him, too, and for the moment had no intention of taking any prohibitive vows.

She caught up with him in the heart of the orchard. Silvery-green pears bowed the branches, and the leaves rustled in the breeze. Sunlight and shade dappled both horses and riders; the chaffering of crickets was loud in the drowsy heat.

"Raoul, wait," she entreated. "I want you to underst—"

He slapped the reins down on Fauvel's neck and the stallion once more lunged ahead. Tears of anger and hurt stung Claire's eyes at the thought that he would not even grant her the courtesy of listening.

Then she heard the sound of a muffled scream and a masculine curse. Something thrashed in the long grass among the trees ahead. Raoul turned his horse, drew rein, and leaped from the saddle. Claire urged her mare with her heels and cantered after him. Pulling to a stop beside the dun stallion, she pressed her knuckles to her mouth, covering a cry of horror and revulsion. Gaping up at her and Raoul, his habit rucked up around his pocked thighs, was Father Otho, and beneath him, torn skirts at a similar level, was Isabelle. Her mouth was bloody and swollen. Bright weals burned her shoulders where her gown and shift had been ripped down to expose her breasts.

"She's a heretic!" Otho panted. "A Devil's minion! She trapped me into sin!"

"The only Devil's minion I can see is you!" Raoul choked. Seizing the priest, he hauled him off the girl and threw him furiously to one side.

Claire flurried down from her mare and knelt beside her maid, tugging down the bunched-up skirts and covering the girl's bruised breasts with her own light cloak.

Raoul looked at Father Otho. "Pack your belongings now. and get off the Montvallant lands," he commanded in a voice thick with disgust.

"You have no right . . ." Otho began, and swallowed to a stop as Raoul's sword half-hissed from its sheath.

"No!" croaked Isabelle weakly as Claire helped her to sit up. "Let him be. It is against the Cathar way to kill for any reason!"

"I am not a Cathar," Raoul retorted grimly, but held the sword at rest in the scabbard. "You will be gone by sunset," he said tersely to the priest. "I will come looking for you, and if I find you still here, I will make of you a eunuch and nail your balls to the church door as a warning to others of your ilk. Understood!"

Otho staggered upright, and tried with no great success to hitch up his dignity along with his gilded belt.

Raoul towered over him, eyes as blue as marsh fires. "Get you gone!" he snarled, and the glint of sword steel lengthened above the scabbard rim. Raoul's fingers on the hilt showed the white of pressured bone.

"Pierre de Castelnau, the papal legate, will hear how you

nurture heretics!" Otho launched over his shoulder as he started to limp away.

"And I will gladly explain all he needs to know!" Raoul took three steps forward, his blade grating free. Father Otho abandoned his bravado and fled.

Claire helped Isabelle to her feet, one arm solicitously around her shoulders. The girl's olive complexion was sallow and she was trembling, but apart from her bruises, she seemed otherwise unharmed.

"What happened?" Raoul asked, sheathing his sword.

Isabelle looked at him and then away. Speaking through teeth chattering with shock, she said, "I went to hear the Good Men preach on the riverbank and decided to return by way of the orchard. He was waiting for me—I think he must have been following me and biding his time." Swallowing, she shook her head from side to side. "He said that he wanted to save my soul from damnation, and when I answered that I had no need of his intervention, or any priest's, he called me a witch and a heretic, and leaped upon me like a wild animal. If you had not ridden past when you did . . ." She buried her face in her hands and leaned heavily against Claire for support.

Claire hugged her and made soothing noises, her eyes meeting Raoul's over Isabelle's bent dark head. "Hush, hush. He'll never bother you again. Come, we'll take you home and I'll find some marigold salve for those bruises."

"You can ride pillion behind me," Raoul offered, holding out his hand.

Isabelle stared at him and swallowed convulsively as if she was about to vomit.

"Better still, behind me," Claire said quickly, her understanding of the situation a bit sharper than her husband's. To have come fresh and cleansed from a Cathar meeting and then to be assaulted by a fat slug like Father Otho was an outrage to the soul. Standing before them, sword hilt gleaming on his left hip, eyes still battle-lit, Raoul exuded a powerful masculinity that was only adding to Isabelle's sense of violation.

He let his hand drop. "I suppose the mare has a gentler pace," he said neutrally, but Claire did not miss the look of hurt that flickered across his face at the rebuff before he caught the palfrey and brought her to the women.

* * *

Raoul slowly descended the stairs from the women's quarters and crossed the hall to a low table. Picking up a wine flagon, he poured a full measure into the cup beside it and looked at his father. Berenger was still wearing his hawking gauntlet and a short cloak of amethyst wool.

"Is she all right?" Berenger asked gruffly. "They told me what happened as soon as I rode in."

Raoul raised the cup toward his mouth. "Bruised and shocked, but nothing too serious." He took a deep swallow as if to wash away an evil taste.

"I heard what you said to Father Otho."

"And I meant every word." His jaw jutted defiantly. "If I trod on your authority, I'll apologize, but for nothing else."

Berenger sighed and tossed his gauntlet and cloak upon a settle bench. "Otho's been given too many chances already. I would have done the same. I only wish it had not coincided with the results of this wretched Papal Council. I was talking to a merchant up from Marseilles earlier today."

"Oh?" Hearing the depressed note in his father's usually sanguine voice, Raoul looked at Berenger in concern.

"Apparently Pope Innocent has written to King Philip of France in the strongest terms, asking him to back a crusade against our Cathars. The merchant actually traveled over the Alps with the Roman envoy bearing the letter. Innocent's exact words were—" Berenger looked at the roof " '—Let the strength of the Crown and the misery of war bring them back to the truth.' " He sat down wearily on the bench, rubbing his knees. "I've been ignoring the rumors, hoping they'll go away, but there has been no easing of the pressure this time. Our Count Raymond is walking into a quagmire, and the only way back is across a path of Cathar slain."

Raoul swirled the wine in his cup and watched the light on its surface break and re-form. "Would you persecute Montvallant's Cathars?"

"How could I?" Berenger said indignantly. "Your mother sponsors them, my head groom's a convert, so is Claire's maid, and you have just thrown our priest out of his living to protect her!"

Raoul gazed uneasily around the hall of the castle where he

had been born and raised. Did it suddenly seem smaller, the shadows darker? He moved closer to the fire for comfort, but it was smoky this evening, giving out little warmth and even less cheer. He had been trained in the arts of warfare—what boy from a noble household had not? But it had only been part of a general rounding out of his education, a chance to work off surplus energy between the reading and writing, the ciphering, Latin, and music. Saving this afternoon, he had never raised a sword against anyone in his life, and the thought of doing so dissolved his bowels.

He turned away, but it was too late. Berenger had already seen. "Mayhap it will yet come to nothing," the older man soothed.

"I am not a child!" Raoul's face burned with more than just the heat of the fire.

Berenger's smile was bitter. "We are all children," he said. "Only we pretend ourselves into men."

CHAPTER SEVEN

Saint-Gilles on the Rhône, Winter 1208

THE JANUARY EVENING was made raw by the wind blowing down the corridor of the Rhône delta, and Raoul was glad of his cloak and the fleece lining to his calf-high boots. The hall belonging to Marcel de Saliers, Raoul's second cousin, was crowded and smoky. The conversation was loud, punctuated by wine-wrought laughter, but Raoul heard the discord of fear and saw the tension in men's eyes.

Some two miles away at the palace of Saint-Gilles, Count Raymond of Toulouse and Pierre de Castelnau, the pope's rep-

resentative, were discussing their enormous differences.
Berenger, as one of Raymond's advisers, had left for the conference before dawn. It was nigh on vespers now and still no
word.

> *At sunrise there is light*
> *Love comes shining*
> *I am one with the brightness*
> *My lady wears a silver girdle*
> *Gleaming like the moon*
> *Love comes shining*
> *We are one with the brightness*

Raoul eyed the jongleur who was singing a spell over the people gathered around him, Claire among them. She was wearing
her velvet wedding gown and a gauzy veil and circlet. Her
chestnut braid, thick as a bell rope, hung to her hips. He imagined it unbound and herb-scented upon the pillow, or stranding
over her rosy-tipped breasts. Sometimes he thought that they
would set the very sheets alight with the brilliance of their passion. The jongleur was making sheep's eyes at her, and she
was giggling behind her hand like a little girl. His stomach
fluttered with love and lust, and a touch of jealousy.

He turned at a nudge on his arm and saw his father with a
young Templar knight at his side. The cold smell of the winter
evening clung to their woolen cloaks.

"I thought you were never going to come," Raoul said. "It
must be full dark by now."

"It is," Berenger growled. "Darker than you know. Raoul, I
want you to meet Luke de Béziers from the preceptory at
Bezu."

The two young men shook hands. The Templar's grip was
dry and firm, his fingers so thinly fleshed in contrast to his
powerful, stocky body that Raoul almost recoiled from the
shock of bone.

"Luke's related through his mother to Marcel's wife,"
Berenger explained, "so that makes him our kin after a fashion."

"Better still, it gives me a reason to claim hospitality here
tonight." Luke grimaced. "Count Raymond's in such a rage,

I'd lief as not sleep at the palace." He tapped his narrow fingers on the disk pommel of his sword hilt. His dark eyes flickered around the gathering with the wary thoroughness of a lynx.

"Has there been trouble?" Raoul asked.

Berenger laughed sourly. "Hell would seem cold by comparison! It started off politely enough, I grant you, but they were soon at each other's throats. The legate said there would be no pardon for Raymond while he continued to nurture the Cathars in his bosom and freely employ Jews and other undesirables. Count Raymond tried to placate him at first, even said he would dig out the worst of the rot, but Legate de Castelnau would have none of it." Berenger thrust his hands into his graying curls, and the anger in his voice intensified. "He accused Raymond of perjury and oath-breaking. Raymond said he had come to discuss the matter, not to be insulted, and before we knew it, they were snarling at each other like a pair of fighting dogs!"

"Raymond ended up by putting his hand on his dagger and threatening to kill de Castelnau," Luke added wryly.

Raoul stared at him in horror.

"Oh, he's not so foolish as to actually do the deed," Berenger said. "That would be tantamount to cutting his own throat and letting the French lap up his blood."

Raoul took a gulp of his wine. For the indolent Count Raymond actually to issue a death threat, he must have been very close to the edge. "What happened after that?"

Berenger spread his hands. "De Castelnau flurried out of the palace in high dudgeon as only he knows how, and Raymond did his best to imitate. Luke and I made our escape. Needless to say, Raymond remains outside the grace of the church, and the tensions are higher than the Garonne after a winter storm." His hand descended from his hair to rub his face. "There's a bitter wind blowing tonight, and no place to shelter."

As if his father's words had actually conjured the cold out of the air, Raoul started to shiver. Luke de Béziers excused himself and went in search of their host. For all his stockiness, he moved with the grace of a cat.

"His father is a senior Cathar Good Man," Berenger murmured from the side of his mouth, "or so I've been told. I tried to draw him out on the subject, but he just looked through me and his face went blank."

"The Templars have always had a reputation for going their own way, regardless of Rome. It's a well-known fact that Cathar families send their sons to the Templars to be educated," Raoul said, and started in the direction of the jongleur whose eyes were smoldering over Claire as he sang a sultry love song involving hands beneath cloaks and white naked bodies in flowery meadows.

That night Raoul slept badly. The bed, as with all makeshift beds, was lumpy and uncomfortable, and the room was shared by several other guests, one of whom snored with a resonance that would have done justice to the bass note of a cathedral organ.

Close to Raoul's side, undisturbed by all the racket, Claire slept, bundled in her fur-lined cloak for warmth. He sighed and shifted, wondering how far away morning was. The snorer turned over and the sound softened to a continuous rumble like a cat's purr. Raoul dozed. His mind became a mosaic of fire-shot crystal. He thought he heard someone call his name from afar, and with a jerk and a loud grunt, woke up again. Claire mumbled softly. Raoul swallowed and stared into the darkness above his head, tantalized by the memory of the gray-eyed pilgrim woman—sitting at his wedding feast, dancing through his dreams, leading him through fire and storm.

"What's the matter?"

"Mmmm?" Raoul turned to Claire with the blank gaze of a dreamer. They were traveling along the marshy banks of the Petit Rhône on the road to Arles. Raoul desired to visit a swordsmith there who had been glowingly recommended by one of their fellow guests at Saint-Gilles.

"I asked you what was the matter. You've scarcely spoken a word all morning."

He moved his shoulders and said diffidently, "It must be the lack of sleep."

Claire frowned, not knowing what was irking him, but certain that it was not lack of sleep. He had been on edge long before they retired last night. Perhaps it had been the boldness of the jongleur; she knew that Raoul had been both pleased and irritated by the attention paid to her, and his kisses in a darkened corner before they retired had been hard with possession and desire. She mulled the thought over for a while and then set it aside. He was playing far too indifferent toward her for jealous passion to be itching beneath his skin. Another thought twitched her brows into an anxious frown. The conference at Saint-Gilles had broken up in discord. What if he knew things about the outcome that she did not, and was keeping them to himself? She had seen him talking to Berenger last night, both of them looking unhappy.

"Raoul . . ."

"Wait!" He raised an imperative hand. Beneath him Fauvel sidled and danced, and he had to tighten the reins.

Mouth open, Claire stared at him. Ahead of them she heard the sound of shouting, the clash of arms. They were approaching a fording point; such places were always susceptible to ambush by brigands and mercenary bands down on their luck. It was the reason why Raoul rode fully armed with a hefty escort of Montvallant troops.

"Roland, Ansil, stay here with the women!" Raoul snapped, and collected the rest of his men about him.

"Jesu, be careful!" Claire cried, her heart beginning to thump so hard that she thought it would surely burst through her ribs.

Raoul had not covered more than fifty yards when a horse came galloping from the opposite direction. Its reins trailed, threatening to bring the animal down. Raoul swerved to meet it, making a grab for the loop of bridle. He missed at first, grabbed again, and tightened his grip. The dagged red leather cut into his fingers, but he held on hard, guiding Fauvel with his knees to impede the runaway's struggles, and succeeded in bringing the horse to a rearing stop.

The bit chains were engraved and gilded; so was the harness. The saddlecloth was of expensive, kermes-dyed wool, the border edged with a design of crosses and crosiers in thread-of-gold, while the saddle itself was a sumptuous affair, ornate and thickly padded.

"Belongs to a priest," said Giles de Lostange, one of the senior knights.

"Not just any priest." Raoul gentled the trembling, foam-spattered horse. It was a showy, highbred chestnut with a chalk-white blaze and hind socks. "This is no meek, ambling nag, and just look at his trappings. Here, Philippe, take him back to lady Claire." He was surprised to hear how calm his own voice sounded when he was as sweating and nervous as the horse.

"Then who . . ." the knight began, but was interrupted by the thunder of more hooves.

"Ware arms!" Raoul bellowed. He grabbed the guige of his shield, ducked it from his back to his left shoulder, and fumbled his arm through the two shorter leather straps.

Six riders came pounding up from the direction of the river and jammed to a halt as they saw Raoul's troop. One of them sat astride a beautiful dappled-gray courser, trapped out as finely as the chestnut—most obviously a recent acquisition.

Clenching his teeth to prevent himself from retching, Raoul lifted his helm from his saddle bow and settled it over his head. His vision contracted down to a narrow slit. His breath roared in his ears, warring with the thunder of his blood and the unsettled circling of shod hooves. He gave Fauvel the spur and cried his challenge, his knights bunching behind him.

The brigands declined to take it up. Turning their mounts around, they fled at the gallop. Fauvel's powerful stride devoured the ground, but the four horses in front had too great a start, and it soon became clear that they would not be caught.

Upon the crest of a low flood-bank, Raoul gave up the chase and drew rein. The slope to the river below was a scene of devastation and carnage that stopped his breath.

"God's love," he whispered. Unable to breathe, he wrenched off the helm and forced down his mail coif. It did not help. He still gagged and fought to breathe.

A loose sumpter mule cropped the grass close to a corpse wearing priest's robes. The linen alb was saturated with blood and the gilded chasuble was missing. Two servants lay dead nearby together with another priest and three soldiers. The contents of disembowled saddlebags were strewn among the bodies like collective entrails. Already, in the pale winter sky, the buzzards were wheeling.

Raoul forced himself to ride closer and look. The scene reminded him of the butcher's quarters of Toulouse, only this time he was not looking at slaughtered pigs and sheep, but at men.

Snorting, Fauvel backed restlessly from a corpse. Raoul wanted to back away, too, to run and not stop until he reached the familiar security of Montvallant's golden stone walls. Instead, he dismounted. The legs that carried him forward seemed not his own.

"There's one here still breathing, my lord!"

Raoul trod across the smeared grass to where Giles had knelt to pillow the head and shoulders of a tonsured young cleric. Blood seeped sluggishly from a bulging gut wound, and his face was gray. Giles looked at Raoul and shook his head. "Dying," he mouthed.

Raoul crouched on his heels. The victim was probably younger than himself, the brightness of acne standing out against the pallor of death. "What happened?"

"We were set upon." His eyelids fluttered, showing sightless white. "Count Raymond's men . . . Raymond of Toulouse. He wanted . . . he wanted my master dead."

"Your master?" Raoul felt himself recoil, knowing what the dying cleric was going to say and not wanting to hear.

"Pierre de Castelnau . . ."

"Impossible!" Raoul snapped with sick fear. "Raymond would never besmirch his honor with such a deed!"

"His men . . . saw them yesterday at Saint-Gilles." The young man sagged against Giles's arm.

Raoul could not speak. He turned his head aside and spat. When he looked again, the young priest had died, and Giles was easing to his feet, his surcoat soaked in blood.

"Raymond would never be so foolish as to do this!" Raoul whispered, struggling to balance himself on a world that had bucked beneath him and tipped him awry.

"And who will believe him even if he is innocent?" The knight looked at the sticky blood on his hands and, grimacing, wiped them on his surcoat. "A hundred witnesses yesterday heard him wish de Castelnau dead. Those men looked like mercenaries, and God knows Count Raymond has plenty of them in his employ."

"And they come and go as frequently as whores in a public brothel!" Raoul gave back angrily. "Look at this; it's more than just murder." He went to stand before what he now knew to be the body of Pierre de Castelnau. "Look at him—no crosier, no ring of office, God's death, not even his robe and cloak! This couldn't have been done by Raymond's command!"

Giles continued to wipe his hand, although it was now clean save for the red half-moons beneath his fingernails. "It may be so," he said, leaving Raoul in no doubt that he was being humored.

"Raoul, what is it?"

He swung rapidly on his heel to see Claire sitting her mare on the flood-bank and taking in the scene with huge, frightened eyes. "It is Pierre de Castelnau," he said abruptly. "He's been robbed and murdered. There's nothing we can do here except get a cart from the nearest village to bear the dead. Don't come any closer; you don't have to see this."

In the distance behind them, over Saint-Gilles, thunder rumbled softly. Feeling as if all the marrow had been sucked out of his bones, Raoul lifted himself wearily into the saddle.

Isabelle was murmuring part of the Lord's Prayer softly to herself, over and again as the Cathars did. *"Deliver us from evil, deliver us from evil, deliver us from evil."*

Raoul glanced toward the accumulating thunderclouds, then down at the wind beginning to seethe through the grass, lifting and flapping the dead legate's garment, giving him the semblance of life. He doubted that a voice in the wilderness was going to hold back the storm about to be unleashed upon them, Cathar and Catholic alike.

CHAPTER EIGHT

Montfort L'Amaury, Northern France, April 1209

Simon DE Montfort narrowed his eyes against the bitter spring gale buffeting into his face, and fixed them upon the dark bulk of the keep rearing before him. A thirty-mile ride from Paris lay behind him in weather that had grown progressively worse. He was tired and saddle-sore, but felt neither as he waited for the guards on watch to open the great gates. The news he bore home from the French court inured him to weariness and pain. Ambition warmed him, buoying him up as he rode into the torchlit courtyard and dismounted. Sleepy grooms came tumbling from the stables to take the exhausted destriers. Stripping his gauntlets, pushing down his mail coif, Simon walked toward the hall, his gait gaining pace and width as his saddle-cramped muscles began to ease.

His body squire, Giffard, held aloft a pine torch to light Simon up the stairs to the women's quarters on the floor above; a second, junior squire brought up the rear. The chape on his scabbard mountings clinked against his mail leggings, and his boots scuffed grittily on the black stone steps. A woman pressed her back to the wall to let them pass, her white undergown lit to yellow by the sputtering torch.

Simon recognized Elise, his wife's maid. "Is Lady Alais awake?" he asked.

"Yes, my lord. She sent me to fetch hot wine."

Simon could feel the woman's nervousness. She fluttered like a bird cornered by a cat. Scornful, indifferent, he let her go and entered the room.

Alais was waiting to greet him, a cloak thrown in haste over her shift. Her fine, light brown hair was unbound around her shoulders. The filaments floated in the candle gleam, betraying a rapid, recent combing.

"Welcome home, my lord," she said in her measured, cool voice, and bowed her proud head.

Simon pinched her chin between his forefinger and thumb, and raised her face to study it. Light hazel eyes and sharp nose, good cheekbones, controlled mouth. A falcon well trained to fly to the lure of his fist. "Not for long," he said, and releasing her, turned to the squires. "Unarm me," he commanded. "Take it all down to Gilbert in the armory and go to bed."

Alais looked at him through her lashes, but held her silence and made herself busy lighting more candles and setting another log on the fire.

The squires hung his heavy mail coat upon a hauberk pole, neatly folded his gambeson and surcoat, and placed the leggings and sword belt on top. Like a warhorse on a tight curb rein, Simon checked his impatience while they undressed him down to an embroidered shirt of Flanders linen and plain braies and chausses.

Even without the armor, Simon possessed an impressive physical presence. He was tall and muscular, not a pad of flesh or fold of age to be seen. His face reflected the man—hard, uncompromising bones made stark rather than mellow by time. Thick, silver hair, black-tinged at brow and nape, was maintained in cropped order. No fancy court fashions of scented oil and curling irons for him. His frowning brows were still jet-black, and gave emphasis to his eyes, which were the cold gray-green of a winter sea.

The youths bowed out of the room. Elise, having returned with the hot wine and given the flagon to Alais, was peremptorily dismissed by Simon. He coveted the privacy of this inner chamber. It was the one place he could shrug off his burdens and, like a man unbuckling his belt, let all confined tension relax. The servants had long since learned not to linger.

Alais presented him with a cup. He took it from her, feeling the heat of the wine through the beveled side, smelling the spiciness of cinnamon and nutmeg in the steam. After one perfunctory sip, he set the drink aside. Free from the constraint of prying eyes, he snatched Alais to his body and kissed her roughly, his hands busy with the lacings of her shift.

Simon was a born soldier, decisive, swift to act and react, and ruthless in pursuing any goal, be it fighting infidels in Egypt, keeping his own fiefs clear of brigands, or satisfying his physical needs after several weeks of abstinence in Paris. He was quite capable of self-denial, but he viewed his body as a machine; occasionally it had to be greased and rested in order for it to function efficiently.

"What did you mean 'not for long'?" Emboldened by his relaxed attitude in the aftermath of release, Alais raised herself on one elbow and leaned over him, the curiosity written openly in her eyes.

Simon gave her a tolerant, slightly superior smile. "A fresh cup of wine," he said. Arms pillowing his head, he admired her length of leg as she left the bed to obey his bidding. "I've been invited to join the crusade against the Cathars as secular head of the army."

Shivering, she crouched to set a poker in the banked fire. Her back was turned, denying him her face to read, but he saw her hand pause on the poker handle, and her voice was not quite steady when she said, "By whom?"

"Arnaud-Amalric, Abbot of Citeaux. Although it was Burgundy who recommended me to him as all that was laudable in a Christian warrior." He watched her thoughtfully.

"Isn't Arnaud-Amalric the papal legate to the Languedoc?"

"He has been ever since Pierre de Castelnau took an assassin's spear in the ribs," Simon said. "We'll deal well enough together providing he remembers that I'm the soldier and he's the priest."

Alais plunged the hot poker into the wine and brought the steaming, fragrant cup to him.

"What is the matter?" Simon's voice was soft, but dangerous rather than tender.

"Nothing," Alais said quickly. "You surprised me, that's all. Are there not other lords who would wish to have the privilege of leading?"

"Of higher degree, you mean? Leave the oily words and

double meanings to the diplomats." He gave her a warning look, then tilted the cup to his mouth. "Anyway, it is not a privilege, it's a pain in the backside. All Burgundy and Nevers want to do is prance along at the head of their troops and show off their best tourney armor. When it comes to pitching tents in the pouring rain and laying siege to pox-riddled towns with the mosquitoes biting to death those parts not already killed by boredom, they'll turn tail and run for the comfort of home."

"But surely you do not enjoy that kind of life yourself?" Alais said, and drew the coverlet with its border of Pyrenean lynx over her shoulders.

"No, but I do enjoy the challenge, and I have the endurance of an ox." He contemplated his cup. "In simple terms, I am made for this and they are not. They are great lords with the difficulties of rulership upon them—they cannot afford to become involved beyond a token commitment." He rotated the cup slowly. "The army's to assemble by midsummer at Lyon. Burgundy's bringing five hundred knights, so is Nevers, and the contingents of Saint Pol and Boulogne are fairly large, too." He made a disparaging sound and set the cup down on the night table. "There are always thousands parading their arms at the start of a crusade and making brave speeches by the dung-load. I know full well that less than a tenth will see it beyond the first two months."

"So they are not worth having?"

"Oh no, they serve their purpose," Simon said. "You just don't use them to build your backbone." Yawning, he rumpled his hair.

"You talk as if you expect this to be a long campaign."

He watched her through narrowed lids. Had it been in her nature, she would have tossed her head and pouted at him. As it was, her expression was schooled to neutrality, but he sensed her annoyance from the rigid way she was holding herself. "You don't rush a banquet," he commented, "and the South is a feast fit for an emperor." He placed a possessive hand on her shoulder. "Or at least fit for the lord of Montfort l'Amaury." Her skin had a silky gleam. Despite the bearing of four living children and two that had not survived, Alais had looked after herself. Breasts and belly might be a little slack, but the use of perfumed oils, a vigorous lifestyle, and close attention to diet left her still supple and attractive in her midthirties.

Taking a handful of her brown hair, he twined it around his fingers, watching it take on gold highlights from the night candle. Then he suddenly tightened his grip and pulled her down to him.

"Simon de Montfort, you are an ambitious man," she said huskily, her eyes bright with desire and tearful from pain. He laughed against her mouth and kissed her hard before releasing her. There were still things he wanted to say; the first edge of his desire had been blunted, and he approved of self-discipline.

"Admit it," he said. "If I were the kind of man to covet the hearth, you'd not be so eager to please me."

"Instead I never see you from one month to the next!" There was genuine grievance in her tone.

"I'll need you with me in Lyon to run my household before we ride down into the lands of Raymond of Toulouse."

"Hah!" she sniffed, digging her fingernails into his dark chest hair. "A camp follower!"

Simon chuckled. "You have no need to complain. My pedestal is yours, and I know your pride and ambition a match for mine. Besides—" he leaned to her ear, his breath a hot whisper "—not every camp follower receives gold collars and bolts of red silk from Paris for their services." His hand strayed down to circle one of her breasts and pinch the nipple. "If you are good, you can have them before breakfast."

"I can't," Alais protested, struggling slightly. "It's still Lent. Indeed, we should not have lain together just now. I'll have to confess and do penance."

Simon's eyes first widened, then narrowed. "I have indeed been absent too long," he growled, and his hand left her breast and grasped her jaw, forcing her head up. "Confess all you wish, do what penance you need to ease your conscience, madam, but Lent or no Lent, you will yield me obedience . . . always."

Her throat worked. "Yes, my lord," she whispered.

Simon nodded, and releasing his grip, set his palm to her cheek. He had not beaten her often—the pride of self-discipline again—but he was full capable if he thought it necessary. Judging her warned into submission, he brushed his knuckles over her cheek and down her throat, returning to her breasts. "I thought I might take Amaury on this campaign with me," he murmured. "He's fifteen, old enough now for the experience of a campaign. Tiltyard training is all very well, but it won't toughen him up like the real thing."

"I am sure it would please him greatly, my lord," she said meekly.

"I'll speak to him at breakfast," Simon said, and pushed her down flat, gratified at the speed with which she opened to him.

CHAPTER NINE

Montvallant, Toulouse, Spring 1209

"BERENGER!" RAYMOND DE Saint-Gilles, Count of Toulouse, hugged the lord of Montvallant ebulliently.

"Welcome, my lord." Submitting to the embrace, Berenger drew his guest into the great hall, his own greeting tempered with caution. There was a friendship of long standing between the houses of Montvallant and Toulouse; Berenger and Raymond had been squires together, but there were still overtones to that friendship of liege lord and obliged vassal.

Raymond wore his years lightly. He had good bones and his olive skin was still stretched tautly across them. He walked on the balls of his feet like an athlete and had a young man's love of gilding and grooming. It was rumored that his jet-black curls owed more to a subtle application of soot than to nature. If so, the camouflage was superb, for the fine-grained skin bore no telltale streaks or stains. His indolent lifestyle and love of luxury should have left him as fat and slack as a slug, but instead, in his red tunic, he was lean and vulpine.

Beatrice and Claire served the men with wine in the solar, and a pair of musicians was fetched to play music in the background. Beatrice excused herself to stir up the household to provide a meal fitting for their guest, but when Claire moved to help, she stopped her.

"No, my dear, in your condition you need to rest. Sit down with your embroidery. I can manage perfectly well."

"I'm all right, Mother," Claire protested. The pregnancy had caused her very little discomfort thus far. She knew that Beatrice tended to fuss, but it seemed an overreaction for her mother-in-law to suggest that she should not help to arrange their guest's comfort when she was only in her third month.

Under the pretense of a maternal scolding, Beatrice drew Claire to one side. "I want you to stay here and listen to what they say," she whispered. "You know what men are like. If I ask Berenger afterward, or you ask Raoul, we'll only get half of the tale, and altered to make it palatable. I know Raymond de Toulouse of old. He can charm the very birds down from the trees, and to no good purpose!"

Bowing her head, Claire appeared to yield to Beatrice's insistence, and returned demurely to her embroidery frame. She felt Raoul's stare, avidly curious, and burning color mounted her cheeks. She had never been good at deception.

"Do I gather from this that some good news is imminent?" Raymond queried affably as he settled himself into a cushioned chair.

Blushing harder, Claire busied herself with her needle.

"In the autumn, my lord," Raoul said proudly.

"My congratulations." Raymond clasped his hands upon the gorgeous crimson velvet of his tunic. He looked at his thumbs, circling one over the other as if their rotation represented the external workings of his brain. Then he raised his grape-dark eyes to Berenger and Raoul. "I wish my own news were as happy as yours."

So now we come to the crux of the matter, Raoul thought. Glancing furtively at his father, he saw that Berenger's face had set like stone.

Berenger said, "We have heard that a French army is assembling in Lyon with the objective of destroying the Cathars."

"Yes," said Raymond. "You have heard true."

"And you want us to help you repulse them?"

Raymond fiddled with an impressive cabochon ruby adorning one of his thumbs. "Not quite. It would be easier for me to stand in the sea and command back the tide with the palm of my hand. The army is enormous. Tens of thousands, my informants tell me, and from all parts of the North and the Low Countries."

"Then what should we do—stand aside and let them do their worst?"

Raymond stopped twiddling the ring, but only to drink down his wine. Without a word, Claire rose and refilled his cup. "No." He wiped his mouth on a kerchief that had been tucked in his undergown sleeve. "I'm taking the cross myself, and I'm advising all my vassals to do the same."

Aghast, Berenger stared at his overlord. "You want me to take up arms against my own people. Is that what you are saying?"

"It's not as simple as that." Raymond replaced the kerchief in his sleeve. "Oh, sit down, Berenger, and stop looking at me as if I'd asked you to roast your grandmother over a slow fire."

"Perhaps not my grandmother, but what about the Cathars on my lands? Perhaps you would like me to roast them instead?"

"It won't come to that!" Raymond gave a short, uneasy laugh, and his eyes slipped from Berenger's.

"Oh, won't it?"

"What did you have in mind?" Raoul asked. His voice was neutral, masking his anger.

Quite misconstruing Raoul's attitude, Raymond turned to him gratefully. "As I have just said, resisting the northern army will be impossible. I have appealed to the pope and promised to mend my ways even down to the humiliation of a public scourging." He grimaced. "I would rather have my hide flayed symbolically than have the French do it for a fact. What I propose is that we all take the cross. If we are crusaders ourselves, then on pain of excommunication, they cannot touch our lands."

"You think that Pope Innocent will not see straight through such a ruse?" Berenger said incredulously.

"That is what the public scourging will be about—proof that I'm in earnest this time." Raymond shrugged his elegant shoulders. "I suppose it's inevitable that a few heretics will have to be persecuted, but if we succeed, we should be able to deflect the wrath of the crusade—from Toulouse at least."

Berenger knitted his brows. "Deflect it where?"

Raymond opened his mouth, but Raoul preempted him, his voice still barren of emotion. "Onto Roger Trenceval, of course, where else? His lands succor twice as many Cathars as those of Toulouse, and he is far too powerful a neighbor for his own good, or ours."

Raymond gave him a sharp look. "I gave Roger Trenceval the opportunity to stand solid with me and repulse the northern army, and he refused. Whatever happens now is on his own head. I have to do what is best for my people."

For yourself, Raoul thought.

Berenger sighed heavily. "You ask a great deal of us, my lord."

"I would not do so if it were not necessary; you know that." Raymond leaned toward Berenger, his voice liquid and persuasive. "At least if we are part of the crusading army, we might be able to soften the blow."

"How strong is the intention of their leaders?" Raoul asked.

Raymond pursed his lips. "Arnaud-Amalric of Citeaux is a fanatic. As to the ordinary soldiers, I don't know. They're being led by some lordling from Paris, Simon de Montfort. If I have read the situation aright, the bulk of the army will march down here, throw its weight around until harvesttime, and then head for home." His dark eyes flickered between father and son. "It is the only way out of this bind, Berenger, believe me. I need your backing when I talk to my other vassals. You're dependable and solid; they'll take notice of you."

Berenger looked at the floor. "Dependable and solid," he repeated, as if he were striving to grasp the gist of an insult. Slowly he shook his head from side to side. "I am not proud to say it, indeed I half think I am damned, but for the sake of all that has been between us in the past, I yield you our support."

Raoul said nothing, appalled, but agreeing tacitly by his silence.

Claire stabbed her needle into the fabric and, her complexion parchment-white, fled the room.

Raymond turned in his chair, momentarily startled by her sudden exit, then he grinned at Raoul. "My wife was exactly the same when she was having our son. Her maid used to follow her around with basins and possets."

"I think there is more to it than that," Raoul said with wooden composure, and excused himself.

It took him no small time to find his wife. Their bedchamber was deserted apart from two maids busy with their distaffs. A quick glance in the garderobe revealed that she had not retreated there to be sick. Nor was she in the kitchens with his mother. He searched the storerooms, bakehouse, dairy, and stables, all without success, and it was not until he mounted the wall walk that he finally discovered her leaning against a merlon and staring across the orchards and vineyards toward the silver glide of the river.

"In God's name, what are you doing up here?" he demanded, brusque with worry and exasperation.

"God's name!" She rounded on him, brown eyes flashing with indignation and tears. "What has God to do with any of this? Make my apologies to the excellent count. Tell him I am sick; it's the truth—sick to the soul!" She rested one shaking hand on the merlon to support herself. "Raoul, if you go to fight Cathars, I will never forgive you!"

"I have no intention of harming a single Cathar, and neither has my father."

"But Raymond has," she said, her voice tremulous with loathing, some of it for Raoul. At the back of her mind lay the knowledge that she was being unfair to him, it was not his fault, but he was here, a receptacle for her feelings of helplessness and terror.

"We are backed into a corner, do you not see?" He spread his hands wide.

Claire looked at them, at the long, tapering fingers. How often had she seen them folded around the neck of a lute, coaxing harmony from the strings; how often had she felt their same persuasiveness on her body. It was an abomination to imagine them fisted upon the grip of a war sword. "All I see is that Raymond wants this northern army to crush Roger Trenceval for him."

Raoul looked heavenward in disbelief. "Were you not listening to anything down there? Whatever we do, the crusaders are coming down on us. We can't resist, we have to deflect, and if Raymond does persecute a few Cathars, it is so that the others will survive. I like it no more than you, but we're caught in a cleft stick."

"So we persecute a few for the good of the whole," she spat. "Tell me, Lord Solomon in all your wisdom, which of our Cathars should we toss on the fire? Isabelle? Pierre the groom? What about the old woman who brings mushrooms to the castle?" Her voice dripped with the corrosion of rage, and she saw him recoil with shock at this change in her gentle nature. "Perhaps we could send for Aimery and Geralda; now, there's a thought!"

"Claire, stop it!"

"Conscience troubling you?" she flung at him.

He grabbed her roughly by the shoulders; she felt the bruising span of his fingers, and through them the shuddering of his own body. She drove her fists at his chest, seeking to escape, but he only tightened his grip. Finally she slumped against him, her throat tightening with tears of anguish and frustration.

"Yes," he muttered thickly, "my conscience is troubling me, and I'm so frightened that I want to shut myself up somewhere deep and dark and never come out. I don't want to wear armor and wield a sword, but this isn't going to go away just for the ignoring." He dipped his head, seeking her lips.

Claire clung to him, responding fervently, filled with remorse for the words she had hurled at him. She was sick with terror at the thought of him going to war. The memory of the bodies on the banks of the Rhône still haunted her, the blood, the indecency of violent death. Raoul might be a knight, he might have been trained in the arts of war, but he was untried and he would be facing men of far wider experience. Her child might never know its father. "Why?" she said, her voice strained and tearful. "Why must they interfere? What harm have we ever done to them?"

He smoothed his hands over her spine and gazed bleakly at the solid stone merlons behind. "We have made them envious and afraid. They have to destroy us before they themselves are destroyed. It is about power and greed and fear."

Claire lifted her head. "Raoul, what about our Cathars?"

His hands stopped at her waist, as yet unthickened by her pregnancy. "They will have to worship less openly for a while. They can take refuge in those old caves in the hills above the vineyards."

"And the Cathars who dwell on the lands of Roger Trenceval?"

"We'll do what we can—stay our hands if nothing else. Claire, you must understand how difficult the situation is. There is so little room for maneuver."

Biting her lip, she blinked up at him through brimming eyes, wanting to agree with him, but unable to bring herself to do so. The bright glass bubble of her world had irrevocably shattered, the jagged slivers turning inward to pierce her heart.

"Will you come back to the solar?" he asked gently, stroking away her tears on the ball of his thumb.

"I cannot." She shivered, feeling the slow bleeding of the mortal wound. "Make my excuses, Raoul. In truth, I am ill." She broke from his embrace.

He stared after her, the wind stinging his eyes. When he followed her into the tower, the contrast between the clear light on the battlements and the sudden blackness of the twisting staircase left him stumbling in the dark.

CHAPTER TEN

"DO YOU EVER think of returning to your mother's homeland?" Geralda asked Bridget. They were seated by the fire in Geralda's bower, rubbing herbs that had been dried the previous summer and autumn, and putting them into clay storage jars. The common, powerful aromas of sage and rosemary mingled with the fragrances of dittany, juniper, and lily of the valley.

Bridget crumbled a sage leaf in her palm and gave Geralda a wistful smile. "Sometimes, yes, but it is a life I left behind a long time ago. I was little more than a child when we crossed the narrow sea." Her mist-gray gaze turned inward. "I would like to celebrate midsummer there once more, among the standing stones, but I do not think it will come to pass. Perhaps one day a daughter of mine will raise the cup in my stead. I hope so."

"Can you not see such things in the future?" Geralda asked, openly curious.

Bridget turned her head toward the fire licking at the logs in the hearth. "Sometimes, but it takes some preparation, and I do not always have the desire to seek the sight. It is a double-edged sword, and if it turns the wrong way in your hand, the blades cut deep. Would you wish to know the time and manner of your own dying?"

Geralda swallowed and shook her head.

"No," said Bridget. "Neither would I." Making a funnel of her hand, she tipped the powdered sage into a jar and reached down for another branch of dried leaves. "But oftimes I have come perilously close."

The women did not speak for a while after that, Geralda's garrulous nature sobered to reflection by Bridget's words. Bridget herself used the silence to ponder the direction of her own life. Since her mother's death, she had been drifting with the current, letting it take her where it would, but that could not last forever. She had an obligation, a terrible duty to her bloodline to bear a child. Mother to daughter, the chain stretched for twelve hundred years unbroken, each link gleaming with ancient knowledge and power.

She had seen the way men looked at her; it would take no persuasion to have one plow her virginity and seed her womb, but she found herself reluctant to take that irrevocable step. There were several personable young men in Geralda's household from good Cathar families, but they did not call to her body in the way that the bridegroom at Montvallant had done. If she was truthful with herself, she wanted to lie with him. And for the moment such a match was untenable.

Geralda said hesitantly, "Is it true that you are descended from the Magdalene? Is that where your sight comes from?"

Bridget smiled. It was a question asked sooner or later by everyone who came to know her. "A little of it perhaps, and yes, she was my ancestor, or so the story has been handed down to me. You will never find her tale in the Scriptures." She could see that Geralda was bursting to know the details, but unsure of her ground were she to ask.

"It is simple enough." Bridget took pity on her. "She married James, the brother of the man the Roman church calls the Christ, and bore him children. When Jesus was crucified, she and her family fled the Holy Land to find a new life. They came here, to these mountains, and settled down—for a time at least. Then the persecutions began. The Christians had turned their Christ into a God, a man's God, immaculate and celibate. They wanted no claims of kinship to detract from the God-head, especially not female kinship—women of the royal bloodline. Nor did they wish to accept that the "virgin" Mary claimed other descendants. We were blasphemers, to be hunted down and exterminated." Her voice had grown bitter. Although she was talking of the distant past, her vision was filled with the image of her wounded, dying mother.

The scent of wine and juniper stung her nostrils. "I'm sorry, I should have had more tact," Geralda said with anxious chagrin, one hand upon Bridget's shoulder, the other offering her a cup.

To please her, Bridget took a small sip. "The wound is there whether I speak of it or not," she said. "Do not blame yourself." She set the cup down on the hearth and resumed rubbing the herbs. "Mary's descendants scattered. Some were caught and killed. Others settled into normal lives and forgot their heritage. My own branch dwelt among the people of Brittany and later Cornwall. Ours has always been a female line, mother to daughter. We have the gifts of healing in our blood, and a raw, natural power. The women of the ancient religion, the priestesses, showed us how to discipline it. Like this." Bridget closed her eyes and stretched her palm toward the fire. The flames licked up, green and gold, as if she had thrown a handful of crumbled loaf sugar onto the logs.

Geralda's eyes widened.

Bridget withdrew her hand and opened her eyes. "It is not always as easy as that. It depends upon how rested I am, how my mind is prepared. And a fire already burning is much easier than a pile of wet sticks and leaves." She sighed softly, a feeling of melancholy, of the inevitable, washing over her. "I am one of the few women left who can raise the fire. The old ways are dying, or being killed. . . ."

Geralda began to speak, then stopped and looked at the door, her nostrils flaring like a mare testing the wind.

Turning, Bridget saw a young Templar knight standing on the threshold, an inverted helm tucked under his arm and his gauntlets stuffed inside it.

"Luke?" She sprang to her feet, her sadness overtaken by pleasure. "Oh, it's good to see you!" Hastening across the room, she took his thin, hard hands in hers and kissed his bearded cheek.

"And you, too, cousin," he responded, his smile uncertain as if it was not often used. He approached Geralda, who was also on her feet, and watching him with raised eyebrows.

"My lady, forgive this intrusion into your most private domain, but your steward said I might find you here and make myself known."

Geralda inclined her head. "If you are known to Bridget, then you are most welcome," she formally replied, assessing him thoroughly. "Cousin, you call her?"

"Yes, my lady. My father is Chretien de Béziers. I understand you are sheltering him beneath your roof, and Matthias the scribe, too."

"You are remarkably well informed." Geralda indicated that he should be seated. He looked round, found a coffer on which to place his helm, and sat down on the edge of a settle near the fire.

"We communicate when we can," he said, his eyes following Bridget as she returned to her own seat.

Bridget felt their darkness upon her. Like Chretien, Luke had taken a vow of celibacy. A pity, but she would not push him to break it for all his suitability to be her consort. "Your father and Matthias are visiting in one of the villages," she said. "But they'll be back before dark."

Luke nodded. "There is news both good and bad," he said. Geralda poured him wine. He took it from her courteously enough, but his movements were guarded, and he glanced quickly at Bridget for direction.

"If you want me to leave the room, I will," Geralda said, her eyes full of reproachful dignity.

"No, no." Bridget motioned Geralda to be reseated. "Our news is yours, too. Luke?" she prompted.

He took a mouthful of the wine, savored it for a moment, then swallowed. His hands held the cup like a chalice. "The good tidings are mainly for Matthias. Our preceptor at Bezu has some more documents for him to translate—ancient manuscripts from the Holy Land recently brought by one of our brethren."

"And the other tidings?" Bridget could feel the heat of the fire strongly against the side of her face. She dared not look into the flames for fear that she would see more than just the simplicity of a domestic fire. But as she turned her eyes from the hearth, her stare was trapped by the gleam of the wine in Luke's cup. Dark as spilled blood, shimmering like a river with each beat of the man's heart.

"The northern crusaders are mustering at Lyons. We are standing on the brink of war. It will only take one small push to send us tumbling over the edge. . . . Bridget?"

From a distance, she felt Luke's concerned touch on her arm, saw the drink splash as he moved. Blood of grapes trickled over his hand like a wound, spilling to the rushes, spattering her gown.

"We are already in the flood," she said hoarsely, and covered her eyes, squeezing out the visions that crowded there all too vividly. "And there is nothing we can do to save ourselves from drowning."

The stars seemed so close that Raoul felt he need only reach out his hand to pluck them from the sky. Cool and silver, they cast blue light over the horse lines near his tent where he had stopped to feed Fauvel a handful of grain. The stallion had a minor foreleg strain, and Raoul had applied a poultice that Montvallant's head groom swore always worked.

The destrier's muzzle was velvet against his palm, and the night was so beautiful that it made his throat ache. He wanted the stillness, the silence, to last forever. He did not want to think about the morning and the order that had been issued by the northern battle commanders to march on the defiant city of Béziers.

Simon de Montfort was not, as Count Raymond had airily dismissed him, "some lordling from Paris," likely to turn for the comfort of home as soon as the grain ripened in the fields. In the short time that the armies of North and South had been joined, Raoul had seen the true caliber of the man and realized how badly Raymond had underestimated him. De Montfort knew how to command men, how to coordinate and control. Against his iron will and fist, Raymond was dismally shown up for the lightweight he was. No matter that he had done penance and sworn allegiance at Saint-Gilles to the church—he was neither believed nor trusted by the leaders of the crusade. Indeed, de Montfort had made it clear that if Raymond put so much as one foot out of line, Toulouse would be the next city to feel the attentions of the northern army.

Raoul stroked Fauvel's golden satin hide and stared into the distance, his heart sick within him. He had no desire to go to war against his fellow southerners for a cause that bore so few particles of goodness or truth—a cause that was an excuse for such men as Simon de Montfort to plunder the Languedoc for their own gain.

He leaned his forehead against the destrier's tawny neck, seeking comfort. Only two weeks ago that comfort had been the softness of Claire's shoulder and breast as she breathed beside him in their bed. It had been the tiny flutterings of their child growing inside her womb. It had been the sight of Montvallant against the sunrise, enduring stone and familiarity. Now he was separated from all that, perhaps forever. When he closed his eyes, he could see Claire standing at the castle gates, tears streaming down her face, her arms around his mother, and there was much more to their grief than the fact that their menfolk were riding away to war. It was the very nature of that war. "Like attacking one of your own limbs," Claire had said.

Like cutting out your own heart, Raoul thought, and turned to watch Arnaud-Amalric, Abbot of Citeaux, and the papal secretary, a monk named Milo, walking together toward de Montfort's tent. Some men did not have hearts to cut out.

"How's the stallion?" Berenger asked when Raoul returned to their fire.

"The poultice is working well. He should be able to walk the distance to Béziers on the morrow." Raoul sat down on a traveling stool and unhitched his sword belt. He had worn it constantly this past week, trying to adjust his body to its weight and feel. Familiarity had begun to come upon him; only his mind recoiled.

Nearby, some northern soldiers were playing dice, gambling for the favors of a camp slut. A wine flask was being tossed from hand to hand, and their language, so different from the southern tongue, grated on the ears.

Raoul and Berenger looked at each other. Words were not possible. To bring their concerns out of the mind and into the open would be tantamount to turning over a corpse and exposing all the maggots wriggling within.

"Raymond stopped by while you were gone," Berenger said into the silence. "He says that the Toulouse troops are to be held in reserve. Any frontline assault has to come from de Montfort's men."

"De Montfort's orders?"

"Yes."

"We're not to be trusted." Raoul looked at his sword belt. The gold wire decorations still gleamed—new and untempered. What he would not have given for a little experience now. "De Montfort's not so far wrong," he said grimly. "I do not believe I could bring myself to press an attack with zeal. If we're left to take care of the camp and the baggage, I'll be more than relieved."

Berenger thrust his hand through his hair. "If it was left to conscience, we wouldn't be here at all. I'm not proud to admit that we're with this army for the sole reason of saving our hides from being flayed by the French."

"Our hides being more sacred than our honor," Raoul said

bitterly. "I'm not so sure that we haven't sacrificed both. Northern ambition won't stop at Béziers and the destruction of a few Cathars. I believe that they are just whetting their appetites for the main feast to come—the entire South! Jesu, Papa, it is more than I can bear!" Knuckles bunched, he swallowed on tears, but still his breathing was ragged.

Berenger slowly rose and fetched a stone pitcher of wine from the camp table. "I know," he said, a wealth of weariness and empathy exposed as he filled the cups and handed one to Raoul. "I know, son, and I'm going to get sodden drunk tonight because it's the only way I'll be able to sleep."

Raoul took the wine from his father and stared into its bloodred, cloudy depths—rough, peasant brew, as spiky on the palate as broken glass. "How many cups between now and oblivion?" he asked.

In a crude shepherd's hut on the low slopes of the Corbier Mountains, Bridget laid her hand upon a child's sweat-drenched forehead. The willow-bark tisane had done its work, and beneath her palm, the damp skin was cool to the touch. Bridget was aware of the shepherd kneeling behind her, watching her every move with anxious dark eyes, of his wife kneading her ragged apron and chewing her underlip from side to side as Bridget ministered to their only son.

"Will he be all right, Madonna? Will he get better?" the mother asked.

Bridget rested her hand on the boy's brow a moment longer, then rose gracefully from her knees and faced the woman. "The fever has broken," she said with a tired smile. "He will live, but he still needs careful nursing. I will leave you the herbs you need and explain how to use them."

The woman knelt at Bridget's feet, trying to kiss the hem of her robe, weeping her gratitude, calling her "Madonna" over and again. The shepherd sat down beside the child and touched him for reassurance, then looked at an embarrassed Bridget, his eyes brimming. "We can never repay you," he said.

"There is no debt," Bridget answered. "As my skills were a gift to me, so I give of that gift to you." The words had been taught to her by her mother, and were ancient tradition, but each time they were spoken, she felt them shake off their dust and resonate.

"But, Madonna, there must be something . . ."

"Nothing more than a crust of bread and a cup of wine," she said with a smile. "I have to be on my way soon." Having raised the shepherd's wife to her feet, Bridget ducked through the low door of the hut into the early morning. The moon still hung in the sky, a glittering silver crescent on a background of luminescent, deep aquamarine. The dew soaked through the leather soles of Bridget's sandals. Moths, like flakes of pale ash, flickered through air scented by herbs and summer growth.

Bridget inhaled deeply, replenishing herself from the bounty laid out before her. The little boy had been very sick, and much of her healing energy had been drained in the effort to destroy the infection that had been killing him. She needed peace, and time alone. Chretien would be here soon to take her back to the Cathar house down the mountain where they had been dwelling this past week. News of their presence always spread faster than a winging eagle. The shepherd was a second cousin to a maid in the Cathar household. Now he would pass the tale of his son's miraculous deliverance to his brother-in-law's cousin in the valley who had the lung sickness, and so it would continue.

Bridget walked slowly through the wet grass, watching the moon lose its luster as the sky paled. Again and again she was obliged to give of her gift. The people talked of payment and debt, but it was she who paid every time, as once her mother had done.

"You must never, ever refuse those who come to you for help." Bridget could still hear Magda's voice, clear, gentle, but stern with emphasis. "Break your body, break your heart, but never your sacred vows." The words came so vividly to Bridget that she looked rapidly round, almost expecting to see her mother standing in the dew beside her. The eastern horizon was ribboned with gold, the moon as insubstantial as a ghost. Her straining eyes caught only the birth of the morning, but she thought she heard the distant tramp of marching feet, the neigh of horses, and the metallic scrape of weapons. The horizon's gold was as fierce as fire now and bloodily tinged. Abruptly she returned to the hut.

Growing by the door was a clump of lilies, the waxy blossoms honey-scented and gleaming with white radiance in the dawn. Bridget stopped and brushed one lightly with her hand. They had always been her mother's favorite flowers and they were sacred to the Goddess, one of the symbols of the fertile chalice of her womb.

"If you wish, Madonna, you may have them," said the shepherd's wife, who had come to the door with a pitcher in her hand.

"No," Bridget said, with a slow, sad smile. "Let them grow and multiply undisturbed."

CHAPTER ELEVEN

Béziers, July 22, 1209

SIMON PAUSED IN the act of lacing his coif, eyes tracing the trajectory of the stone that was curving from the town walls and falling well short of his troops. A howl of invective followed the missile, but did nothing to increase its range. As well as stones, the citizens of Béziers had hurled moldy vegetables and dung at his arriving troops, all falling well short of the mark.

Unhurriedly Simon finished lacing his coif and took the helm that his son Amaury handed to him.

"Missed again," the youth said.

"What does that tell you?"

"That they haven't got strong enough siege machines or the expertise to man them, sir," the boy answered confidently.

Simon nodded with approval. Amaury was a good pupil, swift to learn if a trifle lacking in scope, but that would come with maturity. After all, he was a de Montfort. "They think they have the superiority," he said, "and that is their weakness."

Taunts and jeers continued to rain from the city walls. Most of them were in the southern language, bearing more resemblance to Catalan than French and thus incomprehensible, but some were in the Norman tongue and left nothing to the imagination except the manner of reprisal. Simon gave a wintery smile as he saw his son's ears redden. "Let them have their petty pleasure," he said. "The payment will come soon enough." He turned to mount his destrier. The stallion was a gleaming, spotless white with silver mane and foaming tail. Simon had chosen the color deliberately to stand out on a battlefield, and make a superb background to a dripping red sword. The saddle's high pommel and cantle held him secure, stirrups worn long so that he almost stood in the saddle and possessed all the leverage he needed to deliver blows.

"If matters change and I am sought, you will find me with Citeaux," he told Amaury, and set off through the camp. Now and again he paused to speak to the soldiers, inquiring of their well-being, assessing their morale. A string of small victories along the way from Montpellier and the capitulation of several minor southern lords had increased the loyalty and respect in which the troops held their commander. They looked for him now on his distinctive white stallion, the fork-tailed lion on his shield clawing destruction down upon the enemies of Christendom.

Arnaud-Amalric of Citeaux, papal legate to the troubled lands of the Languedoc, was sitting outside his tent discoursing with a small flock of agitated townsmen who were trying to negotiate a settlement that would leave their comfortable lives intact. With his gray curls and shining, rubicund features, the legate resembled a decadant cherub. He was a man of power who wanted as much from this campaign as Simon did, and that made them uneasy allies and jealous rivals. Among the gathering, translating the southern tongue for the benefit of Citeaux and his scribe, were two southern knights from the retinue of Count Raymond of Toulouse, Berenger de Montvallant and his son, Raoul. Simon eyed them with disfavor. They were typical specimens of the southern nobility—hostile, untrustworthy, sympathetic to heresy, and with about as much fighting ability as he would apportion to one of his own squires in his first year of training. He reined to a halt before the little group and watched the well-fed faces of the townsmen blench. Citeaux, to the contrary, was a sweating, raspberry pink.

"What progress?" Simon demanded.

Citeaux swiveled his chins and looked maliciously at the warlord. "I told you they would not yield . . . except these few, and they're neither use nor ornament!" He gestured contemptuously at the citizens. "Ten thousand of them are still behind those walls, defying God."

From the corner of his eye, Simon saw the younger knight clench his jaw, his blue eyes brilliant with loathing. Rash whelp, thought Simon with disapproval, but he was not surprised. He was fully aware how much the southern attitude clashed with the aims of the crusade. Well and good. Like the rest of their countrymen, the lords of Montvallant would either obey or be broken.

Simon started to dismount, but had gone no further than kicking his feet from the stirrups when he heard a shout and saw Amaury cantering toward him.

"Papa, come quickly!" the youth cried, his adolescent voice cracking with alarm and excitement. "They're attacking us over the river bridge!"

Simon thrust his heels back into the stirrups and spun the destrier in a dusty circle. "Keep them under guard!" he bellowed at Citeaux, indicating the bemused townspeople, and dug in his spurs.

"Attacking over the bridge?" Berenger said in disbelief. "Are they mad?"

Raoul shook his head. His heart was thumping in huge strokes as he watched de Montfort ride away. He was frightened and ashamed to be frightened. He was also very angry. Citeaux had treated him and his father with scorn; de Montfort had made it clear that he thought the de Montvallants of no account. Raoul was sick of their hauteur and sneering superiority.

Citeaux commanded some of his own soldiers to guard the townsmen and went to put on his armor, pausing only to ask

Berenger and Raoul if they wished him to shrive them in case they were involved in the fighting. His eyes glimmered, small and piggy with malice.

"Thank you, but we will make our own arrangements," said Berenger with dignity, his expression wooden.

Knowing that he did not possess his father's control, Raoul walked jerkily away without speaking.

The undisciplined element of Béziers, scornful of the northern army, had taken their arrogance a step too far and attacked a perimeter crusader patrol post, setting fire to some newly erected tents and killing an equerry.

The incensed camp followers had reacted with vigor to the impudent foray. Snatching up whatever weapons were to hand, improvising with tent poles and cooking implements, they launched a counterassault so ferocious that it overturned the townspeople's rash attack and turned it into a panic-stricken rout. The inhabitants struggled to close the city gates in the faces of the camp followers, but a corpse became wedged in the opening. The trickle of crusaders forcing their way into the city became a stream, a river, and then a bursting, unstemmable torrent. Camp followers, mercenaries, and foot soldiers poured into Béziers, swept onward from behind by the mounted steel and muscle of the knights, squires, and great lords. They flooded the streets, carrying all before them in a massive tidal wave of bloody violence and destruction.

Resembling an enormous landed carp in his helm and mail coat, fat legs barely straddling an Ardennes stallion, the Abbot of Citeaux joined Simon to watch the destruction of the city that had dared to insult them. His cherubic features were slack, his eyes fish-round and glazed—not with horror, but with exultation.

Simon, his white horse liberally spattered with blood, rested his clotted sword across his thighs. "Do we stop this slaughter now," he asked, "or do we give our men free rein throughout Béziers?"

"What?" Citeaux blinked at him, only half-comprehending.

"The nonheretics," Simon said with labored patience. "Do you want me to set aside a sanctuary for them? Do you want the wealthy ones—those who aren't already dead—to pay an indemnity and go free?"

Citeaux stared at the butchered body of a woman sprawled near their horses. Blood crawled in the hot summer dust, dividing to become intricate rivulets, reminding him of the sacred mission with which he had been entrusted. Flies already danced attendance on the corpse. A strange smile lit in the depths of his eyes. "No," he said softly. "Kill them all. God will know His own."

With deliberate care, Simon wiped his sword on his thigh and sheathed it. "The decision is yours," he said, squarely placing the responsibility on the legate's fat shoulders. Citeaux was, after all, the nominal leader of this crusade. Simon himself was quite willing to let the slaughter continue. It well suited his plans to have the battle for the first major city of the campaign escalate into a massacre. Other centers of population were likely to capitulate speedily when they saw the fate suffered by those foolish enough to resist. It was useful, however, to have Citeaux take any blame that might later accrue to the decision. Turning in the saddle, he spoke to Amaury and his other two squires.

"Go and relay the order through the city that no quarter is to be given, no one spared. Tell the commanders, too, that I want patrols organized to prevent looting for private profit. Gains will be fairly divided once the city is ours."

"Yes, sir." It was Giffard, the eldest, on the verge of knighthood, who answered. Amaury and Walter were both as pale as flour, but neither of them spoke out in protest.

"Are you coming with me?" Simon asked Citeaux as the youths saluted and rode away to their task. There was the slightest edge of mockery to his tone. "Shall we see what we've gained for Christendom this day?"

Raoul was wearing his battle helm, which meant that he could not be sick, and trying to control Fauvel. The golden destrier was prancing and sidling, thoroughly upset by the stench and sound of bloody destruction.

And I looked and behold a pale horse: and his name that sat on him was death.

Raoul, his father, and their troop entered the city on the final wave, and only when de Montfort's insistence had made it impossible for them to do anything else. De Montfort needed some men who were not entirely overcome with bloodlust and greed to regulate the others.

Raoul felt as if he had ridden through the gates of hell itself. Every building was on fire, even the churches whose future the crusade had supposedly arrived to protect. Smoke roughened his throat and obscured his already impeded vision. Between choking drifts of black air and bright gusts of flame, he saw the bodies of people cut down as they tried to escape—young, old, mothers, fathers, infants. Fauvel stepped delicately over an old woman lying facedown in the dirt, her arms in death still clutching the baby she had been trying to protect. Raoul thought of Claire and their unborn child. "No," he said roughly, his voice breaking, and with it the fragile armor of pretense. His hands were as bloody as the man who had murdered this woman and infant.

Farther up the street his way was blocked by tangled yards of vivid green silk spilling from an open doorway. Sprawled across them were the corpses of a looter and a townsman, each dead by the other's hand.

Berenger rode up beside Raoul. "This is an accursed day for us all," he muttered thickly.

Raoul started to make the sign of the cross, but stopped with a shudder of revulsion.

From a narrow alleyway between the houses, a small troop of northern knights emerged, the sound of their approach concealed by the roar of flames and the crash of falling timber and masonry until they were upon Raoul and his father. Their leader, a fox-faced man broad of build and hard of eye, drew rein before the bodies in the road and rested his elbows on his saddle bow. "I see you've had the orders," he said.

"What orders?" Berenger looked blank.

An expression that was half-smile, half-snarl crossed the portion of the knight's face visible beneath the broad nasal bar of his helm. "No quarter to be given to anyone. The legate says that they're all to die for resisting us. Loot's to be brought to the camp, orders of Lord de Montfort. Anyone caught stealing for their own gain pays like these stupid bastards here." He signaled to one of his troop. The man dismounted and tugged the bolt of green silk out from under the corpses. A dark red stain marred the fabric's rippling shimmer.

The leader watched and unslung a wineskin from his saddle. "Thirsty work," he commented, offering a drink to Berenger and Raoul.

Raoul choked. Berenger gripped his arm and forced it down. "Our thanks, but we have our own," he said, the desire to survive keeping him civil.

"No stomach for this, eh?" The knight removed the stopper and took a hearty swig himself. The wine overflowed his mouth and trickled down his chin like blood. "Better toughen your gut quick. This is only the start." His voice was abrasive with scorn. Stoppering the wineskin, he sat up in the saddle and casually rested his hand on the sword at his hip, but the move was intentional and his eyes were as sharp as flints. "We'll take care of this and check the rest of the houses."

Raoul's fingers trembled a fraction away from the hilt of his own sword. He felt Berenger's grip tighten.

"Do you have an objection?" the knight drawled. He glanced round at his troop, a grin flashing.

"No." Berenger swallowed, and before Raoul could react, booted Fauvel in the belly. The stallion gave a startled leap forward. Berenger pressed his own destrier so close to Raoul's that his son had no room to maneuver and had to continue riding away from the conflict, the sound of northern jeering loud in his ears.

Furious, he rounded on his father. "Why didn't you lick their backsides while you were about it!" he flung with brimming eyes. "I am ashamed to bear the name Montvallant!"

Berenger's tension released itself in a single blow, the full force of his arm behind the hand that connected with Raoul's face. "Don't presume to judge me, boy!" he snarled. "You shame the name yourself with your childish tantrums! You would have died for nothing back there, for a handful of worthless insults. God, he'd have taken you on the first cut!"

Panting, father and son stared at each other. A bell that had been tolling was silenced in midstroke, and in the space where the next note should have fallen, Raoul made his decision. "I cannot be a part of this murder," he said flatly, and wheeled Fauvel.

"Where are you going?" Berenger demanded.

"Home. If I'm declared an outlaw, so be it."

"Raoul, if not for the love of God, then for the love of your family, stop and think!" Berenger said desperately. "I am as revolted as you by what is happening here, but that is all the more reason to stay within the bounds of de Montfort's orders."

Raoul continued to ride away as if he had not heard.

Berenger spurred after him. "What will happen to Montvallant if you desert now? What of your mother and Claire and your unborn child? Do you want to see this happen to them?"

Raoul drew rein before a high brick convent wall. "You can stay with de Montfort if you want," he said, breathing hard. "Disinherit me, bring up my child as your heir—do what you will, the choice is yours. I have made mine."

Berenger reached out to grasp Raoul's bridle and prevent him riding away, but stopped as from behind the wall of the convent they both heard heartrending screams for help and coarse northern voices raw with excitement and lust.

Raoul drew his sword. There was a door in the wall, usually barred with a sliding iron grille so that the nuns could inspect any petitioner before admitting them to their precincts, but today the door hung open at a drunken angle and there was no one to prevent or question Raoul as he rode through the opening and into the neatly set out herb and vegetable garden. Beyond this lovingly tended order, chaos reigned. The convent buildings were well ablaze. Coffers, hangings, vestments, and altar furniture were piled up in the courtyard. A cart had been dragged from one of the outbuildings and the convent's two red and white oxen yoked to it. Soldiers were busily loading the cart with the choicest items. The nuns had been herded into a corner, and Raoul saw that there were children in their midst whom the sisters were trying valiantly to shield with their arms and bodies.

A group of laughing crusaders were toying with the women, taunting and prodding them with their weapons and making lewd gestures. The screams for help had come from a young woman who had been singled out from her companions. One man knelt on her arms, another had spread-eagled her legs, and a third, to loud cheers of encouragement, was hitching up his tunic and loosening the drawstring on his braies.

Raoul's blood boiled over. Scarcely aware of his own ac-

tions, he spurred Fauvel across the herb beds and straight at
the soldier about to commit rape. Raoul swung his sword, felt
it connect with something hard, bite through to something soft,
and then grate upon bone. There was a lot of blood, but his vision was already crimson and he barely noticed. Wrenching his
blade free, he pivoted Fauvel and struck down the second crusader who had been about to leap on him, and then the third.
Behind him, he was vaguely aware of his father leading the
Montvallant troops into the convent grounds and directing
them against the northern soldiers.

The crusader sitting on the cart cracked a goad over the
backs of the oxen. The beasts quivered into motion and the
stout, iron-shod wheels rumbled forward on the pitted earth of
the yard. Raoul turned Fauvel and brought him directly across
the path of the straining oxen, blocking the way out in a swirl
of dust. Raoul's heart was thundering and his mouth dry, but
he found that he was able to think with speed and complete
clarity; indeed, he was aware of a terrible feeling of exhilaration.

The cart driver abandoned the wain and fled across the compound as fast as his body armor permitted. Raoul let him go.
The ox cart was exchange enough for the coward's life. Dismounting, he tied Fauvel to the back of the cart and began dis-
carding the bulkier items of loot, including two chairs carved
of walnut wood from the guesthouse and a handsome oval
bathtub. When he had cleared what he considered to be sufficient space, he clambered into the driver's place.

Occasionally Raoul had driven an oxcart at Montvallant during the barley harvest, but it had been a boyhood delight, part
of the fun of summer. Now, facing death, he found himself
sweating as he turned the beasts in a clumsy circle and brought
the wain around to the women who were huddled together like
a flock of chickens in a coop. Some of them were crying, but
Raoul found it was the ones with dry eyes who were the most
unnerving to look upon.

Berenger had dismounted and, with his hand pressed to his
side, was talking to an elderly nun, who appeared to be in
charge of the others.

"Are you hurt?" All Raoul's previous anger at their difference of opinion was banished by concern.

Berenger gave him a brief, twisted smile. "It's nothing. The flat of a blade caught me across the ribs. My hauberk's split, but no worse damage."

Raoul nodded, not entirely convinced, but prepared to let his concern ride for the moment. "We can't leave the women here; you know what will happen. If they hide in the cart and I pull the cover over, they won't be seen. If anyone stops us, I can say that de Montfort bade us save them to entertain his troops." He frowned at Berenger's harsh breathing. "Perhaps you ought to ride inside, too?"

"It's nothing, I told you!" Berenger snapped irritably. "It's taken my wind, that's all." He swung toward the nun. "Sister Blanche, did you understand what my son said? We are going to try and save you."

"Yes, I understood," she replied in a cool, astringent voice. Her spine was as straight as a rod, her features patrician. Even in extremity, and marked with the horrors of what she had witnessed, they still held their dignity and elegance. "We are of the Cathar faith," she said. "I do not know if that will make a difference to your attitude."

Berenger shook his head and prodded at the dust with the toe of his boot. "I succor Cathars on my own lands," he said gruffly. "I have nothing against your religion."

"And we would not be able to live with the alternative, would we?" Raoul flashed a challenging look at his father.

Berenger raised his head and returned Raoul's look. "No, we wouldn't," he said with a deathly weariness.

"We have a sister house in Narbonne," said the nun. "We could seek refuge there once we are out of the city." Her lower lip suddenly quivered and she made a determined effort to tighten it. "Although God in His goodness knows how long we'll be safe there. How can people who call themselves Christians do something like this?"

"It is what they call themselves, not what they are," Raoul said. "Will you speak to the others? The sooner we leave, the better."

She nodded and briskly returned to the remaining nuns and their charges.

"We're outlaws of a certainty now," Berenger muttered grimly. "As likely to be hunted down as these poor women."

"You can still leave," Raoul said frostily. "I won't stand in your way." He flourished his arm in the direction of the gate.

Berenger shook his head. "I can't," he said. "I'm as much trapped by my conscience now as you." He went to mount his horse. Pain swept through his body, tightening in his chest like a vise and throbbing through arm and neck. Raoul looked distant to him, a little blurred, or perhaps it was just the reflection of the firelight on his mail and the rippling heat haze. This was no time for visions, no time to stand in a daze. Yet his body moved as though he were walking neck-deep in water, on the verge of being out of his depth. His mind saw things with a mystical, sharp clarity, but he knew perfectly well that his eyes had gone out of focus.

"Papa?" Raoul was immediately at his stirrup.

He made the effort for his son. Unable to conceal the grayness and sweating, he nevertheless managed to say with a reasonable degree of command, "You drive the cart, I'll ride the escort. Go on, quickly now!" Convincing himself that the pain was easing, he remounted his horse.

Raoul's anxiety was far from allayed, but there was no time to dwell on it, and he climbed onto the wain and urged the oxen with his voice and the goad.

Half the Montvallant men went in front of the cart, led by Berenger. The other half, under Roland's command, rode rear guard. The small troop emerged from the convent and into the fiery streets of hell. Buildings fell in upon themselves, gushing flame and smoke. Animals ran amok, mad with terror and pain; so did people until they were stopped by sword and lance, by mace and club and dagger.

At the city gates where the crusaders had first broken through, a dozen guards had been posted to ensure that anyone leaving Béziers was on legitimate business and belonged to the northern army.

Pikes clashed, barring the way out.

"Where do you think you're going?" demanded the senior sergeant, eyeing Berenger with disfavor.

Berenger pretended to have difficulty with the language and replied in thick, barely intelligible northern French, "We are told to bring women to camp for soldiers' pleasure tonight."

He gestured at the cart, and when his hand descended, placed it on his sword hilt. "Lord de Montfort's orders."

"Women for the troops, eh?" An unpleasant grin slanted the corner of the soldier's mouth. "First I've heard of it. The lads'll find all the skirt they want back there, and I've no orders to clear any such cargo through these gates."

"It's a special consignment for Lord de Montfort's commanders." Berenger looked over his shoulder at Raoul, who had taken his hand from the reins and was reaching stealthily downward.

"Let's have a look at them, then." The sergeant stepped up to the cart. Pain jolted through Berenger's arm and ran with the heaviness of molten lead into his chest. He gasped and struggled to breathe, his vision darkening.

The sergeant tugged aside the curtain and stared within at the huddled women and children. "This isn't—" he began, but that was as far as he got. Raoul's hunting knife drove through the inferior link mail of the man's ventail and punctured the main artery in his throat. Blood spurted bright and hot. Raoul kicked the convulsing body off the cart and tossed the knife in among the women with the terse command that they use it if necessary. Then he grabbed his shield, drew his sword, and prepared to fight the rest.

Up, down, parry, slash, turn and brace the wrist, present shield, left foot forward, right back. He knew it all from the lessons learned in the tiltyard and the occasional jousts he had attended. But knowing was nothing without the experience of the ultimate trial of war. His breath started to rasp in his throat. His opponent swung low, aiming to shear off his leg at the knee. Raoul leaped. The blade clipped him, making him stagger, but his mail remained intact. He made his counterstroke, also aiming for the legs. The soldier's shield halted the blow, but Raoul used his own shield to batter at the man's face, and then he raised his sword again, this time stabbing upward between the slit hauberk skirts.

The soldier fell, but the scream of agony that rang out was not from his lips. Raoul spun in time to see his father being torn down from his horse by one of the gate guards. "No!" Raoul roared, and sprinted to intercept the descending enemy blade. He clashed the man's sword aside with his shield, and struck hard and low. Dark blood spurted and his opponent doubled over. Raoul straddled his father's body and, snarling like a wolf, fought off all comers.

Then Roland and Giles were at his side, and the remaining gate guards were running for their lives. The street was suddenly and eerily silent, apart from the distant noises of fire and skirmish. Raoul threw down his weapons and dropped to his knees beside Berenger. "Papa?" All fingers and thumbs now, he removed his father's helmet. Berenger's whole face was gray, his lips and the tips of his ears blue. There were dark smudges beneath his eyes, and his face was drawn with pain as he strove to breathe.

"Papa, where are you wounded?" Feverishly Raoul unlaced the throat of Berenger's mail hood.

Gasping, Berenger moved his head from side to side. "No, this is pain from within . . . my chest."

Sister Blanche descended from the cart and touched Raoul gently on the shoulder. "I know the herbs we can give him. They grow locally and they'll ease his breathing."

"He's dying, isn't he?" Raoul said numbly.

She hesitated, assessing him before she replied. "I think so, although I'm not a physician, and there is always the hope and consolation of prayer."

"Prayer!" Raoul spat the word out as though it were as bitter as gall.

"It is man who has violated the word of God," she gently reproved him. "Prayer still reaches out beyond the darkness."

Raoul barely heard her, his attention on his father who was now unconscious. "Roland, take his legs, help me lift him into the cart," he ordered.

Very carefully, they raised Berenger and placed him among the women. Sister Blanche climbed in beside the stricken man and set about loosening his armor and making him as comfortable as possible.

Raoul realized that his face was wet. He wiped away the combination of tears and sweat on the leather cuff of his gauntlet and returned to the driving seat of the wain. Now all he had to do was get them past de Montfort's outer pickets and into the safety of the hinterland between Narbonne and the raging inferno that had once been a proud city called Béziers.

CHAPTER TWELVE

The Templar Preceptory of Bezu, Summer 1209

THE GUESTHOUSE AT the Templar preceptory of Bezu was spacious and comfortable. It was a welcome haven for Bridget, who had spent the recent weeks following Chretien and Matthias from village to village, living in huts, caves, abandoned hill forts, and forest clearings. Here, at least, she could rest for a time and renew her energy.

A glowing hearth, the smell of new bread, pallets freshly made up with linen sheets and good woolen blankets, were luxuries beyond compare. An elderly Templar made them welcome, and when they had unpacked their few belongings and washed the dust from their feet, he took them to dine with the prior.

The meal was simple but substantial—baked fish served with a tart sauce, small flat loaves of crusty golden bread, slashed across their tops, and to wash it down, a local tawny wine. Bridget was invited to break the bread and bless it before they ate. The prior might be head of a preceptory of celibate warrior monks, but the Templars had always acknowledged in their most secret ceremonies that the Goddess had been born long before the God. She was Ishtar, Isis, and Astarte, she was the Virgin Mary and the Magdalene. If the Templars were celibate, it was out of awe for the deity, rather than from fear of being tainted.

Bridget felt the power of their belief settle upon her shoulders like an invisible mantle. To the peasants of the hills she was simply a healer, to the Roman church she was so danger-

78

ous that they sought her death, to the Templars she was the descendant of the Magdalene and the Virgin and to be revered. And to myself? she wondered as she ate and drank. What am I to myself?

When the meal had been cleared away, the prior brought a heavy cedarwood box to the table and unlocked it with a key that had been threaded upon a cord around his neck. "Since last you were here, another book has come into our possession." His words were addressed mainly to Matthias. "While you are staying here, perhaps you would wish to make a copy." With infinite reverence and care, he lifted a small, leather-bound codex from the casket.

Matthias, with equal reverence, took it from him with his good hand and held it close, but not too close, to the nearest lamp. The cover was made of hide that had been stiffened with papyrus and tooled with tiny golden crosses, each set within its own circle. He unwrapped the strip of thonging that was bound around the book. The pages were made of papyrus pasted together in two layers to give a smooth, strong writing surface. The script was a precisely executed Greek, although the language was not Greek, but Coptic.

Chretien looked on, curious, but not lit by the fervor that transfigured Matthias. His own gift was for oratory, for portraying a simple message to simple people, distilling the essence of such works into something that they could understand. "What does it say?" he asked.

The ring finger on Matthias's mutilated right hand trembled across a line of ancient lettering. "It's a Gospel." He raised his eyes to Bridget. "The life of Mary Magdalene."

There was a silence far longer than it took the reverberations of the uttered name to settle into the texture of the room.

Bridget came slowly to look at the small, battered book. Perhaps it did hold between its pages the proof to others that her word-of-mouth ancestress had truly lived and breathed. But it was something she had always known and, unlike Matthias, did not feel a need to prove. Besides, something was badly wrong. Although it was a July evening and the air as warm as new milk, she was cold. Matthias's voice, carefully following his finger along the Coptic letters, seemed to be coming from a great distance, and when she looked at him, the air between them shimmered as if with smoke.

" 'And Mary Magdalene, holy kinswoman to the Savior, went in great fear for her life and the life of her daughters, for they were persecuted for their close knowledge of Him, and for teaching His name amongst the people. And so they fled by night from their home and came with their kinsman Joseph of Arimathea to the shores of Brigantium, where they found succor.' "

They were all startled by a sharp knock at the door. The prior went himself to answer it, and Matthias quickly closed the book, a look of fear upon his face. There was a moment of tension and then the prior murmured words of welcome and stepped aside to let a young Templar enter.

"Luke!" cried Bridget, for his face was gray beneath his tan, and his clothes powdered with the dust of hard riding. "Luke, what's happened?"

His dark eyes were dull with exhaustion. "Béziers has fallen to de Montfort," he said, and dragged his gaze from her to Chretien as though it were a dead weight. "There has been a massacre. . . . Everyone is dead, and the city is in flames."

Bridget gasped, the earlier cold sensation becoming a bone-deep chill. Even before Luke had uttered the words, she had known what he was going to say, for she had plucked the images from his mind. And they had been in her own for several days, deliberately ignored in the vain hope that they would just go away. She saw Chretien put his face in his hands. Béziers had been his home city for more than thirty years before he took the Cathar path, and his roots still clung there.

"I'm sorry," Bridget said, tears filling her eyes, "I'm so sorry," and went to comfort him.

That night, lying on her pallet, the full moon streaming across her blanket, Bridget found her thoughts wandering in the direction of Raoul de Montvallant, something that had not happened since leaving Geralda at Lavaur several months ago. She had dreamed of him frequently then, but since Geralda had often spoken about the Montvallants with affection, that was hardly surprising. And Bridget was still certain that Raoul had a part to play in her life. At one time she had believed that destiny had chosen him to be the father of her child, but as the seasons had passed and their paths had not crossed, she had pushed him to the back of her mind and halfheartedly begun to search elsewhere.

Now, from the back of her mind, his image called to her. She remembered her vision on the battlements of Montvallant, the tide of flame and the bloody sword. He had been at Béziers, of that she was sure, but its effect upon him, she could not know—unless she sought him out. The thought made her heart beat faster. She saw again his vitality, the brilliance of his eyes, the white edge of his laughter. He was not dead, for the space he had occupied at the back of her mind would have been empty, and she could feel him pressing upon her consciousness.

Bridget closed her eyes and relaxed her body, her mind concentrating on the life force of Raoul de Montvallant.

Berenger opened his eyes. At first there was only darkness, but gradually he became aware of the flickering shadows cast by a small clay oil lamp. Chinks of moonlight straggled through a warped shutter and ribboned the blanket at the foot of the bed. The air was close and still in the summer heat, and the room was pervaded by an unfamiliar, frightening noise. Only slowly did he come to realize that it was the sound of his own lungs, laboring like worn-out bellows.

Where was he? He recognized nothing, neither castle nor camp. Pain stabbed through him. The leaden weight still lay on his chest, crushing him. He struggled with his memory, but it was as patchy and as full of holes as an old, outworn blanket.

Something stirred in the shadows surrounding the truckle bed on which he lay, a darker shadow, its garments whispering. For the briefest instant he experienced pure terror, almost expected the thing to turn upon him the leer of a skull, scythe in fleshless fingers as he had seen in the dances of death painted upon church walls. And then the light of the lamp fell across its face as it leaned over him, and he recognized Sister Blanche, whom he and Raoul had saved from the massacre of Béziers.

"Where am I?" His voice emerged as a weak whisper, scarcely as loud as his harsh fight for air. "Where's my son?"

She came within the range of his full vision. Against her dark blue robe a silver chain glinted. Attached to it was a small medallion in the shape of a dove. "You are in the convent of the Magdalene, just outside Narbonne," she replied. "Your son and your knights are lodged here, too. He would not leave you until pressed most strongly, but I could see that he needed a respite. I am here keeping vigil in his place."

Berenger struggled to hold her in focus, but it was beyond his will. His lids were as heavy as destrier shoes, the weight on his chest like a destrier itself.

"Drink." She bent over him and put a cup to his lips. "It will give you ease."

He managed to take two or three small swallows. The brew was so bitter that he would have retched if he had owned the strength. "How long have I been here?" He lay back against the pillows, spent. The lamp flickered and the room brightened and darkened by turns like a faltering heartbeat.

"We arrived here at noon after two days on the road."

He knotted his brow, tried to remember, but his mind did not respond. All he remembered was that there had been a blinding light followed by an equally blinding pain, then this struggle to breathe and an encroaching darkness.

"We were only challenged the once," she added, "and mercifully for us, they were soldiers from Toulouse and let us pass. The only people we met after that were refugees."

Berenger absorbed that in silence. What place on earth was safe from de Montfort and Citeaux? The cave-riddled mountains of the Ariège and Cévennes? Catalonia? Lombardy? Certainly not Montvallant and Toulouse. Perhaps, like his life, the life of the South was guttering out, all culture, color, and intellect killed by the frozen wind from the North. He moved his head restlessly. The potion she had given him had dulled his pain, but he was not so foolish as to believe that he was in any way improved. He was having to fight for every breath and his vision was growing murkier by the moment. "My son . . ." he whispered. "Please, will you fetch him?"

She set the cup down on a crude wooden chest, her gaze suddenly anxious. With a brief nod, she hurried out. Berenger closed his eyes and clung by weary fingertips to life.

"Papa?"

The voice was so young and frightened that it brought him back from the edge, clawing at the crumbling lip of the precipice. He prized his lids apart and, through the narrowest of slits, looked upon his son. The boy was haggard and bloodstained—no, not a boy, but a man. Transition by fire. He swallowed and tried to find the breath for what he had to say. "You must return to Montvallant immediately . . . tend our defenses. Your mother and Claire . . . get them away if it comes to the worst."

Watching his father fight for every word, Raoul felt terror, pity, and the flickering of a terrible rage. Until recently, those emotions had been unknown to him except as pale stirrings of the beast that now dogged his heels, his dreams, his every waking moment. There was no one else to shoulder the burden that Berenger was laying upon him. Yes, there was guilt, too, for his anger.

"We're leaving at dawn," he said, and hesitated. Briefly he looked down at his clenched fists, and then back at his father, tears gleaming in his eyes.

"I won't delay you." Berenger's mouth twisted with the barest hint of a smile. "If I am so inconsiderate as to linger beyond sunrise, you must leave me. . . ."

"Papa . . ."

"We make our farewells now. . . ." Berenger struggled to rise from the pillow to emphasize his point even while the last of his strength ebbed from him. "Tell . . . tell your mother to remember the good years we had . . . not the bitterness of the lees. . . ."

Raoul wept openly then, not just for his father, but for everything that had been taken for granted and was now lost in the bloody destruction of war. Embracing the dying man on the bed, he felt the fragile tremor of response that was overwhelmed by his own shuddering. At last he drew aside and wiped his eyes on the cuff of his gambeson.

Berenger whispered, "All my life . . . tried to be a good Christian. . . . I think . . . now . . . at the end . . . I want to take the *consolamentum*."

Raoul's gaze widened. The *consolamentum* was, among other things, the Cathar version of the last rites. It purified and prepared the believer for a higher, more ascetic plane and was thus taken only by the seriously devout and by the dying, for whom austerity, celibacy, and a meatless diet were no great trials. But to a Catholic, it was the way to everlasting damnation. "Do you mean that?"

Again Berenger smiled. "I've seen . . . the light." Had the whisper not been so weak, it would have held a hint of irony. That light had been so dazzling that it had blinded him as effectively as total darkness. "The nun . . . bring her now."

Utterly bewildered, Raoul backed from the bed. Berenger had never displayed more than a passing curiosity in the Cathar faith. Perhaps because he could not have the last rites of a Roman priest, he was seeking the comfort of another form of ritual. Or perhaps it was a last act of rebellion.

Sister Blanche was waiting outside the door, reading from a tattered copy of the New Testament. "It is over?" she asked Raoul as he emerged from the sickroom.

Numbly he shook his head. "He wants to take the *consolamentum*," he said in a choked voice, and gestured her toward the open door. Then he saw her expression. "You are not surprised?"

Carefully she closed the book and stood up. "Many times I have seen it. The closeness of death opens our spiritual eyes."

Raoul envied the belief and serenity shining in her face, for his own soul was a wasteland of bitterness and uncertainty. She went silently into his father's room. Rubbing his hands over his tired eyes and bristly jaw, Raoul slumped on the chair she had vacated and stared at the outer door facing him. A homespun curtain was drawn across it to keep out the draft. There was a woolen cloak hung upon a wall peg, and beneath it a pile of untidily stacked willow baskets and a pair of old pattens. Ordinary peasant items, speaking to him of an ordinary life that was more like a tale in a book than a present reality. The realities were the aches and pains of his abused, unwashed body, the dried blood on his surcoat and mail, the terrified scream of a child's nightmare as they jolted in the oxcart over the rough, starlit ground to Narbonne, his father dying.

He heard Sister Blanche murmuring, but his father's voice was so weak that the responses did not carry beyond the bed. He could feel no hint of air on his sweating, sticky body, but the curtain across the entrance suddenly stirred and the door opened. He looked up in dull curiosity, and his breath froze. Terror swept over him, for the door that had opened and the curtain that had lifted were superimposed upon a door that was still closed and a curtain that hung unmoving to the floor.

"Jesu's sweet life!" he croaked as the light started to shimmer around him. He wanted to jerk out of the chair and run, but he was paralyzed by the pure brilliance. A draft blew on his face and ruffled his hair.

And then she was in the room with him, aureoled by the light—the dream woman, her black hair flowing and her diamond eyes locking upon his. Raoul pressed himself against the hard back of the chair, trying to retreat into the wood. She wore a white chemise, and around her neck was a red cord from which dangled a circular pendant. Her hair lifted and floated. He could see the individual filaments, could have reached out and touched them had he not been rigid with fright. She looked at him and then into him. It was cold fire. Raoul screamed, but the sound echoed inside his head, never uttered.

"You fear without reason, Raoul de Montvallant." Her voice, in contrast to her appearance, was gentle and ordinary.

"Who are you?" he whispered. "How do you know my name?"

"We have met before, at your wedding. Surely you remember?"

Raoul moaned and shut his eyes, half-believing that he was going mad. Then, because he could still see the glow of light through his lids, he pressed his hands over them.

"It is not your imagination." She sounded almost amused, and because his hands were over his eyes, he was unable to block his ears.

Raoul lowered his hands as far as his mouth. "Yes, I remember you," he said through his fingers. "What are you doing here?" She was beautiful and unearthly, like a goddess. Did goddesses have moles? There was one on her cheekbone, emphasizing the purity of line. And her eyes. He had never known gray to have so many hues.

"When I heard about Béziers, I had to seek you out and

know that you were whole. You have been often in my thoughts."

Her words made as much sense to him as her sudden appearance. "I don't understand."

"You do not need to," she said, and gazed past him into the sickroom where Sister Blanche was leaning over the bed. "Your father has joined with the Light." Her voice was compassionate. She extended her hand. He did not feel her touch his face, but was conscious of the flow of her power tingling through him, restoring balance and energy.

Then she was gone. The door upon the door closed and blended with its solid counterpart. A milky residue of light hung in the air. Raoul swallowed. His throat was parched. He badly needed a drink, preferably some Gascon double-strength wine. Did Cathar nuns keep such a thing or would they consider it decadent? He stood up. Although he felt cold and shaky, the fatigue had ceased to burn behind his eyes, and his limbs were no longer lead weights that had to be dragged around by an equally leaden body.

Entering the bedchamber, he knew what he was going to find even before Sister Blanche turned to tell him, nor was he surprised to see that in death Berenger was smiling.

Bridget reentered her body. There was a jolting sensation as essence and flesh were again made one, and suddenly she was fettered by the weight of bone, cocooned in flesh and warm, breathing skin. Pressing her hands upon the coarse linen sheeting, she felt the stalks of straw in the mattress beneath. She stirred and turned over, her thoughts filled with the quandary of Raoul de Montvallant. He still disturbed her senses. She had seen the depth of his grief and confusion and knew that she could help him. Her conscience reminded her that there were others who needed her just as much, if not more.

"But surely, this once, I have the right to choose," she murmured as, facing the shutters, she waited for the dawn to probe its way between the slats.

CHAPTER THIRTEEN

Montvallant, July 1209

"AND HERE, MY lady, I have an eaglestone all the way from Cathay, a talisman guaranteed to ease the travail of childbirth." A crafty glint in his eye, the peddler offered for the women's inspection an egg-shaped brown stone. The apex of the oval was clutched by four gold eagle talons onto which a ring had been soldered. Through this ring was threaded a velvet ribbon so that the eaglestone could be tied to the wrist in the hour of need.

Beatrice took it from him and examined it curiously. "I asked Berenger for one of these when I was having Raoul," she said to Claire, "but you know what men are, he kept forgetting. By the time he did remember, it was too late. Raoul was born almost a month before my time was due, and so swift was my labor that there was no time for eaglestones or anything else." Misty-eyed, she passed the trinket to Claire.

"How much do you want for it?" Claire asked, trying not to appear too eager.

The peddler named an outrageous sum and justified it by repeating that the stone had come along the silk route, all the way from Cathay, the land where dragons still roamed at will. He expanded on that theme. The tale was entertaining and the women were in sore need of distraction from their cares. Claire offered him less than a third of his asking price and turned the stone over in her hand. It was cool and smooth, pleasant to the touch, and its heart winked with tiny speckles of gold.

She was now in her sixth month of pregnancy and the baby

had been moving for several weeks, the first tiny flutterings becoming more vigorous by the day. She had made new gowns to accommodate her girth and, like a nesting bird, had begun to collect together the articles necessary for childbirth and motherhood. It should have been a time of anticipation and pleasure as the sickness and fatigue of the early months yielded to a powerful, waiting calm.

Sometimes, sitting in the chamber that was hers and Raoul's, stitching swaddling bands, Claire would feel a vestige of that calm. She would envisage the baby, tiny and helpless in her arms, sometimes with Raoul's brilliant blue eyes, sometimes with her own brown ones; a boy, a girl, fair, dark. But then fear would burst the fragile bubble in which she was protecting herself, and her uncertainties would take a different, disturbing turn. Would Raoul be home for her confinement, if at all? What was to be their future? She knew that a pregnant woman was supposed to think benign, placid thoughts and receive no upsets if she was to bear a healthy, undeformed child, but what chance did she have, dwelling on a permanent knife edge?

They had received occasional letters from Raoul and Berenger, but all they contained was daily trivia, no hard facts. She and Beatrice had assumed from this that either there was nothing to report or, more ominously, that the men were keeping them in ignorance to prevent them from worrying. If so, Berenger and Raoul were deluded, for Beatrice and Claire only worried the more. They had heard rumors of skirmishes between the northern army and the forces of Roger Trenceval, their information coming without any reliability from men such as this itinerant peddler. The last they had heard, the crusaders were marching on Béziers. Since then there had been silence. There was silence now. Claire realized with a jolt that the peddler was regarding her expectantly.

"I'm sorry, what did you say?"

"Lady, I offered you the eaglestone for eight silver Raymonds."

Was that a bargain? She did not know, and glanced at Beatrice for direction.

"Six and no more!" her mother-in-law snapped decisively. "I do not believe in dragons."

The peddler gave an exaggerated sigh and spread his hands.

"What can I do? It is a long trudge to Toulouse, and in the meantime I have to eat and buy myself shoe leather. You drive a hard bargain, my lady."

"Rubbish and you know it!" Beatrice retorted. "But in consideration of your fertile imagination, you can rest here the night. My steward will see that you are paid and fed, and show you where to sleep."

"Thank you, my lady." The peddler flourished a bow first to Beatrice, and then to Claire. "May you be delivered of a fine, healthy son," he said, giving her a wink.

Smiling despite herself, knowing that he was a rogue, Claire thanked him and turned toward the stairs, intent on putting the eaglestone away in her coffer. She had taken no more than two steps when she halted and looked toward the hall door. Her heart lurched and began to pound.

"Raoul!" she cried. Lifting her skirts, heedless of all the advice meted out by Beatrice concerning the delicacy of her condition, she sped down the hall and flung herself into her husband's arms, pulling his head down to hers, kissing him, weeping.

His embrace tightened around her, and he hid his face against her cheek and wimple. She felt him shuddering, heard him groan her name, and when he released her, she was appalled at what she saw. It came to her that this was how he would look in old age, a frightening glimpse of what was to come, when he was only three and twenty. Her fingertips caught on some broken pieces of thread on his surcoat, and she saw that the crusader's cross she had so reluctantly stitched to it had been ripped off, scarring the gold velvet.

After a moment, he set her gently to one side, his attention upon his mother, who was watching the knights enter the hall, her gaze searching ever more frantically. Claire's hand went to her mouth as she realized what the expression on Raoul's face heralded. "No," she whispered. "Oh dear God, no!"

"Where's your father?" Beatrice turned toward Raoul, her composure so stiff that it was brittle and Claire could almost see tiny pieces shattering from its edges.

"Mama . . ." Raoul took a step toward her, his hand extended.

She ignored the gesture. Some knights had entered the hall

bearing a litter covered by a pall, and she stared numbly at their approach, her eyes growing wider and wider. "No, it is not true," she whispered hoarsely, and began to back away, shaking her head from side to side. "No, no, no, no!" The sound rose in an eerie, continuous wail that raised the hairs on Claire's nape. Before either she or Raoul could reach her, Beatrice had gathered her skirts and was stumbling toward the turret stairs.

Biting her lip, Claire looked between her husband and her mother-in-law, unsure as to who was in most need of her care. After a hesitation, she followed Beatrice.

Raoul rubbed his face and swung around to the knights who were avoiding his gaze. "Take Lord Berenger to the chapel," he said wearily. Squaring his shoulders, he went after the women, knowing now that the more you ran from death, the faster it gained on you.

Beatrice had fallen into an uneasy sleep, induced by the poppy syrup in wine Claire had given her.

"It was his heart that broke," Raoul said in a low voice as he gazed upon his mother. "He never had a moment of ill health until this war tore him apart."

Claire studied her husband. He had told them very little, only that his father's body had been unequal to the task of bearing armor in the summer heat, but she knew from his stilted, hesitant manner that he had not told the entire story.

She had persuaded him to bathe and eat. Divested of his armor, shaven, and wearing a blue linen tunic, he looked more familiar, but he was still not the Raoul she had grown to love and depend upon during the two years of their marriage. A hard-faced stranger had come home to her from Béziers. When she had touched his hands, she had felt the unholy stigmata of sword-grip blisters, and when she looked into his eyes, they were empty.

He moved from the bedside and went to stand in the thick stone window embrasure. "His end was neither swift nor easy," he said. "For more than two days I watched him die, and knew there was nothing I could do, that if the truth were known, he was better dead."

Claire saw him brace his hand on the stone, saw the pressure he was exerting, and felt afraid. She started forward, intending to offer him comfort, but before she could reach him, he began to speak in a low, clear voice. Every detail of the Béziers campaign poured out of him like blood from a severed artery. Appalled, Claire listened to the tally of death and violence, rape and murder, and felt its stain soaking into her soul. He spoke of the men he had killed, and she heard the bitter triumph in his tone. Burning fluid filled her mouth. Choking, she ran to the chamber pot and was sick. Raoul fell silent. When she raised her head to draw a gasping breath, she saw his braced hand had clenched into a fist on the golden stone wall, and knew that her husband was indeed a stranger.

CHAPTER FOURTEEN

Montvallant, Autumn 1209

I T WAS HOT, too hot, and the thunderstorms too distant to refresh the air. Even Montvallant's thick stone walls were soaked with heat. The leaves of nettle, beech, and plane trees wilted against a sky as blue and hard as a gemstone, the air so still that even an expended breath rippled the atmosphere.

Raoul lay on the bed in his chamber—not the same room that he had shared with Claire for two years. That one had been barred to him for the past month as her time approached. She had shut herself away with her maids, his mother, and the midwives; with swaddling bands, eaglestones, and all the rituals surrounding childbirth. The only item missing from her encapsulation was himself, and he suspected that the omission was deliberate.

He stared at the patch of sky framed by the loop of the narrow window. Blue, solid, opaque. What had happened to the promise? He thought back to his wedding day, to how lovely Claire had looked, how much he had wanted her. But even that was marred by the memory of Father Otho. The Cathars believed that hell was here, that the earth itself was a cage to contain the trapped spirit, and Raoul was beginning to believe that they were right. Only he did not have a deep enough belief or commitment to calmly accept what fate threw at him.

Irked by his thoughts and the clinging, sticky heat, he shifted impatiently on the bed. Perhaps it would be easier after the baby was born. Perhaps the focus of a new life would heal the breach caused by his father's death. . . . Perhaps he was a fool, wishing for the moon.

The three months since Béziers had been very difficult. His mother had taken Berenger's death badly and retreated into herself, grief devouring her substance and leaving her a husk, unable to withstand the blows of daily life. Recently she had donned the plain blue robe of a Cathar croyant and taken increasingly to reading books in the vernacular sent to her by Geralda of Lavaur. Claire, relieved that she was taking an interest in something, had encouraged her and in her turn been encouraged. His women, his family, had retreated into an inner sanctum of their own and closed the door in his face. Did they not know that he grieved, too? Or perhaps, because of what had happened at Béziers, he was no longer welcome.

His chest rose and fell against his damp shirt. Closing his eyes, he willed the other woman to come to him. Sometimes she did, a fleeting shadow skimming through his dreams. He would feel her eyes on him, the trailing ends of her hair, the light touch of her hands and her mind brushing his like soft wing tips. Such sensations were never more than a tantalizing salute. Her visitations were unpredictable and intermittent, and even while they comforted him, they disturbed him, too.

Of late, denied his marriage bed, he had taken to imagining more than just her eyes and hair. He found himself conjuring with thoughts of her hands on more intimate parts of his body, and her mouth pressed to his. Once, in desperation, half out of his mind, he had visited one of his old bachelor haunts in Toulouse. The whore had been experienced and knowingly amused. Young men with wives in confinement were frequent customers of the *maisons lupanardes* that they had abjured nine months before. Eased, but not at ease, Raoul had not gone there again.

The war relentlessly continued against the Trenceval lands. Carcassonne had fallen after a brief siege when its wells ran dry in the summer heat. Unlike Béziers, its citizens had been spared, Cathar and Catholic, but they had been forced to leave their homes and possessions to the victors. The Count of Trenceval had been taken prisoner and languished in a dank cell at Simon de Montfort's pleasure, his heir an infant two years old.

Narbonne had preserved itself intact by severely persecuting its own heretics, among them the nuns whom Raoul and Berenger had rescued from Béziers. All of the women had died, burned at the stake for their beliefs. The day Raoul heard that news turned into the night when he visited the brothel. After the whore had finished with him, he had drunk himself into oblivion. But when he awoke to a gray dawn, nothing had changed. He thought that his childhood had died at Béziers, but he had been wrong. It had died in a Toulouse whorehouse, an empty flagon overturned on the floor.

Raoul stared across the room at his mail hauberk where it hung upon its pole, the rivets bright from harsh scouring in a barrel of sand and vinegar. His sword was propped against the wall beside it, the tooled belt wrapped around the scabbard. Grim companions. Every day he practiced in the tiltyard, developing muscles he had never even known existed. Daily he rode out on patrol and examined the castle defenses for signs of weakness. Sometimes the sense of futility wearied him—he was David facing down Goliath and he no longer believed in miracles. On other occasions the anger came uppermost and seethed so violently that he no longer knew himself, and yet, at its receding, he was left with a growing residue of self-knowledge to which he clung like a drowning man washed up on a foreign shore.

Sitting up, he dragged off his wet shirt, balled it up, and used it to dry his damp body. His gaze returned to his sword hilt, to the irregular bronze pommel and its grip of plaited red and yellow silk. The shape and the colors throbbed at him, and the wall behind the weapon dissolved into white nothing. In the corner of his vision his hauberk, too, was pulsating, licked by tongues of silver flame. Stomach sucked in, the taste of fear in his throat, he sat motionless, unable to look away.

Clearly and distinctly a voice said in his ear, "The destroyers are coming; be on your guard." For a fleeting moment in the pommel of his sword, like a reflection in a distorted mirror, he saw a vineyard and men on horseback locked in combat. Then, as suddenly as it had come to him, the vision was gone and the atmosphere was still. His chest hurt, reminding him to breathe. His eyes had been wide open for so long that they were watering. Outside he heard the shout of an irritated groom and the cheeky retort of his apprentice, but he knew he had not imagined the woman's voice that had murmured against his ear. He had been shown his hauberk and sword, and warned.

Struggling back into his crumpled shirt, he threw open the door and shouted for his squire.

When he went to Claire's chamber, he was admitted somewhat cautiously by Isabelle. He saw the maid's eyes widen as she took in the fact that he was armed. Without a word he strode past her into the room. Two midwives and several women he did not recognize except to know that they were new and Cathar watched him with a mingling of curiosity and fear. That the lord of the castle should enter this room accoutred in full mail spoke of trouble too close to their haven.

Raoul entered the inner room. His mother was stooping over a coffer, putting away linen, and he noticed how much weight she had lost. Her haunches were two bony hillocks against her dark mourning gown, and the fabric was gathered in heavy pleats by her belt.

Claire was sitting near the narrow, arched window, fanning herself and reading. She wore neither veil nor wimple, and her braids were pinned high on her head to leave her nape cool. He saw the graceful curve of her neck, the little loose wisps of chestnut hair, and his heart filled and overflowed.

When she saw him, she jumped to her feet with a gasp and put down her book. "Why are you wearing armor? What's wrong?"

"There is trouble on our lands—a northern raiding party, I suspect."

"You suspect?" She searched his face. "Has the patrol sent word?"

"No, it's a gut feeling, a premonition." His words sounded lame to his own ears. How much less convincing they must sound to Claire.

"I see," she said in a tone that told him she did not see at all.

"Do you not remember our wedding night, that dream I had? I saw Béziers in flames, and ourselves parted by the fire. Has that come true or not?" Taking her by the shoulders, he pulled her against him and felt her flinch as her body made contact with the cold steel rivets of his hauberk. "Look how you shun me."

"It is not you I shun, but what you are becoming!" she replied, tears filling her eyes. "I watch you swinging your sword in the yard, I see the look on your face when you take off your helm, and I grow afraid that you are no different from *them*."

"If you had ridden with *them*, you would not be so righteous," Raoul said in growing anger and irritation. He released her and headed toward the door before he said other things that he would later regret.

Biting her lip, Claire watched his choppy stride. Before he reached the door, she called to him, "Raoul, have a care."

He stopped, took a deep breath, and swung round, his expression schooled to neutrality. "And you," he said.

They stared across the space at each other, but neither made the move. Tears sparkled on Claire's lashes, but she kept her chin up. The bands of muscle supporting her womb tightened painfully. Raoul lowered his gaze and turned away. She watched him leave, her throat tight, her back aching from holding herself rigid. The door closed behind him. Overwhelmed by tension and a terrible sense of loss, she began to cry, her sobs wrenched from deep inside her. The women clustered around, exclaiming, trying to comfort. She felt their love and concern, but it meant nothing and she only cried the harder.

And then she felt a strange, bursting sensation, and water gushed down between her legs, splashing the rushes, soaking through her gown. Her womb felt as if it were tied inside her by a score of tight knots.

" 'Tis the child coming," cried one midwife to the other. "Quickly, help my lady to bed!"

The brief shade of the beech trees gave way to the scantier cover of twisted olive, dark cypress, and holm oak as Raoul's troop climbed away from the castle and its harvested vineyards and barley fields. They headed east on the heels of Roland's earlier patrol, which had been sent out on their daily circuit of Raoul's lands. Sheep droppings, dry and crumbly, were pressed into the nibbled grass by the hooves of the passing destriers. The air was aromatic with the scent of crushed thyme and marjoram. Daisies and pink soapwort splashed the crevices. The air sagged with heat.

"My lord, are you sure this is right?" Giles drew level with him. "Would it not be better to turn north?"

Raoul did not answer at first, concentrating instead on guiding Fauvel over the terrain as it grew steadily more sparse. Farther up the slope, above the path they were following, were some caves, well hidden from casual scrutiny and which he knew were currently being inhabited by a group of itinerant Cathars.

"Do you believe in premonition?" he asked abruptly.

The knight looked startled. "Never thought about it," he growled, and wiped his gambeson cuff over his sweating face. After a pause, he glanced at Raoul. "Why do you ask?"

"I heard a voice in my ear and I saw Roland under attack." Raoul's tone was wooden; he dared not trust it to emotion.

"When?"

"Just before I summoned you and the men."

Giles muttered softly beneath his breath. Had he been a dog, his hackles would have stood on end. "Sometimes the squires scare each other witless telling tales like that after curfew," he said disapprovingly.

Raoul gnawed his lower lip. Now that he had started, he could not stop, even if Giles was not a sympathetic listener. "When she first started revealing things to me, I thought I was going mad," he confessed, "but then they came true. On my wedding night she came to me in a dream and showed me Béziers in flames. And I saw her again when my father was dying, only that time I was wide-awake, and she touched me."

"She?"

"I've never seen eyes so compelling, or that change hue so quickly, and there is a glow around her, as if she is filled with light."

Despite the scorching heat of the afternoon, Giles shivered. He wanted to scoff at Raoul's words, brush them aside as the imaginings of a boy who had listened to too many troubadours' tales, but there was something in Raoul's face that prevented him. The church warned against female demons who sucked out a man's soul through his loins while he slept. "You should talk to a priest," he suggested with a sidelong look.

Raoul's lip curled. "I'd rather remain possessed than let one of those crows sink his talons into my soul!"

"A Cathar, then."

Raoul grimaced and made an impatient gesture. "Leave it," he said. "You don't understand."

For the next ten minutes they rode in uncomfortable silence until they came to a fork in the path. The left one led up to the caves, becoming little more than a goat track and petering out before it reached the summit. The right wove down into the valley, usually a tranquil scene of vineyards and cultivated fields, irrigated by a stream that meandered its way between the hills to join the Tarn. Today that tranquillity was sundered by the flash of armor and the clash of weapons as Roland's outnumbered patrol fought to hold off a larger raiding party of knights and sergeants.

Giles looked askance at Raoul. "Holy Jesu," he muttered, and made the sign to ward off evil.

Raoul pulled his mail coif over his scalp, laced it, and buckled on his helm. His gut was queasy, but the sensation was not as intense as it had been on other occasions. Experience was like another cutting edge on his sword blade, and anger was the burnishing. Not that his sword would be his first weapon. The initial attack would be launched by horse and the full thrust of a twelve-foot ash lance.

Raoul brought the weapon over, resting it on his thigh and across Fauvel's cream mane. He fretted the destrier back on his hocks and drove in his spurs. "For Béziers!" he howled, and charged.

The force of the attack hit the main skirmish and splintered it apart. The knight Raoul had singled out was flung from the saddle, spitted through his hauberk like a roasting fowl. Raoul wrenched the lance head free and swung to meet a challenge on his right. His opponent battered away the bloodied lance tip with his shield and chopped with his sword, splintering the haft.

Raoul threw down the broken lance and drew his sword. He struck and maneuvered, struck and maneuvered, and succeeded in gashing his opponent's shield arm to the bone. The knight tried to back out of the fight, but Raoul followed through hard, rising in his stirrups to bring down his sword and finish it. The man slumped over his pommel, then keeled from the saddle. His terrified horse bolted. Raoul brought the reins down on Fauvel's neck and spurred him into the thick of the battle.

Clods of dry earth and straw churned up by the destrier hooves turned the air into choking dust. He found himself matched against an older man, powerful and battle-wise. The shock of the blows raining upon his shield sent fierce ripples of pain up Raoul's arm. Without surcease he was battered. Desperately he commanded Fauvel with his thighs. The horse disengaged, and a blow that should have taken off Raoul's right arm at the shoulder went wide.

While the knight was still off balance from the missed stroke, Raoul darted into the attack again, cutting two swift blows, neither of which did any serious damage. Vision throbbing with red and black stars, Raoul redoubled his efforts. Luck was with him. His adversary's horse stumbled beneath the onslaught, and the knight was pitched out of the saddle, unable to guard against the blows from Raoul's tiring arm.

Sweat blinded his eyes. His pulse roared in his ears and pounded in his parched throat. He gulped for air, unable to take it in fast enough to serve his starving lungs, and yet he dared not pause for respite. His sword arm was hot and aching, his shield arm felt like lead as he commanded Fauvel with his heels, turning him once more in to the vicious center of the melee. "For Béziers!" he snarled again, reminding himself of what was at stake, and pushed his will beyond the limit of his body in search of survival. "For Montvallant!"

When he regained his awareness, he was standing in the churned-up ruins of the barley field, his sword raw and clotted in his hand, his surcoat splashed with blood, and his helm on the ground at his feet. Fauvel, tawny hide brown with sweat, was being watered at the stream with the other destriers. The dead were spread across the field, several Montvallant men among them. He felt a gray weariness beginning to seep over him, bringing with it the pain of cuts and bruises. A dead sergeant lay near his feet, the red silk cross on his breast reflecting the hazy light of the sun.

Farther across the field, a pair of his own sergeants had taken a prisoner. Raoul swallowed, but his throat was so dry that he choked. He stumbled to the stream. Before he could drink, he had to put his sword down. The state of it churned his stomach, but he forced himself to clean the blade on the barley stubble before sheathing it from sight. At Béziers he had seen men who laughed and competed with each other to see who could cake themselves with the most gore. At Béziers the bloodied sword had been a symbol of honor, of prowess and brotherhood.

Pushing down his coif and scooping his hands into the clear, running water, he sluiced his hot face and sweat-soaked hair, then drank several slow mouthfuls, disciplining himself not to gulp. The water lay in his stomach, heavy and cold. Wiping his mouth, he took Fauvel from the squire tending the destriers and walked the horse across the field to the prisoner.

He was a knight in his late middle years, sporting a full gray mustache and beard to compensate for the sparsity of hair on his scalp. His surcoat was diagonally parti-colored in crimson and brilliant yellow, and his sword belt was as fancy as a strip of gilded gingerbread.

Squaring his shoulders, Raoul set his minor injuries aside to play the victorious battle leader. "You know the rules and pledges of ransom, so we need not waste time on them," he said curtly. "What I want to know is who you are, where you are from, and why you were raiding my lands."

The knight drew himself up. "I am the Seigneur Giroi de St. Nicolas, commander of a reconnaissance detail attached to Burgundy's army," he answered with proud defiance.

It was obvious to Raoul that his prisoner was highly cha-grined at having to surrender to a much younger man, but that he was also concerned for his hide, thus the statement of his value to Burgundy. "By what right do you seek to plunder my lands and attack my patrol like a common brigand?" Raoul demanded, unimpressed. "I'm a vassal of Count Raymond of Toulouse, not of Trenceval."

"I had orders," said Giroi de St. Nicolas stiffly. His scalp glistened with drops of sweat.

"From whom, Burgundy?"

"You are on a list of rebel southern nobles compiled by our commander in chief, Simon de Montfort. The word is that you turned traitor at Béziers, that you aided some heretics to escape, and in so doing, murdered members of the Christian army."

A muscle bunched in Raoul's jaw. "How many Cathars did de Montfort permit to walk free from Carcassonne in return for coin and property?" he snapped. "More than the pitiful score I rescued for certain!"

The prisoner shrugged. "I only repeat what is said of you."

"And you came all this way to plunder my lands because of that?" Raoul arched an incredulous brow. Giroi did not have sufficient men with him to be the advance guard of a siege party, and he could hardly envisage the great Count of Burgundy sitting down before such a minor town as Montvallant when larger cities remained to be conquered. "You find Montvallant worthy of such attention?"

"We were on our way north and just foraging for supplies."

"On your way north?"

"It was always understood that our count would return home once the Cathars had been taught a lesson," Giroi said a trifle defensively.

"One they have learned very well, but not in the manner you hoped," Raoul said, but with only half his mind. The other half was dwelling on the interesting news that Burgundy had quit the field. So it had begun. The great northern army was going home for the cold season.

"Lord de Montfort remains, and you will gain nothing by taking up the sword against him," said the northern knight as if reading Raoul's thoughts.

"Oh, I well know Lord Simon," Raoul said grimly as he mounted Fauvel. From what he had seen of the man thus far, de Montfort would have contingency plans and manage superbly, whatever the numbers of his army, but there were bound to be limitations. Winter would at least provide the beleaguered South with a respite, perhaps even a chance to regroup.

"He is no longer just the 'Lord Simon,' " added Giroi de St. Nicolas as he was granted the courtesy of a horse, although his hands remained securely bound behind his back. "He's now the nominal Viscount of Béziers and Carcassonne, and you are deluding yourself if you think that the Trenceval line will ever rule again. I advise you to make your peace with him before it is too late."

There was a bitter taste in Raoul's mouth. He leaned over Fauvel's withers and spat. "The peace of the grave," he said, his voice intense with loathing. "This has never been a holy war unless the gods have been those of possession and power." Leaving the Burgundian knight, he cantered to the head of the column. His body ached from the violence of battle and his mind had become a dull blade, sawing at matters that it did not have the ability to dissect.

By the time they arrived at Montvallant, the shadows were lengthening. Raoul clattered beneath the gatehouse portcullis and entered the bailey. Grooms ran out to greet the returning soldiers, as did relieved members of the garrison and several wives. Claire's maid Isabelle was waiting for Raoul, her dark eyes very bright.

"My lord," she said, coming to his stirrup as he prepared to dismount, "you have a son."

CHAPTER FIFTEEN

Carcassonne, Winter 1209

IT HAD STARTED to snow again, fine flakes driven slantwise by a bitter wind. Shivering, Bridget drew her thick, blue wool cloak more closely to her body and fumbled in her satchel for a honey and raisin cake and her flask of sweet wine. Five miles to the east across the dusk-blue snow, torchlight twinkled on the walls of Carcassonne, the city that was now the parlor of Simon de Montfort's web. Eating her honey cake, Bridget paused to study the city towers rising in dark silhouette against the frozen landscape.

Chretien halted beside her and sighed. "Once we were guaranteed a welcome there," he said sadly. "There were more safe houses than I could count on my fingers, but that has all changed now. They go in fear of de Montfort and Citeaux . . . and who can blame them after Béziers?"

Bridget touched his arm in quick sympathy and turned her tired mount away from Carcassonne. Two hour's further riding would bring them to a remote village where the Cathars were still welcome and their safety guaranteed. From there they were bound northward, to Toulouse and Geralda for the remainder of the winter months. It was never safe to remain in one place for too long.

Behind her, Matthias cursed as the pack mule balked at being turned in to the wind. The beast sat back on its haunches and whipped its head back and forth, fighting the lead rein and braying as if Matthias had stuck a knife in it. Bridget tried to turn her horse, but something frightened the mare and she shied violently.

Bridget clung to the pommel, the mare's dark mane flying in her mouth and blinding her eyes. It was not until she had recovered enough to sit up and gentle her mount that she saw the body lying at the roadside beneath a light dusting of snow. It was moving, lifting an arm to gesture weakly for help. The mare backed and sidled, her ears flat to her skull, and Bridget was hard-pressed to calm her down.

Chretien dismounted and bent beside the figure, gently turning it by the leading shoulder. "It's a priest," he said, "a black friar," and momentarily recoiled.

Bridget dismounted from the mare, keeping the reins in her hand while she stooped beside her uncle. Her stomach churned as she looked at the ashen, cadaverous features of the young friar. A thick trickle of blood welled from a jagged cut on his forearm where he had landed upon a sharp stone hidden by the snow. He had been bleeding for some time, for his aura was weak with impending death. It was also murkily unbalanced. Like Chretien, she recoiled. Such men as this had murdered her mother and mutilated Matthias.

"Can you do anything for him?" Chretien asked, his tone carefully neutral.

Never had Bridget been so tempted to say that she could not. In another hour the priest would be dead of blood loss and exposure, and better so for the world. And yet it was the sacred duty of a healer to preserve life, and she had no right to withold her skills. For what the priests had done to her mother, she would have passed on by, but for the tenets of her mother's belief, she laid her hand upon the friar's wound. "I do not know that it is my belief any longer," she murmured as she summoned the healing energy from deep within her, and concentrated upon the man's damaged flesh. Behind her eyes there flashed a sudden image of a mountaintop crowned by the sacred lightning fire and the priest staring toward the summit with the predatory eyes of a wolf.

The bleeding slowed and stopped. Feeling chilled to the core and shaken, Bridget took away her hand. "He will live," she said with a shudder, "but we will have to bring him with us."

"And jeopardize the villagers?" Chretien shook his head. "We cannot."

"It is either that or take him to Carcassonne."

Chretien chewed his lip and stared over his shoulder at the way they had come. "I suppose we must bring him to de Montfort's lair," he said reluctantly at last.

The young friar groaned softly and opened his eyes. They fixed and then widened upon Bridget, and his chest moved spasmodically.

"Lie still," she soothed. "You are safe now and help is at hand."

"Ave Maria, Regina Caelorum," he whispered, and fainted away.

"What did he say?" Matthias cocked his hand behind his ear.

"He saluted me as Mary, Queen of Heaven," Bridget said dryly. "He is like all his kind. So near and yet so far from the truth. And if I told him the truth, that her blood is mine, he would burn me for a blaspheming heretic."

Simon gnawed the trimmed end of his goose-quill pen, deep frown lines between his eyebrows. He felt bone-weary, and despite the lynx-pelt robe across his knees and the beaver-skin lining to his cloak, he was cold. Whoever said that the southern winters were mild was a liar. Several times he had been caught in the snow; indeed, there had been a blizzard howling when Albi had surrendered. The Haut Languedoc was a series of sugarloaf humps on the horizon, and at night the howling of wolves sounded like the wailing of lost souls.

Not that Simon permitted either wolves or weather to hold him back. Snow, rain, and hail were concealing mantles through which a small army could move to take an unsuspecting, complacent enemy, and he had need of every ruse at his command.

A ring glinted on the thumb of the hand that was spread across the parchment, holding it flat. Roger Trenceval had died in prison of dysentry, and Simon was now Viscount of Béziers and Carcassonne, a title that sounded impressive but was in fact so precarious that he felt he was tempting fate every time he signed himself thus. In defiance, he did so with a bold flourish.

Despite his drastically reduced army, he had commenced the winter season with some success. Limoux and Albi had both surrendered to him, as well as a complement of smaller towns. But then the sharper local barons had started to realize how few men he actually had, and had pursued rebellion with renewed vigor. Simon had been forced to give ground, and although he had lost nothing strategic yet, he had been compelled to yield several minor fortresses to the rebels.

Infected by the insurrection, the Count of Foix, a former reluctant ally of Simon's, had turned openly hostile and refused to let him have garrisons on any of his territory. Added to this, Pedro of Aragon, Simon's theoretical suzerain, would not accept his homage or recognize his titles. As far as the King of Aragon was concerned, the Viscount of Béziers and Carcassonne was Roger Trenceval's infant son, and Simon had no credibility. Simon might not have his back to the wall, but he was close enough to feel the brick constricting his sword arm.

He stared at the logs in the hearth, lit red from beneath and flaking to gray. It was pear wood, aromatic and clean-burning. A pair of alaunts dozed before it, and Giffard, who should have been polishing Simon's spurs, had fallen asleep with his mouth open. It was late. The triple candlestick near his hand was knobbed with strings of congealed wax, and the candles had burned down very low. Leaning over the parchment to write, he discovered that the ink had dried on the end of his quill.

With an impatient growl, he retrimmed the quill with his penknife and sought the ink horn, determined to finish this letter to Pope Innocent.

The lords who took part in the crusade have left me almost surrounded by the enemies of Jesus Christ who occupy the mountains and the hills. I cannot govern the land any longer without your help and that of the faithful. The country has been impoverished by the ravages of war. The heretics have destroyed or abandoned some of their castles, but they have kept others which they intend to defend. I must pay the troops that remain with me at a much higher rate than I would in other wars. I have been able to keep a few soldiers only by doubling their wages. . . .

Simon paused again to gain control of the frustration that was running away with his pen, and tipped wine from the almost full flagon into his cup. Then he drank slowly, spacing each swallow. When his mind was calm, he finished the letter, sanded and sealed it, and put it on the pile of documents waiting to be dispatched. That done, he drew a fresh sheet of parchment toward him and started writing to his wife. It was a commander's letter to a quartermaster—brisk, efficient, and lacking in sentiment of any kind; nor, when Alais received it, would she expect any. And yet he missed the silver flash of her needle in a quiet corner, her solicitous regard for his welfare, her pride in his accomplishments. Had the winter season not been so fraught with difficulty, and had he not needed her to raise support for him in the North, he would have kept her here at Carcassonne.

He finished the letter. The wine had made him light-headed. Leaving Giffard to sleep, knowing that the boy would be about his duties well before dawn, Simon wound his way slowly down to the great hall, intent on finding a hunk of bread and cold meat to sustain him through at least another candle notch of letter writing.

Here, soldiers and officials were still about their business. Simon ordered someone's squire to bring him food and, rubbing his hands, walked slowly to the warmth of the fire.

Even before Simon had reached the comfort of the hearth, there was a disturbance at the lower end of the hall as two guards came in from the bitter cold, bearing between them the unconscious form of a Dominican friar. They approached the fire, but hesitated when they saw Simon.

"Come hither," Simon beckoned.

Snow melting from their cloaks, the men set the friar down before the hearth. His garments were sodden and water from his tonsure trickled down his ashen, cadaverous features.

"Three pilgrims brought him to the gate, sir," explained one of the guards, surrepetitiously wiping his nose on his sleeve.

"Said they found him on the road in the snow with an injured arm. Put his foot in a rabbit hole, so they think."

Simon grunted. "Foolish to be abroad in this weather," he said. "All right, back to your posts. Fetch my chaplain on your way and let him attend to this man."

"Yes, sir."

The soldiers trooped out. At Simon's feet, the young friar groaned and licked his lips. His eyelids fluttered open, revealing irises of a brown so dark that they were almost indistinguishable from the black of the pupil.

"I saw her," he croaked, focusing hazily on Simon and extended one shaking, slender hand to clutch at the hem of Simon's tunic. "I saw her on the road."

"Saw who?" Simon looked down at the gripping, skeletal claw and felt a mild unease.

"The Blessed Virgin, mother of our Lord Jesus Christ. She appeared to me in a vision and told me that I would be saved." The young man released Simon's robe and struggled to sit up. "I know it was her. She wore a blue robe and her body shone with light, and when she touched my arm, the pain disappeared!"

"You were brought in by three pilgrims," Simon said. "Perhaps you ought to wait for my chaplain before you say anything more."

"You do not believe me?"

"I believe that you are suffering from shock and exposure," Simon said evenly enough, although the friar's words had caused a cold shiver down his spine. "Certainly you may have seen something, but you will be better able to judge reality once you have recovered."

"I saw her, I tell you, I saw her. Do you think I would not know?" Tears filled the young Dominican's eyes, and his scrawny throat jerked. "I had fallen on a sharp stone and was bleeding to death in the snow when she came to me and put her fingers over the wound—look!" He pushed up the saturated sleeve of his habit and exposed to Simon a thin white forearm. The flesh was bisected by a jagged red slash, deep and cruel, but it was not bleeding.

Perhaps, thought Simon, the bitter cold itself had stopped the flow. Then again, like Saul on the road to Damascus, perhaps the young friar truly had experienced a holy presence and been miraculously saved. Such things did happen. Being a pragmatic man, wary of mysticism, Simon preferred to reserve judgment for when the invalid had fully recuperated from his ordeal.

Returning to his chambers with a platter of food, he dismissed the friar from his mind and settled down by the fire to finish his writing.

CHAPTER SIXTEEN

Toulouse, Spring 1210

OUTSIDE THE GREAT hall of Count Raymond's palace on the south side of the city of Tolouse, Raoul unbuckled his sword belt, handed his weapon to one of the guards on duty, and strode into the room on the heels of the steward who announced him.

Raymond did not rise from his seat on the dais and bounce down the room to greet Raoul as he would have done only six months ago. That kind of optimism had been knocked out of him by the endless shock of warfare and Rome's cold rejection of all his recent attempts at conciliation.

Raoul's stride, however, was purposeful. He had learned that to hesitate was to make men take less notice of him because of his youth, indeed to dismiss or patronize him as Raymond had once done at Montvallant. The Béziers campaign and the months since then had taught Raoul his own value, and beyond that, his values.

He bent the knee before the dais, but stood up the moment he was commanded and looked Raymond directly in the eyes.

Raymond had been absent from his lands all winter, attempting to muster support in France and forgiveness in Rome, with success in neither venture. His face revealed the disappointments. Lines that had once been lightly etched were carved deep into skin now sallow and missing its vital glow.

"Welcome, Raoul, and thank you for coming."

It was not the count who spoke the formal words. Raoul turned to regard the youth who, with guidance from his advisers, had ruled Toulouse during Raymond's winter absence. In the time-honored way, he, too, was called Raymond, but to avoid confusion, he had been known to familiars from birth as Rai. He was a pleasant youngster who showed signs of being less indolent than his father, having inherited from his Plantagenet mother a streak of Angevin dynamism. But he was only just fourteen years old, and raw to politics.

Wearily Raoul inclined his head and took the chair and the cup of wine that were offered.

"I was sorry to hear about your father," the count said. "We had been friends since childhood; I was a groomsman at his wedding to your mother and I helped them celebrate your birth." He slowly shook his head and picked up his cup. "I thought we still had many years and gray hairs left to share."

"He was at peace when he died." Raoul gave Raymond a challenging look. "He took the *consolamentum*."

The cup halted on Raymond's lip. He stared.

"He asked for the Cathar rites, and they were bestowed on him by a nun we rescued from Béziers. I learned later that she . . . that she was burned during the persecutions in Narbonne. I believe that my father took the *consolamentum* in defiance of all that we have witnessed in Béziers, but I know that he also found peace."

"Are you of their persuasion?" Raymond continued to stare.

Raoul smiled sourly. "Does it matter, my lord? We are not being harried for our beliefs, but for our lands and titles and our freedom." Bleak humor glinted in his eyes as he put his cup down on the table. "Are you going to clap me in irons and confiscate my possessions? Is that why you wanted to see me?"

"Of course it is not!" Raymond sounded both offended and shocked that Raoul should think such a thing. He leaned across the table, his expression suddenly earnest, and held out his hands in a gesture designed to disarm and placate. "We know that you acquitted yourself well at Béziers, and also that you destroyed an entire Burgundian raiding party on your lands." He paused to let the flattery sink in. The move was so deliberate that it only served to increase Raoul's suspicion, and his eyes remained narrowed.

Raymond looked slightly disconcerted. He cleared his throat. "We need to organize and train fighting men to repulse de Montfort. Now that reinforcements are arriving from the North, he's gone on the offensive again. Toulouse is less than fifty miles from his boundaries."

"You want me to help you organize resistance to de Montfort?"

Raymond gulped a mouthful of wine and nodded. "We've started recruiting men from the towns and from the families whom de Montfort has dispossessed. We also have some Gascon and Spanish mercenaries, and we've been promised aid from the Count of Foix."

Raoul said nothing. He looked down at his hands. Once, not so long ago, they had been soft and manicured, the right thumbnail cultivated for dalliance with a lute. Now his palms were as hard as boiled leather, and his damaged nails were clipped short, almost to the quick. A glance at the count's hands showed him that they were still pliant and cared for. The ruby cabochon ring still glowed on Raymond's thumb like a clot of fresh blood. Everything came back to blood, even his dreams of the gray-eyed woman.

At last, frowning, Raoul looked up. "I was declared a rebel at Béziers and my lands forfeit. Housing and training men will only compound my crime."

"It will also strengthen your position and make you less of a tempting morsel to be swallowed in one gulp."

"Indeed," Rai said with devilish grin, "none but de Montfort and Citeaux will dare tackle you."

"Is that supposed to reassure me?" Raoul asked wryly, but relaxed and began to smile. "My lords, I accept your offer, assuming, of course, that you pay the wages of the men you billet upon me and any expenses I incur beyond my feudal dues." With hidden amusement, he saw them exchange glances.

"Yes," he said softly, "war changes everything familiar. I think it best if we know where we stand from now on."

The count extended a pleading hand—the one that wore the ring. His undergown was tight green silk, the overtunic a blood-crimson damask crusted with gold embroidery. "Your feudal oath, I can have for the acting of a ceremony, but I must know that it goes deeper than the mere mouthing of words."

Raoul bit back the angry retort that his father had died proving his loyalty to the house of Toulouse and that he himself had been branded an outlaw. What more did Raymond want? A hollow feeling in the pit of his stomach, Raoul stared at the hand reaching out from the gilded sleeve. He knew what Raymond wanted, and that it was impossible for him to give it. He was not Berenger, and the halcyon summers between the count and his father were thirty years in the past.

"My lord, I realize that honor is as difficult to find these days as a virgin in a brothel, but I hope that mine is still intact enough that you should not doubt it."

Raymond slowly withdrew his hand. "I doubt everything." The lines bracketing his mouth deepened. He said wearily, "Your father and I had some rare times together."

There was a brief, strained silence.

Rai stood up, stretching like a young cat. "Come to the armory and look over what we've got. You can put in an order to our quartermaster for anything you need."

Raoul nodded and rose with a feeling of relief. He longed to be out of the hall. Even with the candles and lamps burning in every available crevice, the place was unutterably damp and depressing, and the hurt expression in Raymond's eyes was making him feeling guiltier by the moment.

Bowing to the older man, Raoul began to follow the youth out of the hall.

"Incidentally, how is your wife?" Raymond called out.

Raoul's shoulders tensed at the shouted afterthought, and if his expression had been guarded before, the face he turned to his suzerain now was as impenetrable as a cask jousting helm.

"It was a difficult birth, my lord, but Claire has recovered well and we have a fine son, Guillaume." His voice softened on the last word. Guillaume was his at least, even if he seemed to be losing Claire.

"That is most excellent news; I am pleased for you." Raymond's voice was overhearty. "If you want a foster home for him when he's ready for squirehood, you need look no further than my own household."

Raoul smiled, a mechanical stretching of his lips that did not reach his eyes. "Thank you, my lord," he acknowledged stiltedly, and turning quickly, went with Rai.

The rushes carpeting the floor of the Cathar meeting room in Toulouse were strewn with fragrant herbs and gilded with sunshine. Against the walls were stacked bolt upon bolt of fabric. The house belonged to a cloth merchant, and this was one of his storerooms. English broadcloths and plaids, striped damasks and sarcenets from Marseilles, and Italian velvets in glowing gemstone colors provided an opulent backdrop to the voice of Chretien de Béziers.

Seated among the congregation, Claire felt a tingle run up her spine as she listened to his rich, powerful baritone and the simple message of love and encouragement it conveyed. So simple, she thought, that most of the time it was overlooked. Glancing round at the rapt faces of the other listeners, she was assailed by a poignant rush of emotion. Here, in this sun-filled room, it was so easy to believe and to belong. She never wanted these moments to end.

Chretien de Béziers ceased speaking to drink from a wooden cup of water on the table beside him. While he rested, a young woman took his place.

"That's her," whispered Claire's maid Isabelle, "that's the one I saw at the meeting yesterday."

Claire shifted the warm weight of her sleeping son into the crook of her other arm and regarded the Cathar woman. She was small and slender with a neat braid of glossy black hair and a golden skin that caught and reflected the light. Her eyes were a clear, pale gray, her nose and lips finely molded, but her true presence lay beyond mere physical traits.

When she spoke, her voice was low and clear, so controlled that she did not need to raise it to make herself heard. "Even Pope Innocent and the Abbot of Citeaux have the ability to find the Light within their hearts if only they would search."

Her gaze held the crowd, and it was as if she spoke to each person as an individual. "Even Simon de Montfort."

Somebody in the audience muttered angrily.

"Even Simon de Montfort," she repeated with emphasis.

Claire perceived a radiance around her like the glow from a beeswax candle, steady and bright.

"Do you see it, my lady?" Isabelle whispered excitedly.

A tiny thrill ran up Claire's spine. She shushed her maid and stared at the radiance while it expanded from its source to fill the entire room with a golden luminescence before slowly subsiding like rings fading from a ripple in a pool.

The woman smiled in reassurance at the staring, awestruck congregation. "Do not be afraid," she said gently, "it is only that the glow of my spirit is more easily perceived. Everyone carries this within themselves, and they can learn how to set it free."

She spoke for a while longer, then sat down to permit Chretien de Béziers to resume his sermon.

The meeting ended as was customary with a recital of the Lord's Prayer and the laying on of hands. The bolder members of the congregation clustered around Bridget to speak to her, and although the meeting had officially ended, still many people lingered to talk among themselves or to Chretien de Béziers and an older, gray-bearded man who had sat silent throughout the sermon.

Claire knew that she ought to leave. By now Raoul would be back at their lodging after his visit to Count Raymond, but she was reluctant to depart this atmosphere of warmth and companionship for the tensions of her marital hearth. Besides, she was curious about the Cathar woman, and wanted to know how the glow of spirit she had seen could be set free in herself.

As she pinned her cloak and adjusted her wimple, Guillaume woke up and started to cry hungrily. Claire seized upon the excuse to remain in the haven awhile longer. Retiring to a corner of the room, she unlaced her bodice and put Guillaume to her breast, her modesty sheltered by her cloak.

The baby sucked loudly. He was securely swaddled to make sure that his limbs would grow straight, and his downy blond hair was covered by a white linen cap. She looked at his working jaws, at his skin so fine that it was almost translucent. His eyes, a warm caramel-brown, reflected her own as he seriously returned her scrutiny. Gently she traced the line of one feathery eyebrow.

"What a beautiful baby."

The voice, sweet and clear, caused Claire to lift her head and meet the crystal gaze of the Cathar woman. Again she saw her own reflection, but from a different, harder angle.

"How old is he?"

Claire did not ask how the woman knew Guillaume's gender. "He was born in the autumn," she murmured. *And my husband wept at my bedside, his surcoat soaked with the blood of the men he had killed.* The words sprang into her mind unbidden, and as surely as if she had uttered them aloud, she saw the Cathar woman's brows move in response.

"I . . ." Claire stuttered, thoroughly discomfitted. Guillaume had finished feeding and she covered herself.

"May I hold him?"

After a brief hesitation while she fought an irrational feeling of fear, Claire yielded her son.

Bridget cradled him and spoke to him softly, an ache in her breasts and loins. Soon he would not need the swaddling bands; she could feel his small body straining against them even now. As I strain against my own confines, she thought, with a half-rueful, half-affectionate glance at Chretien and the silent, grave Matthias.

"You need not fear for your son," she said to Claire. "His life will be touched by this war, but his destiny lies beyond it."

"You can see the future?" Claire's voice held both eagerness and fear.

"Distantly. Each person chooses the path he takes, but I see your son's road with all its branches attaining full manhood, and he will have offspring of his own." She rocked the baby gently and touched his soft cheek.

"The Cathars teach that the world is evil; I can see that," Claire said haltingly. "But if I become one, do I have to renounce everything? It would kill me to be parted from Guillaume."

Bridget shook her head. "Of course you do not have to renounce him. Only the elect are called upon to go so far, and even then there is room for difference of custom. Chretien de Béziers is my uncle, a strict Cathar, but he loves and cares for me as I love and care for him. You must not feel guilty for the love you bear your son . . . or your husband."

Claire gasped. "Do you see everything?" Her lower lip trembled. "Are we all soul-naked before you?"

Bridget gently returned Guillaume to his mother's arms. "Not everything. If I wish, I can draw a veil across my perceptions. Indeed, sometimes it is necessary, otherwise I would go mad." She deliberated for a moment, then added, "I was at your wedding with my uncle and our companion Matthias. You would not have noticed us because we arrived late to claim a night's hospitality. I felt the attraction between yourself and your husband then, but I think that somewhere between then and now, you have lost sight of each other."

Claire frowned. "Raoul has taken to the sword for his comfort since his father died. I do love him, but to think of him taking pleasure in the spilling of blood sickens me. I . . ." She bit off the words and made a small gesture. "You can see all this anyway, so why am I shaming myself by telling you?"

"There is no shame in unburdening your troubles." Bridget put a compassionate hand on Claire's shoulder. "Sometimes I long to do the same. It can be so lonely even when there are people all around you. It is too easy to reach out and touch nothing." She sighed softly. "The spilling of blood is for his conscience, not yours. Perhaps part of his taking comfort in warfare is the fact that you are shutting him out. I have felt . . ." Abruptly she stopped speaking and blushed.

"Felt what?" Claire lifted a bemused face.

Bridget shook her head. She had felt his need and longing, experienced in the briefest touching of minds, unsubtle and fierce. "I have felt his loneliness,". she temporized. "I say to you that you have time to grow and consider all paths before you take your own road. For now, your doubts make a decision impossible."

"How long must I wait?"

"Live each day as it comes, and when the time is right, you will know."

"How?" Claire stood up, her expression beseeching. "How will I know?"

"Because you will not need to ask." Bridget gave her an enigmatic, sad smile and started to turn away. "Go home to your husband now. He is becoming anxious."

She watched Claire give Guillaume to the maid and go quietly, almost chastened, to the door. Equally subdued, her head bowed, Bridget sat down to recover her own composure. It was difficult to offer impartial advice when she was personally involved, and when the future, whichever branch was chosen, was revealed only as a vast sheet of fire.

CHAPTER SEVENTEEN

Montvallant, Spring 1211

THE FORGE ATTACHED to Montvallant's armory was a dragon's den of red and black shadows—hotter and sweatier than a brothel bedroom, according to Jean the armorer, a pithy sixty-year-old who retained as much brawn in his arms as a man half his age.

The most junior apprentice was working like a demon with the bellows to keep the fire fed with air while Jean's adolescent son stood over an anvil, beating a lance tip into shape with a round-ended hammer. The sweat shone on his corded forearms and in the vee of his strong young throat. Jean himself sat in the adjoining, cooler armory, pitcher of wine to hand as he fashioned hauberk links from strips of wrought wire.

Raoul flexed his shoulders, testing the altered coat of mail for ease of movement. The rigorous training of the past year and the attainment of full physical maturity had increased his breadth so that the hauberk fashioned for him at the age of twenty was no longer the meticulous fit it had been at Béziers.

Having Jean add some extra links was far less expensive than commissioning an entirely new garment.

A troop of horsemen clattered into the ward. Raoul shaded his eyes against the early March sunlight. The leading horse was a red chestnut with distinctive white stockings, and Raoul recognized it even before he recognized its rider. It was more than a year since he had seen Aimery de Montréal, and in that time the man's hair had turned from iron-gray to pure white. His sister Geralda rode beside him on a dappled mare. Raoul vaguely remembered that she had written in the winter, promising to visit his mother, who was ailing with a coughing sickness. Half-pleased, half-apprehensive, he went to greet them.

Aimery met Raoul with a strong handclasp and looked him up and down. "I see you've already heard the news," he said grimly.

"What news?" Raoul had been about to kiss Geralda, but now he stopped and looked round.

"Then you don't know. I thought when I saw your armor . . ." Aimery's voice tailed off.

"I was trying the fit of a new hauberk," Raoul dismissed brusquely. "What news?"

Aimery looked at him sidelong. "Cabaret's fallen. Pierre-Roger yielded two days ago to save his skin. De Montfort's on his way to take us with his entire summer force." His tone was apologetic, as if he felt personally responsible for what was happening. "I thought you knew."

Raoul shook his head, feeling embittered and angry. "I told Count Raymond months ago that he must not let de Montfort drag out negotiations through the winter, that they were a ruse and come the spring we'd all see the falsehood of his good-will." His eyelids tensed. "We should have gone on the offensive. We should have hit him and hit him again while he had no troops."

Aimery sighed. "It is easy for you to say that, Raoul, but Raymond is no warrior and he truly does desire reconciliation with Rome. He's caught by the balls."

"I understand that," Raoul acknowledged on a quieter, but no less bitter note, "and I also understand that unless we organize ourselves, de Montfort will emasculate us all."

* * *

"Geralda's going to take the *consolamentum*, you know," Aimery said. "She's very committed to the Cathar religion." The men were seated before a brazier in the solar, their armor removed and a half-empty flagon sharing the table with a platter of dried figs and raisins.

Raoul stretched out his legs toward the brazier's warmth and studied the fuzz of coney-skin edging the cuff of his shoes. "What about you?"

Aimery smiled and shook his head. "I'm too set in my ways to pass the tests demanded of a fully fledged Perfect. I eat meat, I still enjoy the pleasures of the flesh, and I'm a soldier. Too many sins and not enough remorse to forswear them. Geralda used to argue with me about them all the time, but these days she accepts that we're different."

Raoul sighed heavily. "Claire and my mother are very drawn to the Cathars these days. We have a large community here at Montvallant. I'm always stumbling over their meetings."

"And you resent them?"

"Oh God, I don't know!" Raoul said in exasperation, and hit the arms of his chair. "What they teach is no sin; indeed, they're probably right. This is Satan's domain, and living a pure life is the only way to break your chains, but . . ." He pursed his lips. "I suppose I resent the fact that it is because of the Cathars we are having to fight—they gave the French the excuse they needed." He dropped his eyes from Aimery's all too shrewd scrutiny. "And also they have come between myself and Claire. It is not as difficult for you. Geralda is your sister."

"Ah." Aimery raised and lowered his thick silver brows in sympathy and understanding.

"It's not as bad as it was." Raoul contemplated his cup. "I've grown accustomed to it now, found other things to occupy my time, and Claire, too, has compromised. We manage very well providing that we stay in each other's shallows and don't go wading out of our depth. And I have Guillaume. He compensates for much."

A somber silence fell, both men constrained by the limits of the depths and shallows that Raoul had just mentioned.

* * *

In the women's chambers above the hall, Geralda clucked over Beatrice with sympathetic concern. "You should take hore-hound syrup for that cough," she said. "I'll send you some."

Beatrice smiled wanly. "It has gone too far for that to be of much use." She concealed her bloodied kerchief in her sleeve. "Nor do I desire to fight it. The *consolamentum* awaits me very soon, I think."

Geralda studied her keenly, but said nothing. Claire returned from settling Guillaume in his cradle.

"Asleep?" Geralda queried.

"Yes, at last!" Claire laughed. "He's so inquisitive, hates to think he's missing something!"

"Raoul was just like him at that age," Beatrice said, her gaze misty with reminiscence. "He led us a merry dance, I can tell you!"

Claire gave her a fond look in which there was an undercur-rent of concern. Distant memories seemed to be the most re-warding part of Beatrice's life these days, and she appeared ever more willing to dwell in them and let the present pass her by.

"And he still does," Geralda said, "if the look on your face earlier was any indication."

"I don't like to see him wearing armor." Beatrice com-pressed her lips. "He knows it, but it doesn't make any differ-ence."

"He's a man grown now, with a son of his own. You cannot rule him as you did when he was a child," Geralda cautioned. "I know how hard it is to see your loved ones take the path of war, believe me, but I also know that if you push too hard, you will push him away."

Beatrice stared at a wall tapestry depicting the scene of a hunter's kill. "It will not matter soon," she said softly.

Claire and Geralda exchanged disturbed glances. After a hesitation, Geralda said, "Beatrice, I have a favor to ask of you. It is no light matter, and I will quite understand if you prefer to decline."

Beatrice's attention diverted from the doomed deer on the tapestry. She blinked hard to refocus. "You know that you need but name it and it is yours."

Geralda smiled. "And that makes it all the more difficult."

She drew a deep breath. "I have some Cathars staying with me at Lavaur. The pope is desperate to destroy them above all other members of the Perfecti. May I direct them here to Montvallant as a place where they will be succored if they have need?"

"Of course you may!" Beatrice said, with a glimpse of her former fire. The louder use of her voice caused her to break off, coughing, and fumble in her sleeve for her kerchief.

"Who are they?" Claire asked, hurrying to fetch Beatrice a cup of hot wine.

"Have you heard of Chretien de Béziers?"

Claire felt a thrill of recognition and turned to look eagerly at Geralda. "I heard him preach in Toulouse last year. He has the most wonderful voice—like a soft, warm cloak."

Geralda laughed at the description. "I'll tell him that; he'll be flattered!"

"There was a young woman at the meeting, too. She admired Guillaume and spoke to me for a while." Claire's color heightened as she remembered the steady gray stare and the pull it had exerted on her soul. "I felt that she could see through me as if I were made of glass."

"Ah," Geralda said, nodding, "that would be Bridget. She is not a Cathar, but she and Chretien and Matthias have long traveled together. Matthias translates holy texts and Gospels from the old tongues into Catalan and Occitan. A few years ago, he was captured by papal spies and put to the torture. They cut off the pen fingers of his right hand as a warning. Bridget's mother they murdered by branding her forehead with a molten cross."

Claire put her hand to her mouth in shock.

Geralda looked pensive, a rare expression for her. "Bridget is the most important of the three. She is a healer and mystic of extraordinary skill, and she claims descent from the Magdalene and the Virgin Mary. Rome cannot afford to let her live." She shook her head. "No, I should not have asked you. There is too great a risk involved."

"I do not care what the risks are if I am able to thwart the men who killed my husband." Beatrice took the cup from Claire and drank from it in fast swallows like a soldier. "Of course you must send them to us." A tint of pink returned to the pallor of her cheeks.

"If you are sure."

Claire set the flagon back down upon the hearth. "Raoul is already an outlaw in the eyes of the northern lords. It will make little difference to our standing with them should we harbor three more Cathars among the community already living here." She was eager to see Bridget again, to be bathed in the radiance of her presence. She treasured those moments in the Toulouse meeting house like a jewel, and when she was feeling depressed and frightened, she thought upon them and was comforted. The next words were dragged out of her, but in all fairness, she knew that they had to be said. "Perhaps it is the other way around. Perhaps Montvallant will not be safe for them."

Geralda sighed heavily and closed her eyes. "Child, nowhere is safe anymore," she said.

CHAPTER EIGHTEEN

Montvallant, May 1211

RAOUL NUZZLED HIS lips against Claire's shoulder and played with a strand of her tumbled chestnut hair. The bed curtains enclosed the two of them in shadowy warmth and it was almost possible for him to believe that there was nothing outside this early morning haven—that his life was whole. Almost. Beyond the protection of the hangings, the world prepared to intrude. He could hear the stealthy movements and whisperings of Claire's maids and Guillaume's high-pitched babble.

Making a conscious effort to ignore the sounds, he kissed

Claire's throat and mouth, the dimple in her chin, stroked the soft curves of her body. The caress was not urgent; it was the languorous aftermath of pleasure recently taken. She was often reluctant at first, but he had learned to be cunning, to choose his moment and then to ply her with teasing and cajolery, or with a musician's delicate touch on her sleep-drugged body so that by the time she was fully awake and aware, her stimulated nerve endings were reaching for release and nothing else mattered.

"I ought to go," he murmured, making no attempt to do so. Claire said nothing, passive now beneath his stroking fingertips. After a while he raised himself on one elbow to look at her. She was staring up at the stars painted on the canopy, her mouth rosy and full from his kisses, the love flush still mantling her body, and her expression so haunted that it cut him to the quick.

Uttering a soft oath, he sat up and pushed aside the bedclothes. "Perhaps I ought to take a concubine," he muttered.

Claire flinched and her eyes met his in misery, making him feel guilty, and then all the more angry for his guilt. "What is wrong? Why do you no longer take pleasure in lying with me? Is it because of the Cathars?"

"No, never that!" Her voice held a note of alarm. "Do not turn against them because of me! I will never refuse you!"

Raoul felt as if she had struck him full in the face. "I do not want you out of your fear or sense of duty," he said stiffly. "I want you to come to me as you used to do when we were first wed. You never touch me anymore, or find excuses in the day to seek me out. The approaches are all mine. I feel like a beggar standing at a castle gate seeking crumbs of comfort from a table beyond my reach."

Claire swallowed. Tears glittered in her eyes. "This war," she choked out. "It has changed everything. I feel like a beggar, too. I love you, truly I do!"

Outside the bed curtains, a maid spoke in surprise to someone at the door. The voice that replied was young and light, but undeniably masculine, and it held a note of agitation.

"We'll talk later," Raoul said, unsure whether to be irritated or relieved by the interruption. Perhaps the crumbs were so few and far between because there was no longer a table spread from which to provide them. Pulling on his braies, he parted the curtains and looked at his squire, who was hovering on the threshold.

"Mir, what is it?"

The youth shouldered past the maid. "My lord, there is a messenger to see you from Lavaur. He says that it is most urgent." Mir gestured over his shoulder toward the door.

Raoul saw the glint of mail in the stairwell and knew that for Mir to bring the messenger above to the private quarters, the news must be deeply urgent. "You had better fetch him in." Tying the drawstring on his braies, Raoul indicated a south-facing alcove built into the thickness of the wall where Claire usually sat to do her embroidery.

The man whom the squire ushered into the room was heavily travel-stained. A gray rag of bandage was tied around a head wound and splotches of rust from his hauberk marred his surcoat. "I nearly did not get through their pickets, my lord," he said huskily, and swayed where he stood.

Raoul gestured him to sit on the low stone bench cut into the wall. With his own hand he brought the flask of double-strength Gascon wine from the cupboard and poured a generous measure into a cup. The messenger drank, spluttered, and drank again, then wiped his mouth and looked at Raoul. "De Montfort has laid siege to Lavaur and is on the verge of breaking it. His troops are filling up the moat with soil and brushwood faster than we can empty it, and we cannot stop the sappers from mining the wall. Lord Aimery and Lady Geralda beg you to come to their aid before it is too late."

Raoul frowned and pursed his lips. "I have troops, and well trained at that, but hardly in numbers large enough to tackle de Montfort's entire army."

Guillaume toddled unsteadily into the alcove, a wooden toy grasped tightly in his fat little fist. Raoul scooped him into his arms and looked at the messenger over the child's flaxen hair.

"But enough to tip the balance of the siege if you add your strength to Lord Aimery's." The messenger drank again, sweat shining in the grimy creases of his throat. "The whole area is being laid waste. I beg you, my lord, please help us!"

Raoul deliberated between duty and obligation. The men were not his; they were held in trust for Raymond of Toulouse, but appeal to Raymond would waste valuable time, and knowing his overlord's tendency to prevaricate, he might well be refused. "I'll come," he said with sudden vigor. "Give me some small space of time to break my fast and arm up, and I'll have the men on the road before prime."

"Thank you, my lord, thank you!"

Raoul grimaced at the messenger's gratitude. "Do not expect miracles," he said brusquely. "The women will attend to your wounds and give you fresh raiment and food." He signaled to the maids. The bed curtains flurried and bulged as, behind their cover, Isabelle helped Claire to dress. Raoul brushed his lips against Guillaume's bright, pale hair and set him down. Colors suddenly dulled. Glancing out of the unshuttered window, he saw that clouds had obscured the sun.

Claire watched Raoul buckle on his sword belt, adjust the scabbard at his hip, and reach for his shield, the background a bright egg-yolk-gold on which the Montvallant chevronels stood out in a contrast of stark, black lines.

She hated to see him in armor, for it was a reminder of how she was losing him. Each time he returned to her from a battle, a little bit more of the Raoul she had loved was obliterated. She saw the steadfast gentleness and courage of the Cathar way, and the grim, blood-filled curse of the path of war. She could not bear to see Raoul's feet so entrenched upon the downward road, to feel the distance growing between them. And today it was for Aimery and Geralda that he was donning his armor and losing another small piece of his soul. She could not condone, she could not condemn. And so she watched him in silence.

He seemed to capture the drift of her thoughts, for he glanced up from checking his weapons and met her eyes. "It may be, if we arrive in time, that we can hold them to a truce and save those within Lavaur from another Béziers," he said. "It is what I would hope for."

She nodded stiffly.

"Whatever you think, I do not relish fighting for fighting's sake. If there were another way—a tenable one—I would take it. Do not say anything." He raised his hand. "We have not the time to argue the Cathar ground again."

Claire bit her lip. "I was only going to say, do what you can for Aimery and Geralda . . . and guard yourself. Do you think I do not know how difficult it is for you?"

He folded her in an awkward soldier's embrace, hard with iron rings and the curved jolt of shield edge, the fierce thrust of a sword hilt against her ribs. She clung to him, accepting and returning his scratchy kiss.

"Come home safe," she said. "Come home whole."

He kissed her again, embraced Guillaume, and with a final look, was hurrying away down the stairs to his men.

Assailed by a sense of loss that almost bordered on grief, Claire climbed to the battlements to watch him mount up and ride out.

A storm was coming. Bridget felt its imminence raise the delicate hairs at her nape and tingle through her body. Far, far away, she detected the flicker of dry lightning, and scented its metallic essence. There was danger, too, a long, dark tunnel with only the barest glimmer of light at the other end. Lavaur would fall. Standing upon the battlements, she could see the twinkle of the crusaders' campfires and thought that they seemed almost as numerous as the stars. The smell of death was in the wind, but she was not so foolhardy as to search her mind and find out whose. If her road ended here, then so be it. The presence of the storm was surely an omen.

A light wind fingered her hair, stroking it back from her brow almost maternally. She closed her eyes and lifted her face skyward like a child.

"Bridget?"

The voice seemed to come from a distance, and it was with a great reluctance that she lowered her head and looked round. Geralda stood at her side. She was wearing the simple, dark robe of a Cathar Perfect. A plain white wimple covered her hair. Earlier that evening, Chretien had administered to her the sacred Cathar rite of the *consolamentum*, but for all that, Bridget saw no serenity in Geralda's eyes.

"There are so many of them." Geralda stared as Bridget had done at the enemy campfires encircling Lavaur. "Aimery says that they will attack at dawn and that we will not be able to hold them off." She beat the palm of one hand frustratedly against the heavy wool of her skirts. "I am not afraid for my-self, but it distresses me greatly that I have failed to keep you from harm."

"You have done all that you could; you have nothing to re-proach yourself for." Bridget laid her hand on Geralda's shoul-der in a soothing benediction of her own. "Be at ease. Dawn will bring what it brings."

Geralda bit her underlip. "Aimery told me he had sent a messenger to Raoul de Montvallant, asking for aid. If only we knew if he had reached him."

The name struck through Bridget like a bolt of lightning, and images dazzled across her mind in rapid succession. Raoul de Montvallant astride a rearing golden warhorse, sword held skyward in defiance. Lightning rippled down the blade and into her heart. She saw him standing naked, buffeted by the rain, his erect manhood straining against his belly. His eyes were narrowed against the storm and his face was harsh with lust. She was facing him, and she, too, was naked, her dark hair plastered to her breasts. "He will come," she heard herself say in a breathless voice. "Even now he is riding to us."

"Praise be to the Good God," whispered Geralda, and some of the worry left her expression. "I must tell Aimery; it will hearten him."

Bridget leaned against the merlon for support and clamped her lips tightly shut on the rest of her knowledge. What would it benefit Geralda to be told that he would come too late to save Lavaur?

The sky clouded and darkened as Raoul led his men toward Lavaur. Lightning flickered over the forested hills to the north in a sky the color of sword steel. No thunder pursued the flashes of light and no rain fell. The assault on the senses was silent and thus all the more unnerving.

They stopped for the night in a small hamlet straddling the road. It was an eerie experience. Fearing the approach of the vast crusading army, the inhabitants had fled into the woods with their portable goods and their animals, leaving their houses empty shells, but so recently deserted that the essence of habitation still lived and breathed. It was like bedding down with ghosts, unsettling both men and horses.

All night the lightning blinked silently across the sky, now close, now distant, and a dry, fierce wind gusted over the land, causing shutters in the village to slam, and doors to creak. The strange atmosphere sent tingles down Raoul's spine and throbbed in his temples, making it impossible for him to settle into sleep or join his men at their campfire. Finally, tense as a mountain lynx, he prowled outside and took over the night watch from one of the soldiers on duty.

He had not encountered the dream woman for several months, but tonight he could feel her in the storm-lit darkness. But although he stared until his eyes burned, although he reached out with every particle of his mind, she remained just out of his grasp.

At dawn the wind dropped, but the lightning continued to flash. The sky was metallic, charged with power, and the weight of it was like a lump of brazen metal pulsing behind his eyes. His men made their ablutions and broke their fast in silence. Before full light they had kicked out their fires and were once again on the road to Lavaur.

As they approached the town, the color of the sky changed to a dull bronze. Although the wind had died, Raoul recognized the familiar stink of burning wood, burning fields, and burning meat. No one who had been at Béziers would ever forget that smell and what it signified.

"Ah, God!" wept the messenger, who had chosen to accompany them back to his town. "We are too late!"

"Perhaps it is just the outskirts," suggested one of Raoul's knights, offering words of hope without any conviction.

Tight-lipped, Raoul moved his troop off the road and continued his advance toward Lavaur with increased caution. After a few miles of riding through the woods bordering the road, he halted the men in a stand of pines and, taking Giles, went to reconnoiter ahead. Keeping to whatever cover they could find, they continued to ride parallel with the road and in this manner came upon a procession of baggage wains, cooks, craftsmen, and a general flotsam of camp followers, all heading jubilantly toward Lavaur. Simon's army had struck camp and was on the move.

"What now?" muttered Giles.

Raoul clasped his hands upon his pommel and narrowed his

gaze in the direction of the town. The stink of smoke was powerful, but not as powerful as the certainty that pounded in his temples and trickled down his spine in rivulets of cold sweat. "Now?" He set his hands to the reins and pressed with his thighs to turn Fauvel. "Now we join the procession."

"Have you lost your wits?" Giles's voice rose an incredulous octave. "We'll be butchered!"

"Who is to stop us? Look at them, common northern camp followers, taught to tug the forelock and grovel to anyone riding a destrier and wearing gilded spurs. They will just think we are part of the rear guard detailed to protect them from attack, and we won't disillusion them."

A muttering, reluctant Giles was persuaded to follow Raoul out of the trees and onto the road, but Raoul was right in his assumption that they would go unchallenged. The only difficult moment they had was when a pimp tried to interest them in his girls and had to be persuaded with the sharp end of a lance to try his luck elsewhere. After that, they rode right up to the town walls without incident.

Just inside Lavaur's main gate, their eyes were drawn to the remnants of a collapsed gibbet and the bodies piled around it. They were the soldiers of Lavaur's garrison, their armor stripped and their bodies hacked and mutilated. Raoul could see that the intention to hang the men like common criminals had been thwarted by the broken gibbet, so the sword and the ax had been used instead. Slumped against the gibbet, the rope still around his neck, shirt saturated in his lifeblood, was Aimery, his sightless gaze fixed on the buzzards wheeling overhead. The smoke tore at Raoul's eyes, forcing him to blink, but behind his lids, across his mind, the image was branded forever. Somewhere very close he could hear a crowd shouting.

"Let us go!" cried Giles, revulsion obvious in every plane of his face. "There is nothing we can do, and I have no desire to join these poor souls!"

"No!" Raoul said forcefully, and swallowed his gorge. "Not yet." He urged Fauvel in the direction of the shouting. Blaspheming loudly, Giles turned his mount and pursued his lord.

They came to a square where a throng of townspeople had

been gathered and held at bay by foot soldiers with pikes and swords and by mounted sergeants in quilted habergeons. Through the crowd moved a procession led by priests, a huge, bronze cross carried on high, silk banners of Christ in suffering fluttering to either side. Behind the banners, his crosier held in his fist like a club, walked the Abbot of Citeaux, his corpulent form encrusted with the full, gilded panoply of his office. His face was flushed with righteous triumph and with the effort of bearing the weight of his magnificent garments.

In contrast, the roped line of men and women shuffling in his wake, prodded and spat upon by the crusaders, wore plain, homespun robes in dull colors of gray and blue and brown. Cathars and condemned to death, their faces wore expressions of triumph, too. Their bodies were about to burn, but their spirits were on the verge of release. Bringing up the rear were yet more priests bearing torches to light the faggots.

"Dear God." Giles swallowed.

"Which one?" Raoul asked cynically. "Citeaux's God, or the Cathars'?" He scanned the prisoners, but could not see Geralda among them.

At the other side of the square, a Cistercian monk, his cowl pulled over his face, was pushing his horse through the crowd, forcing a path for his two companions and a laden pack mule. Raoul's sliding glance stopped and jerked back to the horse of the first monk. It was a lean red chestnut with a white blaze and four distinctive white stockings.

"That's Aimery's courser!" he said through his teeth. "That priest is riding Aimery's horse!"

"Doesn't take them long, the vultures!" Giles responded roughly, and spat over his mount's withers.

"Stop them!" An imperative bellow rang out from the far side of the square, and there was a sudden flurry and churning in the crowd as several knights and sergeants strove to thrust their way toward the monks. Whips lashed at the tardy. Shod hooves kicked. The leading destrier was milk-white, and its rider's shield bore the familiar, dreaded device of the de Montfort fork-tailed lion.

"Christ in heaven, it's Simon de Montfort himself, and he's seen us!" Giles croaked, and turned his stallion about. "My lord, this is folly. We must escape while we still have a chance!"

Raoul caught his adjutant's arm. "It is not us they are after. On their last visit, Geralda asked us to shelter three important Cathars." Raoul nodded in the direction of the monks.

Giles looked nonplussed. "And you think they are the ones?" He controlled his sidling horse with difficulty.

"I hazard so, but you are right, we mustn't tarry. No, this way."

"But . . ." Giles began, but Raoul was already cutting across the edges of the crowd, dovetailing his path to meet the three hurrying fugitives. A sidelong glance showed him that de Montfort was gaining, but not as quickly as the warlord might have hoped, for the press of people was still hindering him, in some cases deliberately. That was remedied when de Montfort drew his sword and used not the flat of the blade, but the sharpened edge to cut his way forward.

"Quickly!" Raoul snapped to the monk with the pack mule as Fauvel came abreast of him. "Follow me!"

Smoky eyes glinted within the depths of the cowl. Smooth, brown hands gathered the reins and turned the chestnut.

"Stop them!" The furious command resounded again. "I'll have your balls for ballista missiles if you let them escape!"

Near Raoul, a soldier blinked round, obviously wondering who was shouting and at whom. Before he could make up his mind and act, a burly townsman in the crowd deliberately started a brawl with his neighbor and distracted the crusader's attention.

Raoul led his charges down a cobbled alleyway, across a smaller open space, and then squeezed along a dark entry toward the light of a house garden on the other side. Halfway down the entry, the mule with its bulging load, by now bringing up the rear, became stuck. There was no room to turn. Raoul rode on to the end, dismounted, and came back. His heart was hammering as if it would burst through his ribs, and not because they were being hotly pursued. A cowl might conceal all but the sparsest gleams of skin and eye, but he recognized his dreams made living flesh and bone.

"Leave the baggage mule," he said urgently, "we'll travel much faster without it."

"Impossible!" One of the other monks gestured rapidly, and Raoul saw that his right hand was mutilated. "If Citeaux or de Montfort lay hold on what is contained in these bundles, it will all be destroyed, and it is irreplaceable. Nor would it prevent them from pursuing us to our deaths. We are the guardians and we know too much."

Raoul's scalp writhed. The entry was like a tunnel of light. At the end of it, waiting with the horses, were Giles and the other Cathar. "The mule will hinder us," he insisted. "If you must bring the baggage, let it be divided among the horses, and quickly."

The man opened his mouth to argue.

"Matthias, do as he says." The woman touched her companion's sleeve. "The danger is too close. We don't have time to debate." She nodded at Raoul, giving him leave to continue, and set about dismantling the mule's baggage herself.

"Be careful," moaned the little man, tugging agitatedly at his silver beard as Raoul cut the straps securing the bundles when he could not reach the buckles. "Some of those writings are over a thousand years old!"

"Do you want them to go up in flames?" Raoul snapped impatiently. "Here, take these down to Giles and your friends, and thank yourself for the lesser of the two evils!"

Matthias clutched the bundle Raoul thrust at him as tenderly as a mother would an infant. "You do not understand," he sighed, but made haste down the entry.

Soon they were able to move the mule down the passage to finish transferring the load in the open light of the garden. Raoul watched as the woman secured her own portion of the mule's bundle to her mount's crupper. Aimery's horse, a restive, highly strung stallion, stood as contentedly as a cheeseseller's nag beneath her hands. Raoul found himself staring at them. They were tanned and slim, unadorned by rings, the nails clipped short, so ordinary that they could have belonged to any peasant girl in the Languedoc; and yet they sent a pang through him. Lowering his eyes, he completed fastening his own portion of the mule's burden behind his saddle.

"I assume from your mounts and your disguises that you are the Cathars who were lodged with the lady Geralda?" he asked as he remounted Fauvel. "That chestnut was Aimery's favorite."

"Indeed we are," said the taller man, who had thus far hardly spoken at all. "I gave her the *consolamentum* yestereve when we feared that the town would fall. At least she came to the Good End, even if the manner of it was terrible."

"Then, like Aimery, she is dead?"

"She lives in the Light," Chretien answered firmly without a hint of platitude, speaking with the conviction of his belief.

Raoul thrust his feet into his stirrups and wondered how he was going to break the news to Claire and his mother. He thought of the picnic by the river in the summer of his first year of marriage. The memory was still strong, the colors bold, but it felt more like an illumination from a manuscript than an event that he had lived. "What happened to her?"

"They threw her down the town well and stoned her to death. She denied them entry to the castle—stood in the gateway and read a sermon to Citeaux himself. I implored her, but she would not come with us. If we are here now, it is because she sacrificed herself so that we might escape."

Raoul swallowed and closed his eyes. Poor, forthright, garrulous Geralda, who had cuddled him on her spacious lap as a child. His own son had sat there, too, lulled to sleep by her singing voice, which had been as soft as her speaking tones were harsh. He thought of Aimery and the butchered garrison by the town gate. "Why are you so important?" he demanded fiercely, wanting to understand, but feeling as if he stood outside a locked door behind which there might either be everything or nothing, and not possessing the key to find out. "Why do they hate and fear you even above the hatred and fear they have for other Cathars?"

"Because—" the woman started to say, and broke off, looking toward the mouth of the entry. "They are coming," she said breathlessly. He followed her cowled gaze. The entry was empty. He could see tufts of grass growing out of the stonework and the deserted narrow street at the other end. A cylindrical gleam caught his eye, and he realized that he was looking at a document tube lying against the darkness of the wall where it had been dropped while they were freeing the mule from its load.

Cursing, he dismounted and ran to fetch it. In that same moment the street beyond the entry was suddenly aswirl with horsemen and running soldiers. Raoul closed his fingers around the tube. A quarrel from an arbalest whirred close to his head, struck the wall, and rebounded. Several more followed, bouncing and clattering, missing him by a miracle. He thrust the document tube through his belt and, as the entry darkened with soldiers, ran back to Fauvel, vaulted astride, and drew his sword to cover the retreat of the others.

Once out of the garden, they found themselves in a narrow alleyway that was already filling with soldiers sent round to intercept. With a single blow of his sword, Raoul chopped off the locked latch of a gate set in the wall opposite, and barged the door open. They hastened through a larger garden and orchard, past an empty stable and a ransacked house, and emerged into the next street. Some mercenaries who had been looting the building confronted the little group.

Raoul and Giles clashed with them. By now both men were sufficiently battle-hardened and experienced to take on the extra man without depending on fortune's blessing to keep them alive. They had learned that honor in battle was not the same as honor outside it. Kill a horse if you must, kick a man in the balls, throw sand in his eyes, strike him when his sword blade had snapped. After the victory, then you could afford the gilding of chivalry if it was your whim.

One knight was killed outright, another wounded, and the horse of the third was cut so badly that it was impossible for his rider to fight on. Raoul and Giles wheeled their mounts. A squire had seized the woman's sleeve and was trying to drag her from her saddle. Suddenly, for no visible reason, he screamed and staggered backward, clutching his arm as if in agony. Raoul rode him down.

"Let him be. I am unharmed, and we but delay."

Her voice held a note of such powerful command that Raoul obeyed instantly. He darted a look at her and then the squire. The young man was on his knees, his face gray-white with terror. Above their heads the sky rippled with lightning. Raoul felt a shadow of that terror prickle the hair on his scalp. Knowing that his own expression was giving him away, he lowered his eyes and turned Fauvel.

A sharp right turn, a zigzag, and in a moment the city gates came into view, complete with drunken gibbet, dead men, and buzzards. The birds no longer circled in the sky, but were settling to feed. Bridget stared for a moment at the congealing mutilations, at the brown and cream plumage of the buzzards and curved meat-hook beaks. Then she took a deep breath. "They are only shells," she murmured. "Without the spirit, there is nothing. Let us go."

The last of Simon's camp followers were still straggling into the town as Raoul led the way out of it. Curious looks were cast by some, but the sergeant in charge of the guard was too busy arranging details with the pimp whom Raoul had encountered earlier to take much notice of two knights escorting some Cistercian monks on their way. Citeaux's spies and envoys were always coming and going.

Raoul's company was trotting past the plundered remains of the ramshackle houses built outside the protection of the town walls when a hue and cry was raised behind them and their pursuers burst through the gateway like huntsmen on the trail of a deer. Crossbow quarrels whizzed among the group, by a miracle not hitting anyone. Putting whip and spur to their mounts, the five were quickly out of firing range of the town walls, but the true danger lay in the pursuing soldiers. Raoul knew that he had a reasonable, but not untenable, lead. With twenty fighting men chasing two, if the distance was closed, then capture and death were inevitable.

He tried to remember how far back he had left his men and the safety of numbers. The distance seemed enormous and the leading white stallion of their pursuers was gaining with every stride. *Behold a pale horse.* Raoul felt as if the space between his shoulder blades was an immense target upon which his enemy's eyes were fixed. As he rode, he started to shout the rallying cry that would summon his men, hoping against hope that they were close.

"*À Montvallant! À Montvallant!*"

The road ahead remained empty. Behind them the hoofbeats were thunderous now. The problem was not with the three horses that the Cathars were riding—they were fresh from their stalls—but with the two destriers that had been pushed for two days in haste to reach Lavaur and were heavier of bone than the rangy hunting horses.

"Ride on!" Raoul cried to Matthias, who was abreast of him. "We'll slow them down while you make your escape!" He signaled to Giles and spun Fauvel in a dusty circle to face the oncoming riders. Several times in the last hour he had fully expected to die; now death was such a familiar companion at his shoulder that he scarcely felt any surge of anticipation or dread.

The white horse filled the world, its nostrils red caverns, foam spattering from the bit, hooves striking sparks from the road, a golden shield triangled upon its withers, concealing the joining of horse and man so that they appeared to be one beast. Simon de Montfort, *Rex Mundi*'s soldier. Steel and muscle and the eye of a grim reaper. *Behold a pale horse.* Raoul charged to meet him, flinging his gage in the face of death. White and gold, the horses jarred together. Fauvel twisted sideways. Raoul strove to raise his shield in time. De Montfort's sword hacked a chunk out of the reinforced limewood. Raoul's blade rebounded off the glossy surface of de Montfort's shield. Altering his grip, de Montfort prepared smoothly to kill, but the mail-clad arm never completed its deadly sweep.

A fork of lightning stabbed down to earth, dazzling all around the fighting soldiers on the road and striking two of de Montfort's dead in their saddles. Horses reared, shied, and bolted. The leaf tips of the trees on either side of the road burned like votive candles, and rags of yellow and orange flame danced over the surface of the grass. A new, acrid smell of burning overlaid the stink from the town.

"Montvallant!" came the cry from more than a score of throats. *"Montvallant!"*

Amid the confusion, Raoul was aware of Roland and Mir and his own men filling the road as if conjured out of the storm, but no more than perfunctory blows were exchanged with the enemy. De Montfort bellowed the retreat, for it was obvious that to continue fighting against increased odds in the midst of a dry storm of these proportions was courting disaster. Both northern and southern troops backed off from the encounter, not even bothering to utter the usual rhetoric and threats as they made haste to take cover.

* * *

Two hours later, Raoul's troop rode into a small but still inhabited hamlet and stopped to water the horses and eat. They were offered rough red wine and dark bread, pressed goat's cheese and fat bacon. For the Cathars, who ate neither meat nor anything with the taint of animal, there was thick garlic and bean pottage to accompany the bread.

While Mir watered Fauvel at the village trough, Raoul sat on its stone edge and put his face in his hands. His limbs were shaking and he felt as if his bones were hollow with all their substance sucked out. One arm was sore where a sword blow had slipped past his guard, and although the rivets of his hauberk had held, he had been badly bruised.

"Here," said Giles gruffly. "Best eat something. You're the same color as this cheese."

Raoul eyed the hunk of bread and crumbly curds piled on top of it. His stomach lurched. "I'm not hungry."

Giles considered him. "The reaction's setting in," he said with the comfortable surety of experience. "Always does when a man goes beyond himself as I saw you go today. I'll put it in your saddlebag in case you want it later." Biting into his own food, he started to leave.

"You saw and did the same things." Raoul raised his head to look at the other man. "Don't you feel sick?"

Giles paused and frowned at his meal, then turned round with a shrug. "I'm pretending that this has been an ordinary day out on an ordinary patrol," he said grimly. "I'm pretending that I don't remember things. Sooner or later that defense will crack, but by then it'll probably be safe to get drunker than hell and cry my guts out . . . those I haven't spewed up." Turning away again, he carried on walking.

Wearily Raoul rubbed his hands over his face and stood up. Near the trough, some villagers had gathered around Chretien de Béziers to listen to him read aloud from his vernacular copy of the Gospel of Saint John.

" 'And this is the judgment, that the light has come into the world and men loved darkness rather than light, because their deeds were evil. For every one who does evil hates the light and does not come to the light lest his deeds be exposed. But he who does what is true comes to the light that it may be clearly seen that his deeds have been wrought in God.' "

Raoul was still too benumbed by his reaction to all that had happened to be astounded at the rocklike tenacity of the man's faith. The words poured over him, meaning little, but the Cathar had a voice of such rich beauty that it caught and held him like a shaft of sunlight, and the spell was only broken when one of his men interrupted his listening with a question. Raoul went to deal with the query, passing Matthias, who was muttering anxiously to himself and checking his precious bundles of manuscripts. When at last Raoul was free again, he glanced round and saw the woman standing a little to one side. She was drinking a cup of the rough village wine and had pushed down the cowl of her habit so that for the first time he could see her features clearly.

Hair black as midnight hung loose down her back in the manner that was permitted only to unmarried women and virgins. Glossy black eyebrows and lashes framed eyes of a soft, misty gray, but without the diamond clarity he remembered from his visions. Her face was drained and pale, her shoulders slumped with weariness, and those aspects, too, were difficult to reconcile with his memory.

Tentatively he approached her, and when she did not acknowledge him, lost in her own thoughts, he cleared his throat. "I do not even know your name," he said softly, "although you well know mine, I think."

She took her gaze from the horizon where she had been watching the storm clouds retreating south, and rested it on him instead, a half-smile curving her lips. "It is Bridget," she answered before raising her cup and finishing her wine. When she spoke again, it was more than half to herself. "I'm so tired. Sometimes I wonder if it would be simpler just to give in, to be captured and burned so that I would not have to run anymore, but then the knowledge would die with me, and I made a promise."

"Your companion . . . Matthias; he said that you were the guardians?" Raoul said curiously. "Guardians of what?"

Her smile deepened, emphasizing the tired lines around her eyes. "Each in his way is a guardian of the truths not perceived by the Roman church ... or perceived only as lies and blasphemy. Therefore, each of us must be destroyed."

Raoul was not sure that he understood her. What he was certain of, however, was that she and her companions were in great danger and that they needed help. "There are caves in the hills near my castle, and you should be safe there, for a while at least, if you want to stay," he suggested.

Bridget hesitated, then shook her head. "I thank you, but no. We are intending to go to Foix, to the retreat of the mountains. The Count of Foix is well disposed toward the Cathars, and many of his hills and valleys are so remote that they barely see a single shepherd from one season to the next."

"We will escort you there. With de Montfort's men in the region, the three of you should not be traveling alone."

She gave him a strange look, and the softness of her eyes contracted and brightened. "Then thank you," she said. "We accept your protection."

The prickling in Raoul's scalp had descended to tingle across his loins. He gazed at her mouth, at her wine-moist lips. In her throat he saw the gentle throb of her pulse. The beat of his own was harder, more rapid, coursing into his groin. Although the storm was receding, he still felt charged with its tension. "It is time we moved on," he said curtly. "De Montfort will be on our trail as soon as this storm passes over." And he left her while he still had the control to do so.

Shaken, Bridget watched him go to his knights and issue orders concerning their new destination. Her body was liquid with fear and anticipation. Four years ago at Montvallant she had realized this time would come, but had never known until now the precise moment when fate would set the key in the lock. She could have refused his aid, and sent him home to Montvallant and his wife, but that would be to send him to certain death. This way he had a chance to live, and in return, she would only ask of him the gift of his essence.

When Simon returned to Lavaur, Citeaux's soldiers were prodding through a heap of hot ashes in the field outside the gates where the town's Cathars had been immolated. They were searching for any larger bones that had survived the flames in order to grind them to dust. Citeaux intended nothing to remain, the earth to be purged of their very existence. The broken body of the lady Geralda was still down the well, no one having had sufficient bravery to come and beg its removal. Doubtless she would be taken out before she started poisoning the water.

Tossing his stallion's reins to a groom, Simon entered the keep. A dozen petitioners were waiting for him, among them local lords tendering their submission and adjutants requiring orders. His son Amaury was dealing with some of the less important matters. Seeing his father, he rolled his eyes meaningfully at the dais, where Citeaux was hunched over a platter of pigeons in red wine sauce, his face and the gravy not dissimilar in color.

Simon paused for a moment, mentally raking the earth over his shoulders, preparing to do battle. Then, thrusting his gauntlets and helm at a squire, he stalked up the hall to the dais.

"You lost them!" Citeaux accused, wiping his greasy fingers on a napkin. "You had them in your fist and you lost them!"

Simon braced his arms on the trestle and bestowed the full arrogance of his gray-green glare on Arnaud-Amalric. "Vent your spleen on me and it will be your last act on this earth!" he said through his teeth. He still possessed most of them, a rarity in a warrior of his years, although several were chipped and discolored. "Were it not for the sharp eyes of my own men, they'd not have been flushed from cover in the first place! Your own soldiers were too busy throwing stones down a well and clapping their hands at the bonfire!"

Citeaux's neck, wattle-scarlet, lurched out of his shoulders. "How dare you threaten and insult me!" he blustered. "I warn you I'll . . ."

"You'll what?" Simon's lip curled contemptuously. "Excommunicate me like Raymond of Toulouse? I think not. Sour your gut as it may, you need me and you know it!" With a growl of irritation, he thrust himself away from the trestle. "Besides, I know where to find your heretics and their mentor, and I have a score of my own to settle." He tugged at his coif, for the damp leather lining was chafing his throat.

"Where?" Citeaux licked his lips and leaned forward.

"Gold shield, black chevronels, yellow destrier." Simon raised one thick, black brow. So did Citeaux, in mystification.

He knew the shields of the more important men on both sides, but not all the petty lordlings who came and went like flies on a corpse. Simon, on the other hand, possessed an obsessive, almost finicky awareness of every heraldic device that had ever appeared on the battlefield.

"Raoul de Montvallant," Simon said with a glint of satisfaction. "Fought with us at Béziers, but turned rebel with a vengeance. My guess is that he was riding to Lavaur's aid when he realized it was too late and snatched those Cathars from under our noses instead." Simon took the cup of wine offered by his body squire. His eyes narrowed, calculating. "Time and past time I paid a personal visit to Lord Raoul's home," he said softly, and drank.

CHAPTER NINETEEN

Foix, May 1211

RAOUL WATCHED THE jugglers entertaining the high table toss their painted wooden batons from hand to hand, but although his eyes followed every twirl and turn and graceful arc, his thoughts were far away, and it was only his position as a guest of the Count of Foix that kept him in his place.

Farther along the board, in the lord's seat, the count was deep in conversation with one of his knights, but now and then Raoul was aware of the shrewd black eyes flickering in his direction. Foix was a warrior with a notorious reputation for being hotheaded and as tough and crude as boiled leather. He had taken Bridget, Chretien, and Matthias under his wing with alacrity. To Foix, the Cathars were a symbol of resistance, a rallying point against the northern crusading army.

Here in the mountains, Simon de Montfort was justly feared, but contempt was still the more dominant emotion, together with the belief that in the end he would be beaten. Only last month, so the count had told Raoul, the knights of Foix had ambushed several hundred of de Montfort's German mercenaries in the forest of Montgey and slaughtered them to a man. If the Cathars were going to be safe anywhere, it would be in these mountains marking the foothills of the great Pyrenean ranges.

Raoul's mind dwelt upon Bridget. He knew so little about her, only that she was strange and beautiful and in terrible danger. He desired her so powerfully that even thinking of her brought a rush of heat to his groin. She had not attended the evening meal in the hall, but he could feel her presence, and knowing how close she was set him on edge almost beyond bearing. That and the knowledge that she was not for him.

"I assume," said Foix, leaning across and breaking into his tortured thoughts, "that you will be returning to your overlord?"

Raoul sighed and with an effort brought his eyes to focus on the count. "Yes, my lord. Now that de Montfort has taken Lavaur, all the lands surrounding Toulouse are open to his attack, including my own."

"And Count Raymond, has he the spleen to fight back?"

Raoul was not surprised to see the glitter of contempt amid the speculation in Foix's eyes. Very few if any of the southern lords believed that Raymond of Toulouse was capable of holding his ground. "What choice does he have?" Raoul answered with a shrug. "The church refuses to believe he's repentant, and de Montfort's not open to negotiation while he's winning. He wants Toulouse for himself. It's either resist or die."

Foix was silent for a while. Then he looked shrewdly at Raoul. "Will you bear a letter to your overlord when you leave?" He laughed sourly at Raoul's startled expression. "Perhaps it is time to forget old rivalries. We must unite if we're going to survive, and we must fight. There's only one language that de Montfort understands—the sword!" His fist thumped decisively down on the board with such force that the wine leaped out of the cups.

Raoul thought with irony that the sword was the only language Foix understood, too, the reason he and Raymond had never seen eye to eye. "Willingly I will take a letter, my lord, but—"

"Excellent!" The count whacked him heftily on the shoulder and directed a squire to refill Raoul's cup. "De Montfort's bitten off more than he can chew this time, and we're going to be the ones to make him choke, eh? I'll send out messengers to Comminges and Béarn, too!" His face blazed with eagerness. "What can you tell me about the state of de Montfort's army at the moment from what you saw at Lavaur?"

"Apart from the fact that he's lacking a few hundred German mercenaries he was expecting from Carcassonne?"

Foix's raucous laughter resonated up and down the length of the entire trestle, and he belted Raoul again between the shoulder blades. "I like you!" he bellowed.

Gasping, Raoul wished that Foix did not like him with quite so much enthusiasm.

When he finally managed to escape the hall and its ebullient lord, Raoul climbed to the castle wall walks for a breath of fresh air. Below the great keep, the town slept, only the occasional glimmer of torchlight winking from a bawdy house or tavern, and reflecting on the dark surface of the River Ariège. Alone, but comforted by the unobtrusive, familiar sounds of the guards on watch, Raoul felt his sense of self and perspective return. He blew out through his cheeks and thought that the Count of Foix was about as subtle as a wild bull let loose in a marketplace.

He was suddenly aware that he was no longer alone. Turning, he saw a woman standing close to him in the shadows, her dark cloak embracing her body like a pair of folded wings, her hair a flowing gleam like the river in the darkness. His breath caught and his stomach knotted; even before she stepped toward him, he knew who she was.

"There will be storms tomorrow," she greeted him, her gaze upon the sky. "Do you not feel them?"

The crown of her head only just tipped the level of his shoulder, and her features were delicate. She seemed too fragile to be a vessel for the light and power he had seen her contain. "I did not see you in the hall tonight; I thought you had retired," he croaked, his throat suddenly dry.

"Only to my devotions." A smile, no more than a ripple of starlight, crossed her face. "I have a boon to ask of you before you leave Foix."

"You have but to name it, my lady," Raoul said, swallowing. He knew what his imagination wanted her to say, and that it was impossible.

"There is somewhere I have to go tomorrow without my uncle and Matthias. Would you be my escort?"

Raoul's stomach lurched. Averting his face, he pretended to pick at a loose lump of mortar on the merlon. "Where?" he asked, hoping in the time that it took her to reply, he would be able to compose himself.

"It is a hill fort a day's ride from here, mostly in ruins now. My mother brought me to it when we first came to these lands. Long ago it was a sacred place."

"And it is important to you? I thought the Cathars had no affinity for material ties."

"It is not important to me for material reasons." She studied him gravely. "I do not know if you will understand this, but sometimes, after people have gone, the essence of their hopes and prayers remains. Even in the churches of the Antichrist you can feel the outpourings of genuine belief. And I am not a Cathar in the same sense as Uncle Chretien. I was not raised as one, nor have I taken their vows."

"So how do you come to be traveling in the company of two senior Perfecti with every priest in Christendom decrying you for heresy?" He turned to face her, but did not release his contact with the merlon. Solid, it supported his spine. His hands pressed into the cold reality of the stone, seeking its reassurance.

She stared beyond him into the night, at the dark heaviness of cloud. "My father was Uncle Chretien's brother and a troubadour. He took service with Richard Coeur de Lion at Acre and followed him from Aquitaine, to England, to Outremer, and back to England. My mother was a healer of the old religion who treated my father for a wound he had taken in the Holy Land."

"Did she have the same powers as you?"

"Not as intense as mine, but yes, she had them." Bridget's expression became distant and sad. "Sometimes they are a great burden when I see things that would be better hidden." She took a slow, steadying breath, then sighed it out. "My mother taught me all she knew about healing—showed me how to channel the power. After my father died, we left England, crossed the Narrow Sea, and became pilgrims. We visited the old holy places—Carnac and Compostela, which used to be called Brigantium after my namesake. Then we came to Béziers and sought out my father's family to tell them what had become of him. We met his brother, Chretien, who was a practicing Cathar Perfect, and his son Luke. Matthias was living with him then, too."

Bridget bit her lip and her brow puckered. "Four years ago my mother was captured and killed by the black friars. Matthias was captured, too, and tortured, but he escaped." Her eyes glinted with tears as she raised them to him. "My mother claimed descent from Mary Magdalene and from the Virgin Mary. The Roman church is afraid that I will proclaim it to the world. They would destroy me for blasphemy, for the threat I pose to them. Matthias has the written proof of my bloodline."

"So that was why he was so anxious about his manuscripts in Lavaur?"

She nodded, and took a moment to compose herself. "I can see from the look on your face that you do not know whether to believe me, or to think me dangerously deluded."

"I have never met anyone like you," he said hoarsely. Fear rippled down his spine, warring with the attraction he felt toward her. "What makes you think I am worthy company to be your escort tomorrow? If you knew what I was thinking, you would not be standing here with me now, let alone asking me to accompany you on a journey."

"I know the kind of company I desire," she murmured in a velvet voice, and smiled up at him, the tears still hanging on her lashes. The night settled around them like another cloak. They were alone on the wall walk, not even a stirring of breeze for company. He remembered the soldier in Lavaur who had screamed in terror when he laid hands upon her. But he had not mistaken the invitation in her voice, nor did he want to walk away. Slowly, almost as if daring himself, he took his hand from the merlon and extended it to touch her face, then her hair, and slipped his grasp loosely down a thick strand. His knuckles brushed over her breast as his fingers traveled down to encircle her waist. She did not move, her eyes very wide and her breathing rapid. He pulled her against him, and she came pliantly into his arms, soft and responding. The darkness of night became the darkness of arousal, their bodies entwined, mouth upon mouth and the tactile seeking of fingers.

He stroked her body, touching her, exploring her. Leaning against the wall, he spread his legs and drew her between them to compensate for the difference in height, his hands firmly upon her hips, mouth on her throat, sucking. Frustration at the several layers of clothing separating skin from skin gnawed at his lust with a savage ache. Where could they go for warmth and privacy? Oh God, before he exploded. Hazily he thought about one of the store sheds in the ward, or the stables, although both were open to discovery.

Bridget was making soft sounds and clutching at him, her head thrown back. He thought of laying her down there and then upon the wall walk to slake his craving. God's body, not even on his wedding night had he been so aroused.

He tightened his hold, cupping her buttocks, pulling her against his aching, rigid manhood. Boots scraped on stone as a guard climbed the stairs on his rounds. Raoul felt Bridget struggle against him.

"Not here, not now!" she panted, pushing herself out of his arms and leaping away from him with the agility of a young ibex.

They stared at each other in the weak light from the overcast sky.

Raoul swallowed and pushed his hands through his fair hair. "Jesu, I could die of wanting you," he said, the hint of a tremor in his voice. He could hear the guard coming closer and silently cursed the man.

Bridget's eyes flickered and came back to Raoul as if drawn by a magnet. She took a hesitant step forward, then two back as he reached for her again. "No, wait until tomorrow," she breathed. "It is important, the phase of the moon must be right." She hurried rapidly back along the wall walk. Just before she disappeared into the dark mouth of the turret entrance, she looked over her shoulder and gave him a blinding smile.

Raoul leaned against the merlon and closed his eyes. He could have pursued her, grabbed her arm and pleaded with her, but set against his desire were pride and apprehension. He half-thought about tumbling a maidservant in the straw to ease his need—Foix had offered him one as a matter of course—but there was very little privacy for what would be a sordid, hasty act. As his body cooled enough for rational thought, he abandoned the idea.

The guard passed him on the wall walk with a nod of greeting and a curious look in his eye. Raoul nodded stiffly in response and returned to the pallet Mir had prepared for him in the hall, but it was a long time before he was able to sleep. He thought of Bridget, of how she had haunted him since his wedding eve, and how she was now tangible, within his physical grasp. Inevitably he thought of Claire, of the unbearable closeness and the unbearable distance. His lids tightened, he tossed on the pallet, but he did not change his mind. For better or worse, the die was cast.

The road to Bridget's hill fort wound steeply through forests of beech and dark, resinous pines, home to the boar, the brown bear, the wolf, and the brigand, although Bridget and Raoul were troubled by none of these. Now and then, glimpses through the trees showed them the snow still dusting the peaks of the Plantaurels even though it was early summer. Behind the white-clad crests, the sky was as dark as slate and zigzagged by lightning.

Bridget had told Raoul that they would not reach their destination until sunset. He had queried the wisdom of spending a night in the open when the weather was threatening to unleash terrific violence upon them. She had looked at him sidelong. "There is nothing to fear, we are a part of it," she had said, and her eyes as she spoke were the bright diamond-gray of his visions and her face reflected the clarity of the mountain light. The girl who had melted like wax in his arms last night had become an aloof goddess, and Raoul was in awe.

At noon they stopped to rest the horses. Bridget refused the bread and figs that Raoul produced from his saddle roll, and even a flask of the count's excellent wine, contenting herself with a drink of water from the stream where their mounts were dipping their muzzles. She sat apart from Raoul, saying nothing, her eyes upon the storms over the mountains.

He ate his own food without tasting it, drank the wine without any real appreciation, and like his silent companion, studied the seething mass of cloud that was gathering in the direction they were heading. Had Bridget's manner not been so strange, he would have suggested that they return to Foix. Instead, he held his tongue, knowing that there was no need for him to speak, that she could see every particle of him, as though his substance were made of purest glass.

Throughout the afternoon, they pressed onward through valleys gashed by steep waterfalls, the trees clinging to the hillsides with roots like claws. The pines became sparse and small, giving way to hardy bushes and scrub. Outcrops of limestone thrust through the forests like giant bones, pitted with the dark sockets of ancient cave entrances. Once, in the distance, they saw the lithe, tawny shape of a lynx. It swung its head in their direction, took their scent, and vanished into the scrub.

A herd of feral goats grazed on the steep slope of the mount where the ruins pushed up from the sparse grass like a jagged tooth from a gum. On a tongue of rock, the dominant male regarded his territory with unnerving yellow eyes, his horns magnificent ridged curves, thick as young trees. And behind him the lightning illuminated the molars and canines of crumbling stone.

The fortress had been deserted since the end of the Merovingian dynasty. Owls and mice, predator and prey, had made homes in the limestone walls, and grass sprouted from every opportune crevice. A cold wind like a huge hand pushed Raoul through the ruined gateway, the stone posts of which bore faded designs and symbols. He thought that he could just make out a bear on one of the columns, and beneath it what appeared to be a cauldron. A marmot shot from beneath Fauvel's hooves and scurried across the grass-choked ward. Desolation stalked the ramparts and ruined buildings like a grim sentinel. Overhead the sky rumbled in ominous warning of the storm to come.

Dismounting, Raoul looked round for a sheltered place to tether the horses and make a camp for the night. The remains of a stone-built storage shed caught his attention, but a closer inspection revealed that at least one wall was in imminent danger of collapsing. Hissing through his teeth with irritation, he led their horses into the lee of the main curtain wall and tethered them to a holly oak tree that clung tenaciously to life among the crumbling stones. He supposed that the horses would survive the night well enough where they were, but it was poor shelter indeed for himself and Bridget. This place must be very special that she would seek it even in the teeth of a full-blown mountain storm.

Looking over his shoulder, he saw her standing at the eastern edge of the broken ramparts. The rising wind carried to him the sound of her singing, although he could not make out the words, or even the language. Spine tingling, he attended to the horses, unsaddling them, throwing blankets over their rumps, and giving each of them a measure of grain. All the time he worked he was aware of Bridget standing out in the open, the wind whipping her garments against her body as she sang. His unease grew, and with it a gathering excitement.

He cast his glance round again, searching for somewhere to make a shelter. Finding nothing, he left the horses and went to Bridget where she swayed in a state of half-trance. He started to touch her and changed his mind, confining himself instead to shouting through the wind. "We cannot stay here; there's nowhere to keep dry if the storm breaks. We'll die of cold!"

Her crooning ceased. She stood quite still, breathing deeply, then, obviously making an effort to retrace a mental path to the mundane, gave her attention to him. "There is a cave," she murmured. "It is too small for the horses, but there is room enough for us and there's a smoke hole in the roof. Bring our packs and I will show you." And without waiting for him, she started toward another, smaller gateway at the other end of the fortress. Dragging her gown through her belt, she scrambled over the pile of rubble blocking the entrance with the agility of a mountain goat. As he followed, Raoul admired her slender ankles and calves, the occasional tantalizing flash of her thigh, the suppleness of her body and the swing of her heavy, black braid.

The cave entrance was concealed from the casual wanderer by a dark, abrasive screen of juniper bushes, which Raoul decided were there by design, not accident. Bridget forced aside the bushes and stooped at the entrance. There was a sound like heavy rain on a tile roof and Raoul leaped backward, startled by the bats she had disturbed. A living twist of smoke, they streamed away in the direction of the fort. Bridget laughed and he managed a weak grin himself. He had to bend double to enter the cave. When he straightened and took a gulp of air, the smell of bat droppings and musty stone was so powerful that he nearly retched. Dim light filtered down through the smoke hole, which seemed to be man-made, and there was also a choked, long-disused hearth immediately beneath it. Coughing, hand across his mouth and nose, he gave Bridget an eloquent look from his eye corners.

Her expression was preoccupied, for she was too deeply enmeshed in her own thoughts and emotions to notice anything as commonplace as a bad smell. Her gaze swept the small cave, and she picked her way delicately across it to a shadowed ledge near the rear rock wall. "My mother and I once sheltered here," she murmured. "It was shortly before we went to Béziers, to my uncle Chretien, and I was fourteen years old. She said then that I would return." Reaching on tiptoe, she brought down a small package of waxed linen and unwrapped a red clay lamp and a sealed container of oil.

Raoul found a relatively clean part of the cave floor and unhitched his sword belt. After one brief glance in his direction, Bridget coaxed the tinder to light and set it to the wick on the lamp. Light and shadows danced to life and the smooth sides of the cave became at once more accessible and more mysterious. Raoul felt as if he were caught inside a pulsating womb, the distant roll of thunder like the beat of blood around an unborn child.

"I'll fetch firewood before the storm breaks," he said, and went outside.

Bridget set about unpacking their saddle rolls. She laid out their blankets on the floor to one side of the hearth and set their wooden eating bowls close by. Not that she intended eating anything herself. The fast was part of the ritual, opening the spiritual pathways. She could feel the power of the mystery tingling through her veins and gathering in the bowl of her hips as if she were already great with child.

When Raoul returned with a fat bundle of dry sticks, she had cleared the hearth of the old ashes and rubbish, and had kindled a small fire in anticipation of the larger one to be built. Its smell was aromatic with herbs. His glance lit on the blankets spread together and then upon her as he put the kindling down near the fire.

"We would have been more comfortable if we had stayed at Foix, and I doubt your uncle is deceived by any of this secrecy," he remarked, only half in jest.

She set a small pot over the fire to simmer and scattered into it a handful of leaves. Hawthorn and white lily, fertility plants sacred to the Goddess, cherry laurel and hemp, the plants of visions. "My uncle knows why I am here and my purpose, which is far more than that which I see in your eyes."

Raoul sat down cross-legged opposite her and returned her stare with determination. "And what do you see in my eyes?" he questioned softly.

"A child and a man, a girl and a woman," she answered, the gaze between them holding like a pair of crossed swords. "Light and darkness and fire." Leaning to the flames, without flinching, she lifted the pot straight off the heat. Raoul cried out in warning and started to reach toward her, but she gave him a strange smile and, putting the bowl down, showed him her pink, undamaged palms and fingers. Lifting the bowl again, she brought it round the fire and offered it to him. "Set your hands on mine and you will not feel the heat, nor will you be scalded."

He hesitated, and she saw that he was held on a knife edge between desire and terror. "It is only a tisane that my mother taught me to brew," she murmured to encourage him. "It will not harm you."

He eyed her darkly. "I did not think that you had brought me all this way just to poison me." Placing his hands over hers, he drank. So did Bridget, but sparingly, and urged most of it on him. Then she sat down on her own side of the fire and threw more wood upon it and another scattering of the herbs with which she had infused the tisane.

The smoke clouded up between them, scented like blossom. "Last night at Foix," Raoul ventured, "you said that the phase of the moon must be right . . . that it was important? How so?"

"Women's bodies work to the ways of the moon and the tides. If they have the knowledge, they can tell when their wombs will quicken and when they will lie fallow."

"That seems a very great power to me."

"It is the power of choice." She unwound her heavy black hair from its braid, and removed her gown, tunic, and shift, her eyes never leaving his. "Tonight you will sow your seed on fertile ground; tonight we will make a child between us."

She saw him swallow, saw the look in his eyes as they traveled over her naked body with scorching slowness. "Then the power is mine, too," he muttered, his voice thick with desire as he pulled off his shirt, hose, and braies.

"So it has always been between man and woman." She leaned forward and set her mouth on his, her breasts grazing his chest, one arm around his neck, the other descending to his groin. Of her own accord her action might not have been so bold, but drugged by the smoke, exalted by the violence of the weather outside, she had no inhibitions.

She felt him hard and eager in her hand, felt him touch her and heard the harshness of his breathing combine with her own soft entreaties. His hands, hard from the wielding of sword and lance, parted her thighs, his thumb stroked her womanhood, but she needed no coaxing.

"Now," she panted, taking his quivering shaft in her hand and guiding him home. "Let it be now!"

He pierced her and she cried aloud with the sensation of fulfillment. She was the sky and he was the force of the rain. She was the earth and he was the white-hot stab of the lightning. Closing her eyes, she let the force of the storm take her up so that she became a whirling particle of its vast element—the sheer brilliance of pure sensation possessing her body and removing it from her control, and then the slow spiral down. And before she could grasp anything of self, the spiral reversed and returned her again to the vortex of the storm and the power of the surging life force.

* * *

Early morning brought the high-pitched twittering of the bats returning to their roost, ignoring now the presence of strangers in their abode. The smoke from the fire was a narrow twirl, unscented by any herb, and the light of day glimmered through the hole in the roof and entered obliquely through the screened cave entrance. By its light Bridget turned her head and studied the sleeping man. His arm lay across her, his hand loosely upon the red cords around her neck from which hung the two dove and chalice pendants. Well, perhaps it was appropriate. He had given her the means last night to fashion another such cord. She looked at his short, thick lashes, the sensuous curve of his mouth, his vulnerability in sleep, and her heart ached. What could she give him in return? Only the bitter revelation of something that she had known even before she brought him from Lavaur, and that he would discover when he went home.

Her eyes swept his body, admiring the lean contours of muscle and sinew. How easy it would be to stay here all day with him in dalliance, learning all the subtleties of the new mystery she had discovered—that he had led her to discover. And what would he recall of last night? Her lips curved poignantly. A man and a woman, light and darkness and fire. Very gently she removed his arm from across her body and sat up. Her hair was a wild tangle over her breasts and shoulders. Quickly, quietly, she braided it as best she could, donned her chemise and gown, stuffed her belongings into her own saddle roll, and with a final look at Raoul, went silently from the cave. It was easier this way. If she stayed until he awoke, he would want to talk, to cement the bond they had forged last night, and that could never be. His heart and soul were not hers, and his body had only been a brief lending of the male life force. It had been fine and beautiful. That was what she regretted leaving behind.

It had stopped raining and the sunrise twinkled on the wet grass and covered the fortress ruins in a wash of gold. The air smelled of juniper and thyme and new young shoots. Bridget placed one hand lightly on her belly, feeling an affinity with all things growing. The fecund earth mother; the corn goddess. Humming softly to herself, she began climbing toward the fort.

Opening his eyes, Raoul stared across the empty space beside him at a fire that had gone out. Gradually he came to his senses, his memory floating into place piece by little piece. His eyes widened and he looked rapidly around the cave, discovering that he was alone—not a trace of Bridget remaining. For a wild instant he thought that he had been dreaming again, but when he sat up to put on his braies, he saw the dried blood smearing his manhood and thighs. No illusion could have left such tangible evidence. But then if such intimacy was not an illusion, why had she gone?

He fumbled into his clothing and went outside. A morning alive with birdsong sparkled at him, the sky and land cleansed of dust. The sun stroked his face. Shading his eyes with the flat of his hand, he stared around, but saw nothing save a family of ground squirrels grooming in the new warmth, and a lone lammergeier high in the blue.

Feeling bereft, he stooped back into the cave and began packing his saddle roll. He returned the tinder, flint, oil, and lamp to the shelf for the use of other travelers who might happen this way. As he left the cave and climbed slowly to the ruins on the summit, he wondered if they had begotten the child that she had wanted. Surely so, for he knew that the gifts she possessed were no falsehood, and last night her body had drained his dry.

"Why me?" he had asked her, as they lay close, the sweat cooling upon their bodies. "Why choose me?"

She had smiled, tiny creases appearing at her eye corners. "I could say that it is because you are the most handsome man I have ever seen, and that would be the truth, but not all of it." Her slender hand had moved slowly over his chest, smoothing glistening flesh. His own had responded over the taut curve of her breast. "Once, long ago, I saw you and wanted you," she murmured, "but the time was not right then. You have a strong life force, Raoul de Montvallant, and a will of iron that runs good and true. I want these qualities for a child of mine. Her life will not be easy."

"Her life?"

She had taken his hand and traced his palm and fingertips over her belly to the moist juncture of her thighs. "Her life," she had said, and shortly after that they had ceased to talk.

His horse waited in the lee of the wall, and he saw that Bridget had fed and saddled him. Braided into the cream mane was a red cord from which hung a small, enameled disk bearing the device of a dove and chalice on one side, a spear and cauldron on the other. He recognized it as one of the tokens Bridget had worn around her neck, and which, even in the frantic passion of their lovemaking, she had not removed. Smiling, feeling slightly less bereft, he plucked her farewell from Fauvel's mane, but still he wondered why she had not chosen to stay.

On riding into Foix that evening, it came as no surprise to Raoul to discover that Bridget, Chretien, and Matthias had departed the moment she returned. He was told that she had not even bothered to dismount from her horse, and no one knew where the trio were bound. No messages, no hints.

Curious glances followed Raoul, but he ignored them. His troops saw the set of his jaw and the look in his eyes and knew better than to ask questions. Even Giles and Roland, who dared call him friend as well as lord, held to silence, and exchanging wry glances, hastened to make ready to leave Foix.

At dawn the following day, the count handed over to Raoul the letters intended for Count Raymond. His dark eyes gleamed with malice, for he had no need to put a bridle on his own salty tongue.

"I gather it wasn't a success?" he needled as Raoul put the packets down inside his mail shirt and began pulling on his gauntlets.

Raoul's mouth tightened. "My lord, with respect, that is a private affair between myself and the lady."

"Oh, hardly private," provoked Foix. He leaned back in his carved chair. "Chretien de Béziers was somewhat vexed to discover you and she both gone. He spent the night before last in prayer for his niece, so I hear, but I warrant you and she were worshiping at a different kind of altar entirely!"

The second gauntlet in place, Raoul clenched his fist to ease the leather and contemplated striking Foix in the mouth. He could feel the heat of blood warming his face and pulsing in his throat. But Foix, for all his crude manner, had only spoken the truth, and Raoul knew that his own conscience was on the raw. Carefully he unclenched his fist and turned round. "Doubtless the lady will give her uncle all the reassurance he needs," he said neutrally. "Whatever the lord Chretien's misgivings, he knew our destination. Thank you for your hospitality. I'll make sure Count Raymond receives your letter with all haste." He bowed to make an end of the interview.

"And I wish you Godspeed." Humor tugged at the other man's mouth as he gave a formal response to Raoul's formal farewell. "There's a place for you here among my own knights should you wish to stay. I know a good horse and a good man when I see one."

Panic jolted through Raoul at the very thought of such a fate. "Thank you, my lord," he replied when he could be sure that his voice would not betray him. "You are most generous." And he bowed quickly out into the bright summer morning to take his men home.

And a little to the north, as the sun climbed in the sky, Simon de Montfort went for the enemy's throat and struck at Toulouse.

CHAPTER TWENTY

Montvallant, May 1211

GUILLAUME WAILED AND hit out with his small fists as Claire and Isabelle struggled to hold him still while they finished rubbing viscous brown walnut oil into his skin and hair.

"Hush, oh, hush!" Claire pleaded, unable to bear the sound of his cries but knowing that disguising her son as a goatherd's child was his best chance of survival. She looked in grief at the transformation from blond angel to grubby urchin. An old blanket had been found at the bottom of the press, and a frayed homespun tunic discarded from one of the kitchen boys had been cut down to fit him.

Suddenly overwhelmed by her love and her terror, she took Guillaume in her arms and clutched him fiercely to her bosom, kissing him and weeping.

"My lady, it is not too late for you to come with us," quavered Isabelle, tears magnifying her dark eyes.

Claire bit her lip and concentrated on the physical pain to control the mental. "No." She shook her head. "I cannot leave Beatrice. She's too weak to travel, and in Raoul's absence Montvallant's responsibility is mine. . . . Here, take care of him . . . keep him safe for me. . . ." She returned Guillaume to her maid. In the bedchamber doorway Pierre the groom was waiting. "Go now, quickly. I'll join you later if I can."

Unable to watch Isabelle leave with Guillaume, Claire turned away, her eyes squeezed tightly shut, teeth biting down into the side of her hand to stifle her agony as a piece of her heart was torn out. Her soul was bleeding to death as surely as the soldiers had bled on the town walls when de Montfort had brought his army down on them fresh from plundering Lavaur. She could not blame her people for yielding when threatened. With Raoul absent, they had no commander to coordinate resistance, and they knew what had happened at Béziers and at Bram, where the entire garrison had been mutilated. Apparently Raoul had been too late to save Lavaur, but had rescued Geralda's three important heretics from the town, literally from beneath de Montfort's nose. The lord Simon wanted them handed into his custody or else . . .

Claire's stomach dissolved. How could they give him what they did not have? "Raoul, where are you?" she whispered, and stared at the blood trickling down her wrist where her teeth had bitten through skin. The crusaders held the town. If she refused to open her gates, de Montfort had threatened to raze Montvallant and do on a smaller scale what he had done to Béziers. Claire knew that he did not threaten in vain.

She entered the main bedchamber. The fire had been built up to a huge blaze to keep the room warm. In the great bed that was hers and Raoul's, Beatrice was propped up on half a dozen pillows. Her complexion was bright, but it was the radiance of fever, not the bloom of health. Her ravaged lungs were faltering badly now, the specks of blood on her kerchief had become blots, and her exhaustion grew worse daily. Her mind had started to wander. Sometimes she would speak to Berenger as if he were with her in the room. Claire did not even think of burdening her by telling her what was about to happen or that she would probably never see her little grandson again.

She stood at the bedside. The heat of the room beaded her brow with sweat, but Beatrice's skin was clammy. Her mother-in-law's eyes flickered open, smudged with the fatigue of living on death's edge. "Light the candles," she whispered to Claire. "I can feel the night closing in."

Claire did what she could to give Beatrice ease, and when the sick woman had fallen into a restless doze, went down to give the order to open the gates to the crusaders, her heart heavy within her breast. They came, row upon row, two abreast, their banners snapping in the breeze, their armor glittering. Their horses churned the dust into a white haze so that they rode as if out of a dream, and drew to a halt within the castle's outer bailey. A white stallion paced forward and the soldier upon its back stared assessingly around the golden stone walls. Then he lowered his gaze, narrowed it upon Claire, and beckoned with a raised mail mitten.

Slowly, with dragging feet, her foreboding verging on terror, Claire advanced to tender Montvallant's submission to Simon de Montfort. Her chatelaine's keys were laid across her palms, but she had no intention of kneeling to present them.

De Montfort held his stallion on a tight rein and looked at her with the same hard gaze that had perused Montvallant's walls. Claire forced herself to return that fierce stare and felt as if she had been seized in a vise and squeezed until she could not breathe. This was the man who had overseen the massacre of Béziers and the atrocities at Bram and Minerve, who had taken Lavaur and watched its Cathars burn, and who was now going to do the same to the Cathars of Montvallant, perhaps including herself.

"It is your husband's submission I require," he said huskily.

"He is not here, my lord; I offer you the keys in his stead." Claire was aware of the quiver in her voice. She compressed her lips and, out of sheer, terrified bravado, raised her chin a notch.

A frown brooded between de Montfort's dark brows. He gestured and a young adjutant dismounted from a palfrey to take the keys out of her hands.

"Your husband seems to have a penchant for running away."

"At least he does not steal other men's lands," she retorted. "I count him worth ten of you."

"Do you indeed?" De Montfort curbed his restlessly sidling horse and examined the keys that the young man passed up to him. Then he looked again at Claire. "Then perhaps it is time you were taught to value differently. Giffard, escort Lady de Montvallant to her chamber and make sure that she stays there."

The adjutant grasped Claire's arm. She tried to shake him off, but his grip was of steel. The white afternoon heat, the enemy soldiers, the oppression of de Montfort's gaze, all combined to buckle her knees. She had to cling to the young man to keep herself from falling at de Montfort's feet, making it easy for him to lead her away.

"Berenger? Berenger, where are you?" Beatrice's fever-bright gaze wandered the chamber.

"It's all right, Mother, hush, I'm here." Claire sat down on the coverlet and clasped the sick woman's reaching hand.

"Berenger?"

"No, Mother, it's Claire? Are you thirsty?"

A frown passed like a shadow across Beatrice's flushed brow. "I can feel you!" she whispered. "Beloved, I know you are here." Her hand gripped fiercely upon Claire's for a moment, then slowly relaxed; her eyelids drooped and her words died to a mumble.

Beatrice drifted into an uneasy sleep and Claire gently released her hand from the febrile, translucent fingers. Her chest hurt as she fought not to weep aloud. She wanted to howl her fear and anguish at the rafters, but she knew that it would disturb Beatrice. Besides, outside the room stood an armed guard with his ear to the door, and she refused to give him the satisfaction of hearing her.

Sniffing, still wiping at her eyes and nose like a little girl, Claire went to the stone pitcher and tipped the last of the wine into the wooden cup—not the goblet of earlier. That had been looted by de Montfort's men, and she had been given a crude kitchen utensil in exchange. The wine tasted sour and warm, but then it had been standing in the pitcher since before dawn, and it was well past compline now. From darkness to darkness, she thought, and no glimmer of light in between, although the day she had just endured had been the longest of her entire life.

In agitation, Claire paced to the shuttered window and stared at the bare wall beside it where Beatrice's white hart tapestry had hung that morning. If she looked round, she would see the logs blazing in the hearth, warning her of the fate awaiting all heretics. Before they had locked her in here with Beatrice and stripped the room of all luxuries, she had seen the priests among de Montfort's troops. Smirking beside two friars and Simon's personal chaplains in the courtyard had been Father Otho—a thinner, malevolent Father Otho, who had smiled at her in a manner far from benign. And there had been a young black friar with a fanatical gleam in his eye. She had recognized him from the first months of her marriage when he and another priest had come seeking Geralda's three heretics. Now, apparently, he was a member of de Montfort's retinue.

Claire swallowed the remainder of the wine, uncaring that it tasted like vinegar, but it did nothing to take away the cold lump in the pit of her stomach. No thought was safe. Do not think at all, she told herself.

The door latch rattled and she leaped to face it, the empty cup falling to the rushes at her feet, her eyes huge with alarm.

"Lord de Montfort wants to see you," said de Montfort's senior squire. He was a young man on the threshold of knighthood, hard-eyed like his master, and no older than herself. "Now."

"Why?" Unconsciously she put one hand to her throat, and her eyes darted to the flames in the hearth.

"If you please, my lady. He dislikes to be kept waiting."

If she pleased? And what would happen if she refused? Both the squire and the guard on the door were well fed and muscular, and it would be no difficulty for them to drag her wherever they desired.

"My mother-in-law is sick; I dare not leave her for too long."

The squire just indicated the door, and she saw the impatience flare his nostrils. Smoothing her gown, raising her chin, she went with him down the twisting, torchlit stair to the solar. He banged on the door, waited for his lord to acknowledge, and then ushered her into the room.

Simon was sitting in the chair that had been Berenger's favorite, its cushions worn but comfortable, the wood bearing the patina of lovingly tended old age. De Montfort's large body occupied every inch of it. One knee was raised, boot resting on the cushion, his other leg was stretched out in a relaxed pose, and yet the calculating narrowness of his eyes told her that he was not at ease.

"Come in, my lady," he said, and dismissed his squire with a nod and a brief gesture of the hand not holding a cup of wine.

Quivering like a hunted doe run to bay, Claire took two tiny steps forward. Her hands were clenched tightly in the folds of her gown, her spine so stiff with the effort of holding herself proudly that she only shook the more before him.

Without haste, giving her time to absorb the latent power in his large body, he put his cup down, unfolded himself from the chair, and prowled across the room until he stood over her. "Where is your husband?" he asked, his voice a soft, leonine growl that held the threat of a full-throated roar.

Claire was trapped by the cold ferocity of his eyes, by the dominating bulk that invaded her space and overpowered her will. Her knees shook so much that she could scarcely stand up, and she was cold, so cold.

"You are deluded if you think silence will help you," Simon said.

She returned his gaze blankly, so frightened that her responses were frozen.

"Cooperate with me and your town will not be destroyed. Otherwise . . ." He shrugged. "You should know by now what happens to those who collaborate with heretics."

She bit her lip. The silence was horrible.

"By the rood, answer me!" Simon snarled, and grasping her shoulders, shook her hard. Her head snapped back and forth and her wimple tumbled askew.

The violence restored a spark of feeling. "I do not know!"

she gasped "And if I did, I would not tell you!" Her lips drew back from her teeth in a white snarl.

Beneath the pressure of his fingers, Simon felt her trembling, the fear now mixed with defiance. And oh God, he was so seldom defied. Her hair spilled down her back, webbing his hands with the scent of lavender. Alais's hair was brown, thin and straight, her braids not much thicker than the width of his thumb. This between his fingers was a lustrous river of fire. Suddenly he was intensely conscious of her full, pink lips, the creamy column of her throat, the swift rise and fall of her breasts, his engorged manhood.

Simon prided himself on his control, on his ability to refuse the whores and courtesans whom his own officers used to satisfy their appetites. He had Alais, and as often as not, she was within riding distance, but it had been a long time between visits and she was very close to being brought to bed of the child conceived last autumn. He discovered that for once, he wanted to give his lust free rein, to ride its wildness until he was spent. It was his right to take, to be revenged on Raoul de Montvallant for what had happened at Lavaur.

His hands tightened in her hair and he set his mouth on hers. She jerked, tried to scream, but he sealed her voice in her throat with the pressure of his kiss and forced her back against the wall, pressing himself against her. She struggled grimly and he was filled with the eager need to subjugate. He would brand her forever with his mark as if she were a runaway serf.

He took her savagely on the rushes of her own solar floor, her gown bunched up around her waist like any common whore, her arms pinioned, her body invaded by his male force, flattened by his weight as he surged triumphantly into her. His thrusts raged deep, violating, imprinting. He tasted the salt of blood on her lips as his mouth crushed down on hers, grinding, grinding, hands bruising her flesh, digging bone-deep. As he jammed into her for the final time and his seed pulsed within her, she represented to him the entire lands of Raymond of Toulouse. Raped, subjugated, sown with his will, never to be southern again.

"It doesn't matter about your husband!" he panted, still at his limit within her. "Let him run, let him hide. It can only be a matter of time."

CHAPTER TWENTY-ONE

Montvallant, June 1211

STILL AS A millpond, the Tarn reflected a solid silver moon. Raoul loosened the reins to let Fauvel drink and stared across the water at the light-frosted lands beyond the river's gleam. Montvallant. His home. Crushed beneath a northern fist while he had been riding in the opposite direction to Foix.

The town itself had not been destroyed, but it had been severely purged. The bodies of its garrison rotted on the walls, and the church bell, which had scarcely been swung in the last five years, now called the people to enforced mass and tolled an early curfew. Soldiers, wearing the hated red cross on their surcoats, were billeted upon the inhabitants. De Montfort had established a mercenary camp in the town, displaying to the people of Montvallant what happened when they supported a rebel lord.

Guilt gnawed at Raoul, giving him no respite. In his mind he relived over and again his folly after Lavaur. Instead of returning to Claire, he had pursued a dream and gained nothing but the temporary gratification of his body at the expense of the fabric of his daily life. There had been no warning that this was to come, unless it had been in the voice of the storm, and he had chosen to heed a different kind of message.

The bulk of his troop were swelling the numbers of the garrison at Toulouse, where every man was needed to fight off de Montfort's continuous assault. Raoul had brought only a few picked knights with him to make a night reconnaissance upon lands over which less than a month ago he had ridden in bold

possession. *Je voi bien tuit perdu ai*—Now I see that all is lost.
So the jongleur at Foix had plaintively sung. Not lost, but stolen. On that thought Raoul spoke softly to the horse and urged
him into the gleaming dark water. Ripples arrowed the stallion's legs and breast as he thrust forward against the current.
Behind him, Raoul heard the soft plash of the other horses entering the river. Bit chains muffled, hooves wrapped in cloth,
they rode across moonlit fields, through vineyards and orchards, and took the track toward the caves where Montvallant
had given shelter to the itinerant Cathars of the Agenais.

Crickets chirred in the silence. Rags of cloud drifted across
the moon's silver halo. The men shunned the light, their cloaks
worn over their armor and their faces blackened with mud.
Keeping to the shadows, they climbed the hill and took the
narrow goat track to the caves near the summit. On reaching
them, Raoul felt his heart sink, for they were deserted, their
fires several days cold. An overturned cooking pot, eating
bowls with the food still in them, and a solitary shoe told their
tale only too well. Montvallant's Cathars had been discovered,
and therein died his hope that Claire, his mother, and
Guillaume had been able to hide with them, undetected.

Dismounting, he squatted beside the dead fire, rubbing the
ashes between his fingers. A different cave and a different fire
held his inner vision, and his feeling of guilt increased threefold.

"Listen," Mir whispered urgently. "Someone comes."

Raoul wiped his hand on his surcoat and rose to face the direction of the squire's stare. Very, very slowly, he inched his
sword from its sheath so that no clink of metal or scabbard
mountings would give him away to whoever was abroad on
the hillside.

Their breathing swift and shallow, the men listened to the
sound of other breathing, loud with effort as whoever it was
strove up the rocks toward them from the direction of the
town. The scrape of shod hoof on stone sounded clearly across
the stillness of the night. A woman's voice spoke in the darkness and a man panted a reply. The tongue was southern and
Raoul relaxed slightly. It was very unlikely that this was a patrol out in search of stray Cathars, but still he backed into the
shadows. The starlight shone on dark horsehide and glittered

on the bridle trappings, and as the horse was reined to a halt before the cave, Raoul recognized Claire's bay mare. His heart sprang painfully against his ribs, but the woman who dismounted wore the coarse weave of a peasant and was much smaller than his wife. She spoke again softly to the child wrapped in her arms.

"Isabelle?" Raoul stepped from the shadows. She screamed and her companion's knife flashed and was arrested in midmotion.

"Lord Raoul?" Pierre the groom thrust his head forward and peered into the darkness. The knife flashed again as he sheathed it in his belt, and covering his face with his hands, he started to sob. "You are too late, my lord. They came . . . wave upon wave of them . . . the whole northern army, or so it seemed, and led by de Montfort himself. There was nothing we could do but surrender."

Isabelle drew back the edge of the blanket covering the infant, and in the haphazard moonlight, Raoul saw the face of his sleeping son. "My lady bade me disguise him as a peasant child. We clothed him in homespun and rubbed walnut dye into his hair lest its color attract too much attention, and Pierre and I escaped with him."

Raoul took Guillaume into his arms. An aching lump constricted his throat and he had to force his voice through it to speak. "What happened to your mistress?"

"She was taken prisoner, my lord, and your lady mother with her. The soldiers burned the Cathars and forced us all to watch, and then they took Lady Claire and Lady Beatrice away, and no one knows where." Isabelle's voice was toneless, her dark eyes quenched.

Pierre wiped his face on his sleeve. "They came up here," he croaked, "straight up. They knew where the Cathars were hiding and they dragged them out and back to the town. God's true light, I never want to see such a sight again." He touched the hilt of his knife and his voice hardened. "It was Father Otho who betrayed them to the soldiers," he said grimly. "The crawling maggot returned with de Montfort's troops and set about claiming his revenge. He had people dragged out of their houses and beaten in the streets. He demanded to be the torchbearer when the Cathars were tied at the stake." Pierre's hand went to his knife hilt again, and his face twisted with remembered anger and revulsion. "I knew he would come looking for Isabelle as soon as he was free of his duties, and when I saw the right moment, I took his life. For all that I am a croyant of the true religion, I do not repent the deed. There was another priest with him, a black friar. If the opportunity had arisen, I am not ashamed to say that I would have killed him, too."

"I would have done the same and more." Raoul's voice was now as flat as Isabelle's, but harder. "And you know nothing more of Lady Claire and Lady Beatrice?"

"No, my lord. After they had been forced to witness the burning, they were put straight in a litter under heavy guard and taken away. . . . One of de Montfort's knights feasts in your hall, and the town is overflowing with crusaders and mercenaries. De Montfort is using it as a supply camp. . . . There is nothing you can do."

Raoul closed his eyes, gripped so powerfully by anguish and guilt that for an instant nothing else existed, and he had to ask Pierre to repeat his next words twice before he was able to grasp their meaning.

"We were making our way to Agen, to Lady Claire's mother," Pierre said slowly and clearly, with exaggerated hand gestures and a worried look on his face. "But first we came up here to see if anyone was left. . . ."

"Agen," Raoul said huskily, fixing on the name, while comprehension blundered back into his mind. "I'll escort you there. De Montfort's troops are everywhere." He turned toward Fauvel.

Isabelle held out her hands for the child. "Shall I carry him, my lord?"

"No," he said softly. "Let me have him." Cradling his sleeping son tenderly, Raoul mounted the stallion and felt his loss all the more keenly for the saving grace of the warm scrap of life in his arms.

Perched upon a steep, pudding-shaped rock, its lower slopes forested in pines, the fortress of Montségur was the foremost Cathar stronghold in the Ariège. Lonely, isolated, magnificent, it beckoned the seekers after mystic solitude, and daunted those who had no calling.

A cold wind was blowing off the Pyrenees and the sky was a boiling mass of dark clouds above the fortress, but Bridget's misgivings as she stared at the sanctuary were born of a strange feeling of sadness which was overlaid by far stronger feelings of peace and well-being. This was the place she had chosen to bear her child and watch her grow in wisdom and strength. This was the place that would succor them from a hostile world—for the immediate future at least. She set her hand lightly upon her belly, and felt with pleasure the fluttering throb of the new life quickening within her womb. *See, Mother, I have fulfilled my promise. Your grandchild grows inside me, a daughter of the Light.*

Chretien left Matthias sitting on the grass where they had stopped to eat their noontide meal, and joined her where she stood on the narrow mule track, watching the blending of castle, crag, and clouds. She turned to him with a wistful half smile. "I was thinking of my mother," she said, "and missing her. Sometimes, when I see these mountains, I feel that I can touch her spirit, that she is watching over me."

Chretien returned her smile. "Assuredly she is," he replied, and drew a deep lungful of the pine-scented air. "She loved Montségur. It is fitting that you should come here." He set his arm around her shoulders, and she leaned her head briefly against his stalwart bulk. Chretien had said very little about her pregnancy. Their views differed; neither would ever argue the other into a state of change. He had accepted the inevitable, and offered her his support, if not his approval. If a child was to be born, then let its path be a true and holy one, unstrewn by thorns. Matthias had been more openly pleased at Bridget's news, but then to Matthias, Bridget's fruitfulness was a continuation of the bloodline whose path he had traced and recorded for so many years, a light that glowed despite all efforts to quench it.

Montségur. A place both of kindling and of quenching, quiescent now, couched in power. *I will raise up mine eyes to the light, and I will drink of its bounty. It is my heritage, my life and my death.*

"Come," she said to Chretien, pulling away from him. "There are still many miles to travel before nightfall."

CHAPTER TWENTY-TWO

A N INCLEMENT NOVEMBER wind flung itself against the sides of the four-horse traveling cart that was bearing Alais de Montfort and her ladies toward the town of Castres for the winter season.

The endless swaying and bumping of the wain as it lurched out of one rut and into another made Claire feel sick. The cart was drafty and the furs and pelts with which the women had surrounded themselves in order to keep warm smelled mustily of the clothing chest.

Seated next to Claire was a wet nurse, her ample white breast straining the jaws of Alais de Montfort's four-month-old son as he sucked lustily. Alais's daughter Amice, aged nine, nursed a straw doll on her lap and crooned to it. The sight made Claire feel ill. Shutting her eyes, she repositioned the padded cushions that were supposed to absorb the jolting of the cart, but the grinding ache persisted in the small of her spine. Beneath her ribs, the child kicked and wriggled continuously, taunting her with its presence, reminding her with each punch and thrust of its conception upon the floor rushes of Montvallant's solar.

Simon de Montfort had not touched her since that night. Indeed, he went out of his way to avoid her and regarded her burgeoning belly with as much revulsion as Claire did herself. She knew that he had spoken of the rape to his confessor, for the priest treated her as though she were anathema. From the sermons with which he had lectured the household over the past months, she understood that Simon had been exonerated of all blame and that she was the sinner—a heretic harlot who had used her wiles to seduce an innocent man. Of course, the criticism had all been implied, and only those involved understood the full meaning. Alais remained in ignorance. She thought Claire's child was of the seed of Montvallant. Many times it had been on the tip of Claire's tongue to tell Alais the truth, but on each occasion she had restrained the words, knowing her own vulnerability.

De Montfort had delivered her and Beatrice into Alais's custody. "Spoils of war," he had said in an offhand manner. "Tainted with heresy, the pair of them, but not beyond redemption. I trust in your skills to lead them back to the fold and prove to Citeaux that it can be done. Do not fail me. I've wagered a warhorse on the outcome."

Claire looked through her lowered lashes at Simon's neat, self-satisfied wife. The thin brown braids were concealed beneath a wimple bordered with gold lacework. Samarkand sables trimmed the dark blue cloak, and the thin, predatory hands were adorned with gold rings. The idea, if not the gamble, had appealed to the lady Alais. She was a devout Catholic, and for her own pride and Simon's approval, determined to succeed.

Beatrice had cheated Alais's endeavors by dying within a week of her captivity, but de Montfort's indomitable wife had ensured that Raoul's mother was shriven at the end so that at least her soul could review its errors in purgatory rather than being condemned to everlasting damnation.

Claire was determined that Alais would not claim the victory with her. She knew that she had to be cunning. Open rebellion was not the way. To all intents and purposes, Claire had made herself a meek, biddable mouse. She listened to what Alais and the chaplain said, she attended mass regularly, and she prayed with the rest of the women. They were not to know that as she faced the altar, the stone chapel floor chilling her knees through her linen gown, she was praying not to their corrupt, earthbound God, but to the being of Light worshiped by the Cathars. And the more religious observances that Alais made her perform, the brighter shone Claire's inner rebellion.

They halted at a monastery to water the horses and briefly refresh themselves. Lord Simon, Claire was told, intended pressing on while the daylight lasted and desired to waste no time. She saw him from a distance as she stepped down from the women's cart. He had dismounted and was talking to the prior. Even from here she could feel the weight of his personality bearing down upon her. As if feeling her fascinated, frightened scrutiny, he lifted his head and looked in her direction. His green-gray stare was angry and narrow as it dropped to her belly. Abruptly he turned his shoulder and bent a deliberate ear to the prior. Cold and trembling, Claire followed the other women to the guesthouse. Bile rose in her throat, and she was sick in one of the herb borders that were planted against the stone wall. If only she could vomit up the seed growing in her belly.

A small boy tugged at her gown and pushed a bronze cup of water into her hand. "Gentian says you're poorly because you have got a baby in your tummy," he said seriously.

Swallowing, Claire straightened up and looked at the child. Another of Alais's prolific brood of children. Simon de Montfort, as proved, was a man potent in all aspects of manhood. This one, his namesake, was about four years of age, a serious little boy with gold hair darkening to brown and green-flecked hazel eyes. Claire, despite her hatred of his father, her misery, and her grief, had been unable to bring herself to shun the child, and over the months of her captivity, had even grown fond of him. In a way, because he was close in age to Guillaume, she found that his presence eased the ache of her loss. Besides, it gave her a certain satisfaction to know that the bond that had developed between herself and young Simon was intensely irritating to his mother.

"That is indeed part of it," she said, and to please his anxious gaze, sipped the water.

"Will you be better soon?"

She forced herself to smile. "I think so."

He nodded and cocked his head, assessing her. "I have to ride in the cart when we set off. Amaury says I can't sit on his saddle anymore because I fidget too much. Will you tell me a story?"

Claire knew how much Simon adored to settle down in a comfortable lap and listen to tales until the teller was as hoarse as a bear. But today she was not sure of her stamina.

"The one about the brave knight and the wicked dragon?" he asked hopefully when she did not immediately reply.

Claire bit her lip and looked up at the gray, cheerless sky. The brave knight was golden-haired and blue-eyed with a smile to pierce the clouds. The dragon, had the child but known, was his own father. "In a little while perhaps," she temporized.

He considered her, his hazel eyes narrowing in unconscious imitation of his father's. "Do you promise?"

Claire opened her mouth to say that she would not be persuaded into promising anything, but was forestalled by the appearance of Father Bernard, an itinerant black friar who dwelt in the de Montfort household. Claire had encountered him several years ago at Montvallant in the company of another member of his order when they had been hunting for heretics. He claimed that he had been saved from death in a winter blizzard outside Carcassonne by the Virgin Mary herself, and that it was a sign of divine favor that must be repaid with crusading zeal. He made Claire's flesh crawl, and she could not stand to be near him.

"There you are," Friar Bernard said to the boy. "Your mother has been looking for you. We are waiting to bless the meal." He glanced suspiciously between Simon and Claire, his eyes so black that they seemed to have no pupil.

"I . . . I was feeling unwell," Claire faltered, "and Simon brought me a cup of water." She laid a hand protectively on the boy's shoulder.

"Mayhap you wanted to avoid the blessing," suggested Friar Bernard softly.

"No, Father, that is not so. The babe makes me ill. I will come now." In her own ears, her voice sounded breathless and afraid.

The friar grunted contemptuously. "It is Eve's curse that women should bear children in pain and suffering." He looked at her rounded belly in distaste. "It is a heresy to think that it should be otherwise."

"Yes, Father," Claire said meekly. Lowering her eyes to conceal her rebellious thoughts, she ushered little Simon into the guesthouse. She could feel the friar's stare boring into her spine, replacing the marrow of her bones with ice.

CHAPTER TWENTY-THREE

WITHIN A SMALL hut built upon the lower slopes, Bridget crouched, controlling the pain with her will as she bore down to push her baby into the world. She was alone for the ordeal because she had wished it that way. She had food and water, and there were women at the fortress who took it in turns to check upon her welfare.

The pain came, wave upon pulsing wave, but she did not permit it to overwhelm her. Instead she envisaged a flower bud ripening, swelling, and splitting open in glorious color. Her fingers sought the wet crown of her baby's head. She supported the elastic perineal muscles and panted shallowly, resisting the urge to push. On the next contraction, the head was born, followed by the slippery little shoulders, and finally, in a gush of fluid and blood, the tiny, perfectly formed body.

"Magda," she whispered softly, and stroked the baby's damp natal hair. "Your name will be Magda, as was your grandmother's and her grandmother's before that." And when Bridget had cut the cord with a knife of sharpened flint, she put her new daughter to her breast so that the infant's suckling would more quickly deliver the afterbirth.

The pain was relentless. Claire bit down on the block of wood that one of the midwives had forced between her teeth, the tendons cording in her throat as she fought back the scream gathering there. A moist cloth was pressed to her brow and a voice murmured soothingly in her ear. Between her thighs, hands probed and her spine arched at the agony of the intrusion.

"Well," she heard Alais snap, "how goes it?"

"Slowly, madam. The child is big and the opening is not widening as fast as it might."

"Is she strong enough?"

The senior midwife made a seesawing motion with her hands, which Claire saw as the contraction faded and she opened her eyes. "It depends upon how the baby's head is lying, and that I cannot tell until she has opened further."

"Hah!" Alais said impatiently. "Inform me as soon as you have news."

Claire heard the fading swish of her skirts and gave a sob of relief. She did not want to bear this child conceived of violation, but the less she cooperated with the midwives, the greater became her pain and the more they forced potions down her throat and pried between her legs. The baby's head pressing down the birth channel was giving her an overwhelming urge to push. She resisted it, wondering how long it would take her to die. It was late February now and spring clearly on the horizon, but snow had fallen overnight and continued to sift lazily down. She could see it distorted through the heavy gray glass leaded into the window embrasure. Remote and cold. If only she could detach herself from the struggle and join the swirling flakes in the nothing-white air.

Another contraction built and crashed over her with such force that she felt as if she would burst, and she screamed Raoul's name. Where was he? Dead? Alive? And Guillaume, what of Guillaume? The not knowing tortured her. Oh, my child, my child, the born and the unborn. And as the pain swallowed all thought and reason, the midwives returned to pat and murmur and probe at her.

Simon de Montfort stretched out his saddle-cramped legs and, uttering a deep sigh of relief, took the goblet of strengthened wine from his wife's hands. His gaze was heavy with fatigue as it wandered around the comfort of the room—the tapestries from Béziers, the candlesticks from Carcassonne, the goblets and comfit dishes from Lavaur. They were proof of his victories and were piled around him like a dragon's hoard. Even his wife's working gown was made of crimson velvet and her wimple of cream silk coruscated with gold thread. But they were all summer gains. He seldom brought anything to Alais except his exhaustion in the winter months. This time she had refused to go north with the departing summer army, and despite the hard fighting and some losses, Simon had felt secure enough to let her have her way.

He glanced briefly at his two eldest sons, who were still gorging themselves at the trestle that Alais had ordered to be set up in her chamber. Amice had squeezed between her brothers and was clamoring for their attention as Alais, in her own fashion, was clamoring for his. She was dutifully waiting on him when a maid or a squire could as easily have performed the task of pouring his wine and serving him sweet honey cakes.

"What is it?" He arched his brow a trifle impatiently.

Alais put down the rock-crystal flagon. "Claire de Montvallant was delivered of a son just before vespers." She pursed her lips. "The babe is strong and healthy, but the mother's condition is cause for concern. She refused to push him out until the midwives threatened her with Caesar's cut while she still lived. When she finally did deliver him, he tore her badly."

Simon picked at a rag of meat between his teeth. "Why do you come to me with women's business?" he demanded testily to conceal the swooping sensation in his stomach. "Think you I have the time or interest for such trifles?"

Alais lowered her lids, her mouth tightening, but he judged it a reaction to his manner, not any awareness of the child's paternity.

Her voice when she replied was low-pitched and controlled. "My lord, I desire to take the baby into my household and bring him up with Richard and Simon." Leaning over him, she refilled his cup.

He raised it to his lips and took a long swallow. It was simple; all he had to do was snap a refusal and walk away. She knew better than to argue with him. But he had been raised to acknowledge responsibility and despised any man unable to take the consequences of his actions. He was already ripe with self-disgust over the matter of Claire de Montvallant. Nine months ago he had yielded to the impulse of lust. He still felt the pulsing hunger within himself whenever he looked at their lovely southern hostage, and was invariably filled with anger and disgust at his own reaction.

"Show me the child," he said abruptly, and stood up.

Alais gave him a startled look but led him with alacrity to the chamber where their own offspring slept. Richard, seven months old, was asleep in his crib and tightly swaddled for the night. Beside him on a pallet lay Simon, his father's namesake, his thumb close to his mouth and his gold-brown hair curling on his forehead.

"Of them all, he looks the most like you," Alais said softly, and laid her hand upon her husband's sleeve. Uneasy, he shook her off and cast his glance around the room until he found Mabel, Richard's wet nurse, seated in a corner suckling a new-born infant. The woman started to rise, but he gestured her to remain seated and entered the shadows to look down upon the result of his lechery. She showed him the infant and it bawled at him in protest at being plucked from the squashy, milky comfort of her breast. In the dim light of the terra-cotta oil lamp, the baby's hair and eyes were dark and its puckered skin yellowish.

"Has he been named?"

Behind him, Alais smiled. "As soon as the cord was cut," she purred. "I thought that Dominic was appropriate. Friar Bernard baptised him."

He glanced at her sharply. Her expression was smug. The infant, however he developed, was branded for life with the name of one of the most feared and energetic opposers of Catharism—Dominic Guzman, founder of the order of preaching friars.

"If I cannot save the mother's soul, then I will save the child's," she said, her eyes fixed upon Dominic as he was returned to the nurse's breast.

Simon was not in the least deceived by his wife's piety. While he did not doubt the sincerity of her intention, fostering the child would salve her pride at not having control of Claire de Montvallant's wayward soul. "Where's the mother?"

Alais led him into another chamber, separated from the main nursery by a heavy curtain. Fumes of incense clung to the folds and still pervaded the room, speaking of the recent presence of a priest. On the wall a crucifix was illuminated by a candelabra bearing three slim wax tapers. Sleeping on a pallet, the sheets drawn up to her chin, was Claire de Montvallant. Her form was so still, her breathing so shallow, that Simon thought for a moment she was dead. Her hair, bright with all the russet tones of autumn, was spread abroad on the pillow and framed a face of ice-white fragility. He remembered the feel of her lips, the softness of her skin, her taut muscles as she fought to throw him off, the rake of nails down his face as he pinned her down and thrust into her.

Alais turned to the midwife. "Does she still bleed?"

"Only that which is natural, madam," replied the woman with a nervous glance at Simon's impassive features. "God willing, she will live."

"God willing," Simon repeated under his breath, and started to turn away.

"Whether she lives or dies, I want the child," said Alais.

"Do as you please," he said thickly. "It is your business, not mine!" And he almost ran from the room.

Alais stared after him, a perplexed frown on her face.

Chretien stooped over the fleece-lined basket near the hearth and peered down at his great-niece. She was awake and her eyes, a myopic infant-blue, examined him tenaciously. He touched her hand with a gentle forefinger, and she opened and closed her tiny fist and yawned.

"It seems a long, long time since I saw Luke lying in his cradle like this," Chretien said softly. "My brother was fighting in the Holy Land, and I was the master of an estate in Béziers. A different world." He raised his head to look at Bridget, who was stirring a pot of soup over the fire, her silky black hair caught in a simple knot at her nape, and the gleam of the flames playing upon her smooth, olive skin. "Does Magda's father know that he has begotten her?"

Bridget ceased stirring the soup and reached for a small jar of crumbled herbs. "He knows why I lay with him," she said warily. "Our roads travel parallel; they will seldom cross."

"She is going to have his fair hair."

Bridget said nothing, and scattered the herbs in the soup. The scents of sage and thyme drifted in the steam. She stirred slowly.

"So you choose to raise her alone?" Chretien persisted gently.

Bridget suppressed a sigh. "I need no husband," she managed to say without irritation. "Raoul de Montvallant is a fine man, but he has needs and responsibilities far different from mine. I could hold him, I could keep him, but we would each be imprisoning the other. The soul must have its freedom—as you are always saying." She smiled at her uncle and took some wooden bowls from a shelf. "I could not raise Magda in a better place than Montségur. She will have the best and wisest of teachers."

"And you will raise her as your mother raised you, and her mother before that?"

"I will." Bridget ladled soup into the bowls and set one of them down before her uncle. "And if she does not walk that particular path, you will show her the Cathar way."

Chretien frowned at her from beneath his thick brows, and there was anxiety in his fine, dark eyes. "And the ways of the world?"

"Those she will learn for herself when the time comes. Now, drink while the soup is hot, and then tell me how Matthias is progressing with his translations." She put a spoon in his hand to terminate the present conversation, and plucked her daughter from the cradle to suckle her.

CHAPTER TWENTY-FOUR

The Agenais, September 1213

"PAPA, WATCH! WATCH me!" Excitedly the child dug his small heels into his mount's sides. The pony, which was as small and fat as a pig, obliged by wheezing into a trot for ten strides, before throwing up its head and stopping, eyes showing a white rim. "Papa, did you see, I'm a knight!" The little boy waved his toy lance at the man who stood to one side, smiling slightly.

"A *preux chevalier* indeed," Raoul said, taking the old pony's bridle.

Guillaume rested the lance across his thigh in imitation of his father and sat upright. "When can I have a proper horse?"

Raoul's lips twitched. "When your legs have grown long enough to sit one."

Guillaume considered the reply. He looked at his feet, which just about straddled the pony's fat, barrel sides. "When I'm four?" he asked hopefully. He was four next month.

Raoul hid his smile within his mouth. "Perhaps."

"Can I have a ride on Fauvel now?" And before Raoul could deny him, he added, "Grandmother said you'd let me." He wriggled down from the pony and stared up at the man out of brown, beseeching eyes. The warm wind stirred his shining fair hair. "Please."

Guillaume looked so much like Claire that Raoul thought his heart would break. Stooping, he lifted the little boy in his arms and tried not to think that this might be the last time he ever touched or played with him. Living by the sword inevitably meant dying by it, too. How he hated the day before a parting. On the morrow's daybreak he was due to leave for a rendezvous with other southern troops near the crusader-held town of Muret. Simon de Montfort was trapped there, and an alliance of troops led by King Pedro of Aragon, the Count of Foix, and Raymond of Toulouse had every hope of defeating him this time.

"Papa, can I come with you and see all the soldiers?"

"No, not this time," Raoul said gently as he seated Guillaume before him on the saddle and slid the bridle between his fingers.

"Simon de Montfort's going to be beaten. Grandmother said so!" Guillaume contorted his head to look up into his father's face. "Then we'll get back our land and Mama, won't we?"

Raoul swallowed and ruffled the child's hair. "Yes," he murmured. "We'll get them back."

Reassured, Guillaume forsook the future for the pleasure of the moment and bounced in the saddle. "Make him gallop!" he cried.

And Raoul did, as if he could outrun tomorrow's dawn and a dark feeling of impending doom.

Later, a drowsy Guillaume cuddled upon his knee, Raoul looked across the firelight at his mother-in-law. She was sewing a new tunic for her grandson, each stitch painstakingly placed. He could see that she was straining to focus in the dusk. Her eyes were the same warm brown as Claire's and Guillaume's. In her youth she had been beautiful, and he knew that at least one troubadour had written a song praising her beauty—"Na Alianor al Bel Cors." Lady Alianor of the lovely body. The recent years had taken their toll on that. She was thin and haggard these days with permanent worry lines furrowing her once smooth brow.

As if sensing his scrutiny, Alianor raised her head from her needle. "You are worried about tomorrow," she said. "I have sensed it all day."

"I do not like leaving Guillaume behind." He held up his hand as she drew breath to speak. "I know he is in good hands here with you, Alianor, and that he's happy. It is just that . . ." He shrugged and grimaced. "I want to live to see him grow up."

Alianor put her sewing to one side and looked at him with anxious eyes. "I thought that Simon de Montfort was as good as defeated this time," she said. "He is facing the mightiest force ever assembled against him, and led by the King of Aragon himself!"

"True, but fighting is what he does best. If he has been struggling lately, it is only because his summer supplies have temporarily dried up due to King Pedro's intervention with the pope. Now the balance of papal approval has swung back in Simon's favor. If we do not crush him at Muret, then perhaps we never will."

"You have to defeat him," Alianor said fiercely. Tears glinted in her eyes and she swallowed several times before she spoke. "If you don't, I might never see my daughter again . . . if she still lives." Her gaze went to her sleeping grandson.

"The poor lamb," she whispered, fishing in her sleeve for her kerchief. "What have they done with his mother?"

Looking down at Guillaume, Raoul felt the crack in his heart break wide open. It had been very difficult for him to come to terms with the loss of Claire. Gradually he had learned to live with it like a permanent but not mortal wound. To think or to speak of her made the pain unbearable. "I know that you think it strange I so seldom mention Claire," he said unsteadily to Alianor, "but it is not because of a lack of care. . . . It is because I care too much and too hard to make words for what I feel." Carefully, so as not to jolt his precious burden, he stood up and carried his son away to the small truckle bed at the side of the room. Not the least of what he felt was guilt.

In the tent of King Pedro of Aragon, candles burned to augment the light of a young dawn. A large orange moth blundered around one of the flames. The king shot out his fist and, snatching the insect, crushed it to iridescent dust against his muscular thigh.

"This is what we do to de Montfort the moment he rides out of Muret!" His eyes flashed around the ring of battle commanders assembled in his tent, daring anyone to challenge him. Since he'd overindulged in wine and bed sport the previous evening, his temper was as foul as the headache indicated by the two deep vertical lines between his brows.

The Count of Foix agreed vigorously, prodded by the heat of his own fervor and admiration for the King of Aragon, who was a man after his own heart.

The voice of Raymond of Toulouse, light and irritating, entered the debate like a flagon of meltwater tipped on hot coals. "I still say it is more prudent to wait for him to attack us than to go out and meet him head-on," he said anxiously. "We're in an excellent position here. If we leave it, we will only weaken ourselves. Better to attack him with our crossbows from behind our defenses." He swung to his own advisers for confirmation.

Arms folded, Raoul acknowledged the soundness of his overlord's reasoning even while he saw that fear was more than half the motivation for Raymond's caution.

Foix had seen it, too. "Ah God!" he jeered. "All the enemy has ever seen of you is your arse in retreat!"

The knights of the Ariège and Aragon hooted their appreciation of the crude but accurate sally.

"Peace!" the king's eyes sparked with temper. "We gain nothing by this infantile brangling!"

"There are no second chances with de Montfort," Raoul said into the silence Pedro's glare had engendered. "Lord Raymond is right. It would be better to hold our defensive positions and wait."

"Bones of Christ, our army's twice the size of his!" roared Foix. "I say strike him down now! I've not come to cower behind barricades like a woman!"

"Our armies usually *are* twice the size of his," Raoul retorted dryly.

"Aye, and always running in the opposite direction!" sneered Foix. "I thought you at least were made of sterner mettle. Don't you want revenge for your wife?"

Raoul compressed his lips. His blue eyes were very bright. "I am not unwilling to fight, my lord. All I say is that caution is advisable."

Foix snorted derisively, but his gaze flickered away from Raoul's and he hunched his shoulders uncomfortably.

"We take your point." Pedro of Aragon held up his hand. "But I agree with Foix. We gain nothing by dithering behind barricades. De Montfort will believe that we fear him and are reluctant to engage him, and that will only boost his morale." He stared round the room at his battle commanders and leading knights. "When the French whoreson moves, we go to meet him!"

Cheers pursued the echo of his cry, and the trestle was pounded by fists until it shook and the candlesticks toppled over.

Raymond fired a bloodshot glare around the gathering. "Then you go without me!" he snarled, and shouldered his way out of the tent. His son Rai and his adjutants followed on his heels to the accompaniment of howls of derision and cries of "Coward!"

Tears of humiliation and fury shone in Raymond's dark eyes

as he swung onto the horse an equerry was holding. "I *am* right!" he said vehemently. "I know I am!"

And who would believe him on his past record? Raoul wondered as he mounted Fauvel. Raymond had cried wolf once too often. And riding away to sulk in camp would not enhance his reputation. "Do you want me to keep my men on alert or stand them down?" His voice was carefully neutral.

"Do what the hell you like with them!" Raymond growled viciously.

"Yes, my lord."

Raymond responded to Raoul's impassivity with a full-throated snarl and a dismissive, contemptuous swat of his arm. "Oh, take them and go back to those stiff-necked idiots in there! I'm sick of all of you!" He set spurs to his stallion's flanks and galloped away toward his camp.

Rai winced at the dust kicked up by his father's disappearing entourage. "It will take all day for his temper to cool," he said ruefully.

"He is in the right and they won't listen." Raoul felt both pity and irritation for his liege lord. He was still not sure whether to ride after him or stay where he was.

"And what's more, right or not, they're going to win a great victory and make him look even more of a coward," Rai said softly. "He will have nothing left." He looked at Raoul sidelong, his eyes narrow and black. "Go back to them, Raoul. Break a lance for Toulouse; you're carrying our honor today . . . what's left of it."

Spreading out the parchment, Simon gestured Amaury to weight it down with the stones piled at the end of the trestle. Giffard set down a platter of cold fowl and a flagon, and went to fetch Simon's sword belt. There were so many armored knights in the room that it seethed and glittered like a fisherman's bulging net. They were the commanders and adjutants of Simon's army, the men upon whom he was relying to turn Muret from a potential defeat into a resounding victory— William de Contres, Bouchard de Marly, Baldwin de Toulouse, estranged brother of Raymond, and Amaury, his own recently knighted heir.

Simon's demeanor as he broke fast, donned his mail, and

briefed the men was brisk but relaxed. They were in a difficult, but not hopeless, situation, and the confidence of his knights was essential if he was going to turn potential disaster into triumph.

Tearing a leg off the fowl on the platter, he took a bite and pointed the drumstick at the parchment. "Aragon is assembling his troops here on this rise to the north. This stream is protecting his right flank, and the marsh his left, so not only does he have the advantage of numbers, he also has the advantage of ground." He stared round the gathered commanders, assessing them.

"What makes these advantages null and void are the factors in our favor, namely God, as Bishop Foulquet will assure you when we join the muster in the main square. And southern incompetence. Our enemies have no cohesion. Each man is functioning as a single unit, out for himself. We have the discipline they lack, and therefore we have the fighting edge. This battle is ours if we keep our heads." He paused to take another bite of the fowl, to chew powerfully and swallow, as if the food represented his intentions on the battlefield.

"I propose that we form three squadrons. William, you will command the first, and Bouchard the second. I'll take the reserve. We're going to charge them in three waves, not giving them time to recover between each impact. Apart from coordinating the attack, your task and that of your seconds will be to keep the knights in line. I don't want the impetus of the charge becoming broken up in hand-to-hand glory fights. You hit them, you roll over them, and you crush. After that you can indulge in feats of arms if it is your need." He tossed the chicken bone to a lurking alaunt and wiped his fingers on a napkin before donning the surcoat that Walter presented to him. "It is going to be hard and bloody, I won't lie to you, but I know that we can seize victory. Let arrogance carry the day, not Aragon!" He grinned at his own weak pun.

The hearty laughter it drew from the assembled commanders was out of all proportion to the jest, but it served as a relief from tension. Because Simon was a man who so seldom made jokes, they took it as a good omen, an occasion to be marked, and left the castle for the market square in a confident mood.

* * *

The fair-haired little girl toddled over to the crouching Templar knight and gave him a trusting, joyful smile.

"So you are Magda," Luke de Béziers said, and swung her up in his arms. The child giggled and placed a curious small hand on the chain-mail hood coiled around his neck. Luke's dark gaze fixed upon Bridget. "She is the image of you, apart from the hair."

"No, she is the image of my mother," Bridget contradicted. "The way Magda looks, the way she acts, remind me constantly of her."

"How old is she?"

"She will be two at the feast of Candles in the spring."

Luke nodded. Bridget could see that he wanted to ask about Magda's father, but was uncertain of her response. She was uncertain herself. She still thought of him often. Once or twice she had even been tempted to seek him out, but her duty to Magda came first. And she had only borrowed him for a night. His body and heart were not hers to keep but rightly belonged to another woman.

"What brings you to Montségur?" Bridget fetched two wooden stools from her hut and placed them in the warmth of the autumn sunshine. "Have you come to visit your father?"

Still holding the little girl, Luke sat down. "That is part of it. I've brought Matthias some more books to translate, and news of the outside world for those who want to heart it—but most of you at Montségur don't." He smiled ruefully. "Nor do I blame you."

"Montségur is a haven," Bridget said, her eyes upon her daughter's silky pale hair, her glowing complexion and air of happy contentment. She knew that she would fight tooth and nail to protect Magda from hurt of any kind. "The people here have eschewed the world; they have no need to hear news of it."

"Have you eschewed the world, too?"

"While my daughter is so young, it is necessary. I still travel to the local villages to heal, and sometimes I go with your father to meetings, but my responsibility for the moment is to Magda." Her expression softened. "There is so much I have to teach her, and I want her to learn the good lessons first, before she learns fear."

"There is no need to defend yourself to me," Luke said gently. "More than once I have thought of retreating here myself. Even as a Templar, my cloak of immunity is thin on occasion."

Bridget noted the word *retreating*, but she did not challenge him. Perhaps it was just an unfortunate choice, and she was sure he had not meant to imply cowardice or a shirking of obligation. "Then perhaps you should do so?"

Luke smiled and shook his head. "I would not have the fortitude. If I came to Montségur, I should want to live in a certain hut on the mountainside, and I know what can and cannot be." Setting Magda down, he gave her a gentle push toward her mother.

Bridget looked at her cousin. There had always been an attraction between them. Many times she had explored the thought of deepening their relationship, but had always held herself to caution. She set great store by their friendship, but to make him her permanent consort, she would have to give him more, which she was not prepared to do.

Luke rose to leave. "Don't speak," he said with a rueful smile. "There has never been any need for words between us." Taking her hand, he brushed his lips upon her knuckles. "Tomorrow," he said. "I will call this way tomorrow before I leave Montségur for the world."

Bridget was woken in the night by the sound of Magda's whimpering. Sleep still clouding her brain, she lifted her daughter to cuddle and soothe her. The little girl's eyes were wide open, the pale silver iris completely ringed with white. Under her hand Bridget felt the moisture of Magda's voided bladder.

"Stop!" Magda screamed. "Mama, make it stop!" She buried her face against Bridget's breast, her small body shuddering. "Don't like, make it stop!"

Magda had a good vocabulary for her age, but it was the first time she had ever strung words together. Bridget noted this with a corner of her mind while she sought to deal with the child's nightmare. She rocked and talked to her, murmuring reassurances. Gradually Magda's wild sobbing ceased. Bridget changed the child's damp linens and lay back down with her, the palm of her hand stroking the tangled blond hair. Magda snuggled against Bridget, and secure in her arms, fell into a deep sleep.

Holding her daughter's heavy warmth, Bridget wondered if Magda had begun to experience touches of the sight. Surely not, she was still so young. What had she seen in her dream? What had she wanted to stop? Bridget gazed into the banked embers of their fire, seeking out the tiny red glow under the ash-gray logs. Beneath her stare a flame began to kindle. She ceased to concentrate and closed her lids.

The next thing she knew, the whole room was shaking and filled with the choking dust raised up by hundreds of horse hooves. Bridget's eyes opened wide. She saw the flash and glitter of weapons against a hot morning sky and heard the tumult of savage battle. Men were shouting in Spanish, Catalan, and Occitan. There was a triumphant battle howl in the accent of northern France. A pale gold stallion swirled so close to her pallet that she covered Magda with her body to protect her. The gold horse plunged, and its rider hit the ground only inches from where she lay.

Involuntarily she screamed as the man turned his head and his vivid blue eyes met hers. Contact was lost as horses plunged around him. She saw the legs of a bright red bay, saw blood splash and spatter. In the background, but advancing, was a warrior on a white stallion, his shield bearing the fork-tailed lion of de Montfort. Her frantically searching gaze found Raoul again, and he was standing right in de Montfort's path. She heard her own voice crying, *"Make it stop!"* But de Montfort's sword swung in a killing arc and her vision darkened.

Someone was shaking her shoulder. "Bridget, Bridget, wake up."

Groggily she opened her lids and saw Luke bending over her, his dark eyes full of concern. He was wearing his Templar traveling cloak and his sword was girded at his hip. Her head throbbed as if she had drunk an entire flagon of Gascon wine. She became aware that Magda was missing and looked round wildly.

"It's all right, she's only outside stroking Rosin. He's gentle, he won't harm her. What's wrong?"

Pushing her hair out of her eyes, Bridget sat up. Outside she could hear birdsong and Magda chattering brightly to Luke's horse. "Last night I saw a great battle; it seemed to be here in this very room, and Simon de Montfort was carrying the victory banner."

"De Montfort has been in difficulty of late," Luke said, and poured her a cup of wine from the small pitcher on the trestle. "Pedro of Aragon has allied a huge army of southern lords against him, and there is real optimism that the northerners will be driven out. Are you saying that there is no hope?"

Bridget laced her fingers round the cup and sipped the wine. She felt cold and shaky. "I do not know. There was no indication in my vision of where or even when the battle took place. It could be in the past, it might be in the future, or indeed it might never be." She raised her eyes to his. "Luke, will you do something for me?"

"You need but ask, you know that."

Still cupping her drink, Bridget rose and went to lean against the doorpost. She gazed out on the tranquil, pine-scented morning. Magda's small hand was pressed fearlessly upon Rosin's great brown foreleg, and the horse had lowered his head to breathe gustily into the little girl's hair. "I want you to find a southern noble for me. His name is Raoul de Montvallant. He is . . . he helped me to escape from de Montfort once, and I owe him a debt."

"Raoul de Montvallant?" Luke came to stand beside her, a look of surprise on his face. "You know Raoul de Montvallant?"

"Yes, why?"

"We are kin through my mother—distant cousins only. I met him at Saint-Gilles the year that Pierre de Castelnau was murdered. Of course I will find him for you if I can. What do you want me to say?"

Bridget chewed the inside of her lip. "Warn him to be on his guard against de Montfort," she said after a moment, "and tell him . . ." She shook her head, and looked into her almost empty cup. Tell him what? That there were times when she still felt the heat of the fire they had kindled between them that night? "Just tell him that he is in my thoughts, that I have not forgotten. He will understand what you mean."

"Do you want him to know that you are here at Montsé-gur?"

"No!" Bridget said more vehemently than she had intended, alarmed at such a prospect. "That would be unwise."

Luke's expression remained unaltered, but she sensed his curiosity. "If that is your wish," he said, and kissed her cheek. "I must be going if I'm to reach Mirepoix by nightfall."

After he had ridden away, Bridget scooped Magda into her arms and took her back inside the hut. She tried to put last night's dream-vision from her mind, but throughout the remainder of that day it kept returning to haunt her.

Stinging sweat ran into Raoul's eyes, which were already half-blinded by the constrictions of his battle helm. His sword grip was slippery with blood, his own and other men's. The sword itself seemed to be fashioned of lead, not the balanced Lombardy steel of an hour ago. Two waves of de Montfort's cavalry following close upon each other had swept aside the men of Foix like so many wooden skittles and then plowed into the Aragonese with unstoppable momentum. The cry had gone up that King Pedro himself had been killed, and soon after that the Spanish line had broken up in disarray.

Raoul had been near Pedro of Aragon when he fell, the king in his false humility wearing the armor of an ordinary knight with no distinguishing features to save him from the blades that tore out his heart. It had been impossible to go to his aid, so fierce was the impact of the northern assault. Before Raoul even realized what was happening, their lines had been overwhelmed and surrounded, cut up into small pockets and cut up again. Now, against all hope, he and such of his men as remained were struggling to fight themselves free of the debacle before they suffered the same fate as Pedro of Aragon. Giles was still in position on his left, but Roland had gone down with most of the Montvallant knights on Raoul's right flank.

Raoul parried a blow. A northern knight struck at him with a morning-star flail. The chain spiraled rapidly around his mail sleeve and Raoul was dragged from the saddle and hit the ground heavily. The battle surged around him, separating him from Giles. Fauvel reared and plunged, wild now that he was riderless. He saw the shod hooves and yellow legs dancing close, was almost kicked, and knew that if he stayed down, he would be trampled. A scream not his own echoed through his mind and for the briefest instant Bridget's face flashed before his eyes.

Bruised and winded, but sword still in hand, he lurched to his feet and saw only enemies. A knight leaned down from his high saddle, aiming to decapitate him. His sword sliced through Raoul's shield and the impact threw Raoul back to the ground. He tasted dust, gritty against his tongue and teeth. Eyes wide and smarting, he stared death in the face. Horse legs swirled around him, not Fauvel's this time, but those of a red bay Spanish stallion. As the bay's rider bent over the saddle to strike down at him, Raoul gathered himself and lunged and snatched. The knight shrieked as he struck the ground. Seizing crupper and pommel, Raul hauled himself astride the red destrier.

Too late he sensed an attack coming in from the side, and having lost his shield, tried to deflect the savage blow on his blade. The shock of the impact ran all the way up his arm. He lost control of his fingers, the weapon fell from his grip, and his enemy followed through, slashing open mail and gambeson and flesh. Raoul saw a steel cask helm plumed with scarlet-dyed feathers. He saw the fork-tailed lion on the shield and the ripple of muscle beneath the sinuous skin of mail. *Behold a pale horse and his name that sat upon him was death.*

Pain welled from the wound to obscure Raoul's every conscious function, but even in extremity, instinct made him grip the pommel and squeeze with his thighs. The red destrier reared, striking out, and the young knight on the ground screamed as he was kicked. Raoul felt someone grab the stallion's reins and knew that in a moment he would be dead, knew that he did not care if it would stop this fire in his chest.

But there was no coup de grâce. In its place he thought he heard a southern tongue blaspheming amid the scrape and clash of weapons. The destrier changed pace, the plunging short strides of the battlefield stretching out to a canter. Each stride jolted agony through Raoul's chest. He began sliding toward darkness, but before he could lose his seat or his final grip upon consciousness, he was revived by the icy shock of water flowing over his thighs as the horse plunged into the River Louge.

"For the love of God, my lord, do not let go now!" he heard Giles mutter as if from a great distance.

"I've got him," Mir said close to his ear, and he was vaguely aware of the support of another horse and rider beside him in the water. His lids felt as if they were weighted with stones, but he forced them open. Through the slits in his helm the world seesawed and tilted crazily. He saw his hands on the pommel and they were red with blood. More was dripping into the destrier's black mane. The horse started to strain up the opposite bank of the river and he swayed in the saddle. Mir lost his hold, but Raoul was saved from falling over the crupper into the river and being drowned by the support of a Templar knight who rode up fast from behind. Just before consciousness finally wavered and went out like a snuffed candle, Raoul recognized Luke de Béziers.

CHAPTER TWENTY-FIVE

Toulouse, September 1213

"WILL HE LIVE?" asked Giles.

Luke de Béziers folded his arms and, after a long time, looked reluctantly from the patient to the anxious knight. "He is very sick," he said quietly. "The wound is poisoned beyond what I can do for him with my small training."

Giles bit his lip and stared down at his young lord—the waxen features, the fever-cracked lips, the muscular warrior's body from which the flesh was melting with alarming rapidity. The site of the wound was a suppurating, swollen porridge.

Red streaks like finger marks spread out from the injury, invading the surrounding good tissue. For the moment Giles coddled his dwindling hope for Raoul's life and knew that by eventide, if there was no improvement, there would be no hope at all.

It was two days since Count Raymond's cavalry had taken refuge behind the walls of Toulouse along with the tattered remnants of the armies that had borne the brunt of de Montfort's charge. Luke de Béziers had brought the Montvallant knights to a "safe" house in the city close to the Pont Vieux and the suburb of Saint Cyprien. The dwelling was owned by the Templars, and it was here, while the town negotiated for its life with the wolf outside its walls, that Raoul was fighting for his, and at the moment, both appeared to be losing.

"What were you doing in the heart of the battle?" Luke bestowed Giles a perplexed look. "From what I gather, the rest of the Toulouse contingent didn't come within a mile of the fighting."

Giles laughed sourly. "We were representing them. My lord was trying to explain Count Raymond's viewpoint to Foix, basically trying to make the old fool see the facts beyond his sword point, when de Montfort charged. We had no time to retreat even had we wished to."

"And when it came to the confrontation, he did not wish to, I think." Luke inclined his head at Raoul.

"No." Giles tightened his lips.

"If it comes to the end, do you want one of the Perfecti to be in attendance?" Luke queried gently. "It can be arranged."

Giles shrugged wearily. "I do not think it matters either way."

"Then permit me to send out into the city for one?"

Giles made a gesture both assenting and dismissive and sat down on a stool next to Mir. The squire was knuckling his eyes, his expression tear-streaked and pale. Before he went out, Luke paused at the coffer by the bed to light the oil lamp. As he did so, his attention was caught by an enameled disk that lay beside Raoul's meat dagger and seal ring. Staring, the young Templar picked it up and rubbed his thumb over the dove and chalice symbol engraved within the two-triangle star.

"Where did you get this?" he asked intently.

Giles held out his hand for the token and turned it this way and that. "I don't know. It was around his neck when we undressed him, but I've never seen it before." He passed it to the squire. "What about you? You're the one who helps him to arm and disrobe."

Mir examined the disk and frowned. "It was after we went to Foix with the Cathars that I first saw him wear it. . . . Yes, after he returned from that journey with the lady Bridget."

"What?" Luke stared fiercely at the squire. "Tell me!"

"We—we rescued three Cathars from Lavaur. I—I—" Mir stammered, frightened by the Templar's reaction and overwrought to the state of incoherence.

"One of them was your father, the lord Chretien," Giles interceded, patting the boy's arm. "He had an older man with him, a scribe of sorts, and the lady Bridget. We took them to Foix, and Lord Raoul and she went away on their own for a day and a night."

"And that was when he obtained this?" Luke took the disk back from the squire.

"I . . . I think so," Mir said.

Giles tilted his head to one side. "Why do you ask?"

Luke held the piece close to the lamp to study the interlacing Celtic pattern around the rim. "It belonged to my aunt Magda. Such tokens are rare, to say the least, and if it is in his posession, Bridget must have chosen him to father her child."

"Chosen him?" Giles repeated, his voice and brows rising on the final syllable. "What do you mean?"

Luke replaced the disk on the coffer in silence, and when he turned round, his expression was thoughtful. "Forget that I spoke," he said. "I'll go and find a Cathar Good Man." And he quickly left.

Giles whistled out softly and sat down at the bedside. He dug his hands through his receding hair and looked at Mir. "Can you swim, lad?"

Mir blinked at him. "Why?"

"Because I suspect that we're wading way out of our depth." Picking up a bowl of herb-infused water, Giles wrung out the cloth that had been soaking in it and began to wipe Raoul's burning body. His lord rolled his head from side to side on the pillow and muttered, the sound rising suddenly to a cry.

"What's he saying?" Mir rubbed his hands nervously on his tunic.

Giles refreshed the cloth. "Something about Dominic and fire as far as I can tell."

"Dominic Guzman the black friar?"

"That's the only Dominic I know of."

Mir shivered and looked sidelong at Giles like a balky horse.

"For pity's sake, Mir, go and find some wine," Giles said gruffly as the youth continued to hover miserably at his shoulder. "The stronger the better. We'll have to change this dressing soon."

Raoul was teetering on a precarious ledge of stone, his sword in his right hand, but no shield to balance him. Frost crunched beneath his boots and the sky was crystalline with ice-white stars, the air so cold that it cut his lungs. A chasm gaped below him, black and wide like an open mouth waiting to be fed, its jaws lined with jagged stone fangs. On the ramparts above, torches blazed, outlining his sword edge as he raised it and braced his wrist against the pommel for the final time. Two men, faceless and dark-robed, came at him. His blade clashed on steel and was beaten down in a quenched blue spark. The pain ripped through his chest and he felt himself falling away into darkness, the abyss engulfing him. He clawed at the walls, trying to find a handhold, but they were as smooth as polished obsidian and so cold that their chill invaded his whole body until his limbs froze. His lids started to close; he ceased to struggle.

From a far distance he heard someone call his name. He ignored the sound, but whoever it was persisted and approached. A woman, he thought sluggishly . . . not Claire. Sudden brilliance pained his eyelids, and squinting through them, he saw Bridget, her body haloed with light, her dark hair blowing around her face. Reaching out, she took his hand and led him back toward the light. He flinched and hung back. It was safe in the darkness, but she drew him inexorably onward, and he could not resist.

And then he was in a strange room, looking down from a height on three men who were bending over a fourth lying motionless in a bed. He recognized Giles and Luke de Béziers, but not the dark-robed bearded man beside them. To one side, Mir, his face hidden in his shaking hands, was weeping. None of them appeared to notice Bridget walk to the head of the bed, although to Raoul she was as solid as the coffer and the clothing pole beside it. Leaning over the supine young man, she placed her hand on his chest and pressed her mouth to his, filling him with her breath, and in that moment Raoul recognized his own self and the ground came rushing up to meet him.

"Wait," said Giles sharply as the Templar started to pull the sheet over Raoul's body and the Cathar Good Man closed his prayer book. "Wait, I thought I saw him move."

"No more than the final spasms of muscle," Luke said compassionately. "Surely you have seen it before in your trade."

"No, I'm sure I . . ."

Raoul forced open his eyelids. Bridget was standing among the men and watching him closely, but when he stretched out his hand toward her, she avoided him, and with a parting, sad smile, left the room. His reaching hand was caught instead by Giles, whose eyes were wondering, a little afraid.

"Lord Raoul?"

"Did you see her?" Raoul whispered weakly.

"See who, my lord?"

"Bridget . . ."

Giles exchanged glances with the other men. "There has been no one here but ourselves," he replied hesitantly.

"She was here. . . ." With difficulty Raoul swallowed. His throat was like a tube of dried-out leather.

"I can well believe she was," Luke murmured. "I would have sworn my Templar's vow that I was about to cover the face of a dead man."

Hand shaking, Giles poured watered wine into a cup and offered it to the patient.

Raoul drank thirstily and subsided against the bolster and pillows. He felt exhausted and more than a little disoriented. The Cathar, seeing that they had no further need of his ministrations, departed on the urgent business of his calling. With the remnants of the southern army trapped inside Toulouse, there were many injured and dying men requiring his services.

"He didn't *console* me?" Raoul asked quickly as Luke set about unwrapping the bindings around his wound.

"No. You were not conscious to make the responses, but he prayed that your soul would find a good body to dwell in when it left you."

If Raoul had owned the strength, he would have smiled, but he was as weak as a kitten and the pain was bad. He could remember nothing of the past few days but dark dreams full of fire and bloodshed. "Where am I?"

"Toulouse, my lord," said Giles, peering over Luke's shoulder. "We brought you here after the battle. Count Raymond is negotiating for terms. We can't fight on, but neither can we be defeated while we hold the city."

"It is a standoff." Luke eased away the last unguent-smeared bandage. Raoul groaned and the Templar apologized.

"It's all right," Raoul croaked. "It doesn't hurt like it did before."

"No, the wound has begun to heal," Luke replied, in a distracted voice. Three hours ago Raoul's injury had been an evil-smelling mess bubbling with pus, the infection beyond all containing. Now all Luke saw were clean pink edges and a minor amount of swelling. The red streaks, although still present, were greatly diminished, and the flesh was cool to the touch. Here, if he had needed any more evidence, was proof of Bridget's skills.

"You almost killed de Montfort's son in the battle." Giles fussed around Raoul like a mother hen. "It saved your life. Mir, go and fetch a bowl of broth; perhaps my lord will drink some in a moment when Luke's finished."

"What do you mean?" Raoul watched the squire dash from the room and knew that he would have to disappoint Giles's feverish optimism. He was nauseous with the need for sleep.

"De Montfort was so busy protecting his whelp and picking him up off the ground that he didn't bother to finish you off, and by the time he was free again, we had dragged you out."

"His son?" Raoul's lids drooped. He was vaguely aware of Luke smearing herbal ointment on the wound and applying a fresh dressing.

"Guy, the middle one. You escaped on his horse. Fauvel was lost, but the bay's a real beauty. . . . My lord?" A note of panic in his voice, Giles leaned over the bed.

Luke touched the knight gently on the shoulder. "He's only fallen asleep, don't worry." His glance flickered to the talisman on the coffer. "He will heal now; I can say that with certainty."

"Here's the broth!" Mir hastened back into the room with a steaming wooden bowl and a horn spoon. Then he stopped and stared, for Giles was weeping unashamedly. The youth's horrified gaze flew to the bed and then to the Templar.

Luke smiled in reassurance. "No cause for concern." He held out his hand for the broth. "Here, I'll take that, I'm ravenous. Go and fetch another bowl for Sir Giles. He'll be all right presently, and so will your lord . . ." *In body at least.*

CHAPTER TWENTY-SIX

CLAIRE SAT ON the turf seat in the garden at Castelnaudry, her hands folded in her lap, her eyes on a distance far beyond the herb beds that she was supposed to be tending. She was permitted the occasional moment of solitude, usually when de Montfort and his sons were home from war to occupy Alais and her ladies. Today the entire castle was in a fervor of celebration over the great northern victory at Muret. Claire had closed her ears to their obscene joy and sought the solitude of the garden. Hate, as Geralda had been wont to say, was not a tenet of the Cathar faith. So she must not hate them for taking away her home, for depriving her of her husband and son. She must not hate them for forcing her to watch Montvallant's Cathars burn. She must not hate Simon de Montfort for raping her on her own solar floor and planting his child within her womb, or for taking that child away from her.

She dug her nails into her palms. Sweet Jesu, but it was impossible! How did she find forgiveness in her heart for such crimes? Jerkily she rose from the seat and, picking up her basket and shears, turned to the lavender bushes and began attacking the stems. The aromatic scent of the herb, the motion of her hands, and the silence gradually calmed her turmoil. If she could not find forgiveness in her heart now, then perhaps it would come to her tomorrow. Each day had to be viewed not as a setback, but as a milestone on the road to her goal.

She was placing the final stalks of lavender in the basket when she heard the garden door squeak open, and turned in time to see Simon's huge fawn alaunt spring through the entrance. Black jowls slavering, it bounded straight across the herb beds and launched itself boisterously upon her. Claire screamed and raised her arms to protect her face. The basket was knocked from her arm and lavender scattered in all directions.

"Brutus, lie down!"

The boarhound dropped to its belly, crushing lavender stems, releasing their powerful scent. Claire swallowed, her stomach dissolving in terror as Simon approached with a measured, powerful tread. Today he wore a jeweled robe and belt; his boots were made of the softest kidskin, gilded with small lions on the toes and up the sides. His thatch of iron-gray hair was neatly brushed. Rings sparkled on his great square hands, which held a bundle wrapped in waxed cloth. He set it down on a turf seat and studied her with brooding eyes.

Unwilling but compelled by his presence, she lifted her gaze to his. He might be robed for a feast, might be weaponless apart from the meat dagger at his hip, but it changed nothing. She could still see him astride his white warhorse, his stare impassive as Montvallant's Cathars were burned in the town marketplace. She could still feel the subjugating pressure of his body, his tongue thrusting in her mouth, his engorged shaft thrusting between her thighs.

"You are like a butterfly." His voice was gentle, but husky, as if permanently roughened by the smoke of his victims. He reached one callused palm to touch her thick, russet braid. "What a pity to crush you."

Claire thrust his hand away and took a jerky step backward. "Don't touch me!" she spat, and half-raised her fist, the shears clenched in them.

His eyelids tensed; there was no more warning than that. For all his bulk, his lunge was so swift that she had no time to defend herself. The shears were wrenched from her grasp and hurled across the garden, and he twisted her wrist so hard that she screamed and sagged to her knees. The dog sprang to its feet and bared its fangs within a fraction of her face.

"Please!" she sobbed. "Oh please, no!" She hated herself for her weakness.

He silenced the dog with a terse word. It dropped to the ground, but continued to growl. Breathing unevenly, Simon dragged Claire upright and pulled her roughly against him. She felt the hard bulge of his erect member against her belly. "You are more foolish than I thought," he said with husky contempt. "Or else very slow to learn the level of my tolerance!" Seizing her face between his palms, he angled his head and kissed her savagely. Claire kicked at his shins. Her hands became claws and she tried to scratch him, but he grabbed her arms and forced them down at her sides.

The alaunt ceased barking at them, and began instead to growl in the direction of the garden door. Simon glanced sidelong, saw his squire standing at the entrance, and pushed Claire brutally away. She fell to the ground and hung her head, feeling dizzy and bruised. Her mouth was swollen and numb. She spat into the grass, trying to rid herself of the taste of him.

"I sought you out to bring you these from Muret," Simon said curtly. "Widows should have a focus for their mourning." Lifting the oiled cloth from the bench, he unwrapped it to reveal the splintered remains of a shield and a blunt, badly nicked sword.

Claire stared at the mangled design of interlaced chevronels decorating the face of the shield. Raoul had painted it himself, during the first winter of their marriage. She could still see so vividly his painstaking care, the bright pallet of Italian dyes, and the satisfaction in his eyes as he stepped back to examine the finished result.

"I killed him myself," Simon said as the color drained from her face and her stare widened and widened. "He lies in an unmarked grave on the battle plain with all the other fools who never knew what hit them—apart from the wrath of God." He smiled nastily. "At least he has an heir to inherit his lands, one who is being raised in good Catholic traditions."

"You are of the devil!" Claire whispered, her gorge rising as she took his meaning.

Simon drew himself up to his full, proud height. "I serve my God faithfully," he pronounced. "You are the traitor, and I've been more than lenient thus far ... but all that can soon change."

She flung away from him with a cry like a wounded animal and hung over one of the flower beds, retching.

He watched her for a moment, a perplexed frown on his face that slowly became a grimace of self-disgust. Snapping his fingers at the dog, commanding it to his side, he turned on his heel and left the garden.

When the spasms of nausea finally subsided, Claire collapsed onto the grass beside the seat and sobbed. Her grief, terror, and revulsion were a raw pain within her. *His* God, not hers. She saw the distinction most clearly. *Rex Mundi*, eater of souls.

For a wild instant she contemplated suicide using the dull, damaged sword he had left on the bench. She set her hand to the leather grip and felt the ridges indented by the regular pressure of Raoul's fingers. How many men had this instrument killed before it had led him to the moment of his own destruction? Shivering, she released the hilt and instead touched the broken shield beside it. Her fingers traced the bold, black design lovingly. The tears came, but within herself, at her core, she was aware of a transformation, as if she had woven herself a chrysalis out of experience and only now was it complete.

Leaving the lavender strewn where it had fallen, leaving the shears and the broken weapons, she went out of the garden, and although she still wept, she carried her head high. From this day forth she would walk in the light of the Cathar way, and no one would stop her.

CHAPTER TWENTY-SEVEN

Montségur, The Mountains of the Ariège, Summer 1215

"Do you remember what this plant is for?" Bridget asked the attentive fair-haired child sitting beside her in the dappled sunshine among the pines.

"To stop coughs, Mama."

"That's right. And what do you do with it?"

"Pour hot water on the leaves and when a candle notch has passed, it will be ready to drink," the child repeated faithfully. "We don't want this leaf; a caterpillar's chewed it."

"No." Bridget smiled and watched her daughter select the best leaves from the white horehound and place them in the basket. "Magda, what about this plant?" she persisted gently after a moment. "What do we do with this?"

The little girl frowned at the clump of common plantain for a moment and then her brow cleared. "The leaves make burns better," she said brightly.

"Well done!" Bridget praised, hugging her. Although Magda was not yet four years old, her aptitude for learning and absorbing through every pore was prodigious, and she loved nothing better than to be out on the mountainside in the freshness of the early morning woods, gathering herbs and plants and discovering their lore.

"Mama, why does this . . ." Magda stopped, for her mother's attention was upon the path that could just be seen through the feathery sweep of the trees.

Hoofbeats thudded on the beaten soil and echoed in Bridget's heart. For a moment she tried to deceive herself that they heralded soldiers looking to be hired or delivering messages from the Count of Foix; or perhaps a supply train of mules from the foot of the mountain. But the deception was thinner than a Mass wafer. She knew even before they came into view what she would see. The leading horse was a striking red bay. The man astride wore armor, but his helm hung from the saddle and his tawny hair, dark-tipped with sweat, framed a sternly handsome profile. A profile she had last seen by dying firelight in the afterglow of passion. At his side rode the knight Giles, balding and dour, and a little behind them the squire kept a watchful eye on a slender boy of about six years old.

"Who are they, Mama?" whispered Magda, to whom visitors were a novelty.

Bridget hesitated. The distant future, she had foreseen, but not the manner of this meeting. Indeed, she had tried to keep her presence at Montségur a secret. Now, without warning, she needed to collect herself for what might be a rite of passage as stormy as the night on which Magda had been conceived. "Messengers from Foix," she answered shortly. "Put the plants in the basket; we have to go home."

Magda thrust out her lower lip. "I don't want to; I like it here!"

"Do as I say!" Bridget snapped.

Magda stared at her mother in hurt astonishment, and tears filled her wide, gray eyes.

The bewilderment in Magda's face brought Bridget's reeling emotions back into focus. She was aghast at her own behavior. "Ah, sweetheart, I didn't mean to shout at you." She gathered Magda quickly into her arms, kissing her temple and cheek and smoothing the pale gold hair that was all her father's legacy. Magda's rigidity melted, but when Bridget held her away and looked at her, a vast question underlined the trust in the immense gaze.

"I know the knight on the bay horse and I had not expected to see him here, not so soon anyway," Bridget explained, willing Magda not to be difficult.

"Don't you like him, Mama?"

"I like him very much." Bridget continued to stroke

Magda's hair. "He is a good man. I don't want to hurt him . . . not any more than he has been hurt already."

Magda screwed up her face. "But you're a healer, Mama. . . ."

Bridget smiled wearily. "If only that were the beginning and the end," she murmured, more than half to herself, and her eyes went pensively to the slope above them where the party of horsemen could still be heard.

It was in the afternoon, the hottest part of the day when everyone was asleep, that Magda heard the horse on the track above the hut that she and her mother shared. Bridget was inside, resting, but Magda, even as a tiny baby, had never slept except for the darkest hours of the night. Just now she was occupying herself by arranging a collection of white shells and stones in one of the sacred spiral patterns her mother had shown her.

The sound of hooves grew louder, approaching at what sounded like an injudicious canter. Magda set the keystone into the pattern and stood up, dusting her hands upon her homespun skirt. Squinting against the sharpness of the sunlight, she saw a chestnut pony coming directly toward her, its shoulders and flanks dark with sweat and its nostrils wide red caverns. Astride it was the boy she had seen earlier with the knights. He was clinging to his mount's back like a burr, his expression a tense mixture of exhilaration and fear. Behind him the towers of Montségur were on fire. The pony became a warhorse, its hide grooved with muscle, and the boy became a man in armor, a sword shimmering in his hand, his expression gaunt and terrible. Other men were with him, one with eyes of green on gray and a face of rugged beauty. From the shadows stepped a creature in a long, black robe, a hunting dagger shimmering in its thin fingers. Magda was filled with such an overwhelming feeling of terror that she screamed and pressed her fingers across her eyes.

Magda's shrieks brought Bridget running from the depths of the hut, her loose hair streaming around her shoulders, her feet still bare.

Peeping through a gap in her fingers, Magda saw that the pony had stumbled and the boy had been thrown. He lay so still that she thought he was dead. His mount was limping badly and uttering small grunts of distress. The sun shimmered on the pines and the shadows were somnolent and empty.

Her mother knelt beside him and gently probed his skull. Beneath her fingertips, he groaned, and Magda burst into tears. "Will he be all right, Mama?"

"I think so. He's bumped his head, but nothing is broken as far as I can tell." Bridget glanced at the sweating, trembling pony. "This is what comes of abusing the life force," she muttered darkly.

"It wasn't his fault, Mama; I was in his way. I saw . . . I saw him . . ." she broke off, biting her lip.

"What did you see?" Bridget demanded with swift concern.

"He was older . . . on a big black horse with a sword in his hand . . . and the castle was on fire. . . . I saw a man in the shadows with a knife." Her voice disappeared into a whimper of fear, and she clung to her mother. "A bad man; he was coming for me."

"You are overly young to be having the visions so powerfully," Bridget murmured, making her voice low and soothing as she held and rocked her. "Often the sight comes without warning—like a bad dream with your eyes open. I will teach you to have control over it." She kissed Magda's brow, and when she was sure the child had calmed, said, "Now, do you think you can find my flask of comfrey lotion and the marigold salve? We'll talk about the dream later and what it could have meant."

"Yes, Mama." Magda hurried down toward the hut, and Bridget frowned after her. In Magda the sight was very strong. There had been several incidents like this, going back as far as her father's wounding at Muret, but this was the most powerful yet. She returned her attention to the injured boy. His eyes had opened and she noted that although his lids were heavy and his complexion ghastly pale, his pupils had reacted to the light.

"What happened?" he mumbled.

"You were galloping your pony when you should have known better," she said in a voice gentle but stern.

His breathing caught and he sat up, looking wildly around until he located his trembling mount.

"He's taken the skin from his knees and strained his shoulder, to look at him. I'll see to his needs in a moment."

The boy nodded gratefully and lay back down, his eyes filling with tears. "I didn't mean to," he said in a choked voice. "The slope was steeper than I thought." He set his hand to the lump on his head, then regarded the smear of blood on his palm. "Are you a Cathar?"

"No, but I live among them. I am Bridget, and this is my daughter, Magda, whom you nearly rode down."

"I couldn't help it, she just stood there."

"Were you running away?" Magda asked forthrightly as she gave her mother the remedies she had requested.

"Of course not!" He scowled indignantly. "I came out for a ride on my own, that's all!" And then, as if aware of how ungracious he sounded, he firmly closed his mouth and dropped his lids.

Bridget considered him. Perhaps not running away, but seeking release, she thought. Let a pup off the leash and its first energy was usually expended in a bout of frantic gamboling. "Do you think you can walk over to that tree?"

He nodded and made the effort, although his legs were groggy and he had to hold on tightly to Bridget as she led him to the shade offered by the whitebeam's branches. Magda followed them, clutching a waterskin she had thought to bring from the hut along with the salves. Bridget settled the boy against the tree trunk and briefly left him while she caught the pony. He propped his head against the smooth, gray bark, his complexion a nauseous yellow.

"You will feel sick for some while," Bridget warned him. "Best if you try and sleep while I fetch your father from the castle."

His lids flew open. "How did you know that my fath—?"

"I saw all of you on the path this morning, and I recognized him. He helped me escape from some priests a long time ago." She smiled. "I even know that your name is Guillaume because I held you in my arms when you were still in swaddling and your mother brought you to one of our meetings in Toulouse." While she spoke, she poured a small amount of comfrey lotion onto a pad and pressed it against the lump on his forehead. He flinched, and then she felt his muscles lock as he steeled himself to resist more than just physical pain. She sent out waves of healing calm to penetrate his troubled aura. Gradually, under the soothing influence of her fingers and her mind, his lids drooped and he fell asleep.

"Where is his mama now?" asked Magda. "Is she up at the castle?"

"No, sweetheart, she is a prisoner in another place far away."

"Oh." Magda looked thoughtful, not quite sure that she understood, but knowing that their patient was in sore need of comfort. She watched her mother go down to the hut and return with one of their blankets to tuck around the sleeping boy. This was no ordinary incident to be absorbed into their lives as a minor memory, Magda realized, but was part of some important thread of fate as yet too intricate for her young mind to comprehend.

"Magda, I want you to do something for me," Bridget murmured so as not to disturb Guillaume. "I have to go up to the fortress and tell his father what has happened. Do you think you can look after him until I return?"

Magda nodded solemnly, feeling slightly afraid, but also very important. She had helped her mother tend the sick before, had sat with them for short periods while herbs were ground and potions mixed, so this was just a small extension of that responsibility.

Bridget kissed her. "I won't be long," she promised, "and you know how to summon me if anything happens."

"Yes, Mama," Magda replied dutifully, then ruined her serious demeanor by scurrying up the path to pick up her collection of shells and stones so that she could play with them to pass the time. An involuntary glance at the trees showed her only soft green shadows, protecting and benevolent.

The Seigneur de Perella, commander of Montségur's garrison and the man responsible for building the fortress into its current formidable state, turned to the young knight standing beside him in the castle's crowded bailey.

"Are you traveling to Rome, too?"

Raoul smiled acidly. De Perella was referring to the council that had been called by Pope Innocent to discuss various issues troubling the Christian world—the continuing crusade in the Languedoc being one of them. The Count of Foix would be attending to make his views vociferously known, as would be the other interested parties, the exiled Count of Toulouse among them. "Yes, I'll be in Rome, funds permitting. Unlike Count Raymond, I don't have King John of England for my father-in-law to pay my expenses."

"Do I detect a hint of bitterness?" De Perella brushed a lean forefinger back and forth across his mustache.

Raoul pursed his lips. "Not against Count Raymond himself. God knows, he must feel the taking of charity far more keenly than I. Once he was the peer of kings; now he's reduced to begging from them." He rested his hands on his worn sword belt, its gilding mere memory and equal partner to the thread-bare nap on his velvet surcoat. "If I am bitter, it is because I'm forced to sell my sword in order to make a living for my dependents. I run messages for Foix in exchange for the cloak on my back and the bread in my mouth. I watch my son growing up and wonder how he will make a living when the time comes." His jaw clenched. "Nay, that's wrong; I don't wonder, I know. By the lute or the sword he will earn his crust, and probably occupy an early grave. I doubt that the pope will use this council to revoke the powers of the men who have bled us dry in the name of Christ." He expelled his breath harshly. "Rome will only set the seal on de Montfort's theft!"

"I thought that the pope was annoyed with de Montfort for quarreling with Citeaux."

Raoul shrugged. "A storm in a pitkin. In matters of broader policy and intent, they all think the same." Raoul stared across the courtyard without really seeing its bustle. It was two years since the defeat at Muret, two years spent on the tourney circuits and at the courts of other men, living on the crumbs of their charity. He had disbanded such of his men as had survived the disaster of Muret, retaining only Giles and Mir. While convalescing with Claire's mother at Agen, he had deliberated whether to leave Guillaume with her, but had finally decided against it. The boy was all he had and just as safe, if not safer, living an itinerant, nomad life than he was dwelling in a city ripe with volatile rebel sympathies.

For one year they had dwelt in England among the entourage of Raymond of Toulouse at the court of King John, but Raoul had sickened for the warmer climate of his homeland, for the sight of vines and olives and the ripe southern sun. He had returned to the Languedoc and taken up the offer of employment that Foix had once extended to him. He was a *faidit* in truth now, a dispossessed mercenary.

"I've done my best to make this place impervious to siege," de Perella murmured, examining the austere gray walls as if checking the very substance of every stone, every trowel-load of mortar. "No French or Roman whoreson will do to my Cathars what they did to Aimery's at Lavaur." His expression grew hard and determined. "A sanctuary, this is, and so it will remain as long as I am able to defend it. These are good people, and the Light has to be protected." Suddenly self-conscious, he slapped Raoul's shoulder. "I'm an old fool; I talk too much. Come and look at the new winding gear on the portcullis and tell me what you think."

Together they walked toward the stone tower housing the equipment, but were only halfway across the courtyard when Raoul suddenly stopped, his whole body tense, his breathing arrested, and on his face a look of heartrending yearning and disbelief. "Bridget . . ." The sound was the merest whisper.

De Perella followed the direction of Raoul's stare. A look of disgruntled surprise crossed his face. "You didn't tell me you knew our healer."

Raoul paid him no heed, and making a rapid excuse, started across the ward.

She raised her head, saw him, and took a step forward. His sense of the unreal increased, for he had thoroughly expected her to run away, or even walk through a wall. Instead they came face-to-face, and she took his hands in a warm, sure grip.

"Your son fell off his pony outside our hut," she said, cutting across his drawn breath. "He hit his head and concussed himself, but there will be no lasting damage. I left him sleeping and came to fetch you."

Questions, hundreds of them, flashed through Raoul's mind and robbed him of the ability to think properly or to speak. All he could do was stare at her, taking in every aspect of her appearance, from her loose, silky hair and the clarity of her eyes, to the plain robe and even plainer wooden shoes on her feet. She started to withdraw her hands and involuntarily he curled his fingers and gripped.

"I am real," she said with gentle amusement. "And I promise not to vanish on a whim. Your son will need you when he wakes up."

Raoul shook his head. "There is so much I need to ask you," he said, but relinquished his hold and forced himself to pay attention to what she was trying to tell him. "My son? He's supposed to be with Mir."

"Well, he's given him the slip and come a cropper for the prank. Come, I do not want to leave him for too long."

"He is alone?"

She paused and stood to one side to allow a mule train of firewood to enter the courtyard. The muleteer made her a reverent salute, which she returned with the ease of long usage. "No, my daughter is watching over him, but she is young for the task."

"Your daughter?" Raoul followed her past the huts of the Perfecti that were clustered outside the walls of the fortress. "So you did get your wish?"

"She was born here at Montségur." Bridget did not elaborate, but bent her concentration upon the stony path before them.

Raoul walked beside her so that he could see her face. "Why did you leave after that night?"

The scent of pine resin wafted over them with each ripple of breeze. "Our lives were not destined to go forward together from that point." She spoke impassively, but averted her head, avoiding his scrutiny.

"That is not an answer."

She looked at him then, her eyes like gray lightning as she drew herself up. "Why I left and where I went are my own concern. I belong to no man. Yes, I shared my body with you once, but that does not give you the right to question me or seek to buckle a halter around my throat."

Raoul's lip curled. "So I have to stand back and humbly adore like all the rest?"

Her look crystallized, freezing him. She quickened her pace. Cursing softly, he hastened to catch up, and she let him.

"No one has to stand back and humbly adore," she said in a tone less fierce. "It is a step too close to being enslaved."

Raoul gestured ruefully. "I was just hitting out in anger. I owe you my life, do I not?"

She looked a question, wariness in her eyes now.

"After Muret, when I was mortally sick, you came to me. Giles said that I was in a raving fever, but I knew you were there." He looked over his shoulder. "And it was this place I saw, but on a winter's night, I think."

She shivered a little and hugged herself defensively. "You must try to forget. Sometimes we are permitted glances through windows that should be shuttered. Did your wound heal cleanly?"

"There's a scar that pains me sometimes, and occasionally I dream, but on the whole, I barely notice." He half smiled. "Few men can boast to have taken a sword blow from Simon de Montfort in the thick of battle and survived it."

"And do you boast?" she asked neutrally.

Raoul eyed her. "Not to Cathars," he said with a straight face, and she was surprised into laughter. He laughed with her, the expression altering his whole face, revealing the young man still clinging to a tenuous existence beneath the warrior's hard exterior. He took her arm to steady her over a patch of rough ground, and the vibration of their bodies, one upon the other, blended to become one harmonious chord. His hand tightened and he pulled her round to face him.

"Thin air or lightning?" he murmured, and kissed her. Out of time, the moment hung suspended. Longing, aching; question upon question without coherent answer. As they drew apart, Bridget's certainty was shaken to the core. Without a word, she pressed herself out of his arms and continued rapidly down the path.

Magda came running toward them as they approached the hut. "He's awake again!" she cried excitedly. "I've given him a drink of water." Her gaze flashed over Raoul. "Are you Guillaume's papa?"

"Yes, I am." The little girl was a replica of Bridget in miniature; the same paradox of sturdiness and fragility. But Bridget's hair was midnight-black, and the child's was moonlit silver, paler even than Guillaume's. His own daughter, By the Light.

"He says that you're the bravest knight in the world!"

"Did he also mention that I'm the poorest?" Raoul smiled.

"What's poor?" She gave him a look of such puzzled innocence that he felt suddenly humbled and a lump came to his throat.

"Poor is not understanding what wealth really is," he said wryly, and went down the path to Guillaume.

They spent the remainder of the day and the night at Bridget's hut on the mountainside. Mir came looking for them, directed by de Perella and half-mad with worry. He was reassured, fed bread and soup by Bridget, and sent back to Montségur with instructions to return on the morrow with Raoul's horse.

Mostly Guillaume just wanted to sleep away his headache, but for a while he played a game with Magda, using her white stones for counters. She proved herself adept, with a level of concentration far in advance of her tender years, and he was the first one to tire.

The children were put to bed in the smaller second room of the hut. Bridget dropped the thick, woven curtain that served as a partition, quenched the oil lamp, and returned to Raoul at the central hearth of the main room.

He arranged more twigs on the fire with unnecessary care. She watched the movement of his hands and remembered their touch on her body. A small shiver rippled through her. He should not be here. She should have made him stay at the fortress, but she did not have the willpower. Her throat was dry and her loins were liquid. Tonight there was no thunderstorm to charge the air; tonight there was only the sighing of the wind in the pines and the stamping of the pony outside the hut, but the human tensions were the same.

He looked up from the fire and it was as if he had absorbed the heat into his body, for his stare burned. Then he came to her. One arm curved around her shoulders, the other plucked at the simple drawstring of her gown.

"Please," he said when she hesitated, holding him off. "Please, I need you. . . ."

Often people said *need* when they meant *want*, but she knew that was her downfall, not his. She wanted him badly, but she did not need him. Pushing his fingers aside, she unlaced the drawstring of the gown herself, and went into his arms.

* * *

This time when Raoul opened his eyes, she was still beside him, her body pressed close to his. The fire glowed in the central hearth like a forge, and dawn was a long way off. He lazed in elusive pleasure. Not since losing Claire had he indulged his senses thus. Thinking of his wife touched within him a sudden sadness and a feeling of guilt. He still thought about her, but her memory had to compete with the everyday struggle to live and eat and raise Guillaume, and it was inevitable that it should fade to a background discomfort.

Awake herself, Bridget tensed as she caught the trace of what was in his mind. With a soft sigh, she withdrew from their intimacy and silently began to dress.

"Why the haste?" he asked, a warm languor in his voice. "We have all night."

"Would you have Magda or Guillaume waken and stumble in upon us like this?"

He slid a coil of her hair through his fingers. "I do not see that it would cause any harm." He gave her an assessing look. "If you let me stay here awhile to mend my wounded heart and soul, they might even grow accustomed to such a sight."

Bridget stiffened. How easy it would be to agree, but in all conscience she knew that she had to tell him the truth, and that in so doing, she would send him away and perhaps lose his friendship. "You cannot stay," she said. "Your wife still lives. She is locked up at Beaucaire on the Rhône."

Raoul stared at her. Soundlessly his lips formed his wife's name.

Leaving his side, Bridget crouched to mend the fire, and remained there, staring into its deep red heart.

"Can you see her?" he croaked.

"Not tonight. My sight is weak, my body holds the mastery, but I know that she is there. Your mother died from the coughing sickness soon after they were captured." Emotion burned in her throat even as the heat of the flames was burning her face, and her sixth sense became totally blocked.

He was silent. Then she heard the whisper of cloth and the clink of his belt buckle as he pulled on his garments. "How long have you known?"

She bent her head and briefly closed her eyes. Now came

the most difficult part, the cup from which she would rather not drink. "Since before Lavaur."

"Then in the name of Christ, why didn't you tell me!" The words were softly spoken, for there were two children a mere partition away, but they were raw with anguish.

"You would have returned to Montvallant with your troops and have been killed outright. Your wife would still have been captured by de Montfort. Nothing would have changed except your death and my . . ." She did not finish the sentence. Her hair curtained her face, and behind it she hid her vulnerability. "You will be reunited, I promise you. At least this way Guillaume has a father."

Raoul pushed his hands through his hair. "Am I supposed to thank you for that?" His voice was dangerously flat.

"I did not know we would meet again so soon. I thought that you and Claire would be together before you came to Montségur, I thought—"

"Then your power is fallible," he interrupted scathingly.

"I never realized how fallible until now." She met his scorn with a swift, miserable glance.

Without another word he went to the door, raised the bar, and banged out into the night.

Shivering despite the heat of the fire, Bridget bent her head. Gradually her heartbeat slowed and she remembered that everything had its pattern, its measured rhythm even in the act of change. A permanent bond with Raoul was untenable. They had little in common except the lightning spark that struck between their bodies and made them briefly one white-hot flesh. He wanted to know the mystery when he hardly understood a word of its language. With a leaden sigh, she rose from the hearth and went out to him.

He was crouching beside the pony, checking the poultices that had been applied to its grazed knees. She knew that he was aware of her presence, but he did not turn round and acknowledge her.

"I love you," she said to the starlit curve of his spine, "but I cannot give you what you are asking. I can heal your body, I can soothe your mind, but I cannot make you understand. That has to come from within. I am sorry I did not tell you about your wife, but there was nothing you could have done, truly."

There was a drawn-out silence, interrupted only by the sound of night crickets and the pony's restless stamping. At last he stood up and turned round, and she saw that his face was wet. "Sometimes I think that there is nothing left within," he said wearily, his anger gone.

She grasped his hands, afraid at what she saw in his face. "You must not lose your spirit; there is much more than you realize!"

Raoul looked down at their linked fingers. "If it is this painful to draw it out of me, then I do not think I want to know," he replied. "I'll take Guillaume back to the castle tomorrow. There's no point in prolonging the torture." Gently he removed his hands from hers. "It's late," he said, "and I'm very tired."

She watched him return to the hut, her emotions in turmoil. Choosing not to follow him within, she took instead the track toward her favorite ledge of stone that jutted out moss-grown among the trees above the hut. Here she sat down in the moonlight and sought for peace of mind, but it eluded her. In its place she was troubled by the old images of fire and lightning.

CHAPTER TWENTY-EIGHT

Toulouse, Winter 1215–1216

A BITTERLY COLD rain was falling on Toulouse, sky and stone and human feeling blending into one bleak atmosphere. Dagger glances were cast by the citizens in the direction of the Château Narbonnais, from which their new count imposed his iron rule.

Simon had little regard for their opinion. His was the power, his the choice to caress or to strike as the mood took him. Today in the rainy, overcast dawn, he was drinking mulled wine while his squires dressed him for the journey north. Each rivet of his hauberk had been individually burnished. His spurs glittererd on his polished, gilded riding boots, and his shirt was edged with the finest Flemish lace as befitted a lord who officially owned all the land between Toulouse and the Rhône.

The ecumenical council in Rome had found in his favor. Count Raymond was to live in exile on a pension of four hundred marks, having been judged incapable of ruling his hereditary lands. It was a pity that his son, Rai, was to have for his portion the Marquisate of Provence on the eastern side of the Rhône when he came of age, and that the Count of Foix had managed somehow to slip off the hook and retain his lands intact, but they were only minor flies in Simon's ointment. What did they matter when the rest of the world was at his feet?

A sound in the doorway made him glance up from his wine to see Alais advancing on him, a garment draped over her arm. She was dressed for traveling in her warmest gown and mantle, the latter edged with ermine tails and fastened with a heavy amethyst brooch. A gold circlet bound her wimple to her brow, and heavy gold earrings clinked at her lobes. Their journey was to be a victory procession, a slow progress north to do homage to King Philip Augustus for Toulouse and its environs and to accept the adulation of the French homeland.

"I made you a new surcoat for the occasion," she said, and unfolded the gold silk, appliquéd front and back with the snarling fork-tailed lion that was the de Montfort device. "The best Montpellier silk." Pride shone in her eyes as she helped him don it and stood back to admire the result. "How far we have come," she breathed, and closed the distance again, her fingers greedy on the rich fabric and the bulge of his muscles beneath the thick mail shirt and padding.

Simon gestured and Giffard brought his sword belt. Taking it from the youth, he gave it to Alais. "Buckle it on," he commanded. She met him stare for stare, and lifting it out of his hands, slowly passed it around his waist, latched it, then knelt to attach his scabbard. The pressure of her fingers, the look in her eyes, the language of her body, aroused him, but he gave no outward sign, holding himself motionless until she stood up again. Impassively he held out his hand for his cloak. "Is everything ready?"

"Yes, my lord," she murmured with lowered eyes, her color high. "We but await your pleasure."

Simon grunted, forced the pin through the thick wool and fur of his cloak, and taking his gauntlets from the squire, preceded her out of the door.

In the courtyard, Gentian, one of the nursemaids employed to keep the younger de Montfort children from being an inconvenience to their noble parents, was wringing her hands and biting her lip, and the instant that Alais appeared, descended on her, almost weeping.

"Oh, madam, madam, something terrible has happened! I took my eyes off him for one moment and he was gone. I've searched and searched, but I can't find him anywhere!"

"Who?" demanded Alais coldly. "And stop sniveling. I cannot understand a word you're saying!"

Simon, one foot in the stirrup, made an impatient sound. Decisive in all matters, he hated to be kept waiting, especially in the pouring rain.

"Master Dominic, madam. I swear I only spoke to Elise about a spare cloak and he gave me the slip!"

Alais cast her eyes heavenward and slapped the maid sharply when she continued to blubber. "Don't just stand there, go and look again; he can't have gone far!" She cast a swift glance at her husband.

Simon gained the saddle and adjusted his stirrup straps, his expression stony. Alais pursed her lips. "I swear that child has a devil in him!" she snapped. "If ever there is trouble, he is always at the root of it!"

He heard the petulance in her tone and knew that its source was not so much Dominic's behavior as the boy's uncanny physical resemblance to himself. Despite the fact that the child was officially known as the son of Raoul de Montvallant, all could see for themselves the direction of his true siring. Alais had made it her business to remove the temptation of Claire de Montvallant from the household, and to that end she was kept under house arrest at Beaucaire on the Rhône. After an initial pang of guilt, Simon had neither questioned nor contradicted the move; indeed it was a relief not to have the thorn of Claire's presence in his side. Nothing had been said between himself and Alais; the partnership of their marriage remained as staunch as ever, but in the deepest corners there were shadows.

The child's name rang around the courtyard as the maids shouted and searched in vain. A man-at-arms went pessimistically to investigate the well. Another squelched in the direction of the stables and the sludgy midden heap.

"Oh, let the brat rot here in Toulouse if he won't come!" snapped Guy de Montfort, his voice rough with adolescence and the remnants of a heavy cold. He wiped his dripping nose on one of his gauntlets. "I don't know what all the fuss is about! He's only another rebel heretic's whelp!"

A brown-haired boy of about eight dismounted from his pony. "I'll check the kennels," he said. "Dom was mad keen on those brach pups born a few weeks ago."

"Jesu God, not those whelped by Douce!" Guy's face took on a look of loathing as his younger brother Simon started across the courtyard. "Misbegotten, the lot of them!"

"Guy!" Alais's voice was as sharp as a whip.

Guy, totally insensitive to atmospheres and quite without imagination except when it came to swearing, continued to rub salt into an open wound. "Well, it's true!" he protested. "They should all have been drowned at birth. God's death, they're part wolf at least!"

"I would have drowned you at birth," Simon said acidly, "if I had guessed the difference in size between your mouth and your brain."

Guy stared at his father in bewilderment, wondering what he had said. Unable to think of anything, and being too fond of his own hide to argue, he sulked into the fur collar of his cloak.

As the younger Simon had suspected, Dominic was in the kennels, crouched down in the straw with Douce and her three pups. The bitch was a brach, elegant and lean with a smooth coat the color of clotted cream. Her pups were a motley collection of leftover scraps from every other breed within Christendom, and a few outside it, too, for their yellow eyes and long, fuzzy limbs were decidedly lupine. Douce and the kennel boy who had left her unattended at the critical moment of conception were in disgrace for the crime. That the pups had not been drowned at birth owed more to the kennel-keeper's curiosity to see the grown result than any misplaced soft-heartedness. Dominic had taken to the pups as he had never taken to anything or anyone in his entire small life, as if recognizing that they, too, were misfits.

"Dom, come on, they're all looking for you. Gentian's nearly wetting herself! They'll have your guts for garters if you don't hurry up!" Simon warned.

The child raised his eyes to the older boy and thrust out a stubborn lower lip. "Don't want to." His scowl outdid Guy's. Grasping one of the pups, he hugged it ferociously.

"You've got to."

"I won't," Dominic repeated mulishly, but then his head tilted and his look became sly. "Not unless Loup can come, too."

"Dominic, he can't! You know Elise doesn't like dogs, and he's not even trained. He'll piss all over the litter cushions!"

"Don't like Elise," he said as if that were the end of the matter, and continued to cuddle the pup while it licked him frantically.

Simon didn't like Elise much either. He also knew that his father was less than impressed with the maid, and decided to take the risk. At worst Dominic would throw a tantrum, but if they were in the courtyard, it would be the women's task to deal with it, and at best Dominic would get his desire and Elise's haughty nose would be put out of joint.

The older boy returned to the bailey five minutes later, complete with his small half brother, a leggy pup gamboling and snapping at the string attached to the infant's wrist. Elise was silenced in the midst of her vociferous complaints by Lord Simon himself with a furious command that sent her scurrying into the litter like a flustered hen into a coop.

Simon rested his eyes briefly on his namesake's innocent expression before gesturing him to remount his pony. He flickered an even more perfunctory glance over the little boy wriggling away from his nurse as she tried to fasten his cloak and avoid the pup at the same time. Straight hair as black as his own before it had grayed, sea-storm eyes, and the promise of bold Norman bones; Dominic de Montvallant was the living proof of one wild moment of lost control.

Simon cleared his throat and spat over his mount's withers. Alais was watching him. He pressed his knees into his palfrey's flanks and urged it forward. Mud sprayed from the hooves. A groom dodged, but not before he had been well spattered. Simon fixed his stare on the road flanked by the towers of the Château Narbonnais, on the gray sky and the bright silk banners rippling against it, until the sight of the black-haired child and the dog had vanished from his mind's eye.

CHAPTER TWENTY-NINE

Provence, Spring 1216

THE SOLDIER SHOOK his fist, blew on his knuckles, muttered an incantation, and flung the dice into the center of the circle. They clicked together and fell in the dust. Amid cheers and curses, a fine cambric shirt changed hands.

A short distance from the gambling mercenaries, Raoul groomed his bay stallion, teasing out the last of the winter coat until the hide reflected the sun like a mirror. Nearby Guillaume was practicing his horsemanship with a group of squires and pages. Raoul paused to rest his arm and watched his son with pride in his eyes. Guillaume set his riderless mount to a circling canter, himself in the center of that circle. Judging his moment, he took a running leap at the pony and grasped the coarse mane and the padded sack he used for a saddle. His thigh slipped smoothly across the pony's back and he sat up, fists punching the air.

"Your lad's making a fine horseman," Rai commented,

strolling to Raoul's side. He was lightly dressed in shirtsleeves and hose, the day being hot, but nevertheless managed to look as elegant as a cat. Behind him on a leading rein plodded a dun cob—a plain workhorse with saddle galls and an expression of weary docility on its broad face. Raoul eyed it dubiously, for it was scarcely a mount worthy of the Marquis of Provence and leader of the southern army.

Rai had landed at Marseilles at the beginning of the month to gather a rebel army of Provencals and dispossessed southerners to his banner. He was the Languedoc's rising star. His father had diverted to Spain in order to raise a second army to strike at the northern garrisons, leaving Rai to reap the adulation of Marseilles, Avignon, Orange, and every Rhône town through which his growing army had passed. He was poised now to march on de Montfort's stronghold of Beaucaire. The lord Simon was still conducting his victory parade throughout the North, secure in his belief that the South was defeated. What did he have to fear from a broken old man and a feckless youth?

"Guillaume is something of a daredevil," Raoul qualified. "He took a bad fall last year at Montségur, but it doesn't seem to have knocked much sense into him." He was smiling as he spoke, with no real censure in his voice.

Rai's teeth flashed. He well understood the "watch me" element in the boy's nature since it was an integral part of his own. Rakish good looks coupled with charm meant that most of the time, Rai's desires were gratified.

Raoul watched Guillaume for a moment longer—the wiry agility, the nimbus around his sun-bleached hair—and with an indulgent smile, shook his head and returned to grooming the stallion.

"I want you to do something for me," Rai said.

Raoul worked his way down the bay's powerful haunch. "It concerns that nag of yours, I think?"

Rai grinned. "How did you guess?"

"Pure mischance," Raoul retorted. "If it's a sweetener to get me to do your will, you'll have to do better than that!"

Rai's grin became outright laughter. "I knew that's what you would say!" He slapped the dun's neck and tethered it at

Raoul's horse line beside two pack mules. "No, seriously; do this for me and you can name your price."

"You know my price," Raoul said with quiet intensity, all humor flown. "Montvallant and my wife." His blue gaze rested on the distant walls of the castle of Beaucaire, visible on its high rock above the Rhône.

"I'll give you them both if you but trust me." Rai followed the direction of Raoul's stare. His own eyes narrowed. "It is time for the reckoning to be made."

"What do you want me to do?"

"Take a message to the citizens of Beaucaire, giving them the where and when of our attack. There's a goldsmith, Pierre the Saracen, with a workshop near Saint Paque. He's our contact, and he'll organize the people to repel the garrison and open the gates to us." Rai indicated the dun cob. "You'll ride into town as a laborer."

Raoul looked from Rai's glinting dark eyes to the spavined nag, and rubbed the back of his neck to ease the beat of the sun.

"You can leave tonight," Rai added. "That way you'll be ready to enter the town gates at dawn. I'll give you detailed instructions later." Then he slapped Raoul's arm the way he had slapped the dun's neck and nonchalantly strolled off.

Raoul crouched in a doorway, his shoulder resting against the carved stone arch of the porch, a shield propped to one side and a sword balanced across his thighs. Both weapons had been borrowed from the rebels in the town. To have borne his own into Beaucaire beneath the suspicious gaze of the northern gate guards would have been asking for trouble. They had stopped him entering the town and made him empty his pack on the ground. It had revealed nothing more incriminating than a patched shirt and braies, a tatty spare tunic, a hunk of stale bread, and an onion. Not satisfied, they had examined his palms. Fortunately, Raoul had spent two hours in camp roughening his hands on a grindstone and then rubbing them into the soil, a precaution that had paid its reward. The soldiers had let him pass, mocking the *ac* and *az* sounds of his southern accent and jabbing their lances at the old dun nag in a vain attempt to make it sidle. His anger had boiled up, but he had swallowed it scalding down into his belly. He could feel it now, trickling through his veins as he waited in the doorway, dressed like a peasant—a wolf in sheep's clothing.

Two other men waited with him—Thomas and Jeffrey, the sons of Pierre the Saracen. Their father was at the city gates, ensuring that all would go smoothly for Rai's knights when they attacked.

Thomas coughed nervously. He had been sick twice already that morning. "How much longer?" he croaked.

Raoul glanced at him. He was a gangly youth with the baby down of a first mustache on his upper lip. It was the waiting that was getting to the young man as much as the fear of what might happen once the fighting began. From what Raoul had seen, the people were eager for battle. The citizens of Beaucaire were fiercely cosmopolitan, and de Montfort's attempts to rule them by the feudal laws of the North had fanned a bitter resentment. "Not long," he said with a glance at the luminescent rim of the eastern sky. A church bell rang out, summoning the pious to mass.

"Is your wife really locked up in the castle?" Jeffrey inquired, curiosity overcoming prudence.

Raoul rubbed his forefinger gently back and forth over the sword grip. "I have heard it is so," he said without inflection.

"Our sister had to take some gold buckles up to the castle for the Countess de Montfort a few years ago, and she told me that there was a southern lady among her women. Hair like an autumn forest, she said.

Raoul lowered his gaze to the motion of his finger. In his mind's eye he saw his hands webbed by Claire's glorious russet hair, her beautiful heart-shaped face lifted to his.

"She was greensick," Jeffrey added. "My sister said that you could tell she was with child."

"With child?" Raoul went cold.

"Yes, she . . ." Jeffrey stopped, his garrulousness arrested by the expression on Raoul's face. "I . . ." he stammered as Raoul rose jerkily to his feet. Whatever else Jeffrey had been about to say was drowned out by the clamor of the tocsin that suddenly started clanging from the castle walls.

Ignoring it, Raoul seized a fistful of Jeffrey's padded leather jerkin. "Do you tell me my wife was pregnant?"

"My sister said so, but she might have been wrong." Half-choking, he tried to push Raoul away. "Perhaps it was one of the countess's other women. It was a long time ago."

"My lord, the alarm!" Thomas grabbed at Raoul, his young voice cracking with anxiety.

Breathing hard, Raoul opened his fingers. Cold dread seeped from his gut into every vital part of him. Claire bearing the burden of pregnancy and childbirth in the den of the enemy, isolated and afraid. She had said nothing of pregnancy to him in the days before Lavaur, so if the child was not his ... He voided the thought in the rapidity of sudden physical action. There was a garrison in that castle, a garrison that had to be prevented from reaching the town gates.

Claire sat up on the narrow straw pallet and listened to the bell that was summoning everyone to mass. Prayer had been as much in evidence recently as food had not. Yesterday's ration had consisted of the end of a loaf and the lees from the last tun of wine. Yesterday, too, they had slaughtered one of the knights' horses. Claire had been allotted some thin slices of the tough, undercooked meat, but in revulsion had given it away. Cathars did not eat meat, and she knew herself to be one now in all but the final confirmation. Mind and spirit held the certainty; only the body was afraid.

It seemed an aeon since Rai's knights had galloped through the gates that the people of Beaucaire had so willingly opened for them. The crusader garrison had belatedly realized what was happening and rushed into the city to repel the southern troops. They had reached no farther than the northern quarter by the church of Saint Paque, for the people were out in the streets and their blood was up, thirsty for vengeance. The garrison was met by a barrage of arrows and stones. Deciding that discretion was better than death, the crusaders had fought their way back to the keep to secure it against the citizens. Now the castle of Beaucaire was moated by a massive southern army, and its garrison prayed as they had never prayed before for Simon de Montfort to come to their aid.

Hollow-eyed with hunger and lack of sleep, the people trapped inside the castle endured the daily pounding of the walls by Rai's massive stone-throwing trebuchets. Most of the upper defense works were gone. From what remained of the battlements, the hopelessness of the crusaders' situation was obvious. The rotting corpses of northern soldiers dangled from the branches of the olive trees in the town vineyards. De Montfort's relief army could not get near the castle, for Rai had learned from the disaster at Muret and refused to be drawn into a pitched battle on open ground. Instead he had constructed extra defense works to the west of the castle, and behind these, he kept Simon at bay.

Claire heard the gloomy reports and she saw the growing frustration and despair of the garrison as, day by day, week by week, their hope was whittled away. Last night, as so many nights before, she had slept in her clothes. She had no change of garments now. Her spare shift had been torn up to make bandages, and someone had stolen her other gown. Once she would have been horrified to appear in public looking the least bit dirty or unkempt. Now it did not seem to matter; indeed, in some ways it was a comfort. Men no longer looked at her as if they would like to eat her alive.

What would it be like to be free? To come and go as she pleased? That thought until recently had been an exotic flight of fancy. Now, with each passing day, it was becoming more feasible. In her imagination she set one foot outside her cage, then the other, taking cautious steps. She would go to Agen, to her mother, and she would see Guillaume again, her beautiful little boy. For a while she would stay there, regaining her strength, and when she felt ready, she would depart for the hills of the Ariège to serve the Cathars and become worthy of the title of Perfect.

But then her imagination would take a darker turn. What if her mother was dead like Raoul's mother, or what if Guillaume had never reached her safely and his bones lay scattered and bleaching somewhere on the road between Montvallant and Agen as Raoul's bones lay bleaching on the plain of Muret? The doubts rushed at her like a pack of harpies and she fled back to her cage, locking herself inside it, terrified that, like a bird with clipped wings, she had lost the power to fly.

Rai's surcoat was a confection of immaculate wine-dark velvet extravagantly adorned with thread-of-gold. It well suited his saturnine features, which were further enhanced by the dazzle of his smile. Feline, smug with triumph, he regarded his enemy across the trestle. A hot wind gusted his black hair, but it was Simon de Montfort who was being forced to squint into the sun.

Standing among Rai's commanders, Raoul stared at the northern warlord with a hatred so powerful that it brought tears to his eyes. Even now in defeat, de Montfort's face wore a look of superior arrogance, as if he were condescending to yield, and not being forced.

"We are agreed, then," Rai said. "You withdraw your army and yield me Beaucaire, and in return I let your garrison depart intact with their families and possessions."

Simon stared coldly at Rai as if he had spoken out in front of his betters. "Agreed," he said curtly, his lips barely accommodating the word. Inking the quill, he signed the document of surrender with bitter, forceful strokes and thrust the parchment back at Rai. Declining the offered wine, he levered himself up from the trestle. "We have nothing more to say to each other; let the bargain be fulfilled. Amaury, my horse." He reached for his gauntlets and glared darkly at the knights surrounding Rai as if marking each one for future retribution.

The moment came when his stare collided with Raoul's like a lance striking a shield on a tourney field. Both men recoiled from the impact and then sought each other again. Raoul steadied his glare, his fist tightening on the cheekstrap of the red bay destrier that had originally come from the de Montfort stables. He braced his left hand on his scabbarded sword and offered up a wordless but no-less-potent challenge.

De Montfort snorted and turned his back in a gesture of contempt and supreme indifference, but not before Raoul had trapped the glimmer of fear in his eyes.

Claire huddled in a corner of the chapel, silently praying, her heart thumping so loudly that it almost obliterated her thoughts. The dead silence that had fallen after the garrison had departed had been eerie, a pause in time. Terrified that the troops might take her with them and hand her over to de Montfort, she had hidden here, behind the altar, the last place they would think to look for her.

There had been a frightening moment when some soldiers had come to remove the candlesticks, pyx, and altar cloth. She had realized that her foot was protruding from the edge of the stone and it was too late to tuck it under her, but they had been in far too much of a hurry clearing the valuables to notice.

Now she could hear voices again, and the footsteps approaching her sanctuary were unhurried and casual this time.

". . . very generous of you, my lord, to donate new furnishings for the chapel," she heard someone say, and daring to peep around the altar stone, saw a priest talking to a slender young man wearing a crimson and gold surcoat.

"I have appreciated your prayers and good offices among my men," the latter replied gracefully, and walked toward the altar. Claire curled up behind it again, afraid that the thud of her heart and the sound of her shallow breathing would give her away.

A sword chape scraped on the stone floor as the young man knelt, and the priest must have knelt with him, too, for in a moment she heard his voice intoning in Latin the words that she herself had learned by rote as a small child; words that revolted her now—not for their meaning, but for the memories they evoked. Alais de Montfort and Friar Bernard forcing them at her, stuffing them into every orifice . . . eyes upon the cross, wafer on her tongue, incense in her nostrils, the devil's spear reaming her body, *Credo*. Claire bit down into the fleshy side of her palm to prevent herself from crying out, and squeezed her lids tightly shut until her vision was filled with bright starbursts of color. There was bile in her throat and her own blood in her mouth.

At last it was quiet. She dared to remove the improvized gag of her own flesh and opened her eyes. Cream beeswax candles now flickered on the altar, a cross casting its long shadow between them, and staring down at her over the top of the altar table were the priest and the young man.

"Sweet Jesu!" The latter came around the side of the stone and, crouching, extended his hand as if to a wary animal. She shrank from him with a whimper.

"Claire?" whispered a horrified voice she had thought never to hear again. Behind the priest and the man in the surcoat, she made out the shape of a third person. The light glimmered on his tawny hair and gaunt bones. His spurs clinked on the floor tiles, and as he advanced, his link mail flashed. "Claire?" he said again, his throat working. "Dear Christ, what have they done to you?"

Rai, the bright mockery in his nature subdued by the enormity of his horror and pity, cleared his throat, and making a tactful excuse, drew the staring priest away with him out of the chapel and posted guards at the door to give the two within a modicum of privacy.

An echoing silence descended. Raoul advanced and knelt beside her. She felt his tentative touch on her snarled, matted braid. The days when she had taken a pride in her appearance were long gone, but her hair had been her vanity and Raoul's particular pleasure. She could feel the grief in his fingertips. She raised dull, haunted eyes to his face. "They have done nothing to me," she whispered, "nothing. What they did was to *her*. After you die they cannot touch you. . . ." Her eyes slipped from his. "But sometimes, despite yourself, you remember."

Raoul's face showed fear. He set his hand to her shoulder and shook her. "Claire, in God's name, stop it; don't look at me like that!"

She flopped back and forth against his hand without resistance. "In God's name?" she said in a faraway voice. "*He* said that it was in God's name, when he came on his white horse, but I know which God *he* meant." With an effort she focused on him. "*He* told me that you were dead, that *he* had killed you."

"He lied," Raoul said, knowing only too well which *he* she meant. He gathered her to him and she came limply into his arms like a child's cloth doll. "We fought on the battlefield, but I was only wounded. Beaucaire is ours, and you're no longer his prisoner. Did you hear me, no longer his prisoner!" He clutched her tightly.

Chin upon his shoulder, Claire shut her eyes so that she would not see the gilded ornaments belonging to the false God, her body riven by tremor upon tremor.

Raoul removed his cloak and wrapped her in it. "We can't stay here, love; they'll be needing the chapel for the services.

I've a room in a house in the town. Once you've eaten and rested, you'll be all right."

She felt nothing at his touch or his words. When he pulled her to her feet, she swayed against him, weak as a kitten. "I'll always be *his* prisoner; don't you understand?" she said in a distant, dejected voice. The chapel whirled before her eyes, the candle flames becoming an intermittent wheel of fire, quartered by the cross. Faster and faster, brighter and brighter. Light burned behind her eyes, searing through her body. Raoul's voice came from far away, edged with panic, and then there was black oblivion.

Claire woke to a strange room that was pervaded by a smell that seemed familiar but which she could not immediately identify. Bunches of drying herbs and flowers hung from the rafters, and bundles of rushes were stored between the beams. Molten August sunshine bathed the floor and slanted across the bed in which she lay. She recognized the smell as that of freshly laundered linen. On a coffer beside the bed stood a candle on a pricket and a polished bowl of fruit—pears, oranges, and green figs.

Her gaze was drawn back to the brightness at the window and she saw a man sitting in the embrasure looking out through the open shutters. . . . Open shutters? How long since she had been permitted such a dangerous luxury? She frowned and put her hand to her forehead. The scent of soap on skin filled her nostrils. She sniffed her wrist and stared at the blindingly white linen chemise clothing her arm. A thin thread of memory slowly began to unravel, and she clutched at it.

"Raoul?" she said faintly.

The man at the window turned, and she saw that indeed she had not been hallucinating in the nightmare darkness of Beaucaire's chapel. It was Raoul, although he was more hard-boned and sinewy than the Raoul of her memories, and his mouth no longer wore a smile in repose.

"Where am I?"

He came to the bed, his expression one of mingled anxiety and relief. "In the house of Pierre the Saracen in the town . . . of Beaucaire," he added, unsure how confused she still was.

"Are you hungry? You haven't eaten anything in three days except an egg posset, and we had to force that down you."

Claire examined the familiar, hollow feeling in the pit of her stomach. Was it hunger, or an emptiness of a different kind? She did not remember the egg posset, but neither did she remember the three days.

Taking her silence for assent, Raoul fetched half a loaf and a crock of honey from the sideboard, and with his eating knife, cut and smeared a slice.

Claire sat up, her head swimming. Raoul's face blurred and cleared by turns. She took the bread from him and bit into it. Saliva filled her mouth and the feeling in her stomach resolved itself into ravenous hunger. The anxiety in his eyes softened as he watched her devour the food, and he turned to pour wine into two cups.

"You have slept almost solidly," he said. "You hardly even roused when we bathed you. . . . I'm sorry about your hair. Pierre's wife says that it will grow again, but it was so matted and dirty and louse-infested that she could do nothing with it."

Claire put her free hand to her scalp and discovered herself as closely shorn as a midsummer sheep . . . or a nun. "It doesn't matter." A brittle laugh broke from her throat. "I've long outgrown vanity of that kind. When you stand to lose your soul, your body does not matter." She pushed away the last of the bread and honey. Her stomach, unaccustomed to such bounty, felt queasy. Glancing at Raoul, she saw that he was fiddling with the stem of his goblet, his eyes lowered. But then what did they have to say to each other when so vast a gulf separated them?

"De Montfort has retreated," he said awkwardly. "The town is safely ours for the time being." He hesitated, obviously floundering. Several times he started to speak, then with a grimace, stopped himself. "God's life," he finally burst out, "I should never have ridden to Lavaur!"

"It would not have made any difference to the outcome; there were too many of them, and your duty was not to me alone."

"No." He turned his head aside, his color heightened. "I swear I won't leave you again." His voice was low-pitched, ripe with guilt.

Claire sighed. "Nothing can ever be the same," she said wearily. "Too much has changed. I love you, but I am not the girl you married, and for a long time you have been a stranger to me . . . since before Lavaur."

Raoul rolled the goblet between his fingers and did not contradict her. She saw the way he was frowning, the set of his mouth, and her damaged heart ached. He rose to his feet and paced to the window. For a long time he stood motionless, just staring out, but at last he turned and looked at her.

"Pierre's nephew told me that while you were kept prisoner here, you were with child. Is it true?"

Claire felt her stomach plummet with shock. Dear God of Light, how was she going to bear this? She closed her eyes. "Yes, it's true," she heard herself say in a tight, small voice. "Four years ago at Castres, I bore Simon de Montfort's son." She heard Raoul make a stifled sound, but could not tell if it was disgust, outrage, or pure fury, nor at whom it was directed. Drawing a shaken breath, steeling herself, she continued, "Simon de Montfort took Montvallant, and when he realized that you were not there and I did not know where you were, he quenched his lust and his rage upon me. Then he gave me to his wife so that I could be taught the error of my ways, become a good Catholic again. When I started to be sick in the mornings and my gowns grew tight, I let Alais believe that the baby was yours, conceived before Montvallant was captured, but it wasn't true." She swallowed, fighting her gorge. "They took him away from me the moment he was born, and all that I know of him is that he is named Dominic and they are bringing him up in their traditions . . . as the true heir to Montvallant." She drank her wine and choked. "I wished so hard to die that part of me did."

Raoul turned and strode to the bed. Snatching the wine from her hands, he pulled her fiercely against him. "Ah God, Claire," he said hoarsely, one hand upon her cropped hair, the other around her pitifully thin body.

At first she struggled against him, against the liquid burning of her eyes and the pain of dissolving from stone back into flesh. Her nose was pressed against the worn linen of his tunic and she absorbed his familiar smell. His warmth and closeness evoked bittersweet memories and suddenly the tears were running freely down her face. The last time she had cried had been in the garden at Castelnaudry when Simon de Montfort had violated her again with Raoul's sword and broken shield.

Raoul murmured her name over and over, interspersed with endearments, while she clung and shivered. His own thoughts were tortured with guilt. While she had been enduring the hell of rape, he had been begetting a child, too, perhaps not in rape but nevertheless in lust and with never a thought for his wife.

Gradually she calmed and so did he, the first shock waves diminishing to ripples.

"It is over now," Raoul said with bleak determination. "We have to build on what remains. If we keep looking back, we'll be destroyed."

What did remain? Claire wondered. The changes in each other were too great to make bricks and mortar out of the debris, but for the moment she was too weak and tired to fight him. She let him hold her and closed her eyes.

The door opened and a boy danced into the room. "Papa, Lord Rai wants to talk to you about . . ." He stopped in midflow and stared.

Claire stared back at her son. She had carried the memory of his soft, blond hair, pudgy limbs, and dribbly, gap-toothed smile throughout her trials. The child eyeing her now was slender and tanned, and possessed the wiry grace of a young deer.

"Guillaume," she breathed, a world of pain in that one word. "I would not have known you."

He nodded in response to his name, and after only the briefest hesitation, and a flicker of a glance at Raoul, advanced to the bed, his manner exuding a confidence bordering on boldness. Tears shone in Claire's eyes, blurring his image. "Last time I saw you, you were barely walking. . . . Oh God, how many years have I lost?" She moved her head from side to side.

"I'm nearly seven," Guillaume obliged. "Papa's going to give me a new pony and teach me to joust." He cocked his head on one side and pushed his sun-streaked hair off his brow. "Are you feeling better now?"

"Yes, much better," Claire said as a matter of form. In fact, she felt worse. She had lost both her children. The baby conceived in rape had been snatched away at birth, and this child of her heart had become a self-assured individual, already aping the behavior of the older boys who were pages and squires. A dagger sat on his hip, and his liquid brown gaze was knowing and worldly-wise. War dragged children far too swiftly into adulthood.

"Your mother is very tired; she needs to rest," Raoul said with a quick look between mother and son. "Perhaps we can all talk later. Did you say that Rai wanted to see me?"

"Yes, Papa. About a foraging party, I think. Can I come, too?"

It was Raoul, not Claire, who tousled the boy's fair hair. "I don't see why not," he said, and grinned at Claire. "You should see him on horseback!"

She responded with a wan smile. "I am not surprised. It used to bring me out in a cold sweat of terror to watch you gallop him round the tiltyard at Montvallant."

The unspoken words hung between them like beads dangling precariously on a broken necklace. One careless move and they would be scattered abroad without hope of ever being restrung.

"It did, didn't it?" he agreed, and the grin faded. He squeezed her hands. "I'll stay if you want me to. Rai can always find someone else to do his foraging."

"No." Claire shook her head, squeezing back. "Go, both of you. I am indeed very tired, and I'd like to be alone for a while."

Raoul gnawed his lip and hesitated, but at last he kissed her brow and went to the door. Guillaume kissed her, too, performing his duty to a stranger, and followed his father.

She heard them speaking below in the yard—Guillaume's voice loud with excitement at the prospect of accompanying the men, Raoul's response amused and chiding at the same time. Sunlight upon bright, shallow water. She sought the cool, peaceful depths of the sacred word.

Truly, truly, unless one is born anew, he cannot see the kingdom of God. Unless one is born of water and the spirit, he cannot enter the kingdom of God. That which is born of the flesh is flesh, and that which is born of the spirit is spirit.

She decided that when Raoul returned, she would ask him if there were any Cathars in Beaucaire who would be willing to visit her.

CHAPTER THIRTY

Toulouse, Spring 1217

DOMINIC TENSED HIS narrow shoulders as Friar Bernard leaned over his work to examine what he had written. The results were not impressive. The five-year-old had an excellent degree of control for his age when he was allowed to use his left hand, but Friar Bernard said that the left hand belonged to the Devil and that he must not use it for eating or writing, nor in practice swordplay. Especially he must not use it for genuflecting in church. However, Dominic frequently chose to use it behind Father Bernard's back in signing gestures at his tutor that were far from holy, for he hated the friar with all the concentrated passion that smoldered beneath the surface of his deceptively quiet nature. The musty smell of Friar Bernard's black robes disgusted the child. The fanatical sparkle in the black eyes, and the veins bulging like worms on the high, pale brow, both fascinated and repelled him. Most of all he was terrified by the willow switch that Friar Bernard was never without, and with which, in tyranny, he ruled his domain.

Fiat voluntas Tua . . . Thy will be done. The words straggled across the slate, barely legible. Dominic bit his lip, not daring to look up into the cold, fathomless eyes.

"Do you see that spider above your head?" Friar Bernard jabbed his stick at a web in the corner of the room. "Do you? Answer me, boy!"

"Yes, Father Bernard." Dominic squirmed on the bench, only too aware of the bony white hand so close to his ear, clenched and quivering with anticipation on the smooth willow switch.

"That spider could write a better hand than I see on your slate! You do this deliberately to test me. . . ."

"I don't, Father, I can't use my—"

"Silence, boy! Are you insolent as well as stupid!"

Dominic's bottom lip quivered. He stiffened it, knowing full well that the friar wanted to make him cry in front of the other boys so that he could further taunt him. Some of them, the sons of de Montfort's knights and retainers, had bullied him before now, calling him a heretic and a whoreson, although they made sure never to do it in front of the adults. Dominic knew what happened to the odd one out in a dog pack—either it was harassed to death by the other dogs, or it became their leader. He did his best to appear indifferent to the taunts and ridicule when they came his way, but his best was not always equal to the occasion—and never good enough for the fanatical Friar Bernard.

The priest picked up Dominic's slate and held it with the tips of his fingers as if what it contained were contagious. "Write this again," he said coldly. "Three times." And he pushed the slate back into Dominic's hands, bruising him with the force of the thrust.

Dominic swallowed the painful lump in his throat, hatred shuddering through his small frame. Beside him on the bench, Simon, four years his senior, gave him a sympathetic nudge and a swift look. Dominic risked a grimace through the suspicion of tears.

Friar Bernard turned away, his jaw grinding, and went to stare out of the window. Dominic eyed the switch tapping impatiently behind his tutor's back. He willed it to jerk from the priest's fingers and belabor its owner about the head and shoulders. So strong was the emotion concentrated in his stare that he saw Friar Bernard begin to turn his head, the black eyes narrow with suspicion. Hastily Dominic bent over the dreaded slate and fumbled with his stylus. His right hand refused to cooperate, and the lettering it produced was twofold more clumsy than before. After another glance at the friar, this time furtive, he changed the stylus to his left hand. A transformation took place. The words flowed upon the slate as smooth as silk and the pained expression left Dominic's face.

As if gifted by eyes in the back of his head, Bernard whirled round. His expression blazed with righteous fury and he took three leaping strides across the room to bring his stick swishing down across the knuckles of Dominic's left hand. The stylus flew from the little boy's fingers, and with a cry, he snatched his hand away. Again and again the enraged friar struck him, the blows landing upon Dominic's shoulders and head, stinging across his face. Dominic curled himself into a defensive ball. After the first shriek of pain had been surprised out of him, he did not utter another sound. On the tiled floor, the slate lay broken in two pieces, the words *fiat voluntas Tua* flawlessly written.

"If you weren't Lord Simon's own son, I'd break every one of your fingers!" Bernard panted as his arm rose and fell. "I'll drive the Devil out of you somehow, I swear by Jesu's blood I will!" He raised the switch on high to strike again with all the force in his arm, but the blow never descended. In the shocked silence, Dominic peeped through his fingers and saw the lord de Montfort himself watching the proceedings with cold eyes.

Slowly Bernard lowered the switch. "My lord, I did not know you were here." After stating the obvious, he licked his lips nervously.

"I think the boys can be excused from their lessons for the rest of the day." Simon's voice was the husky growl that the men under his command had most learned to fear. Without waiting for the friar's leave, he jerked his head at the children. "Out."

One and all, they fled with alacrity, except for the younger Simon, who paused to persuade Dominic out of his fetal ball and to his feet. De Montfort looked at the boy's face, at the scarlet stripe branded upon the pallor of shock, at the rigid mouth and jaw, but it was the eyes that bore the most eloquent testimony to what had just been accomplished. Tears brimmed in them, but so did the pride and the hatred. His father's face wearing his mother's expression.

"Take him to the women and get one of them to put some salve on that bruise," Simon instructed his son brusquely. When the older boy had led Dominic away, he turned to Father Bernard. "I hope you have a good explanation for what I saw just now."

"Dominic was using his left hand again, my lord, and he defied me before the others."

Simon regarded the shattered slate at his feet, the childish characters perfectly formed. "There is a world of difference between breaking and schooling. Ask the meanest of my grooms." And then the soft voice curled like a whip, and struck to draw blood. "If you ever open your mouth before your mind again in front of an audience, I'll cut out your tongue. I do not acknowledge him as mine. He is heir to the lands of Montvallant; is that understood?"

"Yes, my lord," Bernard said stiffly.

"I hope that you do." Simon turned on his heel. "Because I never threaten, I promise."

Dominic crouched against the wall in a corner of the bailey, his arms around Loup, the hot tears he had refused to shed earlier now darkening the hound's wiry silver coat. He touched the throbbing place on his cheek where Friar Bernard's whip had slashed him, and then looked at his fingertip, which was shiny with the lady Alais's herb and goose-grease salve. He had desired neither salve nor attention, only to be left alone to cry in peace. Instead there had been an inquest with all the grisly details laid before the women by Sim, whose desire to comprehend was as insatiable as his curiosity. Not that any answers had been forthcoming from Alais, whose response had been positively glacial.

Dominic tightened his fingers in the dog's ruff. Loup might not understand, but he was loyal, big and warm, and made no demands of intellect as Sim did. Did the priest's words mean that he and Sim were half brothers? Was he a bastard like the children born to the soldier's women? He had heard the word often enough to know that it stemmed from some irregularity of birth. Loup licked him exuberantly and whined. Friar Bernard said that Loup was a dog of the Devil's creation, but Dominic knew that for a falsehood. Young as he was, he understood that his hated tutor was capable of seeing the Devil in a bucket of water or a horse dropping if the mood was upon him. He even claimed to have encountered the Virgin Mary in a blizzard. Perhaps everything he said was distorted and false.

Gradually, as he cuddled the dog, Dominic started to feel better. His was a resilient, self-contained nature. Like a snail retreating within its shell at moments of danger, so Dominic had the ability to retreat within himself, thereby surviving the crisis. Indeed, he had recovered enough to be thinking of visiting the kitchens to see if Hubert, one of the apprentice cooks, would spare him a bone for Loup and a piece of marchpane for himself if he pleaded with wide enough eyes, when some soldiers from the town entered the bailey, dragging three men and a woman in their wake. All the prisoners were roped together and in consequence stumbling and staggering off balance. They looked drunk, but they were not. If anything, it was the soldiers who had been drinking, to judge from the way they were poking and prodding the captives and making ribald remarks.

The foremost man wore a handsome green tunic and hose, and his graying hair and beard had been curled with irons and slicked with pomade. His three companions, in contrast, were dressed in the garments of Cathar Perfecti—unembellished hooded robes of dark blue wool, relieved only by the silver buckles on their girdles. Their faces reminded Dominic of Father Bernard—undernourished and fanatical—but unlike his tutor, he felt no threat from these people.

He had seen these sorts of prisoners on several previous occasions, and in a relatively short space of time. It had been autumn when the de Montfort household had come to Toulouse, after the defeat at Beaucaire. Sim had told him that the count believed the citizens of Toulouse were traitors who had supplied arms and money to the rebels and that they had to be punished. Occasionally he and Sim had sneaked down to the dungeons to peek at the people who had been arrested by the troops. Sometimes the blue robes were amongst them, but they never lasted very long. Dominic Guzman, the leader of the black friars, would come and talk to them, then he would either weep or become very angry at their obstinacy, but the end result was always the same. The ones who called themselves

"Perfecti" were taken out and burned. Dominic did not understand why. Friar Bernard said that they were very bad people, but then he said that Dominic was bad, and Loup also. What was good? Was it the stench of Cathars roasting? If the wind was in the wrong direction, they could smell it sometimes in the countess's rooms, and she would make them all kneel and pray.

A flurry of activity near the main door caught Dominic's eye and he froze, cowering against the wall, his stomach clenching as Friar Guzman and Friar Bernard issued from the keep and approached the prisoners. The fat man in the green tunic fell on his knees and wept at the feet of the churchmen, crossing himself, kissing the dusty hems of their robes. Dominic saw the switch tremble in Father Bernard's thin fingers, saw the cadaverous expression on his face, and knew that all the captive's tears and pleadings were for naught. Small whimpers choked his own throat, and he clenched his teeth and tightened his lips so that no sound should betray him into another beating.

The Cathars neither begged nor wept, their reaction indifferent, bordering on the contemptuous, and Dominic admired their courage. *Heretic* was suddenly a word plucked from a vague awareness in his vocabulary and elevated to the shining levels of *knight* and *chivalry* and *honor*.

He watched as they were dragged away to the dungeons, watched until the glint of the last soldier's hauberk had been quenched in the shadows, and the black robes of the friars no longer endangered the courtyard. At his heels, Loup whined and pawed him beseechingly. The look of narrow concentration vanished from Dominic's gray-green eyes and once more he was only a small boy in a dusty tunic, his mind diverted by thoughts of marchpane and marrowbones—but only diverted. Memory was as strong as the pulse beat in the throbbing weal on his cheek.

Simon de Montfort raised his eyes from the pile of parchments and tallies in front of him—paperwork concerned with the war he was preparing to open again in Provence—and stared at Friar Dominic Guzman with ill-concealed irritation. "Did you wish to speak with me?"

The friar scratched his tonsure. Simon noticed a fierce, blotchy rash that welted Guzman's throat and assumed the friar was wearing a hair shirt again.

Guzman interlaced his fingers and bent his thoughtful, sorrowful gaze on Simon. "A brief word, if you please. It was wrong of Friar Bernard to say what he did this afternoon in front of so many young ears. I have spoken to him most strongly, and I hope that will be the end of the matter."

"I have warned him myself," Simon said flatly. "You are right about it being the end of the matter."

Guzman sighed. "Bernard's zeal sometimes carries him further than is wise, but he has a genuine concern for the child's continued defiance, not to mention the persistent use of his left hand."

Simon ceased writing and scowled at Guzman. "Better to let it remain," he said curtly. "If it were just his calligraphy at stake, I would say do your utmost to correct him, but since he is to wield sword and lance, he will perform better by doing what comes to his nature."

Guzman's brown martyr's eyes widened. "You intend him being a soldier, my lord? I thought that under the circumstances, you would want to give him to the church."

"What circumstances?" Simon challenged softly.

"Those of his begetting . . . I think you know what I mean, my lord."

"As far as I'm concerned, Guzman, the child is the rightful heir to the estates of Montvallant, a position he can hardly claim and keep if he takes holy orders." Simon's gaze was bone-chilling. "He is to be given a thorough grounding in the military arts the better to serve God." Reinking the quill, he started scratching at the parchment, indicating that their interview was terminated.

"You will not officially acknowledge him, my lord?" Guzman persisted. It was this dogged aspect of his nature coupled to a diamond-sharp brain and a flair for meticulous detail that made him so invaluable to the papacy as an eliminator of heresy.

"No." Simon did not look up. "I will not." His breath emerged heavily down his nose in a sigh of impatience. "Do you not have work of your own to pursue?"

"Indeed, my lord ... God's work," Guzman replied in a voice as cold as chapel flagstones on a midwinter evening, and left the room in a whisper of musty black robes.

Simon stared at the blot of ink spreading onto the parchment from the quill he had split with the pressure of his grip. He ripped the parchment across and across. Reaching to the wine flagon on the trestle, he was not pleased to discover that his hands were shaking.

CHAPTER THIRTY-ONE

BRIDGET WATCHED HER daughter examining the shepherd boy's swollen knee. Magda's fingers moved quickly and lightly. "The pain is worst here?" she asked, looking at the curly-haired youth.

He nodded, biting his lip.

Magda glanced at her mother for permission, and Bridget nodded. It was only through the experience of touch that Magda would learn to control the healing energy.

Magda closed her eyes and put the tips of her fingers to the core of the shepherd boy's pain. Bridget felt Magda's concentration and knew the moment when the bright river of gold rose in her body and flooded out of her and into the youth. It was too much; Magda did not yet have the fine control. The boy would not be hurt—indeed, it was much to his benefit—but Magda would be drained. Bridget moved to break the contact, but even before she did so, Magda herself disengaged.

Her face was as pale as flour and her hands were trembling. Her gaze, however, was steady and filled with a new understanding. "How do I make it do what I want?" she asked.

"That will come in time. You have to think of a steady, soothing flow, not a river in full spate."

"But I tried to do that."

"Have patience," Bridget said. "You have done very well; I'm proud of you." She gave Magda a kiss, and examined the youth herself. Beneath her gentle probing, he scarcely winced, and she could see that most of the swelling had gone down.

Bridget and Magda shared a meal of pottage and bread with the shepherd lad's family, and accepting more bread and a flask of wine to sustain them on the road, went on their way.

Bridget noted that Magda was still a little pale and subdued and decided not to press too far that day. It was a month since they had left Montségur to travel the mountains, their direction leading them ever more northward toward Toulouse. Bridget knew that it was important for them to go there; again and again she had dreamed of the city spires, of the River Garonne, of Raoul and Simon de Montfort. The dreams were only vague and half-formed, but they were persistent. And Magda had been dreaming again, too. On several occasions before they left Montségur, she had woken screaming in terror from a nightmare about a dark-robed specter hiding in the pines of the mountain slope, a long dagger in its hand. And once, in her sleep, she had sobbed the name *Dominic* as if her heart were breaking.

It had been time to leave Montségur for a short while at least. Once on the road, she and Magda had slept more soundly and been more at peace. The outside world was still a dangerous place, but with Simon de Montfort's fortunes in war at an ebb, it was safer than it had been for several years. Magda had to know that a world of both good and evil lay beyond the boundaries of Montségur.

"Mama, will I ever have a husband and children?" Magda asked, jolting Bridget out of her reverie.

She looked at the child's earnest little face, the bright gray eyes. "If that is what you wish, then surely it will be so," she answered, and smiling, gently smoothed Magda's shining blond hair.

"But you don't have a husband," Magda frowned. "Didn't you want one?"

"Not enough to make it happen," Bridget said, on her guard now.

"What about my father?"

"He was already someone else's husband. I had no right to keep him. One day, when you are older, I will tell you about him."

Magda nodded, a thoughtful, serious expression in her eyes. "I am going to find someone to marry, and I'm going to keep him," she said, with determination.

Bridget sighed, knowing conflict. She hoped that Magda did find a husband, but he would have to be more than special to accept her gifts and the heritage that went with them. And such men were rarer than enlightenment. With the exception of Luke, who came very close, Bridget had yet to meet one.

In the very first glimmer of an autumn morning, Raoul lay on his pallet in the small tent and listened to the growing mélange of sounds as an army came to life. Soldiers on horseback and on foot, knights and squires, archers and arbalesters, oxcarts laden with baggage; all were on the move, heading for the last obstacle between themselves and Toulouse—the ford on the Garonne at Bazacle. Today the city was to be liberated from de Montfort's rule and returned to the governance of its rightful lord.

Raoul touched his lips to his sleeping wife's temple, his eyes bright with desire, although not for her. These days all such urges were channeled into making war on de Montfort, where vigor and passion were permitted and bitterness could be purged on the edge of a sword. For Claire, he dared feel only a grieving compassion.

She was studying hard to become a Cathar Perfect. Frequently her apprenticeship took her away from him to other parts of the camp where she attended meetings and found the companionship of ideas in common. She had spoken to him of drinking from a deep well of tranquillity, and her face had reflected the peace of mind she was tentatively beginning to discover. He did not begrudge her that spiritual grace, but it saddened him to see her drifting ever further from his grasp.

The bond between Claire and Guillaume had never been reestablished either. Claire was ill at ease in the presence of her slender, predatory son, and Guillaume himself had made little attempt to form bridges across the chasm. Indeed, sometimes in defiance, almost as if he resented her presence, he would show off his riding skills and swagger in front of her, imitating the soldiers, knowing how much the Cathars disapproved. She would pretend not to notice, but Raoul would see her eyelids tense and her mouth compress.

He squinted down at her head, which was pillowed on his arm. She had continued to crop her hair, but the luster and rich coppery chestnut color had returned. It still gave him sad pleasure to touch it, but she preferred him not to. Indeed, were it not for the chains of obligation that still bound her to him and the fact that in an army camp it was unsafe for a woman, even a holy one, to sleep alone, he knew that she would not be here in his tent at all.

"Lord Raoul." Mir poked his head through the loose laces of the entrance flap. "I've saddled up the horses." His voice was a loud whisper. A newly cultivated dark mustache and beard were gray with water droplets, for there was a thick river mist enclosing the encampment. "Guillaume's with me."

Raoul nodded and gently set about rousing his wife—but not gently enough. Thrashing wildly, she screamed at him to let her go.

"No, please, no, don't hurt me!" She let out a shriek so piercing and full of terror and pain that it brought Mir back to the tent flap, his eyes round with anxiety. Behind him, unseen, a boy's voice questioned, the sound coming indistinctly as if through a mouthful of food.

"She's dreaming again!" Raoul said over his shoulder. "They're always worst just before she wakens. Claire beloved, you're all right, no one's going to hurt you." He patted her cheek. Mir retreated again and Raoul heard him speaking to Guillaume. Their voices receded. "Claire?" She had ceased to struggle. Gingerly he released her.

Sitting up, she put her head in her hands. "I was shut up in a darkened room," she panted. "And *he* was there with me and *he* said that I had to tell him where you were, and when I said I did not know, *he* . . ." She desisted on a sob.

It was always *he*, never de Montfort, Raoul had noticed, and her nightmares were always about what he had done to her.

Over and again, a hundred different ways, she relived the violation that not even her new faith was strong enough to purge from the unquiet corridors of her inner mind. What chance did Raoul have?

"Is it time?" She made a visible effort to collect herself, wiping her eyes on the back of her hand and sniffing loudly. She forced her mouth to smile.

Raoul avoided her eyes. Some wounds went too deep for words or a touch to heal, each moment of contact trickling blood. "Yes, it's time," he said, a hint of unutterable weariness in his tone.

Through the fog the army of the former Count of Toulouse moved in shadowy formation, row upon row. Armor and harness jingled. Muffled hoofbeats thudded into the soft autumn soil, conversations were brief and whispered. Men from Aragon, from Bigorre and Comminges, marched and rode with the dispossessed of the Toulousain, and astride a dappled gray Andalusian stallion at their head was the most important *faidit* of them all—Raymond of Toulouse.

For the first time since the judgment in Rome of two winters past had gone against him, Raoul saw that his overlord's head was carried high. The glow from Raymond's ruby cabochon thumb ring was reflected in his eyes, albeit that those eyes were now sunken deeper in their sockets and the once fine, smooth skin surrounding them was webbed with wrinkles. Suffering and experience. Raoul knew that Raymond was aware what was and was not possible, the reason he had led this small army by unfrequented roads and crossed rivers at minor fording places rather than using main bridges. It was also the reason he had avoided the towns that were populated by de Montfort's vigilant garrisons, and had waited until his intelligence reports put the hated usuper firmly out of the way on the other side of the Rhône at Crest.

The day Raymond had chosen to enter Toulouse could not have been better. The fog rising from the Garonne and drifting across the land was as thick as a horse blanket, obscuring everything. Raoul could remember other entries into the city in times of peace and war—the heralds, the panoply, the buntings and celebration; wine running in the streets, gold coins showering upon the crowds in display of Raymond's largesse. And now the secretive return, cloaked in silence and fog. Raoul could see from the glow in Raymond's eyes that his blood was singing with triumph, but then Toulouse belonged to the house of Saint-Gilles. The possession was bred into them blood and bone, countless generations deep, and no northern soldier, no matter his expertise and brutality in war, was going to usurp it on the bought word of a meddling priest in Rome.

On this day Toulouse, Raoul thought, tomorrow Montvallant.

Chin propped on his right hand, Dominic used his left to toy with a piece of bread, for he was no longer hungry. Beneath the trestle, Loup waited hopefully for whatever tidbits might come his way, one eye cocked upon his master's swinging legs, the other watching Amice's snappy little terrier for any treacherous sudden moves.

The Château Narbonnais was gloomy even in the fierce clarity of high summer. In late autumn when the whole of the city was swallowed in a grainy, thick fog, it was unutterably damp and dark; even covered by tapestries, the walls seemed to ooze depression.

From the corner of his eye Dominic watched the lady Alais dab at her mouth with a snowy napkin and reach to her goblet. On her long, elegant fingers, rings twinkled in the candlelight. Her lips were pursed as if pulled tightly together by a drawstring, and she was glowering at him. Guiltily he stopped swinging his legs and removed his hand from the bread, knowing that she abhorred bad manners and fidgeting. It was very difficult to sit still knowing that as soon as the household had finished breaking fast, he was due to attend weapons practice, something that he enjoyed immensely. He was allowed to use his left hand, and was proving so adept that he was almost as good as Sim, who was a full four years older. Sir Henri Lemagne, the knight who tutored him, professed himself exceedingly pleased with Dominic's progress, and had promised that if his skills continued apace until Christmas, he could start practicing with a proper steel sword after the festival.

Following weapons practice came lessons with Friar Bernard, but even these were tolerable now. Since the incident with the slate in the springtime, the priest had kept a rein on his tongue and his stick. Only once had Dominic been thrashed—for putting a ladder snake in Friar Bernard's hat following a lesson about the serpent in Eden. It had been worth it just to see the look of sheer horror on his tutor's cadaverous features. Dominic smiled at the memory and his fingers crept out to play with the bread again.

Beside him, ten-year-old Sim suddenly tugged on his sleeve. "Listen, what's that noise? It sounds like fighting." His light hazel eyes were full of alert curiosity, but no fear.

Dominic raised his head and looked at the door. Everyone in the hall had stopped eating now. The sounds came vaguely, but once noticed, they could not be ignored. Not just the everyday shout and rattle of men at drill, but the wilder, higher clamor of battle and of a mob.

He saw Alais clutch at the jeweled cross that hung from her neck on a broad, gold chain. She commanded a knight to go outside and see what was happening.

The man had not even risen from the trestle when her inquiry was answered with terse brutality by Nicholas de Riems, a knight billeted in the town, who staggered into the hall and half-collapsed, half-knelt at her feet. Blood welled from an ugly cut on his cheek, and his sword hand was lacerated to the bone.

"Madam, grave news. Raymond of Toulouse has invaded the city with an army of *faidits* and the people have risen to greet him. We have been overwhelmed . . . destroyed."

Alais swallowed. Her face had gone as white as her napkin. "And the château?" she asked through lips that barely moved to encompass the words.

"Safe for the moment, madam; we can hold out against them here, but the city is lost. You must send to Lord Simon immediately."

Eyes flashing, she drew herself up. "I know what I must do. Do not presume to lecture me!" She concealed her trembling hands in the folds of her gown and tightened her jaw until the tendons in her throat stood out like drawbridge pulleys.

"Madam, they came at us through the fog. The first we knew of their arrival was the moment they were upon us."

Alais made an impatient sound and turned away to snap her

fingers at a scribe who was still holding a piece of bread, one cheek bulging in arrested mastication. "Fetch quill and parchment!" she ordered. "Henri, find me some messengers! I'll not be held to ransom by a heretic rabble!" Her eyes narrowed. Hastily Dominic avoided their sweeping glare.

"My lord will come," she said, her voice low and furious. "And then we shall see once and for all who is the master of Toulouse."

CHAPTER THIRTY-TWO

MASSIVE AND THREATENING, the siege machine known as "The Cat" towered against the burning blue of the summer sky like a creature from The Revelation. Its lair was the carpenter's compound of the Château Narbonnais, and it had been designed for the sole purpose of battering a breach in Toulouse's eastern city wall.

The core of The Cat was an enormous tree trunk rigged up in a pair of uprights, with crossbeams on top of each pair. The trunk was slung on ropes from the crossbeams and between the uprights. One end of it had been sharpened to a point and reinforced with iron plates. The entire contraption was contained within the ribs of a wooden shed with an upper housing to hold the archers. Its roof was thatched with green hides to protect the men who would have to work for hours on end, thrusting the iron head against the stones in the city wall. The carpenters had nicknamed it "Lord Simon's prick," a title they kept to themselves in view of de Montfort's current unstable temperament.

For nine months Toulouse had resisted Lord Simon, and he

was scarcely any closer to breaching the city defenses than he had been at the beginning. His only good fortune was that the Château Narbonnais remained in his hands, and because of its position, had open access to the outside world. Toulouse was still *virgo intacta*, and Simon's frustration was undermining his judgment.

On this particular August morning, Simon, his advisers, and his adjutants were inspecting the siege machine after its final fettling. Dominic and Sim were present, too, having unofficially attached themselves to the group, but they stayed well out of their elders' way.

Simon and his adjutants gave The Cat a thorough examination, then went to look at another siege machine across the compound. When they had gone, Dominic stepped curiously inside the wooden housing of The Cat and tried to imagine himself as a soldier working it. The smell of new wood and untanned hides was so powerful that it almost cut off his breath. He sat down on the oak trunk, then bounced on it several times.

"Will this really break down the wall?" he asked the older boy, who was exploring the machine as gravely as the adults had done.

"Papa says so."

Dominic looked doubtful. He had been brought up to regard Lord Simon's will as law, and until recently, had looked upon him with the awe that he knew should be reserved for God. Then, last month, a trebuchet stone had crashed into the chapel of the Château Narbonnais while they were at mass, killing one of the cardinal legate's chaplains. Dominic had been standing near the man; indeed a moment earlier he had been kneeling at his feet and would have joined him in death if the stone had smashed through a fraction sooner. The immediacy of death, the bright splash of blood, the dust of fallen masonry hanging in the sunshine—these things held far more weight than the count's command. He had learned to dread the *whump* of the counterweight, the pause, and then the heavy crash of the stone missile against its target.

"Dom, stop bouncing!" the older boy said impatiently. "If you don't behave, you'll be sent back to the women. Look, do you understand why the head is tipped with iron?"

"Course I do!" Dominic sniffed scornfully. "If it was wood alone, it would just splinter against the walls!" He jumped off the trunk, his nose wrinkling. "It stinks in here," he said, and ran back outside.

One of the carpenters, a rough, jovial man, winked at Dominic and offered him a drink of wine from his skin. "What do you think of it then, lad? Will it broach a hole in the heretics' wall?" His eyes flashed with laughter and an innuendo that was beyond Dominic's comprehension, but not that of the other men, who erupted into bawdy guffaws.

"It's very big," Dominic said politely, and the men's mirth became uproarious. Dominic laughed with them, although he did not understand why. Then he ran across the compound to where a lean, wiry-coated hound was dozing in the shade. Loup raised his head from his white forepaws, stretched, and trotted over to nuzzle his young master. Dominic made a fuss of him, and seeing that no one was watching, decided to escape for a while. Loup needed a run, and on a fine day like this, Dominic could not bear the thought of returning to the gloomy darkness of the women's rooms in the château and the tongues sharp as needles with anxiety and bad temper. Untethering his pony, he mounted up, told the groom that he was going home, and set off in that direction. As soon as he was out of sight, however, he doubled back and trotted his small cob in the direction of the river, Loup moving springily at the pony's heels.

Claire gently wiped the brow of the heavily pregnant woman and gave her a few sips from the cup of water a passerby had fetched.

"You should not be working so hard in this heat with your time so close," she admonished. "It is small wonder that you fainted."

"I'm all right, m'lady, truly. Just give me a minute and I'll be back on my feet. The men have to eat."

Claire glanced at the laden baskets of food that the woman had been delivering to the soldiers on duty at the city walls. This was probably her third or fourth journey thus encumbered, and it was obvious to Claire that she could not continue. She was not young. Her congested face wore the lines of early middle age, and the frizzy hair escaping her wimple was more gray than black. "No, you must rest or you will do yourself and the babe a lasting harm. Let me take the baskets up to the men. Isabelle will see you home and cared for." She gestured at her maid.

"Thank you, my lady, God bless you." The woman pressed Claire's hand between her own. "My man's in charge of the stone thrower near the Montoulieu gate; his name's Isarn. There's wine and bread and meat pasties for him and his team in the left basket. Tell him I'm all right.

"I will." Claire patted the woman's arm and picked up both baskets. The entire town was determined to hold out against de Montfort, and to that end everyone from the smallest child to the frailest octogenarian was doing his part to help. Claire's main task thus far had been tending the sick and the wounded, although she had also carried supplies to the walls and run messages. She kept herself as busy as possible, and when she was not busy, she prayed, but her ghosts still hovered, awaiting their moment.

The sun scorched down and her body prickled with sweat inside her shift and heavy Cathar robe as she climbed toward the trebuchet posts on the eastern city wall by the Montoulieu gate. Small wonder that the pregnant townswoman had collapsed. Perhaps they were in for an early thunderstorm. A glance at the sky filled her vision with a fierce, clear blue, and because she was not looking where she was going, she stumbled.

"Careful, mistress," a soldier said gruffly, and grabbed her arm to steady her.

Claire thanked him but quickly freed herself from his grasp. Ever since de Montfort's violation of her body, she disliked to be touched, even in concern and courtesy. He was small and wiry with twinkling brown eyes and a dark beard salted with gray. Sweat gleamed in the creases of his throat and trickled down his naked chest.

"I'm looking for someone called Isarn," she said as she regained her balance and her breath.

"Then look no further!" He took her arm again, but only to steer her aside from a pulley load of rocks that two panting laborers were securing and unloading. "Ammunition for the old girl." Fondly he patted the huge trebuchet. "There ain't much left of anyone she kisses!" Then he noticed the Cathar robes and sobered. "I know you don't hold with killing, but I can't say I'm sorry to send any of them bastards to hell!"

"We don't believe in hell either," she said gently, and indicated the basket. "Your wife sent provisions for you and the men. She was suffering in the heat, so I sent her home to rest."

"That's my Garsenda, all right. She'll work until she drops. I've told her meself to slow down, but she'll not heed me. Her first man was killed by de Montfort's lot a few years ago. Hates 'em, she does." He wiped his hands on his filthy chausses and, stooping to the basket, grabbed a pasty.

Claire said nothing. Learning not to hate, not to fear, were the most difficult lessons of her new religion—too difficult at the moment for her to surmount.

"So where do the wicked go if not to hell?" Isarn asked as his men gathered round to plunder their share from the basket.

"Into another human or animal body so that they may work out their sin in another life. Those that come to understanding become pure souls, no longer enslaved by matter and the God of matter."

Isarn chewed thoughtfully. His eyes gleamed. "So one day Simon de Montfort might become a worm feeding upon his own former body?"

"It is possible." Claire tried to match his lightness with a smile, but she could not. Even the mention of the name made her feel nauseated.

"I've offended you now."

She shook her head. "It's not that. Do you mind if I have some of your wine?"

"Help yourself."

Gratefully Claire unstoppered one of the skins and took several swallows. Her panic subsided and she was able to thank him in a more natural tone. Putting the flask down, she reached for the other basket, which had still to be delivered farther along the ramparts. She was just taking its weight when Isarn forgot that she was a Cathar and a woman, forgot everything but the sight of what was advancing on them from the camp around the Château Narbonnais.

"God's bleeding eyes!" He showered out a mouthful of half-chewed meat and pastry. "What the hell's that!"

His companions came running, and leaned over the walls to look, exclaiming as colorfully as their captain. Abandoning the basket, Claire ran to the parapet and stared at the huge siege engine that was rolling ponderously toward their section of wall. It consisted of a wooden housing covered with iron plates and thatched with raw hides, and seemed almost to be moving of its own accord, for the men propelling it forward were concealed within its bowels.

"The whoreson, it's a Cat! Helias, Rob, help me load Le Catin!" Wiping his mouth on the back of his hand, Isarn thrust past Claire to the trebuchet, muttering the word *bastard* under his breath in a continuous litany.

The enormous ram crept nearer to the walls. Rooted to the ground, Claire watched it approach. Riding behind it was a man on a white stallion. He was wearing his battle helm, three red plumes tossing on its crest, and he was surrounded by a host of adjutants and squires, but she would have known him anywhere. Her belly heaved and she clapped her hand to her mouth. Something dark swished past her head and thrummed into the wooden structure of the trebuchet. The sky overhead was suddenly dark and there was a noise like a hundred birds in flight. She was seized from behind and, in the sweaty grip of one of the laborers, was dragged down to the wooden flooring upon which the trebuchet stood.

"Ware arrows, my lady!" he yelled.

Claire lay too winded and shocked to move. The laborer crouch-ran to the trebuchet and began turning the windlass frantically to lower the sling on the long end and wedge it so that Isarn and Helias could load it with a rock.

"All right, Rob, let her go!" Isarn bellowed. The wedge was knocked out of the fastening on the arm, the counterweight smacked down, and the loaded long end whipped through the arc of a circle, flinging the stone missile with great force out toward the enemy. It fell short, landing with a loud thud. All along the town wall other trebuchets fired, but were not close enough to do anything but threaten. The Cat continued to creep toward the ditches, closer and closer, while the arrows whirred overhead. Claire huddled on the ground, sick with terror.

Around her the men were working feverishly to reload the trebuchet. The smell of hot stone dust and tarred wood overpowered the air. Again a stone was launched and again came the groans of disappointment. Isarn's voice was hoarse as he directed his crew to reload. The weight came down and was pegged. Into the sling went the stone.

"Wait for it, lads, wait for it. . . ." Isarn raised his arm. An arrow burned past his boiled leather pot helm and he swore through his teeth. "Now, *now!*" he shrieked, his arm chopping down. Out came the peg, down slammed the counterweight, over the wall sailed the huge stone. This time a different, crunching, splintering sound hit their ears. Isarn ran to the wall and peered over. A massive cheer went up from the trebuchet crews on either side of Le Catin.

"It's a hit!" bellowed Helias, capering around the stone-thrower and hugging the other men. "Up yours, Montfort! Up your arse!" He gestured eloquently. All along the wall soldiers jeered and gesticulated at the crusaders below and the broken Cat. The trunk itself had not sustained any damage, but part of the housing had been crushed and some of the supporting ropes had snapped. A soldier was carried out of the housing, his leg badly mangled. Slowly, like a wounded wild beast, the siege engine was withdrawn under a final sally of arrow fire.

Isarn and his crew sat down upon their trebuchet, all talking at once and capping jest with jest as they gave release to their tensions. Claire shakily stood up. Her knees were weak and she still felt sick. She dared not look over the wall lest she glimpse the man on the white stallion.

"Hey," said Isarn, frowning. "You're as white as my wife's new-washed linen. Have some more wine."

Claire shook her head and picked up the second basket. "No, I'm all right, and I'll be better if I give myself something to do. Besides, until I arrive, your friends have nothing with which to toast your victory." She found a genuine smile for him and moved off along the wall, stepping over the arrows littering the ground like so many dead twigs. As she walked, she timed her footsteps to the mental chanting of a prayer, and gradually her fear of de Montfort faded to a dull but persistent niggle like a rotten tooth.

* * *

Absorbed within himself, Dominic rode much farther from the château than was wise or than he had intended, but when he realized his folly and made to turn back, he discovered that he had lost Loup. Shouting and whistling brought no results, and the confidence of his voice had started to waver and develop an edge of panic when he heard a whine from a clump of reeds and sedge close to the water's edge. Urging his pony forward, he saw a movement among the tall stems. He also thought he heard a voice, and his hand went to the small eating dagger at his belt.

"Who's there?" he demanded, trying to make his voice as deep and assertive as Lord Simon's.

There was a long hesitation during which his hand tightened on the hilt of the dagger. He had even started to ease it from its sheath when a girl of about his own age rose up from the rushes and faced him. Loup was with her. Her hand rested lightly on his collar, but the dog was making no effort to free himself. Indeed, he had that almost smug expression on his canine face that usually meant he had managed to get the better of Amice's nasty little lap dog.

"Who are you?" Dominic demanded, rude because he had been frightened.

"Magda," she answered simply, as if that were explanation enough, and tossed her hair away from her face. It was as pale as moonlight, the color that Alais's women were always trying to achieve out of an alchemist's bottle, with varying shades of disaster. Her eyes were a clear, bright gray, and her skin golden from the summer sun.

"What are you doing with my dog?"

"He had a thorn in his paw, so I drew it out for him." She smiled. Her front teeth were missing and river mud bedaubed one cheek and the front of her gown, giving her a waifish quality.

"Loup would never let a stranger do that!" Dominic dismounted and clicked his fingers, summoning his pet.

"He let me," She patted the dog and released his collar. Loup licked her hand and lingered at her side, and she had to use her voice and point before he would return to his master.

Dominic felt betrayed. Loup's loyalty had always been singularly for him. "What are you doing here?" he challenged, jaw thrusting in a fair imitation of Lord Simon's.

"Helping my mother pick herbs. These marsh marigolds have more flowers on this side of the river." She showed him a basket filled with an assortment of plants. "Why are you so angry?"

Dominic scowled. "I'm not."

She gave him a clear, steady look, and he dropped his gaze and scuffed his toes on the ground, color burning his face. Loup pushed his moist muzzle into his hand, but he ignored the treacherous hound. When he looked up again, his eye was caught by a dark, oblongish shape half-concealed among the rushes, which he suddenly realized was a small boat.

"You're from the rebels, aren't you?"

Her poise slipped and she looked quickly over her shoulder as if searching for someone.

"Are you a heretic?"

She faced him again, her shoulders tense. "I am not a Catholic if that is what you mean," she said with dignity.

"Friar Dominic burns heretics," he said. "I'm named after him."

Although the words might have been construed as a threat, the girl did not take them as such, and the tension actually left her body, as if whatever danger there was had passed. "So your name is Dominic," she said, and when he did not answer, scooped her hair behind her ears and set about plucking some more stems of marsh marigold. "Do you want to help me?"

Dominic hesitated. The proud, masculine side of his nature, affronted by her easy mastery of Loup, wanted to say something scornful and ride away. His reasoning mind and his imagination bade him override his hostility and remain. He had never spoken to a real heretic before, and with her silver hair, river-gray eyes, and delicate features, she reminded him of a half-elven, half-human creature from one of the tales of the romances. "All right," he said gruffly. "What do I have to do?"

She showed him. Gradually the hostility melted into a companionable silence, curiously adult in its quality. The pony grazed. Loup explored the reed beds, startling a heron into heavy flight and ruffling a family of grebes. He splashed in the shallows, sending up silver sprays of water, and shook himself unsociably close to the children so that they winced away, arms upheld, and broke into the common bond of laughter.

"What sort of dog is he?" Magda brushed water droplets from her gown.

"I don't know, a mongrel. Sim says he's got wolf blood, so that's how he got his name. They were going to drown him, but the count let me keep him."

"Who's Sim?"

"Simon, Lord de Montfort's son. He's older than me and he bosses me a bit, but we're friends really."

"Do you live with him, then?"

"Yes."

Magda gave him a searching look, for there was a wealth of meaning in that one quietly spoken word. Several questions hesitated on the tip of her tongue, kept there by the knowledge that it was probably not polite to ask them. She could have used her mental abilities to divine some of the answers, but that would hardly be fair and certainly less interesting.

"They say de Montfort's my father, too." Dominic peeled away the green outer casing of a reed stem, his movements jerky.

"Do you believe them?"

He shrugged and started shredding the white pith with his thumbnail. "I suppose so. Sometimes they tell me that my father is a southern noble, a *faidit*, and that his lands really belong to me, but I know they're lying. Lord Simon took me to see his castle once, at a place called Montvallant. The people stood in silence when we rode past and then they spat in our dust. Lord Simon had the ringleaders hanged, but it made no difference to what they thought." He tossed the reed aside, his brows drawn down in a frown. "I'm like Loup, a misfit."

"No," said another voice, gentle and adult. "You are yourself, and that is your strength."

Dominic turned round quickly and found himself looking up at a slender black-haired woman with the same crystal-gray eyes as the girl. In her hand was a large, shallow basket full of plants, and her gown was kilted to midcalf, the hem dark with moisture.

"Mama, I've found a friend; his name's Dominic, and his dog's called Loup. We've picked all these for you." Magda showed her mother the fruits of their efforts.

"You have been working hard, both of you." The woman smiled. Dominic felt as if he were being pulled inside out and examined piece by little piece. For a moment he resisted, then changed his mind and opened himself to her stare. It was not cold like the Lady Alais's, but encompassing and warm. Around her he thought he perceived a faint glow, and around Magda, too, and then he was drawn into it. It was extremely pleasant, like basking in sunshine. He sensed approval from the older woman, something very rarely meted out to him at the château, and he felt himself stretching and expanding to absorb it. But then there was a sudden disturbance in the golden field. Turning his head, Dominic saw a horseman riding toward them, his own halo a murky black with pulsing red edges.

The moment was broken and the sensations of pleasure and contentment vanished.

"Mama, who is that?" Magda pointed toward the rider.

"It is the Lord Simon," Dominic said dully. "Probably he's come looking for me. I'll be in trouble now."

"No, he is seeking solitude." Bridget bit her lip as all the rage, pain, frustration, and hatred engulfed her in a fetid miasma.

"Look at his life force." Magda shuddered. "It's horrible. . . . Why can I see death?"

Dominic began to feel sick and cold. The jagged, murky glow still surrounded the count. Loup was growling, his hackles standing on end.

"Quickly, Magda, go to the boat!" Bridget gave her daughter a push.

"Mama . . ."

"Go!" Bridget cried urgently, and as Magda raised her skirts to her knees and hurried to their small craft, Bridget stood beside Dominic and faced the brooding, dreadful darkness of his father. A brief glance showed her that the boy's aura remained steady and confident. He was apprehensive, but he did not fear the approaching man, and that was all to the good.

De Montfort saw them, recognized Dominic, and put his already blowing horse into a renewed gallop. Dominic took a single step back and then stood his ground, his shoulders square and straight, his face as taut as the skin across a shield.

"What in the name of Christ's ten toes are you doing here!"

Simon demanded huskily, and drew rein bare inches from Dominic and Bridget. Foam spattered from the bit hinges and the stallion sidled, rolling its eyes. Simon's face was dark with the temper that was swelling up in him like rapidly proving bread.

"I brought Loup out for some exercise, sir," Dominic said. Behind his back, his hands were clenched one upon the other, squeezing tightly.

"That was not what you told the grooms at the carpenter's compound!"

"I . . . I changed my mind."

"By the rood, I should have let Friar Bernard have his will with you!" Simon maneuvered the horse closer and leaned down from the saddle to grab Dominic's arm. As his fingertips closed, Loup attacked, snarling ferociously. His teeth sank into the count's hand, puncturing skin, drawing blood. Simon's rage erupted at this final insubordination. His sword rasped from the scabbard, and the yard-long blade dazzled in the sun.

"No!" Dominic shrieked, and protected Loup with his own body. Simon reversed the weapon, intending to club the boy away from the dog, but suddenly cried out in pain. His fingers opened and the sword slid over the stallion's withers and flashed in the grass. Gasping, Simon clutched his wrist, and Dominic saw agony writhe across his face. He lost control of the horse. Rearing, it threw him, and as Simon struck the ground at Dominic's feet with a solid thud, the stallion galloped away in the direction of the château as though it were morning-fresh and had not been pushed for half the day.

Simon threshed on the ground, clutching at his midriff. Bridget stood over him. "What you give to others has been turned back upon yourself," she said with icy calm. "It will destroy you unless you stop what you are doing now and seek the Light."

"Who are you?" Simon gasped through clenched teeth, his body shaking.

Bridget tossed her head. "Who am I? Do you not recognize the radiant illuminatrix in all beings?" The light danced all around her, lifting the ends of her hair, gilding her. "I am Bridget, of the line of the Magdalene and the blessed Queen of

Heaven." Simon's eyes widened. Then he cried out again. His body writhed and was still.

"Mama!" Magda emerged from the boat and ran to clutch her mother, the tears running down her face. Bridget put her arms around her daughter, but her gaze remained somberly on the unconscious man. His aura was still murky, but the most destructive flashes had drained away, channeled through his own body.

"Is he dead?" Dominic asked, his face flour-pale, eyes huge.

"No, just stunned. When he wakes up he'll remember nothing of this." Bridget freed one hand to set it comfortingly upon Dominic's shoulder. He felt a pleasant tingling, and the rapid pounding of his heart subsided.

"Best, I think, if we go and you let his grooms find him. They'll think he took a fall from his horse . . . and so will he."

"Are you sure he won't remember?" Dominic looked at her anxiously. "What if he knows that Loup bit him?"

"He won't. Do you trust me?"

Dominic bit his lip. His glance flickered toward Magda and he nodded slowly. "Yes."

She brushed the damp black hair off his forehead in a gesture that was almost maternal. "And it is not something given lightly, I see," she murmured. "Go now, quickly."

Feeling disoriented, slightly dizzy, Dominic went to his peacefully cropping pony. Simon twitched and groaned and he made haste to mount. Magda and her mother were already in their boat and rowing toward the other side. The girl raised her hand in farewell, and Dominic responded before whistling Loup to heel and setting off at a gallop to meet the grooms whom he could just see on the horizon.

Bridget ceased pounding herbs and grease into ointment in her mortar and looked at her daughter with troubled eyes. Magda's bright nature had been subdued of late, and frequently her face wore a distant expression.

"You were dreaming again last night," Bridget said, touching Magda's arm. "Was it the same one as before?"

Magda shook her head and, swiftly glancing at her mother, continued to strip the leaves from the plants they had gathered.

"Then what?"

The child bit her soft underlip. "I don't remember, except that I was hurting here so badly that I couldn't breathe." She fanned her hands over her belly, in the space between her navel and the juncture of her thighs. "It was at Montségur, though, and the presence was there." She gave a little shiver, and one hand left her stomach and traveled to the reassurance of the dove and chalice medallion she wore around her neck.

Bridget resumed pounding the ointment, a frown troubling her brow. She, too, had dreamed recently of Montségur. Magda had been lying upon a pallet as still as death, and for the first time, Bridget had felt the presence, too—the dark, hollow hunger of an unbalanced mind. She had tried to reach Magda and protect her from its searching greed, but found herself powerless. Instead, it was a black-haired young man who had stepped forward and offered himself as a shield.

And today they had encountered Simon de Montfort's bastard son, begotten upon Claire de Montvallant—a black-haired child with an aura as powerful as his father's, but clear and pure and fierce. She suspected that his fate was closely interwoven with Magda's, that he was the reason they had been drawn to Toulouse. But the threads of life and death were so narrowly blended in this instance that she could not separate one from the other.

Concussed, head bandaged, limping from a twisted ankle, Simon refused to do as his physicians suggested and remain abed. Alais had no better success, and when Simon threatened to convince her of his determination with his fist, she abandoned him to his temper. He stumped around the carpenter's compound, swearing at all and sundry, kicking at tools and pieces of wood, and reviling the workmen when they told him that the damage to The Cat and the extra strengthening that he required to its structure would take them at least ten days to make good.

At first Dominic was frightened that Simon would remember what had happened on the banks of the Garonne, that he would connect the healing marks of a bite on his hand with Loup, but the heretic woman had been right; Simon remembered nothing, or nothing but his hatred. Sometimes Dominic would see it, a dull, red-edged cloud, eating into him, destroying balance and judgment. On those occasions he avoided Simon altogether if he could. Indeed, most of the time he made himself quiet and scarce, hoping to be overlooked, and most of the time he succeeded. The times he did not, he set himself to a stoic endurance.

As the great Cat grew closer to restoration, so did the murky cloud enveloping the count's being.

CHAPTER THIRTY-THREE

"SOMETHING HAS GOT to be done about that siege machine." Rai glared at the long loaf of bread in front of him as though it were the offending article. "He's serious about reinforcing it, and we can't depend on another hit like the last one."

Since his arrival from Provence, Rai had taken over the command of military operations in Toulouse from his father. He had the youth and vigor that Raymond lacked, and a far better grasp of warfare. A signal brought his youngest squire, Raoul's son, Guillaume, hastening to refill his cup and take away what was left of the meal.

"How long have we got?" Roger of Foix leaned on his folded elbows.

"A couple of days at most. I don't want him getting any closer to the Montoulieu gate than he did last week . . . and that was too close." Rai's dark gaze crossed the room and sought a seasoned blue one. "Raoul, you're the most experienced at quick in-and-out fighting. Will you command a raid?"

"Willingly, my lord." Raoul rose from his bench to look at the plans laid out on the trestle.

Drawing his meat dagger, Rai used it as a pointer. "We have to break into the carpenter's compound here, preferably when as few people as possible are about."

"Morning mass, then."

"Ideal."

Raoul nodded. "A decoy attack just before the main one to draw off the guards would be useful."

"Leave that to me," said Bernard de Cazenac with a wolfish grin.

Raoul returned his grin, and then added to Rai, "I'll need some pots of Greek fire and some tar-soaked brands. That thing has to be set alight in the shortest time possible. We dare not linger."

"Whatever you need is yours," Rai confirmed. "I'll let you organize it, just keep me abreast of the details." Looking round, he stretched his arms above his head. "Any other business? Otherwise I'm for my bed." Which was currently filled by a luscious merchant's daughter, and Rai could not be blamed for wanting to retire early. No one thought the most recent letter from Pope Honorious worth mentioning. It was a whining admonition with neither the power nor the conviction to move any of the gathered men beyond a cynical shrug.

When Raoul departed, Guillaume held his horse for him while he mounted.

"Does Lord Rai keep you on your toes?" Raoul asked his son with a smile.

The boy responded with a good-natured grimace. "He works me to the bone."

"What else are squires for?" Raoul laughed. It had not really surprised him when Rai had offered to take Guillaume into his household to train to arms. The Raymonds owed the Montvallants a debt for their unwavering support, a debt that could hardly be repaid in money or land given present circumstances, and so Guillaume had been favored with a knighthood apprenticeship in Rai's own mesnie.

Guillaume returned the laugh. "I'm not really complaining. I'd rather have a lot to do and people around me all the time."

Rather than what? Raoul wondered as he gathered the reins.

Rather than enduring the strained silence between parents who had grown so far apart that they could no longer even look each other in the eye?

"Good luck with The Cat," Guillaume said.

Raoul saw through the boy's smile to the underlying anxiety. "Watch for the smoke." He grinned, and tousled the sleek blond hair.

Isarn's wife, Garsenda, groaned and writhed on her pallet in the throes of another fierce labor contraction. Moistening the woman's lips with a sponge soaked in watered wine, Claire wished that the midwife would hasten back from attending another patient. It seemed that every pregnant woman in Toulouse had decided to have her baby tonight. Claire had been summoned from her slumber to this particular bedside because the midwife could not be in ten places at once, and Garsenda, remembering Claire from the previous week when she had helped her in the street, had asked for her.

Raoul had not returned from his military briefing when she left the house in response to the summons. She knew that he was going on a raid at dawn and was worried about him. For all the differences between them, for all the heartache, she still loved him and would have liked to wish him the talisman of walking in the Light.

"Ah . . . ah!" groaned Garsenda. "I want to push!" Naked, she crouched on all fours on the bed, gray hair hanging down, sweat rolling off her unwieldy bulk. The thought of Raoul slipped from Claire's mind, and she gave all her attention to the laboring woman, wishing again vehemently that the midwife would return. Bearing two children was not the same as delivering one, but it was rapidly becoming obvious that she had no choice.

Garsenda gasped and wailed aloud to God and the saints to help her, and in the next breath swore the vilest blasphemies against those to whom she had just been pleading. The mucus-wet crown of the baby's head started to bulge at the entrance of the birth passage, and Claire had no time to panic. "You must pant," she commanded Garsenda firmly, "or else you will tear yourself!"

Garsenda sobbed and swore, but withheld from pushing

down too hard. Claire bent over her and, with a moistened cloth, cleaned the baby's face as it was born. On the next contraction, amid a gush of fluid, blood, and slime, the infant slipped out onto the bedstraw, a bluish-red bedraggled scrap, as wrinkled as one of last season's apples.

"Is it all right, my lady? What is it, a boy or a girl, what is it?" Garsenda cried, and collapsed on her side, her slack belly wobbling like a mound of tripe.

The infant wailed lustily, arms and legs thrashing like windmill sails, the cord still attached and pulsing. The sound echoed in Claire's head. "A boy," she heard herself say. "And he's perfect." Where had she heard those words before? Alais de Montfort with malice in her eyes.

"Let me have him, oh, let me have him, he's so beautiful!" Garsenda's plump arms stretched out, her pain already relegated to the back of her mind, tears of joy streaming down her face, mingling with the sweat of her travail. She took the baby onto her breast, crooning in absorption to the slippery, blood-streaked little body.

A new soul trapped in flesh, Claire thought, but the feeling of weepiness did not stem from that, but from her own aching loss. She had never been able to grieve for the child conceived upon her in rape and taken away the instant that the cord was cut. The wound remained open, festering. Sometimes her dreams were haunted by a crying baby like this one. On other occasions he was a little boy, laughing and dark-haired, dressed in the black robes of a preaching friar, a skull in one hand and a burning torch in the other. She woke from those nightmares screaming hysterically.

The midwife returned in time to deliver and examine the afterbirth, and hear Garsenda's praise for Claire.

"I couldn't have done it without you, my lady," Garsenda declared stoutly, and smoothed a gentle forefinger over the baby's soft, damp hair. "My Isarn's on watch until prime. Will you take him a bite to eat and give him the good tidings? He'll be so proud!" She put her new son to her breast, cradling him tenderly, creating a new bond to replace that of the cut umbilical cord.

Swallowing on tears, Claire busied herself preparing a basket of provisions to take to the men—bread, olives, cheese, and wine. She was glad to perform the task, for she knew that if she went home, it would only be to worry about Raoul or to fall asleep and endure the attack of nightmares that would begin the moment she closed her eyes.

When she stepped into the street and closed the door behind her, the sky was paling toward dawn over the suburb of Saint Cyprien. People were stirring from their beds—those who had not been on night watch. The smell of fresh bread filled the air, and on the walls and among the dunghills the cockerels crowed, vying with each other. It was the hour of stillness before the streets filled with the rumble and bustle of activity, both military and domestic. Claire slowed her walk to suit the atmosphere, taking advantage of the cool half light as she strolled toward the Montoulieu gate.

It was then that all hell broke loose.

Raoul gave de Cazenac five minutes to draw off the guards with his attack on de Montfort's camp, then led his own assault upon the carpenter's compound.

While the soldiers posted around The Cat had not been expecting an attack, they rallied rapidly and put up a spirited resistance. Raoul realized after the first vicious exchange of blows that here were no raw, expendable troops, but handpicked professionals, nursemaiding their commander's last hope of conquering the city. It was still half-dark, hard to judge when to strike and when to duck, or identify whether it was ally or enemy who screamed in sudden pain. Raoul was surrounded by fighting, confusion, and the blaze of torches. From his eye corner he saw Mir lob two clay bombs of Greek fire at the giant Cat. One missed and burst like a fiery marigold on the compound floor. The other hit the green hides and cracked open. As its volatile burden dripped in shreds of silver flame down the side of The Cat, Raoul cut beneath his enemy's guard, leaped over the falling soldier, and ran to help Mir. Seizing a pitch-soaked torch, he hurled it into the open mouth of The Cat where the tree trunk protruded like a tongue.

The sun burst over the horizon and leached the color from the flames, giving it instead to mail and surcoats, to wood and stone and steel. "*À Montfort! À Montfort!*" came the furious rallying cry, and crusaders started to pour into the compound from the camp around the château.

"Sound the retreat!" Raoul bellowed at Giles, who was carrying the horn, aware that they could not hope to hold off the full tide of the counterattack. Fighting hard, they backed toward the safety of the Montoulieu gate. When they reached the defensive ditches before the walls, the trebuchets began to fire into the northern troops, and arbalest bolts whizzed overhead, proving a hazard to both sides.

Raoul slashed and thrust and struck, all the time backing slowly toward the safety of the gate. He was challenged by a heavyset knight who kept bellowing, *"À Montfort!"* through the slits in his helm to rally and direct the crusaders. One of Simon's senior battle commanders, Raoul surmised through the roaring of blood in his ears and the harsh draw and release of breath as he continued to back away. The heavyset knight pursued him grimly. Smoke gouted from the direction of the siege machines, blinding and choking, spangled with heat. Raoul almost lost his sword to a twisting motion made by the knight, but recovered and retorted. An arbalest bolt whined past his helm and sank into his opponent's upper arm. Crying out, the knight buckled to his knees and Raoul raised his sword on high to finish him, only to find himself violently engaged by another warrior who had forced himself forward out of the northern melee. This time there was no doubting his identity. Three red plumes danced on the crest of the helm, and the fork-tailed lion snarled across his shield, claws unsheathed, and Raoul looked upon the image of death.

As the light brightened with the dawn, Claire stood beside Le Catin on the wall at the Montoulieu gate, her view of the fighting clear. She saw the bursts of flame explode on The Cat and flare upon the barricades protecting it.

"Look at 'em." Isarn smacked the wall. "We've stirred up a regular ants' nest! Go on, lads, show 'em who's master here!" His eyes were dark-rimmed for want of sleep, for he had been on duty all night, but his grin was white and savage before his lips closed around the neck of the wine flask she had brought him.

"My husband is down there," Claire murmured, hands

clasped so hard that the knuckles were bone-white. "He was coordinating the raid."

Isarn's gaze turned to her and softened. "He's a right brave man, my lady."

Claire looked down at the wall, knowing that he would not understand if she tried to explain. Raoul was running away from his ghosts, as surely as she ran from hers.

"Look sharp, lads!" yelled Helias. "Here comes the counterattack!" He stood by the peg on the windlass as the crusaders began pouring into the compound. Arbalesters ran to man the walls either side of Le Catin and aimed their fire as best they could.

The area below became a confusion of struggling men—the knights in mail and brightly dyed surcoats, the ordinary soldiers in leather hauberks and padded gambesons. Weapons clashed amid a cacophony of shouts and screams. Along the walls the stone throwers cast their missiles into the far reaches of the melee. Le Catin hurled its first stone. Helias and Rob hastened to reload, not waiting to see if they had done any damage.

Claire stared down at the confusion of battle and saw the familiar shield and helm of de Montfort in the forefront. She watched the muscular mail-clad arm sweep down in a killing blow. A soldier crumpled and was trampled upon. Sick and cold, but unable to look away, she followed de Montfort's progress through the melee, and suddenly her heart seemed to stop beating because Raoul blocked de Montfort's way, refusing to give ground. She screamed her husband's name in anguish, her fingers digging into the wall.

Rob ran to help Isarn wind the empty sling back down. The latter was muttering his usual litany of "bastards" beneath his breath, with a few choice epithets besides. Suddenly Rob screamed and staggered, a crossbow quarrel protruding from his chest. He collapsed on all fours, then keeled over, blood trickling from the corner of his mouth. Isarn ran around the trebuchet and, raising Rob's shoulders, cradled him, slapping his face and shouting, but it was no use.

Claire watched Raoul and de Montfort exchanging blows. Being less powerfully developed, Raoul was coming off the worst. "Run!" she screamed at him, but even as the words left her mouth, knew that he would not, for he and a small core of his men were protecting the retreat of the others into the safety of the city.

"Come on!" Isarn snarled, grabbing her arm, his eyes wild. "Help me prime her. This one's for Rob!"

"What do I have to do?" Tears streamed down her face, making everything a blur.

"Just turn the windlass, fast as you can. . . . Hurry!"

Feverishly Claire snatched at the wooden handle as if snatching at sanity. It was a machine of war, of destruction, but it was also something to occupy her hands and mind, prayer being no solace. The wood burned against her hand, her shoulders nearly tore from their sockets, but the sling came down and Isarn pegged it before running to help Helias load the stone.

"When I shout, pull out the peg!" he cried to Claire.

Face white with strain, she nodded. Over the wall she heard the increased howling from the crusader mob and the diminishing cries of *"Toulouse!"*

"Now!" bellowed Isarn.

The peg resisted her tug. She set both hands to it and yanked with all her might. It flew out, gouging a deep splinter into her palm, and she fell backward, hitting the platform at the same time as the counterweight *whump*ed down and the boulder flew over the walls in the direction of the ditch. She heard the crash as it hit, and then a strange, hollow silence. Slowly that silence was filled by cries of disbelief and ragged cheers. Claire crawled to her knees and, clutching the wall for support with bleeding hands, staggered to her feet and looked over the parapet. The fighting had stopped. Raoul was standing alone, his sword and shield both lowered, and no one was making any attempt to come at him. Instead the crusaders were retreating, dragging something with them—a man's body, but even from here she could see the blood, the flattened helm encasing a red pulp.

"God's eyes!" croaked Helias. "You've hit de Montfort!" And then, voice growing stronger as belief took hold, he cried over his shoulder to Isarn, "Here's revenge for Rob; de Montfort's dead!"

The word spread along the walls like wildfire. Fists punched the air. The ragged cheering rose in volume to a sealike roar of jubilation.

The words *"de Montfort"* and *"dead"* unlocked a door in Claire's mind. She glimpsed light and air and suddenly recognized the moment in her dreams when she set foot outside her cage and advanced to make her own life ... or else retreated into the darkest corner of her cell. The cheering reached out to her, and the pealing of church bells. Looking over the parapet, she sought her husband. He was limping toward the gate, his shoulders slumped. As she watched, he stumbled and almost fell. Whirling round, gathering her skirts, she left the trebuchet and pelted along the wall and down to the gate. She had to fight against and through a seething crowd of citizens. Several times she was grabbed and hugged and once was drawn into a wild dance. Euphoria crested, broke, and surged anew, wave upon wave.

> *"Montfort est mort!*
> *Montfort est mort!*
> *Montfort est mort!*
> *est mort est mort!"*

In the middle of the crowd, sitting on an upturned barrel, his head in his hands, was Raoul. When only a yard separated her from him, she spoke his name and he raised his head. A deep scratch was beaded with blood between eye corner and jaw where a fragment of the exploding stone had caught him. The rest of his face was colorless.

"It's true," he said woodenly. "He's dead. I saw him hit ... like a ripe plum struck by a mallet." He clenched his teeth, fighting his gorge. "If I hadn't given ground a moment before, it would have been me. . . ." He looked her in the eyes, his expression bewildered and weary. "How is it possible not to believe the truth?"

"Oh, Raoul!" Weeping, she threw herself into his arms. He caught her and they clung together grimly, as if to save each other from drowning, while around them the sea of jubilation roared toward a full-blown storm. De Montfort dead was like having a constant plucked out of the firmament. Everything had to be readjusted, realigned, and in the meantime there was a frightening void.

"I was helping to man the stone thrower that killed him." Claire wept. She was assaulted by terrifying and conflicting emotions. She had violated the Cathar creed of nonviolence and was sick and ashamed of the surge of exultation that had coursed through her as the stone flung over the wall, that still ran in her veins at the knowledge that Simon de Montfort was dead. It seemed only justice that she should have a hand in killing him. But whose justice? The Cathar God was above the creed of an eye for an eye. That doctrine belonged to the crusader's God, *Rex Mundi*.

She heard the rejoicing, the howls that seemed like bloodlust. The scent of war and destruction was in her nostrils. She gripped it tightly in her arms and felt it shuddering through her own body. Her beloved husband, who had almost been the blood sacrifice. Their tears mingled, and some were for joy, and others were for the terrible grief of parting, for the pain of a wound that Simon de Montfort's death had only deepened.

CHAPTER THIRTY-FOUR

AFTER THE DARKNESS of the chapel, the bright sunshine was a shock to Dominic. He blinked and squinted and raised his hand to shade his eyes. The courtyard was packed solid with wains and carts, sumpter horses, destriers, and palfreys. Six dappled gray horses champed between the shafts of the ladies' litter, and six black cobs were harnessed to the sumptuous open cart that bore Lord Simon's pall-covered coffin.

Dominic admired the gold tassels fringing the pall, the

bright limewood and linen shields nailed to the side of the cart, the silk banners and richly decorated harness and trappings. What lay beneath all this gilding was not so pretty. He had seen Lord Simon's corpse when the knights brought it back from beneath the city walls—the torso unmarked, the helmet crushed into the head and oozing bloody matter, white with minute slivers of bone. Sim had been sick, and Amice hysterical. To Dominic, the sight of the body had not been pleasant, but he had seen nothing to frighten him now that the awful black cloud had dissipated from around it. It was only a body, no different from a butcher's carcass on a block.

Friar Bernard, the priests and chaplains, said that Count Simon's soul was now in heaven, its bliss assured by the great service he had performed for Jesus Christ. Dominic wondered what Jesus Christ really thought of it all. He even asked Him in the chapel when he was supposed to be praying for Lord Simon's soul, but there had been no reply except for silence itself.

A month had passed since the stone had crushed Simon's skull, a month in which the siege of Toulouse had been half-heartedly pursued by Amaury de Montfort and then abandoned. A month of disbelief and indecision for the adults, a month of wandering freedom for Dominic and Loup. They had visited the place where they had encountred the heretic woman and her daughter, and Dominic had stared across the river until his eyes ached, but there had been nothing to see except the glitter of the sun on the water and the breeze stirring the reeds to a muted whispering. He committed the longing to memory and occasionally brought it out to examine with a mingled feeling of pleasure and pain.

This morning at dawn, the main camp had been burned, including everything that might be of use to their enemy, the gutted frame of the huge Cat among them—a funeral pyre saluting Simon de Montfort and his ambition as his remains took the road to Carcassonne for official burial.

Friar Bernard was traveling with the entourage. Dominic eyed him sidelong and contemplated putting a burr beneath the orante saddlecloth. As if reading his thoughts, his tutor turned his head and fixed Dominic with his icy, black stare. Dominic returned the look, but not for long enough to bring retribution down on himself, and busily adjusted his stirrup strap.

Alais emerged from the château with Amice and the maids. She was somberly gowned and wore no jewelry apart from the gold cross on her breast and the coral rosary beads that clicked ceaselessly through her fingers. She still walked as if she owned the world, her voice autocratic and powerful, but Dominic had seen behind the mask she held up to the world, had seen her straggle-haired, a wine flask in her hand, her face puffy and bloated with weeping. Her nighttime alone face, the price paid for showing pride to the world when all her pride was really rotting beneath a pall of purple velvet.

They left Toulouse behind, the ancient château and muscular sweep of river, the gold and pink town scarred but secure behind its ditches and ramparts. Simon's triumph and Simon's downfall. Of them all, only Dominic looked back, and he was not thinking of Toulouse, but of two people he had met upon the banks of the Garonne.

At the crossroads upon the hill, Raoul rested his hands upon the raised saddle pommel and looked out over his Montvallant lands. A broken wain lay at the roadside and some peasants were picking it clean. It had belonged to the crusaders, but they had abandoned it in their haste to leave. All over the Toulousain and the Agenais, the northerners were departing, retreating into towns that they knew they could hold for certain, slipping away north. The second siege of Montvallant had been as rapid as the first, only this time it was Raoul who had appeared beneath the castle walls with southern troops in overwhelming numbers and offered the defenders surrender or death.

The northern commander had been sour but sensible, and Montvallant once more belonged to a lord of that blood, but like an insecure child, Raoul kept looking over his shoulder, expecting at any moment to see a crusader force marching down on him. Rumors clustered thicker than a cloud of flies in a fresh patch of dung. Amaury de Montfort was coming from Carcassonne with fresh troops. The pope had called a new crusade. Philip of France was coming to put an end to Rai's string of successes. The last rumor was the one most likely to bear fruit. Beware, be on guard, do not relax for an instant. Hold the soil in your fist, the clay of which you were made, and let no one take it from you.

And Claire said let everything go. The spirit is what matters.

She joined Raoul now where the road branched. Isabelle followed at a discreet distance on her palfrey, and behind her rode the soldiers whose task it was to escort the two women on their chosen road. Raoul turned his gaze from his lands to his wife. "Are you sure?" he asked softly.

She returned his stare, her eyes traveling slowly over his face as if memorizing every feature. "Yes, I'm sure. I have to leave for both our sakes, or else we will bleed forever. I wish I could make you understand."

Stretching across the horse, he took her hand in his. Her fingers were brown and firm, devoid of rings, testimony in themselves to her commitment to the Cathar way. He sighed deeply. "I have tried being blind, I have tried being angry, but I was just blocking out the truth, not destroying it. Take your path; I will not stop you."

Her eyes were luminous with tears, but there was a tremulous smile on her lips. "You do understand!"

Raoul kissed her fingertips. What use except to cause more heartache to say that he did not? "Walk in the Light, Claire," he said huskily. "And think of me sometimes." Abruptly he released her, and turning his horse around, set him to a canter in the direction of Montvallant.

Tears spilled down Claire's face as she watched him go. A warm wind tumbled and gusted, billowing her cloak, drying the moisture to salt on her cheeks. "Walk in the Light," she repeated softly. The wind took her words and danced away with them. She turned her mare southward.

Raoul rode toward his castle, its walls golden-red in the autumn sunshine. He felt the sleek power of the glossy courser beneath him, the leather in his fingers, the sun on his face, and the desolation of having no one with whom to share them.

He forded the river, low now after the hot summer. Brownskinned children played in the shallows, and women pounded their linen on white stones beside the bank. Difficult to imagine from this scene that there had ever been a war or foreign occupation, but the scars were there all the same, deep and bitter. One of the women glanced up from her laundry. She had copper hair of a similar shade to Claire's, a winsome smile, and abundant curves, accentuated by the damp patches on her gown. Slowing the horse, he approached her, seeking solace.

CHAPTER THIRTY-FIVE

Toulouse, Summer 1234

HALF-OPENING HIS eyes, the young man squinted against the intrusion of daylight from the window embrasure. Linen sheets and a rumpled plaid coverlet were tangled around his body. An unaccustomed warmth pressed against his spine, and a hand not his own curved over his ribs. Fingers tugged at his chest hair, then traveled lower. A satiny thigh arched over his own. Normally he would have responded with alacrity to such an invitation, but after last night's overindulgences, all inclination was defeated by the hammering pain within his skull and the gurgling pit where his stomach should have been.

Undaunted, the woman persisted and was rewarded with a token response, his body functioning on the raw, physical level of early manhood. "You want me again, Lord Dominic?" she purred.

Her accent was Catalan. Very gingerly he rolled over to face her and in the gray light from the embrasure saw that she had a mass of auburn curls, magnificent dark eyes, and even more magnificent breasts. What was her name? Peronelle? Williametta? He couldn't remember, didn't want to. Last night, his first in Toulouse for more than ten years, had been passed in convivial celebration—wine, song, gambling, more wine, and then the woman. At the time it had seemed an excellent idea. The area below his waist still thought it was, but his stomach threatened to react violently against any such prospect.

"No," he muttered, shoving aside her busily kneading hand. "Just . . . just go away."

"You didn't say that last night," she whispered throatily, and poked her tongue in his ear.

"I wasn't sick last night," he groaned. "Please, just leave me alone."

Tossing her head, she sat up, torn between petulance and sympathy. For five years, ever since the treaty of Meaux when the young Count Raymond had submitted to King Philip Augustus of France, the Château Narbonnais had been occupied by French troops. Business was always brisk when there was a change of garrison, the homeward-bound men celebrating their release, the incoming ones drowning their sorrows.

Lord Dominic was a young knight attached to the new garrison, and a very personable one at that, better than the stinking graybeard who had taken her for his regular bedmate last time. Her new partner still possessed all but one of his teeth, and his breath last night had only smelled of wine, nothing more obnoxious. He was darkly avised like the native southern men, and the bold expression in his eyes as he had looked her up and down proclaimed him an heir to the troubadours. His payment had been generous, too, although that might just have been the drink. What a pity his home was the Île-de-France, his allegiance to the North, and that he would not be staying at the château above a few months.

"Shall I come back tonight?" Reluctantly she started to dress.

Hovering on a very delicate brink, knowing that if he did vomit, his head would explode, Dominic made an inarticulate sound, his eyes closed. She took it to mean yes, because that was the best way to do business, and having shunned the temptation of extracting whatever coins were left in his pouch, kissed him lightly on his throbbing temple and tiptoed out of the room.

Dominic heard the door gently close behind her, and with a suffering groan, buried his head beneath the pillow, wishing to die. It was not often that he drank to excess, but last night he had needed the oblivion. The Château Narbonnais held too many boyhood memories, and to have them land on him all at once had been too much to bear . . . but then so was this headache, and he thanked Christ that his duties did not officially begin until the morrow.

When finally he dared to move, the first cool of the morning had been burned away by the hot, bright southern sun. In the château, however, the shadows were as dingy as he remembered, and everywhere the ghosts whispered at him. A small boy with a red weal burning on his cheek, and a young and eager mongrel dog trotting at his heels, escorted him through the various chambers. Passing the schoolroom, where the echoes were at their darkest, he discovered it still occupied by children struggling with their Latin and tutored by a Dominican friar—a young man with a fluffy red tonsure and an eager, freckled face. Not all of them were bad, he told himself, but his throbbing skull still carried too powerful a memory of pain and humiliation for him to be convinced.

The chapel was dark and cold, busy with priests. The smell of incense hit his nostrils and threatened to upset his slowly settling stomach. Here, too, were memories—his father lying in state, although, of course, they could not display his face in blessed repose because there had been no face left to display. A swift death, and an inglorious one. Live by the sword, die by it, but there were worse ends. He had his own share of battle scars, but these days no one flung at him the taunts of *bastard* and *whoreson*. No longer was he Dominic de Montvallant or Dominic FitzSimon, but Dominic le Couchefeu—the banked fire. His was a nature of smoldering coals over intense heat. The doubt, insecurity, and misery of an unloved child drove his ambitions. He acknowledged it, knew his failings, and kept them on a tight rein lest he become like his father, which was both his hunger and his dread.

The breaking of fast in the hall was long over; the trestles had been cleared and stacked against the walls, and people were going about their daily business. Some young knights with whom he had been carousing the night before had gathered in a morose huddle near the hearth to nurse their fragile heads and stomachs. Not relishing the prospect of recounting last night's follies, Dominic edged around them, avoided two

Dominican friars with a perfunctory right-handed signing of the cross, and headed for the kitchens to rekindle a certain old acquaintance.

Hubert, who had been a senior apprentice during Dominic's boyhood, was now a fully fledged cook in his late twenties, florid of face with close-set eyes that displayed an alarming tendency to cross when he concentrated. He looked Dominic dubiously up and down and wiped his hands on his apron.

"Can I be of service, my lord?"

"Don't recognize me, do you?" Dominic grinned, lounging against the doorpost. "Would it make things easier if I begged a piece of marchpane and a marrowbone? I haven't got Loup with me. He died last year and I've yet to find a pup to replace him."

"Master Dominic?" Hubert's eyes grew as round as tart cutters, and the pupils shot toward each other. "By all the saints!" He hesitated, obviously wondering whether to bow or adopt the familiarity of their former relationship.

"I'm not sure that the saints have anything to do with it!" Dominic laughed, and slapping the cook on his heavy dough kneader's arm, peered into the dark, hot depths of the kitchen. "I missed the breaking of fast. I don't suppose you can spare me a crust of bread and some wine?"

"At least your appetite hasn't changed!" Hubert laughed, deciding on familiarity. Ushering Dominic inside, he tipped a sleeping tabby cat off a spare stool.

"It's only just returning to life," Dominic confessed ruefully. "I made a night of it and my gut's as sour as the bottom of an English vintner's barrel!" He sat down on the stool. The cat, a champion mouser and thus permitted the run of the kitchens, glared balefully at Dominic and stalked off to inspect the trestle next door where an apprentice was gutting fish.

Hubert set a brimming cup before his visitor, a loaf of bread, and some goat's cheese. "Get outside of that," he said cheerfully. "You'll soon feel better."

Dominic eyed the cheese dubiously, but cut a weighty chunk from the loaf with his eating knife.

"I remember you sitting there when your eyes scarce reached above the level of that table." Hubert shook his head.

"You'd make two of me now!" He returned to chopping herbs with rapid, unthinking expertise.

"I'm not as tall as Simon or Amaury." Dominic raised his cup.

Hubert eyed him, not deceived by the light tone. The quiet, self-contained child had not suddenly become a garrulous extrovert, unless by way of a shield. "So how are the other boys?" he asked.

Dominic swallowed a mouthful of wine. "Amaury's King Louis's constable now, although you probably know that already. He arranged for me to be taken into the royal household as a squire after the Lady Alais died, and of course, he's ceded all rights in the South to the French Crown—nor can I blame him. He had a rough time after the siege of Toulouse. It's hard to live in the shadow of a dead paragon, particularly when he's your own father, and your every movement compared and found lacking." He shrugged and drank again.

"Is that your problem, too?"

"God no!" Dominic laughed sourly. "I'm just the overlooked bastard, and tainted at that with southern blood. They expect me to be trouble, and I don't disappoint them. Amaury sent me down here, you know—decided that posting me to Toulouse was the quickest way to settle the most recent dust."

Hubert stretched across the table for a bundle of chives. "What did you do?"

"Dallied with a lute and someone else's wife and got caught by her husband."

Hubert clucked his tongue against the roof of his mouth and shook his head.

"I was transferred to the garrison here, and Clemence was packed off to a nunnery. Not that she minded. Her husband was sixty years old and as odious as they come, but Amaury didn't like the scandal." A spark of devilry bordering on relish glowed in Dominic's eyes.

Hubert gave him a censorious look. "What about the others?"

Dominic lifted his shoulders. "Amice is married now, Guy was killed at Carcassone—but you must know that—and Richard died of fever in Paris a few years ago. Simon's doing well for himself."

"Yes?"

"He's been able to claim the Earldom of Leicester by an old hereditary right. I've an offer of employment there any time I want it."

"Leicester?" Hubert fumbled his tongue around the name and looked at him blankly.

"It's in England," Dominic said. "A far cry from here."

"Will you go?"

"I might." He broke off another chunk of loaf. "I haven't decided what to do with my glittering future. Amaury would always keep me—I've got better manners than a mercenary when I think to use them, and a family connection. The same goes for Simon's offer. . . . I don't know." He grinned. "I'm like a Gascon wine; I need time to mature."

"Hmmph," Hubert muttered, and brows puckered, returned to chopping herbs, the sound blocking off all conversation.

When he had finished and swept the results into a bowl, Dominic asked, "What about Toulouse? What's been happening here?"

Crossing his ankles, Hubert leaned one arm on the trestle and rested the other against his hip. "Well, the new pope's certainly keen on rooting out the heretics here. Guzman might be dead, but his kind are everywhere. You can't take a step these days without tripping over a friar with his ear to the ground and his nose on a scent. 'Tis no wonder they call them the dogs of God." He tut-tutted for a moment. "At least the Cathars let you make up your own mind. If you disagree with the black friars, they take you away for questioning and you're never seen again, unless it's chained to a stake or tied to a whipping post outside the basilica."

"I remember," Dominic said softly, his mind filling with the image of Friar Bernard.

"You don't," Hubert contradicted grimly. "'Tis more vicious these days than it was when you dwelt here. Pope Gregory's got the bit between his teeth, all right. Have you been out in the streets yet?"

"Only ridden through them yesterday."

"Well, take a good look. Black robes everywhere and folk wearing cloaks sewn with yellow crosses to show that they're repentant heretics, and for no greater crime than passing a true heretic in the street. These days it is best to be seen going to mass every day and adoring the cross. Wear one round your neck and stitched to your surcoat. Sign yourself like mad when you're out." Hubert wiped the back of his hand across his upper lip. "Do you know what else, lad?"

Dominic shook his head.

"They won't give permission for old Count Raymond to be buried in consecrated ground. Nearly nine years his coffin has lain in the precincts of the Hospital of Saint John, and he was never even convicted of heresy." The cook grimaced. "I'm a good Catholic, wouldn't want anyone to think otherwise, but they have taken matters too far." He pointed his knife at Dominic. "Don't go using that left hand unless you're forced; it'll be seen as the Devil's mark, and the count ain't here now to throttle the opposition."

"I can look after myself," Dominic replied defensively, and draining the cup, rose to his feet.

Hubert studied him with pessimism. "How old are you, lad?"

"Two and twenty last Candlemas."

"Well, if you want to live to be three and twenty, better gentle your attitude."

"Don't worry, I'll be as meek as a washed lamb," Dominic said in a tone that did nothing to reassure the cook, and thanking him for the food, strolled from the kitchens.

The city of Toulouse beckoned him and he left the gloomy environs of the château for its busy streets. The walls and ditches that had ringed the town during his previous sojourn had been demolished or filled in, in accordance with the treaty of Meaux. Some dwellings for the Dominican friars donated by a pious citizen of Toulouse stood sentinel directly opposite the château, and black-robed figures could be seen industriously entering and departing like swarming ants.

Everywhere towers thrust at the sky, armoring and enhancing the private homes of the rich, or proclaiming the pride of the Roman religion—the square towers of St. Etienne, the Romanesque spires of the basilica of St. Sernin. In every quarter, from the city to the burg, to the sprawling suburbs on the west bank, the bells called the faithful to bear witness.

Dominic allowed the city to seep into his pores. Memories

competed with the hot dazzle of the present. New buildings had appeared in places he remembered as grassland or decimated by war. Urban bustle had returned, and prosperity. The hatred and the fear were as they had been before. He could sense the wounds festering beneath the scabs. People looked at him, noting his fine tunic and the sword on his hip, suspicion and speculation in their eyes. Was he one of them, or a northern oppressor? If he opened his mouth, he knew that his accent would damn him, and so he did not pause to listen to the troubadours in the marketplaces or inspect the wares in the merchants' booths, nor did he stop to hear a Dominican friar haranguing the crowds from a podium outside the ancient church of Notre Dame de la Daurade, but hastened to complete his circuit of the city and return to the château.

Before the great gate, a crowd had gathered to witness a spirited brawl between two of the château's guards, a friar, and one of the townsmen, although it took Dominic a moment to discern exact numbers because of the entanglement of arms and legs. The friar flew backward and landed almost at his feet, blue-veined shins exposed, his dignity in tatters. A soldier followed him to the floor, his mouth and nose a scarlet smudge.

The townsman stood his ground, brown eyes blazing, blond hair ruffling like a cap of feathers. His shoulders were heaving violently, not just with exertion, but with the force of his dry sobbing. "Good God!" he choked out. "Can't you even leave the dead in peace, you black kites!"

The other soldier drew his blade. Glancing around, Dominic saw that members of the crowd had picked up stones, and the atmosphere was volcanic with tension.

"Hold your sword!" he snapped to the soldier.

The man turned with a curse on his lips, recognized Dominic's rank and accent, and protested instead. "He's to be arrested, my lord."

"What for?"

"Interfering with the lawful progression of justice and God's law!" snapped the friar, struggling to his feet and dusting himself down.

"God's law!" spat the young townsman. "Is it truly God's

law to dig up the dead and burn them? What's the matter, haven't you got enough living heretics to keep your fires fed?"

"Blasphemy!" squawked the friar, pointing a bony finger. "Arrest him now!"

Fear coiled and tightened unpleasantly in Dominic's gut as he recognized Friar Bernard, his former tutor. The priest had changed little except to become more cadaverous in appearance, flesh drawn tight and ivory-pale over his skull and bony beak of a nose. He had left the de Montfort household when Dominic was eleven years old, and had returned south to the task of pursuing heretics. Dominic could perceive a murky haze around his body, almost like smoke, as if the hatred in the priest's soul were incandescent.

The injured guard groggily sat up, wiped at the blood pouring from his nose, and looked in surprise at his red hand. The crowd began closing in. From the direction of the château, Dominic heard the clash of pikes as reinforcements ran to contain the disturbance. The townsman was seized, the first stone flew, and the brawl renewed itself on a greater scale. Dominic raised his arm to protect his face, and a sharp stone slashed his hand to the bone. Friar Bernard, his lips curled back from crowded yellow teeth, incited the crowd to new heights of bitter violence by howling hellfire and damnation at them.

"By the rood, shut your foolish mouth!" Dominic bellowed. "You will get us all killed!"

Friar Bernard stopped in midtirade and stared at Dominic. His pupils contracted, and as recognition tardily dawned, he silently mouthed his former pupil's name.

Dominic snarled a mirthless grin. "Deliver us from evil!" he mocked, dodging another stone.

The arbalesters arrived then, crossbows primed at the crowd, and the townspeople gave up the fight, retreating in a last defiance of flung stones and insults. The prisoner was manhandled roughly into the château and dragged away to the cells.

Friar Bernard gave Dominic a basilisk glare as he beat dust from his robes and sought to reassume his dignity. "What are you doing here?"

"Being stoned," Dominic retorted, defiantly flippant because inside himself he was quailing beneath that flat, black stare. "Look, it's my left hand." The blood dripped steadily into the dust like a sacrifice. "Would you not say there was judgment somewhere?"

Bernard's eyes narrowed. "Take care," he hissed. "You're no longer a child, I'm no longer your tutor. You're a man answerable for your sins, and I'm an inquisitor."

"Fiat voluntas Tua," Dominic said, crossing his breast, and with a look of cold scorn, stalked off in the direction of the leech's quarters to seek attention for his hand.

Later, in the cool of the evening, Dominic ventured down to the banks of the Garonne to pay a poignant homage to the place and the day from his childhood that he had never forgotten. Little had changed. He stood, breathing in the scent of river and meadow. Among the reeds, a herd of brown and white cows stood knee-deep in the shallows, swishing their tails against the flies, and snatching at succulent green shoots on the bank. A heron stood sentinel, its intense yellow gaze trained on a frog ripple among the reeds. Slender marsh marigolds grew in abundance. Half-smiling, Dominic plucked one with his good hand and thought of the strange silver-haired girl. How long it had been, and how powerfully she still tugged at his soul. A golden moment amongst so many dark ones.

He wondered what had become of her. Had she survived to grow up like himself, or had she been caught and killed as a heretic? He stared out across the river to the opposite bank, the reeds and grasses gilded by a flamboyant crimson and gold sunset. Here it was that he had first discovered his ability to see the life force that dwelt in all living things. The tones of harmony, soft and rich, the more intense hues of power and determination, and the jagged, dirty shades of imbalance, madness, and evil.

It was a fickle gift. He was often too preoccupied to be receptive and was unable to summon the faculty at will, but sometimes it came upon him so strongly that he was always surprised to learn that others saw nothing at all, and thought him touched by devils. These days, he kept it to himself. Tonight it was strong. He could see a soft golden haze rising from the backs of the cattle, from the grasses, from the heron, even from the flower in his hand.

He was back in Toulouse. He could not call it home, and yet the place exerted a strong pull on his soul, and this place, this plain stretch of riverbank, the strongest pull of all. He cast the marsh marigold into the water and watched the slow-flowing water spin his offering around the bear it away in the direction of the water mills downstream.

The following morning saw Dominic established at a trestle in the great hall, a scribe to one side of him and a mountain of paperwork to the other. As he was the youngest knight of the relieving garrison, the most mundane and tiresome tasks were quickly foisted upon him, nor did his bandaged left hand provide any excuse, for he still had the use of his fingers.

He scrawled with rapid impatience, now and then pausing to ask the scribe a question or clarify a point. Sometimes the pauses were longer because the more experienced men kept directing external queries to Dominic's trestle and he would have to stop and deal with them—demands for payment of kitchen supplies, of oxcart hire, an irate father looking for the soldier who had got his daughter with child. As the morning wore on, so did the pressure of Dominic's fingers on his quill, and on a hard downward stroke it snapped, spraying ink across the close-written sheet of vellum.

Cursing through his teeth, Dominic trimmed a fresh pen, then sat back, opening and closing his aching fist. A servant put a cup of wine down in front of him and made to move on. "Leave the flagon," Dominic commanded tersely.

"But, my lord . . ." the servant started to protest, changed his mind at the look in Dominic's eyes, and did as he was told. Sighing, Dominic took a deep swallow from the cup. In the corner of his vision, he saw a helpful official directing yet another query in his direction, and swore again. The scribe smothered a grin behind his hand and bent diligently over his parchment.

The man who came to Dominic's trestle was tall and lean with a face too old for the proud, athletic carriage of his body. An embroidered tunic, gilded belt, and rings upon his fingers professed his nobility; a musty smell informed Dominic that the finery was not habitual.

"I have come to inquire about my son," the southern noble said, and nodded over his shoulder. "They directed me to you."

Dominic took another swallow of wine. "They would." He grimaced. "I'm today's scapecoat. Have a stool."

"I prefer to stand," came the cool reply.

Dominic put the cup down. His ears grew hot as he was neatly put in his place, which was not even on the lowest rung of the southerner's ladder. *He thinks I'm a bored upstart; probably he's right, and I think he's a pain in the backside.* The faintest hint of amusement curved Dominic's lips. "Your son?" he said.

"He is locked up in your cells for fomenting a riot yesterday noon, or so I understand. I want to see him."

Dominic met the piercing blue gaze with a kindling of interest. "As a matter of fact, I was there." He held up his bandaged hand. "I'll warn you now, he's not just clapped up for brawling in the street. He said some very unpalatable things to a Dominican friar and knocked him to the ground. It is likely that he'll be charged with heresy." Dominic indicated the stool again. "Sit, I pray you."

Slowly the man did so, as if any swifter motion would break the shell of his pride. "What precisely did he say?"

Dominic took the scribe's empty cup and poured the southerner a measure from the flagon. "I didn't hear all of it, but the gist was that the friars had no right to go about digging up corpses and burning them because their owners had been heretics."

The older man closed his eyes for a moment, the lids squeezed tight as if he were in mortal pain. Then, opening them, he took the wine that was offered. "They did that to his grandfather last year," he said wearily as he put the cup down. "He died a Cathar, so they came and took his body from the crypt and burned it in the center of the town. We had to pay a heavy fine. Guillaume would rather run a black friar through on the tip of a lance than genuflect to him."

Dominic smiled without humor. *So would I,* he thought, and then realized that the southerner was staring at him with a strange, almost painful intensity. "I wasn't laughing," he said quickly, thinking that perhaps his expression had been misconstrued. "I have no love for the friars myself."

"And no inkling of what we have suffered!" The blue eyes flashed and the fierce pride burned up high. "Good God, my own wife was . . ." He bit off whatever else he had been about to say. "Ach, go home, lad; you don't belong here. Get out and play your knighthood games where it's safe."

Dominic tightened his lips. "Don't judge me by my appearance," he said curtly, and drawing forward a fresh sheet of parchment, began rapidly to write. "My mother was . . . or is from the Agenais, and I spent my childhood here in Toulouse." He dipped the quill in the ink horn. "Your son's name?"

"Guillaume de Montvallant, son of Raoul."

Dominic wrote the name on the parchment in a fierce burst of pressure. The quill split again, and raising his head, he met the blue stare and saw his own recognition mirrored.

"Holy Christ," whispered Raoul de Montvallant, gripping the trestle with both hands. "You're Claire's son, aren't you?"

"They never told me her name." Dominic was surprised to hear his own voice emerge level and calm, as if he were discussing the price of wine or an ox-load of faggots. "How did you know?"

"Just now . . . the way you smiled, and what you said about her being from the Agenais."

"I was raised by Alais de Montfort and fostered out to the French court by Amaury when she died. . . . They used to tell me that my father was a rebel southern lord and that his estates belonged of right to me."

"You are not mine," Raoul said harshly. "I grant you no claims on the Montvallant lands!"

"Christ, do you think I want them!" Dominic snarled, and this time his voice was ragged.

"Your true father didn't care upon whom he trampled to take what he wanted!"

"No, he didn't," Dominic agreed, "so that's reason enough to cover me with the same fleece, isn't it?"

"What are you doing in Toulouse, then, if not examining the possibilities?"

"I was posted by my half brother for being troublesome at home. That's the problem with mongrels; they don't conform to the ways of thoroughbreds." Jerkily he sanded the document he had just completed and stood up. "Come with me."

Raoul stared at him. "Where?"

"To the cells, of course. This is a warrant for your son's release, but I might have to do some browbeating to get him out ... but then, I'm not Simon de Montfort's bastard for nothing." He glinted Raoul a slightly malicious look.

The older man cleared his throat and looked uncomfortable. "I'm sorry, I should not have spoken as I did."

Dominic shrugged. "A bastard gets accustomed to abuse at a very early age." The tension in his shoulders belied his indifferent tone of voice. He set off purposefully across the hall, aware that the southerner was having to lengthen his stride to keep up. In a gloomy, unguarded corridor, Dominic slowed his pace and tried to calm the frantic racing of his heart and mind.

"My mother," he said carefully. "Does she still live?"

Beside him, Raoul de Montvallant slowed, too. The bitterness in the man's expression suddenly softened with a compassion bordering on pity. "Yes, she still lives, although perhaps for you it would be better if she did not." He drew a deep breath. "She is one of the Perfecti, a preacher of the Cathar faith. She was of that inclination even when we were wed, but what Simon de Montfort and his wife did to her pushed her that final step."

"What did they do?" Dominic was compelled to ask with a feeling of hollow dread. He stopped and faced the older man.

"Your father captured Montvallant. It was me he wanted, but I was absent in Foix, so he took out his frustration and anger on Claire—raped her and gave what remained to his wife to do with as she pleased. She tried to turn my wife into a good Catholic, but after you were born, the Lady Alais realized why she would never succeed and had Claire locked up in Beaucaire. Poor Claire," he added softly. "She wanted to weep for losing you, but she could never forget the violation."

Dominic was silent for a long time. "I never knew," he said at length. "No one ever told me. I was never allowed to ask questions about her. The little I do know has come from my half brother Simon. I thought perhaps that she had been his mistress." It took a tremendous effort, but he looked Raoul in the eyes. "You must have hated him."

"Yes."

There was another long silence. Dominic looked away. What

could he say? That he was sorry for his father's sins? That he wished he had never been born?

Finally it was Raoul who placed his hand lightly on Dominic's arm. "We cannot bury the past when the priests keep digging it up, but perhaps we can see some of it in a different light," he said. "I lay no blame at your door. You are as much a victim as any of us who are left from that time."

Dominic shook his head. "I came to Toulouse to escape, and find that instead I'm caught fast!" His laugh was ironic, slightly shaky, and pulling away from Raoul, he began striding out again. "Dallying here solves nothing," he said curtly over his shoulder. "Let us go and secure the release of your . . . of my brother."

CHAPTER THIRTY-SIX

DOMINIC LEANED DOWN from his horse and took a lance from the stack propped against the tiltyard wall. In the center of the practice ground, Guillaume was hanging a wooden ring on the quintain post. The wind ruffled his blond hair and caused him to narrow his eyes. Otherwise his expression was carefully neutral.

Dominic knew that Guillaume's feelings toward him were ambivalent. His half brother bore an implacable hatred for the northern invaders who had wrecked the symmetry of his life, and toward the de Montforts in particular. Dominic was a de Montfort and thus to be reviled, and yet they were kin by blood and Guillaume owed him his life. If not for Dominic, he would still be languishing in the cells of the Château Narbonnais, awaiting trial for heresy.

Vividly aware of Guillaume's critical scrutiny, Dominic couched the lance, collected his horse to a steady, bouncing canter, and assaulted the quintain. To his relief, he succeeded in lifting the ring off the post as delicately as a lover lifting a lock of his lady's hair. At the time all the hours of training had seemed tiresome, but now he was glad of Henri Lemagne's insistence on the mastery of technique.

"Good!" Guillaume applauded with a forced smile and placed another ring on the quintain. "My turn now." He ran lightly to his horse and vaulted nimbly into the saddle. When he took the lance from the stack, he twirled the shaft round and round, his dexterity making of the tip a silver blur, and before he charged down the tilt, he made the horse perform several intricate moves, using only his thighs for guidance. And if Dominic's touch had been delicate, Guillaume's was positively ethereal.

His face flushed with triumph, a challenge in his hot, brown eyes, Guillaume faced Dominic. "Want to run a tilt lance to lance?"

Dominic grimaced and shook his head. "I think not," he said gently, and handed his blunted weapon to a squire.

"What's the matter, scared of losing?"

"It wouldn't just be to prove valor, would it? If you unseated me, you would be insufferable with triumph; if I unseated you, you'd bear a grudge far greater than the one you bear me now." Dominic dismounted and gave his horse to a groom.

"Coward," Guillaume hissed through his teeth.

"I'm not the one running away," Dominic said in a quiet voice that his de Montfort half brothers would well have recognized, for it was so much like their father's.

Turning way, Dominic started to pull off his gauntlets. The look on the groom's face warned him and he spun and ducked, but Guillaume, with the suppleness of a born athlete and the killer instinct bred in the nomadic life of an army camp, adjusted the blow even as it was launched.

Dominic went down, the air *whoof*ing out of his lungs, and Guillaume was immediately on top of him, hands digging into the embroidered collar of Dominic's tunic, raising him up, slamming his head back down on the tiltyard floor, once and then again. Dominic's knees arched. He twisted, got his arm under Guillaume's, prizing, and with a sudden spurt of pressure, threw him over and scrambled to his feet, his breath coming in short, painful gasps.

Guillaume made a fluid recovery and drove his bunched fingers straight at Dominic's face. Dominic blocked the move with his right forearm and punched with his left fist. The blow literally stopped Guillaume in his tracks, for he had not been expecting a retaliation from that direction. Blood started to drip from his split lip. He touched the place with his fingertips, looked at the smudge of dark, bright red, then at Dominic, who was nursing his grazed knuckles.

"If I hit you again," Dominic panted, "I'll not be able to sign any more releases, and I certainly don't want you to hit me. You've got a punch like a mule!"

Guillaume eyed him suspiciously, his body still keyed up to fight, but the explosive tension was draining away. He discovered that he no longer wished to murder Dominic. A test had been passed, and new parameters set. "You're left-handed!" he accused.

"It doesn't do to take me for granted," Dominic agreed with a smile, and held out his right hand. Guillaume shook his head, and grinning reluctantly, held out his own across the space separating them.

The two young men sat their horses on the hilltop, the lands of Montvallant spread out before them, fields and vines baking in the sun.

"Truly," said Dominic, "I lay no claim to any of this. I can have lands in the North for the asking—one day I probably will."

Guillaume gave Dominic a brown, sidelong glance. "Lands for the asking," he said with a bitter note in his voice. "I suppose it makes a difference to lands for the taking."

Dominic tightened his lips and maintained his control, managing not to rise to Guillaume's bait. He had been trying to conciliate, but he realized he had not been very subtle. The Montvallants' own struggle for their lands was written in sweat and blood.

"My father fought a battle down there against the crusaders," Guillaume said after a moment, and pointed toward a meadow of bleached yellow hay, "and he won. He told me about it. It was the day I was born." He narrowed his eyes at Dominic. "By the time I was three years old, your father had possession of Montvallant, and mine was reduced to a life in our army camps, fighting for our bread. I lived with my grandmother for a while, and then I lived on the road with him. When we regained Montvallant I did not know how to call it home anymore. I still don't," he added over his shoulder as he guided his horse down the goat track leading toward the river. "Every day I look around me and seek the feeling, but it doesn't come. I'm lost." He shrugged. "Where do I belong?"

Dominic followed him down the twisting path. "I have asked that question a hundred times myself and been drawn into more trouble seeking the answer than most men would find in a lifetime," he confessed, and screwed up his face, partly against the strength of the sun, partly in self-mockery. "I've sought it in all the wrong beds, hoping to find the right one. . . . That's one of the reasons I'm in Toulouse now, avoiding a furious husband."

Guillaume snorted with amusement and just a hint of superiority.

"I've sought throughout all the taverns in Normandy and France, on several battlefields and in castle and camp, and the restlessness only increases," Dominic continued. "I understand what you mean—about belonging."

They paused again at the foot of the hill to drink from their waterskins and briefly rest their horses. "Sometimes I think about joining the garrison at Montségur," Guillaume said, as he wiped his cuff across his lips. "Prayers alone won't keep the Cathars safe from the pope and the French king. Besides, Montvallant is becoming dangerous for me. That black friar of yours would love to roast me at the stake."

"He is not my friar," Dominic growled. "He used to be my tutor, and he would beat me black and blue for the smallest misdemeanor. I hated him. He would love to roast me at the stake, too; I do not speak in jest."

Guillaume's smile was mocking as he banged the stopper back into his waterskin. "Yet another thing we have in common." His expression grew conspiratorial. "You say you have searched throughout all the taverns in Normandy and France. I know a few in Toulouse that bear investigation."

Dominic immediately brightened with devil-may-care anticipation. "Then you had best lead on," he said.

The young woman checked her satchel of herbs for omissions and reached on tiptoe to the shelf above her head for the vial of lavender oil. "I think that is everything," she said, and flicking her silvery hair over her shoulders, turned to smile at her mother.

The older woman smiled in return, but Magda could see that she was afraid. Bridget always hated it when Magda went away from Montségur, even when she was in the safe hands of her great-uncle Chretien.

"You have given me your wisdom. Now I have to learn my own." Magda put the satchel to one side and crossed the fire to kiss her mother's smooth cheek. Her pale hair lay against her mother's tresses, in which the first silver strands were marking the passage of the years.

"Yes, I know that," Bridget answered quietly, "nor will tomorrow be the first time of your leaving. It is only a mother's anxiety for her fledgling in a world full of predators. Here, sit and eat; the food is ready."

Magda and her mother shared a loaf and bowl of thick herb and vegetable stew in companionable silence, savoring the food and the company, knowing that it would be the last time they would be together until the first winter snows powdered the mountain passes.

When they had finished and cleared away their bowls, they sat beside the fire, preparing freshly gathered herbs for storage, as if this were any ordinary evening. "I must make some more rub for Matthias," Bridget murmured, more than half to herself. "His joints are so stiff and sore these days. I can ease them a little with my touch, but I have no cure for old age."

Magda watched her mother's smooth, tanned fingers deftly strip the leaves from a stem of sage. Her mind's eye was briefly overlaid with the sight of those hands illuminated in lightning, outlined in fire. She blinked the vision out of her mind, for it bore echoes of the nightmare that had haunted her for as long as she could remember.

"What do you see?" asked her mother with swift concern.

"Fire and lightning, love and death," Magda said, then looked curious. "You were in a cave with a man, and a storm was all around you. And then I saw you on the battlements of Montségur calling out to the lightning."

Bridget's gaze grew intent. "And have you seen this before?"

"No, Mother, this is the first time . . . although the other vision, the dark dream, is very close." She gnawed on her underlip and said hesitantly, "The man in the cave . . . I remember seeing him when I was a little girl. He came to Montségur with his son."

"You remember it?" Bridget asked warily. "You were not even four years old then."

"I remember it well. It was the first time I had the dark vision. And the man said to me that being poor was not knowing what wealth really was. I remember that, too."

Her mother's gaze brooded on her for a long moment, and then she drew a deep breath. "He is your father," she said. "His name is Raoul de Montvallant, and he is lord of estates close to Toulouse. He is a fine man, an honorable one, but we never had enough in common to make a life together, and besides, he was already married."

"But enough in common to lie together?"

"Do you moralize, daughter?"

Magda shook her head and lowered her eyes. "No, Mama."

Bridget rose, and stepping lightly around the fire, enfolded Magda in her arms. "Your father had a vitality about him, a spark that I wanted my daughter to have. Yes, I could have chosen another man, but even then I would not have considered marriage—it was not for me."

Magda leaned into her mother's arm. "I have often wondered who my father is," she said. "I thought perhaps he was one of the Cathar men on the mountain, but I know that they are sworn to celibacy."

"Perhaps I have been wrong in not telling you before. I always intended doing so, but you never asked, and you seemed happy enough with what you had—your uncle Chretien and Matthias, and sometimes Luke."

"I have not been unhappy," Magda said quickly, not wishing

to distress her mother over what could not be changed. "And I already have a sense of belonging—to you, to Montségur, and everyone here." She glanced at Bridget. "Does he know about me?"

"He knows. I told him on the night you were conceived, and when he came to Montségur, he saw you, and he was proud."

Magda wondered if she would have greeted him any differently if she had known he was her father, if she would have looked at him more closely or tried to sit on his knee the way she had once done with uncle Chretien. Strange to think that she had a half brother, too, and that he was a grown man.

There is something else I have not told you," Bridget said, "but since you know the one, you might as well know the whole. Your father's wife dwells here at Montségur—Sister Claire."

Magda stared at her mother, her gray eyes widening. "Sister Claire?" she repeated, thinking of the quiet, chestnut-haired woman who spent so much time in prayer, and who had dwelt at Montségur for the past fifteen years at least.

"She came to us after the final siege of Toulouse. Your father and she had been separated by the war, and by the time they were reunited, they had each traveled too far in different directions. Claire took the *consolamentum* and became a practicing Cathar."

"Does she know about me?"

Bridget frowned. "No, daughter. Often I have pondered about telling her, but what purpose would it serve? She has scars enough already from the war. Do you remember that day by the river outside Toulouse when you met the dark-haired boy?"

Magda smiled. "Yes, I remember." A soft note entered her voice. "His name was Dominic."

"His father was Simon de Montfort, and his mother is Claire de Montvallant. She was de Montfort's hostage and he raped her."

Magda looked at her mother with a mingling of horror and compassion. How could such knots ever be untangled and made smooth enough to weave into life's tapestry? She thought of the boy, trying to shrug and pretend his parentage did not matter. She thought of the suffering of Claire de Montvallant.

Then she thought of the walls of Montségur ablaze with lightning, and shivered.

CHAPTER THIRTY-SEVEN

DOMINIC HAD JUST begun to realize that he was lost when his horse went lame. Cursing fluently, he dismounted and gently ran his hand down the chestnut's foreleg. The animal flinched and sidled as Dominic's fingers encountered the hot, slightly swollen knee. Further examination revealed that the shoe was loose, too, missing a nail. Dominic cursed again. Cobweb drifts of mist were beginning to cling together, threatening fog, and the sun had vanished from a grainy sky. It had been shining brilliantly that morning when he had bidden farewell to Guillaume and set out on the road back to Toulouse. Only somewhere, he had taken the wrong turning, and instead of approaching the outskirts of the city as the afternoon drew on, he was in the middle of nowhere, with not so much as the clonk of a goat bell to tell him that he was near civilization.

Following a period of convivial exploration of the taverns and stews of Toulouse, the two young men had gone hunting together in the purer air of the mountains, seeking more of the common ground that Guillaume had said they shared. Dominic was not sure that he agreed with his half brother. Certainly they had found many grounds for differences of opinion and taste, and even with the best will in the world, suspicion and envy still lurked in the shadows of the campfires they made. Still, each had learned from the other. Guillaume had begun to think a little before he opened his mouth, and some of his spontaneity had rubbed off on Dominic's cautiousness. They had parted on wary but friendly terms, Guillaume riding off to visit friends of his father's from the old days of the war, Dominic taking the road—the wrong road—to Toulouse.

Grasping the chestnut's bridle, Dominic started to lead the horse along the track. Downward, he told himself with a grimace at the mist, go downward. People lived in valleys, not on the top of mountains, and he had to find some kind of shelter for the night.

The mist drifting up the river valley had gradually thickened during the day into a moist fog, enclosing the village and concealing it from prying eyes. It lay off the Toulouse road between Foix and Palmiers, a hamlet of the Plantaurel foothills, red-tiled roofs swaddling squat amber stone and tightly barred shutters.

Magda was glad of the roaring fire in the hearth of the shoemaker's cottage, and the bowl of hot bean soup, thicker than the fog, cupped in her hands. She sipped with relish. A meeting had been held earlier that evening, and two of the villagers had taken the final Cathar vows from her uncle Chretien. One of the converts had been so old and weak that his relatives had to carry him into the cottage, and it was obvious that the *consolamentum* was but a deathbed comfort. The other, however, had been a widow of middle years, healthy and strong, with a need to devote her life elsewhere now that her husband had gone.

There were many believers in the village, and Magda and Chretien had been welcomed with open arms and invitations to stay for as long as they wanted. That, of course, was unsafe. Even in a village of believers, there were those who would betray a Cathar to the Inquisition for the bounty payment of a mark per head, and the Dominican friars had their spies and informers everywhere.

Magda knew that her heritage made her especially vulnerable to persecution and that if she was caught, she would be subjected to inquisition, torture, and death at the stake. She and her mother stood accused of blasphemous heresy and witchcraft. What was the difference between their powers and the powers of a saint—the sanction of the Roman priests who were so blind that they could not see the plain truth in blazing splendor before them? No, all they saw was the blazing splendor of their own bigotry in the flames to which they committed those of different beliefs. Anger surged within her, but she sternly quashed it. Love, not rage, was the ultimate immolator.

There was a momentary lull in the conversation around the hearth. The fire crackled and the sound of the ladle that the shoemaker's wife was stirring in her cauldron was very loud. Outside, a horse whinnied.

"Hola!" shouted an impatient voice. "Is anybody there?"

Magda felt a powerful tingling in her veins. The traveler was impatient because he had tried several houses in the village already and found them empty; she could read his thoughts as if they were her own.

The shoemaker, his face as pale as whey, went to the door and opened it the merest crack. "What do you want?" he muttered, his attitude at complete odds with the Cathar doctrine of love to every man.

"A farrier to shoe my lame horse, a bed for the night, and directions to Toulouse in the morning," came the curt reply. "A little courtesy would not go amiss either. If it's dependent on silver, I'll pay."

The tongue was southern, but horribly mangled by a French accent. As wide-eyed as a trapped rabbit, the shoemaker turned to his guests for guidance.

"There is no danger," Magda said with quiet certainty, and setting down her bowl, stood up.

"No danger, my lady, but . . . ?"

"I promise you." She fixed the gibbering craftsman with her steady, gray gaze.

"If you want, we will leave," Chretien offered. "We can always make do with the goat shed or the threshing floor."

"No, no, I wouldn't dream of turning you out!" The shoemaker shook his head vigorously.

"And if the Christ came knocking on your door?"

Shamefaced, their host widened the gap in the door by a thumb width. "There's stabling at the back," he said gruffly to the stranger. "I've no room in the house, you'll have to sleep with your horse, but I'll bring you a bowl of soup."

"My thanks," came the sarcastic response, followed by the slow clop of hooves and the jingle of harness. Magda saw the firelit chestnut hide and the plain but high-quality saddle trappings as the horse was led across the ribbon of light from the doorway and around to the dilapidated goat shed at the back of the dwelling.

Pushing through the uneasy throng of villagers to the hearth, she ladled some steaming bean soup into a wooden bowl. Chretien watched her with a mixture of apprehension and approval. She cast him a swift, reassuring glance. "It is all right, truly," she murmured. "You know that my sense is as keen as my mother's."

"Yes, child, if not keener," Chretien's deep voice rumbled, "but you are also very beautiful and too lightly made to put up a struggle."

"I have nothing to fear from him," she said confidently, and briefly squeezed his hand. "Do go and talk some charity into these people while I administer some to our guest."

He was busy unsaddling his horse and swearing softly beneath his breath. Magda hung the horn candle lantern on the hook provided and put the soup bowl down on the milking stool. Beyond the lantern light, separated precariously from the first section of the shed by a rickety wooden partition, was the shoemaker's goat flock, ready for culling and market.

"The villagers do not mean to be rude," she said. "They are just afraid. I've brought you that hot soup."

Light flashed on the saddle mountings he was setting down in the corner, and reflected in his eyes as he stood straight again. She could not determine their color, but knew from a day long in the past that they were green on gray like the Cornish sea-stones set into her cloak brooch.

"Small wonder they are afraid if this is how skillfully they cover up illicit meetings," he said scornfully, and unrolled a blanket from his pack to cover the horse. "If I wasn't suspicious before, then I'd certainly be suspicious now." Crouching, he ran his hand down the courser's foreleg and clicked his tongue with annoyance. "I'll have to walk him tomorrow, even with a new shoe."

"Let me look at his leg; I'm a healer," Magda offered. "And you can drink your soup before it goes cold."

"I don't need to be a healer to know what's wrong!" he said

testily, but stood aside to let her pass, and picking up the bowl from the milking stool, sat down.

Magda felt the swelling just above the cannon on the chestnut's near foreleg. Gently she rubbed her fingers upon it, closed her eyes, and concentrated. The horse snorted and plunged once, then quivering, stood still. Heat flowed from her fingertips into the damaged tissues. Once, she had thought never to be able to control the force within her, but now it came as easily and unconsciously as breathing.

She felt the man's gaze upon her spine, knew that he had yet to recognize her, and was eyeing her as he would any peasant girl in a stable at night. She sensed that there had been many such moments and many such girls, and because she had come out alone to bring him the soup, he thought that she was one, too. Smiling into her hood, she finished with the horse and, rising from her crouch, turned round.

"The leg will be better by the morning," she said. "It won't give him any more trouble."

He lifted his brows. One corner of his mouth tilted cynically. "Impressive," he said. "Perhaps I could persuade you to lay your hands on an old war wound of mine and ease the ache." His aura flickered softly with glints of vitality and small, impatient sparkles. She projected her own to meet it and saw him register the challenge with a rapid blink of surprise. He set the bowl down beside the stool and stood up, his eyes never once leaving her shadowed face.

"Tell me your name." His voice was as soft and intimate as velvet as he raised his hand to touch her cheek and push down the hood of her cloak. Her silver-fair hair tumbled to her hips in the loose cascade permitted only to virgins. In the wake of his fingertips Magda's skin tingled and warmth suffused her body.

"It is Magda," she said. "Do you not remember?"

His hand fell from her hair and his breathing faltered, and she knew with a quickening at her core that he did indeed remember. "Magda?" he whispered, looking her up and down with a different expression in his eyes from that of a moment since. "Holy Mary, tell me I am not dreaming!"

"You are not dreaming," she answered with a hint of impishness.

He gazed and gazed, drinking her in. "I've never forgotten that afternoon. I even went down to the river when I returned to Toulouse in a sort of pilgrimage—made a wish and threw a flower into the current, but I never thought . . ." He broke off and shook his head bemusedly. "Jesu, but you're beautiful!"

"You didn't think that last time." A dimple appeared at the corner of her mouth. "I was a muddy heretic girl who had stolen your dog."

"And I was the son of the most powerful man in the Languedoc," Dominic said, and his eyelids tensed. "I've never forgotten that part of it either—what happened to him. I knew he was going to die when I saw him on the ground at your mother's feet. It was his only way of escape."

"He had a choice," Magda contradicted.

"But he never saw or understood it. For my father there was only ever the power of the sword. Sometimes I see myself following him down that same road. He is in front of me leading me on, and I know that when he turns round, he won't have a face." Restlessly he turned from her to pace the small hovel.

Magda watched him, sensing his complexity and tension, the hair-thin line he trod between darkness and light, past and future. She reminded him of a caged lynx that she and her mother had seen on a feast day in Foix.

He ceased pacing and paused beside his horse to stroke its satin chestnut hide. "Are you one of the Perfecti?" he asked on a more level note.

"Not in the orthodox sense."

"What does that mean?"

Magda hesitated, bemused, a little frightened by the speed at which events were moving. "My mother and I live among the Cathars, but our beliefs are not entirely the same. Our bloodline carries the blessing . . . or curse of adept skills, and it is my duty, as it was my mother's, to continue it."

"Are you spoken for?"

Warmth rippled through her body in response to the rich huskiness of his voice. "The women of my line speak for themselves," she said proudly.

He left the horse and came to stand in front of her. "And how say you?" he asked softly.

Between their bodies was a resistant barrier of physical heat, demanding to be broken and reforged. There had been temptations before at Montségur as her womanhood came upon her and she started to notice men, but no one had ever attracted her with this kind of intensity before. Was this how it had been for her mother and father? "That I am no man's property, nor ever will be except of my own desiring." She stepped away from the seductive danger of his proximity. "And you? How say you?"

He released his breath and his tension relaxed a little, but she was aware of the predatory gleam in his eyes. "I have no pledges to break."

She regarded him warily. How easy it would be to seek an hour of gratification with him. The moon phase was perfect, she would be assured of conceiving, but beyond that immediate realization, a deeper concern held her back. She wanted to know more of the man than the magnificence of his body, which had been squandered many times on many different women. The road branched here. She could have this one night, or the opportunity of a lifetime commitment. The path her mother had trodden, or the one that she herself desired to take. "You could travel with us awhile," she suggested, and bit her lip nervously as he began to frown.

"Travel with you?" he said slowly. "To make of me a Cathar?"

"No." She looked at him steadily, willing him to understand, not to turn away, and then because she knew the power of her own mind, lowered her gaze and blanked out that will. Whatever his decision, it was his alone to make. Once before they had stood like this in a water meadow, she offering, and he at war with himself.

He inhaled to speak and she lifted her head, but his reply went unspoken and his gaze cut from her to the crude shed doorway.

"Uncle Chretien," she said with a mixture of relief and disappointment.

Chretien's deep-set eyes raked over herself and Dominic while he assessed the situation. "Are you coming back within, Magda?" His voice was more of a command than a question. "It is time to bolt the door."

"Yes, Uncle," she said so meekly that his brows lifted in

speculation as she brushed past him into the cold night. She looked round once at Dominic, an unspoken question hanging in her eyes. Dominic returned that look inscrutably and inclined his head.

"Demoiselle," he saluted, then added softly, "until tomorrow."

She caught her breath and her eyes widened on his before she turned away, decently drawing up the hood of her cloak.

The glow left Dominic's eyes as he faced Chretien. "Are you her guardian?"

"I am." Chretien handed him a coarsely woven blanket. "Here, it is going to be a cold night out here alone." Heavy emphasis pressured the final word.

Dominic laughed shortly and took the blanket. "You are quite right to be suspicious. I won't say that any such lewd thoughts did not enter my head, because they did. She is beautiful, but then you Cathars would say that beauty is just another snare of the Devil."

Chretien studied their guest thoughtfully. He could see why a young woman might find him attractive with his strong, regular bones and fine eyes, but there had to be more than that for Magda to want him. "The beauty of the soul, we do not deny," he murmured, "just its fleshly covering. Without love, there is naught but corruption."

Dominic spread the blanket on the dirty straw of the stable floor. "Then I have led a very corrupt life," he said lightly, but the remark itself was not light at all.

"You are young, you have time. All you have to do is open yourself to the truth."

"The truth?" Dominic lifted a cynical brow. "If you are going to preach me a sermon about good Gods and evil Gods and spirit and matter, you will be wasting your breath."

Chretien looked amused. "The breath is wasted anyway unless it bears witness," he said. "The core of the message is simple enough—deed, not word; example, not hypocrisy." His eyes lit upon the sword, shield, and rolled-up hauberk propped against the harness.

Dominic followed his glance. "I am not of your creed even while I applaud its merits," he retorted with amusement of his own, and sat down on the blanket.

"You're a good French Catholic then?"

"Hah, none of those!"

Chretien stared at him, and Dominic laughed. "Well, I never claimed to be good, and I'm only half-French—my mother's from Agen. As to being a good Catholic . . ." He spread his hands. "My tutor was a black friar and he was convinced that I was a minion of the Antichrist. Whatever devotion I had to offer was beaten out of me at a very tender age. I pay lip service, no more." A pensive, almost defiant, expression crossed his face. "Magda asked if I would travel with you for a while."

Chretien sucked in his breath. "And how did you reply?"

"I more or less accepted. I have no commitments in Toulouse . . . well, none that matter. I left my post with the garrison more than a month ago."

The older man frowned heavily. "If you came with us, it would be because of your interest in her, would it not?"

"I would be lying if I said I was driven by religious fervor." Dominic met the Cathar's stern gaze steadily. "But if I agree to travel your road, I will be making a commitment far beyond idle dalliance, and at her behest."

"Magda is no ordinary young woman. There is a blood price on her head way beyond that upon any Cathar, indeed way beyond mine. I advise you most strongly to think with your head, not your loins."

"I am thinking," Dominic said softly, "with my heart."

In the morning the chestnut's foreleg was cool beneath Dominic's hand, and there was no evidence of swelling. "I do not suppose that you can conjure a horseshoe out of thin air?" he inquired of Magda when she brought him a bowl of hot, honey-sweetened gruel and a cup of wine to break his fast.

Her gray eyes sparkled. "I have never tried," she said impishly, and sat down on the stool to watch him eat. "But there is a smith in the village. He'll be here as soon as he's broken his fast." She hesitated, then spoke again. "Uncle Chretien doesn't know whether or not to approve of you."

Dominic sampled the gruel and found it more appetizing than it looked. Besides, he was starving. "I hope you set his mind at rest." He looked at her from beneath his brows as he lowered and lifted the spoon.

"No, that is something you will have to do yourself—if you have not changed your mind?"

"Why should I do that?"

Color flooded her face. "Last night everything happened so quickly."

Dominic sucked the end of the spoon and gave her a considering look. "I have not changed my mind, unless you have changed yours," he said after a moment. "It doesn't matter how quickly things happened, only that they did. And for all your cleverness, you are wrong."

Magda raised her brows. He pointed the spoon at her. "Seventeen years," he said. "I have been waiting seventeen years. There is nothing swift about that."

She laughed and then she grew sober. Their eyes met and held. "No," she said. "There is nothing swift about that."

They rode together that day, side by side, sometimes in animated conversation, sometimes united by a silence more profound than the speaking of any words. He told her about northern France, the cooler, unpredictable summers, the gray, heavy winters, about life at Montfort l'Amaury, and then later at the French court—although he was somewhat circumspect about his adventures there, particularly with respect to women. And Magda told him about her childhood at Montségur among the Cathars, and a little about her upbringing, and she, too, was circumspect.

At eventide they came to the next village on their path and were welcomed with food and lodging. Sidelong glances were cast at Dominic, for Cathars did not usually travel in the company of armed soldiers, but Chretien explained that the young man was a fellow traveler, a friend who had joined them for a while on the road, and Dominic was accepted.

When Chretien preached his sermon to the village gathering in his deep, mellifluous voice, he enthralled the people, filling them up with his vision of a purer life. Such were his gifts of oratory that even Dominic, who had learned the power of the sermon from the black friars and grown cynical and disillusioned, felt his breast fill with optimism.

After Chretien had spoken, bread and soup were served and the people came to Magda, asking for her healing touch, for potions and balms and advice. Dominic watched and listened, absorbing this, too. He saw how they trusted her, and how she gave of herself unstintingly until she was white and drained. He thought about sending away those who still waited their turn, but checked himself. It was not his place to do so, it was hers.

She raised her eyes to his and gave him a brief, secret smile of approbation. Unobtrusively he brought her a cup of sweetened wine, pressed it into her hand, and with a light touch on her shoulder, went and sat down next to Chretien.

"It is always like this," Chretien said, as much by way of a warning as informing. "News of our coming travels before us, and the village numbers swell to twice their size."

"The French court is the same whenever the king is in residence," Dominic said with a shrug. "But of course, the people wait on the king's pleasure, not he on theirs."

"Are you saying we should do the same?"

Dominic met the straightforward dark stare. "No, sir," he answered quietly. "There is a difference between being the taker and being the giver. I do not think that the King of France would recognize it."

Chretien nodded thoughtfully and a half smile relaxed the severity of his mouth. "Have you never thought about taking up preaching yourself?"

Dominic laughed and shook his head. "That is for other men with a deeper conviction than mine—and a greater skill. To give people belief, that is a very great power, but I do not know that I trust it. Each person's own truth is different from the truth of his neighbor."

The half smile faded, but not with disapproval, and the thoughtful look remained. "There is more to you than meets the eye," Chretien said, and glanced toward Magda.

Dominic followed the direction of his stare. His own eyes settled on her willow-slim body, the tired droop of her lovely gray eyes, the shape of her mouth. Desire flickered through him, and a deeper need. The desert wanderer discovering an oasis. "There is more to everyone than meets the eye," he responded.

Two nights later, between villages, the three travelers made camp for the night beneath the stars. The air was sharp with encroaching autumn and the breeze nipped and pinched maliciously at exposed flesh. They had been gathering firewood along the road as they journeyed, and while Dominic picketed the chestnut and the pack horse, Chretien prepared the fire.

The fickle breeze was blowing in the wrong direction and Chretien's tinder had little inclination to light. Although the day had been fine, and the evening sky was clear, the misty weather of the last week had dampened the firewood. Dominic finished tending the horses and came to help Chretien, kneeling down to blow beneath the tenuous flicker of the last of Chretien's tinder.

"It is no use," announced Chretien with a sigh. "It will not light."

Magda approached them, a loaf in one hand and a skin of wine in the other. Gracefully she knelt upright before the fire, put down the provisions, and spread her fingers over the damp branches and feeble guttering of tinder. Her eyes were closed. She drew a deep breath and released it slowly. The flame steadied, wearing a single eye like a candle, and then, before Dominic's astonished eyes, yellow flowers bloomed among the caverns of firewood. Heat spread outward in a golden aura, amid the crackle and spit of a living fire.

"How did you do that?" He gazed at her, not a little daunted. That she was a healer of considerable skill, he had accepted, but that she could kindle a hearth out of damp wood set her abilities in a different dimension entirely.

"My mother taught me to control it, but it is something I have always been able to do. It's not really much different from laying my hands on a sick person."

She spoke so normally that Dominic's skin prickled. What other skills did she take for granted? Perhaps, as he had once thought as a child, she was indeed half-elf. She scooped her hair behind her ears and turned to the food. "Bread," she said, breaking the loaf, "and wine. It is all we have until we reach the next village."

Uneasily Dominic consumed the food of the sacrament, and pondered what he had seen, measuring his strength to cope with it. Chretien announced that he was tired and rolled himself in his blanket early, leaving Dominic and Magda to watch over the fire.

"You are troubled," Magda said softly. She moved closer and he found himself stifling the urge to recoil.

"It is nothing," he lied, and avoided her eyes, which would draw the thoughts straight out of his own.

"It is because I raised the fire, is it not?"

He tossed another branch on the flames and listened to the hiss and spark, guarding his thoughts while he mustered them. Then finally he dared to look at her. "Most women bake and spin, tend the household and the vegetable plot. Do you do those things, too?"

She pursed her lips and asked a question of her own. "Most women? How many have you known?"

Dominic shrugged. "More than I can count, or even remember their names. Life at the French court when you are Simon de Montfort's son is akin to being a bee in a garden full of flowers."

"Truly known? I mean beyond flesh?"

He thought about getting to his feet and walking away from the conversation, but knew that if he did, he would be walking away from far more than that. "I doubt any of them," he capitulated. "But then I did not want to know them beyond flesh, or else they could not give me what I needed."

Magda studied him gravely. In the firelight, her eyes were dark pools with glimmers of flame in their depths. "Yes," she said. "I can bake and spin and tend vegetables like other women." She leaned toward him, touching herself for emphasis. "I am a woman, ordinary in most senses of the word. I hate it when my gifts set me on a pedestal. I accept you as you are, so you must accept me."

"What do you expect me to do when out of nowhere you stretch your hand above damp branches and cause them to light?" he demanded.

"The way you speak, to return to Toulouse."

Dominic gazed into the fire that she had raised. Why not take one of the safe, ordinary heiresses whom his brother Simon was always offering him? Why not, as Magda suggested, ride back to Toulouse, report for another stint of garrison duty, and seek out auburn-haired Peronelle, she of the smothering cleavage? Then he looked at Magda and clearly saw his reason for staying. They were half of each other, could never be whole unless they were together, a complete and eternal circle.

"There is nothing for me in Toulouse," he said. "All I want is here with you. All I need." He set his arm around her waist and drew her toward him. She came into his arms, eager and shy, her faced raised. Dominic kissed her brow, her eyelids, her cheeks and chin, returning finally to the soft cushion of her lips. Heady as strong wine, sweet and sweeping. As if he were kindling to her touch, he felt the fire lick through his body and center at his core.

The kiss broke for want of breath, and was renewed. He wove his hands in the silk of her hair. She pressed herself against him, the formerly unfocused yearnings of her body now given sharp clarity. This man. Forever.

Again they broke apart. Dominic swallowed, and very gently released her. "Seventeen years," he said with a tremulous smile. "A little longer will not matter. I want to know you, Magda, all of you, little by little. All at once would overwhelm me." He stroked her cheek, traced the outline of her face with his forefinger.

"It is the same with me," she whispered in reply. "It is frightening, to feel so much, so strongly."

Sobered, they remained staring at each other until the fire choked loudly on a knot of resin, and spat out a shower of sparks. Both of them jumped. Chretien, wakening, sat up, looked at Magda and Dominic, and turned over.

Magda leaned toward Dominic, kissed him gently, and after a final look, rolled herself in her cloak. "Good night," she said softly.

Dominic touched a strand of her silky hair. "Good night," he responded, but made no attempt to sleep himself, preferring to remain awake, watching the fire, and the stars, and distilling from the open night a sense of power, calm, and great, great joy.

CHAPTER THIRTY-EIGHT

Tiny flakes of snow danced in the air, starring the travelers' cloaks and ticklishly settling on their faces. The powdery ground muffled the chestnut's hoofbeats and recorded each imprint of shod hoof and human foot on the village road. Winter had come early this year to the Plantaurels, and although the cloud was not thick, the snow was a portent of what was to follow. This journey was Chretien's last before returning to Montségur for the harshest winter months.

Behind Dominic, sharing the chestnut, Magda dozed, her cheek against his spine, her hands beneath his cloak, taking purchase in his belt and drawing comfort from his body warmth. He smiled to feel her presence, and bore the bitter wind with equanimity.

For two months he had been traveling with her and Chretien, but it seemed as if it had been forever, so quickly had he become attuned to their way of life. He had been wary of pursuing a dream, of revealing too much of himself, but gradually, as the dream took on texture and reality, he had become absorbed into it, opening to Magda's scrutiny his heart and his soul, something that even his half brother Simon, who had come closer to him than anyone, had never been permitted.

The physical tension was still present; he had only to look at her, or feel her looking at him, for his breath to quicken and his loins to tighten pleasurably, but he was willing to wait upon a time that was ripe, rather than purely convenient. Besides, the fact that he had proved he was not about to pounce on Magda and ravish her behind the nearest rock had much improved his standing with Chretien, as had his perseverance. He was full aware that the elderly Cathar had half-expected him to tire of waiting, make his excuses, and leave in search of easier game. These days Chretien was less reserved with him, and despite the older man's presence and gravity, Dominic detected a salting of mischievous humor in the deep-set eyes.

When they arrived in the village it was almost dusk. The headman, Jean le Picou, a wool merchant, welcomed them into his house and served them bread and a rich vegetable stew, fussing obsequiously over the three of them. His nervous, jerky manner was more than Dominic could stand, and on the pretext of needing to empty his bladder, he excused himself and went outside.

Le Picou's goat flock was penned in a rickety shelter close to the house—beasts that had grazed well all summer and were sleek and strong. Their breath steamed in the night-blue air, and their horns gleamed as they moved. It had stopped snowing and the first stars glimmered on a turquoise horizon. Dominic inhaled the frozen tranquillity of the evening, his eyes on the dark humps of the surrounding mountains while he waited. When he heard the sound of the door latch clicking, his lower lids tensed with amusement, and without surprise, he turned his head to watch Magda walk up the path to join him.

"What's your excuse?" He grinned, unfolding his arms.

"You." She reached on tiptoe to kiss him and stole her hands beneath his cloak. He returned her kiss, his body suffusing with warmth. They held on to each other, the embrace deepening, losing its playfulness, while above them the sky darkened and the stars glittered, huge and ice-white.

In the village a door slammed and a dog barked frantically. Breaking the kiss, Dominic raised his head. Magda swayed against him, her eyes half-closed, her lips parted, the bodice of her gown in disarray under her cloak. He looked down at her, remembering other such occasions with different women. Snatched moments in dark corners, one ear cocked for a footfall.

> *A wonderful gift she gave to me*
> *her love, her ring. God end the strain*

Beneath her mantle my hand will be
If yet enough of time I gain.

"Magda?" he said gently, and rearranged her cloak. Her eyes lost their blind look and she raised her head.

"You did not have to stop," she said.

"Where would we go? In with the goats? Sneak past your uncle and our host?" His voice was full of wry amusement and not a little frustration.

She glanced round and acknowledged with a soft sigh the truth of what he said. "It will be different when we reach Montségur," she murmured, rubbing her cheek against his hand.

"Montségur," he repeated, and withdrew into himself a little. Magda was overjoyed to be returning to her mother and her people, bringing with her the man with whom she had chosen to share herself, but for him it was not so simple.

"You are worried about meeting your mother, aren't you?"

He lifted one shoulder. "It will not be easy."

Magda leaned against him, offering comfort. "It will not be easy," she agreed. "But you have the strength, and so does she."

"You know her well, then?"

"I was only a child when Sister Claire came to Montségur, but my mother often visited her. She was much troubled with nightmares and a burden of guilt and grief that were not even hers to carry. I think she recovered from them enough to find a measure of peace and take the *consolamentum*, but I do not believe that she has ever been really happy. If she could come to terms with what happened in the past . . ."

"Stare it straight in the eyes, you mean," Dominic said grimly. "I am told I look like my father."

"Looking is not being." She sought his hands and squeezed them. "I think that once she has seen you, she will be cleansed . . . and so will you."

Dominic smiled. "Oh, Magda," he said with a gentle shake of his head, and took her face in his hands to kiss her again, tenderly. "Where would I be without you?"

Her arms encircled his neck. A glint of light caught the corner of his eye and he turned his head, half-expecting to see

Chretien in his role of guardian of Magda's welfare. Instead he saw the cloaked figure of a woman leading a pack mule down the village street. She wore stout leather shoes, and the nailed soles clicked loudly in the silence and created a pattern of sound that wove in and out between the clop of the mule's small hooves.

Magda craned over his shoulder and her hands suddenly gripped upon him. "It is my mother!" she said in astonishment. "I felt she was close to me, but I thought it was because we were on our way to Montségur!"

The mule and the footsteps ceased. The cloaked figure turned in a half circle and looked directly at the lovers.

"Mama!" Magda cried, and grasping Dominic's hand in hers, tugged him toward Bridget.

She was as he remembered, her gray eyes warm and bright, her smile tender. When she put down her hood, he saw that her once black hair was ribboned at the front by a single wide moonbeam of silver.

"It is but a few days journey to Montségur," she said as she kissed Magda and held her close. "I decided to come down and meet you. I knew this time your homecoming would be special." Her eyes went to Dominic as she spoke, and once more he felt the cleansing glow of their scrutiny.

"Be welcome into our family," Bridget said, and embraced him, too. "Magda has chosen wisely and well."

He felt how lightly boned she was, her frame sparrowlike beneath his hands, where Magda's was sturdy. He could almost see the flame of her spirit within the shell of her flesh. "I will strive to be worthy," he said.

Magda smiled and folded her arm through his. "So will I." She looked up at him with such a radiance of love in her eyes that it took away his breath and prickled his lids. His early years had been so bereft of affection that to have it poured upon him now was almost too much for his heart to bear, and he thought that it would burst.

The wool merchant was delighted to welcome Bridget into his house, and his nervous hand-rubbing increased threefold. He insisted on going out to fetch more bread and wine, and when Bridget protested that what he had was entirely adequate, he fluffed up like a cockerel, declaring that it would be slacking his duty as a host to do otherwise.

Magda could sense Dominic's irritation, although it did not show on his face, which remained politely expressionless. She herself had a feeling of impending danger. It crawled unpleasantly on her skin, leaving a trail of fear. She looked at her mother.

"Yes," Bridget said softly. "It will be wise to stay here only this one night, and to travel fast on the morrow."

"We have been little troubled thus far," Chretien said, his dark eyes flickering to Dominic. "A Cathar journeying in the company of an armed warrior is a sight to behold and to be treated with respect. Of course, it is not the first time I have done so by far."

Dominic smiled, but looked slightly uncomfortable. "I know that you would rather I discarded my sword, but it has been a part of me since infancy. One day I might indeed beat it into a plowshare, but for the moment it remains, especially if there is a danger." He rose to his feet. "Le Picou's been gone a long time. "I'm going outside to look for him."

The scabbarded weapon was leaning against the doorpost, and on his way out, he paused to grasp the hilt.

Magda stared at the door he had just gently closed. "When we reach Montségur, the moon time will be right," she said, and laid her hand upon her flat, taut belly.

"Then you have not lain with him yet?"

Magda shook her head. "In the beginning I was afraid of losing him—he has had many women before." Her chin came up and she looked at her mother defiantly. "I did not want him for just one night of rutting fever even if it would better have served our bloodline. And if that is heresy, then so be it."

"I do not believe you would have lost him."

Magda sighed. "Neither do I now, but at the time I was not to know. He was so determined to have his own way, and I was equally as determined to prove I was more than just a wench for tumbling in the straw."

Chretien cleared his throat and, muttering something about relieving himself, went out of the door.

Mother and daughter exchanged rueful glances and smiled. The Cathar belief that celibacy was a prerequisite of spiritual enlightenment did not sit easily with their own belief in celebrating life's forces at the given time.

"Does he know about us, about the Virgin and the Magdalene?" Bridget inquired.

"A little. He has seen that I have the gifts to raise the fire and heal the sick. I will tell him the story of our bloodline when we arrive at Montségur. I—" She stopped speaking and her head jerked up as they heard a commotion outside the house. The door burst open and Chretien hurtled in on a draft of freezing white air.

"Quickly!" he panted. "Le Picou has betrayed us. The Dominican Inquisition is here in the village with a troop of soldiers!"

Weapons clashed outside the house. Magda heard a scream, and then Dominic was in the room with them, his sword stained red. She ran to him. His lips touched hers in a single hard kiss, and then he was pushing her away. "Go with Chretien," he commanded. "I'll join you later!"

"You will be killed!"

"Go!"

Bridget grabbed her daughter's arm and jerked her away toward the low door that led through into the merchant's stables.

"In the name of our Lord Jesus Christ, I command you stay where you are!" A black friar loomed upon the threshold, a bony forefinger pointing at the occupants of the room.

Magda froze, all her childhood nightmares suddenly solidifying as she stared upon the face of the dark presence of her dreams. She was powerless against it, could feel her will draining away. It was her mother who spoke, her voice colder than Magda had ever heard it. "Perhaps you should invoke the Virgin Mary, since you claim it was she who saved your life on the road to Carcassonne one harsh winter's night," she said, giving him stare for stare. "If it were not against my teaching, I would have left you to die."

The friar blenched. His eyes were blacker than a void. He tried to articulate, but no sound came from his jerking throat. Bridget dragged Magda through into the stables.

Dominic raised his sword and blocked the advance of two foot soldiers who had ranged themselves on either side of the stuttering Friar Bernard.

"Get out of our way, you accursed heretic," snarled one of the men.

Dominic heard the neigh of his chestnut horse and the thud of hooves in the dirt yard behind the house. The soldier attacked.

The shriek of sword upon sword carried across the frosty night. Blue-white sparks flashed off the blade edges as they slid along each other. Dominic twisted and cut. His opponent, trained to deal with a right-handed adversary, made the wrong defensive move and paid for it with his life. Dominic leaped over his falling body and engaged the second man, feinted right and struck low and left, ripping open his leg.

Then he lunged at Friar Bernard. Someone pushed the priest out of the way. Dominic's sword screeched upon mail rings, and then he found himself looking down a loaded crossbow that was aimed directly at his heart.

Slowly Dominic lowered his sword, and cast it down in the dirt. Magda, Bridget, and Chretien were safely away; it did not matter what happened now.

Friar Bernard strode over to him, forefinger trembling, accusing. "If it is the last thing I do," he panted in a voice shaking with emotion and fear, "I am going to hold you up to the world for the filthy heretic you are! Take him!"

The soldiers handled him roughly, but Dominic hardly responded. He retreated within himself, closed the drawbridge, and presented the foaming Friar Bernard with an impervious facade.

CHAPTER THIRTY-NINE

Toulouse, Spring 1235

TORCHLIGHT. VOICES. A key screeching in the lock. The occupants of the cell who were capable crawled away from these portents as rapidly as they could like insects panicked from beneath an overturned stone.

Dominic curled his left fist, testing the pain of his raw nail beds against his palm. At the time that they ripped out his fingernails, it had not seemed too difficult to bear because he had been in a semitrance, backed against the far wall of his snail-shell of retreat. Magda had come to him through the door and past the priests; they had not seen her and she had taken him away, leaving only the husk of his body to the inquisitors. But the moment had arrived when he had to return to his body and what they had done to it. Suddenly and sharply, with no time to accustom himself.

Time had lost all meaning. He might have been in the cells of the Château Narbonnais for three days, three months, or three years. He had been beaten, tortured, pushed and pushed to confess to heresy by Friar Bernard, whose assaults, both physical and mental, had become increasingly vicious as Dominic refused to yield so much as an inch of ground. They were back in the schoolroom, will locking with will. *Fiat voluntas Tua.*

The soldiers picked their way across the musty straw, searching the darkest corners of the cell and the rags of life cowering there, until at last they discovered Dominic hunched against a dank wall, staring blankly at nothing as he so often did. Obtaining a response from this one was nigh on impossible. They hauled him to his feet when he ignored their command to rise, and thrust him before them out of the cells and up the twisting stairway. Dominic took little notice of where they were dragging him, all his being concentrated upon summoning the light, upon reaching out to Magda. He could sense her presence, but she was far away, barely glimpsed by his spirit.

Fear and privation made his limbs weak. His teeth chattered uncontrollably, and the arms that were grasping him tightened to brace him up as they mounted another set of stairs. Through a gray haze Dominic realized they were not taking the usual direction to the inquisitor's rooms, but were entering the private chambers belonging to the garrison commander and his officers, a place that Dominic himself had much frequented in the past, in another life, his fingers stained with ink, not blood.

"Good God!" he heard someone say in a shocked voice. Squinting through gummy lids, he recognized Henri Lemagne, one of his brother Amaury's adjutants. "Give the lad a blanket and pour him some of that double-strength wine. . . . Quickly man, don't just stand there!"

Dominic swayed. A hand held out a blanket toward him. He took it with his right hand, could not hold it, and it slid to the ground. "Henri," he said hoarsely, and his knees buckled.

Swearing volubly, Lemagne sprang from the comfortable X chair in which he had been awaiting Dominic's arrival from the cells, and knelt beside the young man. He was still conscious, but obviously disoriented and in a dreadful condition. His bones protruded alarmingly through his sallow skin and there were some horrifying sores where chains and manacles had chafed him raw. The left hand was the worst, and Lemagne's oaths became yet more blasphemous as he realized what the priests had done to it.

Amazingly, Dominic managed a mirthless shadow of a smile. "Don't let Friar Bernard hear you say that. He'll have you in thumbscrews faster than a whore lifting her skirts for business. . . ." He squeezed shut his eyes, gasping with effort and nausea. "Have you come to watch me burn?"

"You're not going to burn, lad!" Lemagne declared vehemently. "I'd light a torch beneath the black friar who did this to you if I could! Can you sit up?"

Grimacing with pain, Dominic struggled to raise himself. Lemagne watched him, a lump thickening in his throat. Left-handed himself, his skill proven by the fact that at the age of five and forty he was still alive and barely scarred by a life of fighting, Lemagne had been responsible for much of Dominic's early training in the use of weapons. Dominic had learned swiftly and displayed a real talent in arms. The good wages paid by the Count de Montfort and a genuine affection for Dominic had bound Lemagne to that employment for more than ten years, and to see his handiwork thus abused was like seeing a beloved blade that had become battle-mired and broken.

The wine arrived. Dominic extended his left hand, remembered, and used the right. "What are you doing here if not witnessing my execution?" His speech was slow and difficult, for his lips were swollen where he had been struck across the mouth, and two of his teeth were loose. Bruises blue and yellow discolored his face and puffed the skin beneath one eye.

"Simon sent me to get you out. What else would I be doing in this godforsaken cesspit?"

"Simon did?"

"And Amaury. The de Montfort kinship is a powerful bond, and your half brothers powerful men." Lemagne took a roll of parchment from the trestle and waved it at Dominic. "This is your release. You've been signed into my custody by Friar Seilha himself, senior inquisitor for the district."

"So I'm not a heretic?" Dominic said bitterly, and took a shuddering drink of the wine. "God pity me if one of my brothers were not the high constable of France, and the other an English earl."

"God pity you indeed," Lemagne said with a frown, and rubbed a twist of his gold and gray beard between his fingers. "They say you were caught traveling with some Cathars in the mountains and that you killed an inquisitor's guard so that the Cathars could escape. What were you thinking of?"

Dominic looked, and then dropped his gaze. "If they had caught her, she would have burned," he said huskily.

Lemagne's tight mouth relaxed. He took his hand off his

beard, made an exasperated gesture, and sighed heavily. "Dominic, Dominic! A woman. I should have known! Those friars almost had me thinking you truly had taken to heresy. God's sweet love, will you never learn!" He shook his leonine head. "Women are trouble, more than any man can handle! Look what happened in Paris when you tangled with Clemence de Veyran. You were lucky to be banished to Toulouse with your jewels intact. Didn't you learn any discretion!"

Dominic knew that it was pointless explaining his motives to Lemagne. The man was forthright, honest, and had about as much imagination as a loaf of bread. Besides, at the moment, Dominic was in no condition to make him understand anything. Let him believe it was the folly of hot blood. Easier for everyone. The warmth of the room was bringing his injuries back to throbbing life as the cold receded from his bones. He flexed his left hand, and gritted his teeth against a red wave of pain. "What about Friar Bernard?" he said hoarsely.

"What about him?"

"Didn't he protest about my being freed?"

Lemagne shrugged and teased at his beard again. "He's away at a conference in Albi. Seilha's zealous, but he's not too blind to see reason when it knocks on his door bearing the seal of France's constable. Don't let it concern you." He splashed more wine into Dominic's cup. "Once you're out of this place, your paths won't cross again."

Dominic kept his eyes on the wine and held his tongue, but his precautions were useless. Lemagne was a seasoned enough soldier to see straight through him.

"If you were thinking of riding out of Toulouse and straight back into trouble, let me disabuse you of the notion now. There are terms to your release," he growled.

"Such as?" Dominic's gut clenched.

"You're to remain in my custody until handed over to Amaury or Simon; you're to wear the yellow cross of a repentant heretic on your garments for a period of three years, and you're to take an oath to go on crusade as soon as you are recovered enough." He sucked his teeth and frowned at Dominic's obdurate expression. "Look, forget her, lad. You're playing with fire, the real thing, not the slush that troubadours drip through their lute strings. Do you want to burn in hell?"

Dominic bent his head, assailed by violent wingbeats of pain that threatened his consciousness. He was to be released from prison but still kept within the shackles of Friar Bernard's forging, and doubtless closely observed—for his own good, they would say. He dared not endanger Magda or her family by making contact, not yet at least. "This is hell," he muttered, his eyes blinded by scalding salt. He curled his fingers tightly around the goblet, and with the last of his strength, abandoned control and hurled the cup across the room. The sound of it shattering against the wall, and Lemagne's exclamation, were the last things he heard for a very long time.

CHAPTER FORTY

Montségur, Spring 1242

THEY SAID THAT he was dead, but staring out on a landscape of green spring buds, Magda knew that it was not true. She would have felt the emptiness in her soul. Sometimes she was aware of his presence so clearly that it was as if he were standing beside her. She would feel his breath against her hair and the touch of his hand upon her shoulder. Many times she had cast her mind abroad, seeking him, but on every occasion she came up against a stubborn, solid wall that would not permit her beyond its daunting barrier.

In the early months of their parting, she had found him in the dungeons of the Château Narbonnais in Toulouse, and she had done what she could to help him endure. It was for her sake and her mother's that they were breaking him, and watching him suffer had filled her with guilt and grief. Then one day, when she sought him through the paths of the mental bond they shared, he was gone, and in his place she found the wall. One of their number who could move freely in Toulouse had made discreet inquiries at the Château Narbonnais.

They said that he was dead, but she did not believe them.

Magda wiped the tears from her cheeks and rubbed her eyes with the back of one hand. She could see one of the women from the fortress coming toward her through the trees, and she did not want to be discovered weeping.

As the visitor came closer, Magda saw that it was Claire de Montvallant, and she was carrying Sancha, her small two-year-old granddaughter, in her arms. The child was the result of a liaison between her son Guillaume and a capricious Spanish mercenary's daughter who cooked for Montségur's garrison.

Magda put aside her contemplations and went forward to meet them, a smile of greeting on her face. She was always pleased to see Claire, for she was a tenuous link with Dominic. Sometimes Magda could see him so clearly in the Cathar woman that her heart turned over with pleasure and pain.

Whimpering, the little girl curled against her grandmother, her hair a snarled mass of dark curls, her eyes a huge, liquid brown. One cheek was bright red.

"She is teething, poor lamb," said Claire as Magda led her down to the hut that she and Bridget shared. "Constanza says that she kept her and Guillaume awake all night with her crying. I thought that you might be able to ease her pain."

"Give her to me." Magda took the little girl's solid, warm weight into her arms, and sitting down, settled her on her knee. Sancha thought about screaming, but her wails were only half-hearted, and after a moment she forgot them and peeped a shy, dimpled smile at Magda from beneath coquettish black lashes. Magda laid the palm of her hand to the child's burning cheek and summoned the healing flow in the gentlest trickle to soothe the tender gum. "I will give you some ointment of honey and cloves to rub on it," she said, and inquired politely after Claire's well-being and that of Sancha's parents.

Claire's fine brown eyes narrowed with pain. "I fear for my son," she said sadly. "Today he rode out of Montségur with Pierre-Roger and some others. They were all dressed for war and spoiling for a fight. He feeds on his hatred of the French. I know why he came here in the first place. Toulouse and

Montvallant had become unsafe for him, so he retreated to the mountains and offered his sword to Pierre-Roger in return for food and shelter and the wherewithal to make war. Many times I have tried to reach him and make him understand that what he is doing is wicked, but it seems that we speak a different language."

"His conscience is not in your keeping," Magda warned gently. "If you goad him, you may drive him further away."

Claire sighed helplessly. "Yes, I know," she murmured. "Your mother told me as much about Raoul once, and she predicted that Guillaume would reach manhood with many roads open before him. It breaks my heart to see the one he is choosing. Is there nothing I can do?"

"Listen quietly to the voice of your own soul," Magda said. "Look at the paths of your own choosing." She gave Claire a sad smile. "That was what I was doing myself when I saw you coming toward me. A part of me says that it is time to leave the old road for a new one before it is too late. But another part lingers, waiting for someone else to catch up." She tightened her arms around the child, and brushing her lips over the silky curls, imagined that Sancha were her own. Sometimes the emptiness in her loins and breasts was a physical ache. I have been fallow for too long, she thought.

They say he is dead. I do not believe it.

Guillaume kissed Constanza, squeezed her rump, drank from his goblet, and sat down with an exaggerated movement beside his mother, who was watching Sancha sleep, free of teething pain. Guillaume's blood was still up. Claire could almost hear it fizzing in his veins. Eyes bright with drink and excitement, he seemed to loom over her, not her son, but a stranger, one of the false God's servants.

"You'll be able to travel the roads in peace now," he told her proudly. "Safe from the black-robes!" Laughing, he gulped at his wine.

"What have you done?" Her stomach turned over at the smell of wine and meat on his breath. It was one of her denial days and only water had passed her own lips.

"You've heard me mention Alfaro? He's Rai's bailiff in Avignonet and married to Rai's half sister?"

"I . . . I think so."

"Well, he hates the Dominicans and the French very badly indeed, so when an Inquisition of eleven of them turned up in Avignonet, he sent word here straightaway . . . and we rode out and dealt with them." He patted the sword on his hip and held out his empty cup for Constanza to refill. "I've got a fine new horse and harness out of it, and a spare hauberk." Grinning, he addressed his mistress. "They'll fetch enough money to keep you and Sancha in silk gowns for a long time to come . . . or perhaps you'd like a necklace and earrings of Byzantine gold, hmmm?" He snatched a fondle and a kiss.

Claire heaved. She clenched her teeth and swallowed bile. Raoul had wept when he killed men, had used his sword with reluctance, shielding himself with the tatters of his honor and pride. Guillaume was openly bragging. Oh God, how he had been twisted by this lifetime of war. Occasionally she glimpsed the remnants of the decent young man he could have been staring through a chink in *Rex Mundi*'s black armor, imprisoned, bewildered. It was the way she remembered her own past before the salvation of the *consolamentum*. But Guillaume was unable to see the shining light beyond his desperately outstretched fingers. All he saw was a red, killing darkness.

"Do you think such an act will stop them?" she asked tiredly. "Fighting evil with evil only begets evil."

Guillaume's eyes flashed. "You are quite content to have the soldiers protect you up here on your sacred mountain!" he sneered. "What do you think would happen to this community without a garrison of sinning souls to guard it?" He struck his fist upon his knee, a warrior's fist, the knuckles slick with scar tissue.

"I am not content, but I tolerate it," she replied, and smoothed her own hands over her knees in a repetitive motion, struggling to remain calm. "What disturbs me is when you ride out to kill and return gloating over what you have done. It frightens me. Your soul will be lost."

Guillaume cut off her concern with a harsh laugh, grasped his goblet, and walked unsteadily away. Grief wrapped its tentacles around Claire until the pain was too great for her to contain and she let out the wail of a woman mourning for the dead. But Cathars did not mourn the dead. They sang with joy for their release, or prayed that in the next life they would find the enlightenment that had eluded them in this.

She was not aware of the moment that Magda's arms embraced her like a comforting cloak, only realized suddenly that someone was there, someone who understood.

CHAPTER FORTY-ONE

Gascony, Summer 1243

A FIERCELY COMPETITIVE chess game was in progress, the atmosphere less than brotherly. Dominic picked up the ebony knight between forefinger and thumb, hovered for an instant, then set it suddenly and decisively down.

"You underhanded, sly . . ."

"Bastard?" suggested Dominic, grinning at his half brother Simon. Leaning back, he stretched his arms above his head. His shirt, transparent with perspiration, clung to his muscular body. He wore braies and chausses, but had long since discarded hose and shoes. The heat was stultifying, without so much as a hint of a storm to clear the dusty air, the clouds high and distant, out of reach.

"That as well." Simon glowered at the board and then at Dominic. "Ach, it's too hot to play chess!" He waved dismissively.

"Too hot to do anything else. Do you concede?"

Simon was saved from an ignominious declaration by the approach of one of his squires. Trailing in his wake came a jongleur and two dusty, exhausted-looking women.

"Luck of the devil," Dominic muttered, and lowered his arms. One hand descended farther to fondle the silky ears of the dozing young wolfhound near his feet while he appraised the women and found them about as appetizing as two barnyard hens in molt. Frayed robes drab with dust, worn shoes, worn faces. The man was a draggled cockerel, faded ribbons twisted in a limp bunch at the neck of his lute, and a cap set at a jaunty angle on his obviously dyed yellow curls.

The news had continued to spread in widening rings from the original impact that Henry III of England was lingering at his court in Gascony and spending money as if it were water. Every juggler, tumbler, sword swallower, huckster, buffoon, trickster, and troubadour in the world had made their way here in the hopes of a share in the largesse. Most numerous were the men of the Languedoc, where the living was no longer easy and well patronized—where frequently there was no living at all because the nobility there were impoverished and struggling to survive. Simon, besides being the Earl of Leicester and one of the most powerful men in England's domain, was also married to the king's sister Eleanor, and thus well worth cultivating.

"We already have troubadours coming out of our ears," Dominic said indifferently, "although perhaps the soldiers might pay them for a ditty or two."

Looking exhausted, near to tears, the women slumped against each other. They were hardly the kind of fare to tempt the appetites of men jaded by a life of idle good living for the worst part of four months. Pity stirred Dominic's conscience along with disgust for this sybaritic malingering, which fed on itself like a Celtish circle, teeth devouring tail.

"My lord Earl, we have news," declared the minstrel, flourishing a performer's bow, obviously forcing the effort through his weariness. "All the way from Toulouse!"

Simon looked mildly interested. Dominic's heart quickened as it always did when the South was mentioned. He ceased fondling Lynx's ears and beckoned a squire. "Bring wine and food," he commanded. The squire's lip curled, displaying what he thought of being sent on an errand for such riffraff, but he was not so foolish as to refuse.

"News?" Simon motioned the three of them to be seated on the floor near his chair. "Tell me." He lifted a silver penny off the gambling pile beside him and flipped it to the troubadour.

The musician caught it in midair faster than the snap of a starving fox, and it vanished with equal rapidity into his scrip.

His news was commonplace and some of it was stale. Simon's hazel eyes began to narrow and he raised his hand, preparing to dismiss the motley trio. Then the word *Montségur* dropped into the narrative. It meant nothing to Simon and he snapped his fingers.

"Wait." Dominic arrested his brother's impatience and leaned forward, eyes intent. "What about Monségur?"

"Good my lord, there is an army marching from Carcassonne to take it once and for all." Sweat trickled down the minstrel's tortured face. "The Cathars are to be burned if they don't recant, each and every one. It's true, I swear it. We were in Carcassonne when the troops were assembling, at least a thousand men. It is because of what happened at Avignonet, when the holy friars were massacred. The Cathars don't really want peace, they just employ other people to do their killing for them!"

"Well informed about them, are you?" Dominic said silkily, and Simon's gaze switched to him in sudden speculation.

The troubadour had not missed the threat in Dominic's gliding tones. "I don't know anything about them, my lord. I'm a good Catholic, I am! I go to mass every week, so I do!"

"Then do not go making judgments you cannot uphold," Dominic bit out. "Who's commanding the army?"

"Hugh d'Arcis, my lord."

"The seneschal of Carcassonne," Simon said. "One of the best there is. Once his teeth sink in, he doesn't let go until his opponent is dead."

The squire returned with the food. Dominic abruptly rose from the chessboard and went to stand in the window embrasure. Thrusting his shoulder against the cold stone, he stared down into the pleasance below. Under the watchful eyes of their nursemaid, Simon's two small sons, Henry and Simon, romped with a ball. Some gaily decked women were clustered around another of their number who was playing a lute. The notes drifted up, as sweet and light as one of the king's angel wafers, and as superficial. Dominic examined his left hand—the lean brown fingers, a jagged white scar where a falcon had once clawed him, a small mole . . . the ridged, misshapen fingernails that had never properly grown back, the thickened skin. He became aware of his half brother's silent presence beside him.

"Simon, I have to go to Montségur," he said without turning round.

"Oh yes?" Simon said neutrally.

"My mother is there ... and someone else. If there is the slightest chance of getting them out, then I have to take it. I thought they were safer without contact from me. I was wrong. I should have gone there years ago."

Simon frowned at Dominic. Reaching across, he raised the irrevocably damaged left hand. "And if fortune fails you? It won't just be your fingers, Dom, it'll be your life and your soul. I won't be able to protect you this time."

"My life and soul will be forfeit anyway if I don't try," Dominic said softly.

Simon snorted, but let him go. Turning, Dominic saw the deep lines carving his brother's forehead and the perplexity in his stare. "Have you ever wondered why I have turned down offers of marriage over the years?"

"It had crossed my mind. I thought you were mad to reject that Breton heiress. Intelligence, beauty, a superb dowry, and all you did was shrug and reject the offer cold."

"Lukewarm," Dominic protested. "I did consider it for a moment, but there is someone else and she has lived in my heart a long time."

Simon was swift to pick up on the repetition of "someone else." "A Cathar!" he surmised on a falling cadence. "So Henri Lemagne was right. Jesu, Dominic!"

Dominic smiled ruefully. He was always Dominic, never Dom, when he did things of which the more responsible Simon disapproved. "No, not a Cathar, but living among them. She has the sight and healing skills and other gifts that I'm not even going to try to explain to you. Don't stare at me as though I'm contagious; I am not possessed, if that's what's in your mind ... well, no more than you are by your wife and sons." He looked out of the window at the women below, and sighed. "I want a woman I desire to call wife, and children by her to inherit the English lands you have bestowed on me. You wanted Eleanor from the moment you laid eyes on her. Do not deny the same feeling in me for Magda."

"Eleanor is the king's sister," Simon pointed out dryly.

"And you're a de Montfort out of a Montmorency!" Dominic retorted. "The rules are different for you. I'm only an unacknowledged by-blow and I can mate where I choose. My mind is made up. I'm riding out at first light. If you won't give me leave from my command, I'll resign it."

Simon rubbed his fingertip slowly back and forth across the sweaty groove of his upper lip. "You mean it, don't you? All right, gather what you need, we'll leave at first light."

"We?" Dominic twisted in the embrasure and stared. "You can't enter the Languedoc with all your retinue."

"I mean you and I alone, perhaps one squire."

Dominic's eyes narrowed suspiciously. "Why?"

Simon shifted uneasily and cleared his throat. "I'm not sure I know the answer to that myself. Perhaps because I'm bored stiff here dancing attendance on Henri day in and day out. It's bound to be cooler in the mountains, and the hunting should be good and . . ."

"And?"

Simon rubbed the back of his neck. "Ah Christ, I don't know. I was four years old when you were born, but I remember it clearly. Your mother was very pretty. She had shiny hair just like a horse chestnut for color, and a beautiful soft voice that was never raised like my mother's. I was smitten, lovelorn. The other women spurned her and I could tell she was bitterly unhappy, but she always had a smile for me. My mother found you a wet nurse and banished Lady Claire from her household. I was bereft at first, but then I realized that I had you to look out for. I suppose I transferred my affections, but I never forgot her. She was greatly wronged, Dom, and it needs to be redressed."

Dominic left the embrasure and clicked his fingers at Lynx, who was attending hopefully on the three entertainers for scraps, but with little success. "You will never redress what has gone before."

"But I can ensure that the future is more evenly weighted," Simon responded with all the forthright honesty in his nature.

"Then thank you," Dominic said quietly. "I'll welcome your company . . . but now I think I'd rather be alone for a while."

For the first time in many nights, Dominic went to bed sober and alone. Despite the news of the danger to Montségur, he was aware of a feeling of peace within himself. The sense of purpose that had led him to bury the past and live an exemplary Christian life for the eyes of the Dominican friars who spied upon him was gone, destroyed by the resurgence of that which had been subdued for so long.

He closed his eyes and opened his mind and she came to him, crying his name like a stumbling pilgrim lost in the desert, or a storm-tossed ship on a wide, empty ocean. He grasped her, and she clung to him. Joy and grief mingled so powerfully that he could not tell where one began and the other ended.

"I am coming to you now," he told her, but even as he tightened his hold, she slipped from his arms and began to fade away. Their fingertips touched as he stretched out to try and hold her. He received the image of flames and death, the dark oppression of a dreadful danger, of an army encamped at the foot of a steep mountain and a powerful dark beast hunting. Lightning sparked and he opened his eyes with a jolt to the fading echo of his own voice crying out her name and the sound of thundery rain sluicing off the tiles and into the courtyard. The room was gray with early light, as gray as her eyes.

CHAPTER FORTY-TWO

MONTSÉGUR AT DUSK: the pines a vivid green just on the visible side of darkness, their scent distilling on the summer air, making it as resinous as Greek wine. The powerful silence was broken by the husky calls of hoopoes and the sigh of the wind through the trees like a voice calling. The metallic clop and scrape of shod hooves and the champing of horses sounded a note of discord.

The hairs lifted along Raoul's spine. He felt as if he were in a vast cathedral in the presence of some dark being with a thousand invisible eyes. The Old Testament God of war, the Cathar's *Rex Mundi* laying siege to the tiny point of clarity and light crowning the mountain. His horse pranced nervously, and behind him, one of his knights muttered something about not liking the atmosphere one little bit.

The sky darkened; swags of cloud like witches' tresses drifted across the moonrise. The men continued to climb, drawn by the comforting pinpricks of light above, driven by the heaving darkness that surrounded them. Raoul almost leaped out of his skin when the trees rustled at the side of the path, and a slight figure emerged to stand in shadows and silver before them.

He gasped with relief and released his instinctive grip on his sword hilt when he saw that it was a young woman with unbound flaxen hair. She wore a pale robe that gleamed softly in the darkness, and around her neck a medallion flashed. In this bad light, he could not see its design, but he knew instinctively that it would bear the dove and chalice symbol. "Magda?" he ventured.

"My mother said you would come when you heard about the army they are sending to destroy us." She stroked his mount's nose, calming the horse with the hidden strength in her hands.

Raoul stared at his daughter. She had Bridget's beautiful eyes and graceful features, but her build and coloring were his. He wondered if she knew. "She sent you here to wait for us, on the mountainside?" he asked with a hint of censure.

"No, I was seeking someone else, and I heard your horses. Come, I'll take you up." She felt his concern for her, and heard the question that he did not ask. Her father; the man her mother had chosen above other men, but not for a permanent life-mate. His lined face was handsome and his aura glowed with a steady strength, but she saw great sadness there, too, and his eyes were weary, as if they had seen far too much.

"I do not know who you were seeking," he said. "There is no one here except us. We have seen scarcely a soul since leaving Foix, and we are the only ones on the mountain path tonight."

"I know that. The man I am hunting is beyond physical reach for the moment." A mischievous note crept into her voice. "He is in Gascony, and it is easier to call to him in the open than it is surrounded by walls."

"In Gascony?" Raoul repeated.

"I knew he wasn't dead." She smiled at Raoul and stepped on lightly before him and his troop, her pale hair and robe glimmering almost like a lantern to guide their way up the steep southwestern approach to the fortress.

Guillaume's attention diverted from his dice game as the horses entered the bailey. His brown eyes narrowed on the newcomers and he rose from his crouch. "Papa?" he queried to himself with surprise and not a little trepidation. He hurried from the shadows and ran to grasp his father's bridle. "It is you! What are you doing here!" His eyes flickered to Magda. She looked swiftly between him and Raoul, hesitated for a moment, and then excused herself, walking gracefully away into the depths of the fortress.

Raoul dismounted and he and Guillaume clasped each other in the exchanged steel and muscle of a soldier's embrace. "There is trouble afoot. I'm here to talk to Perella and my family. Ah God, Guillaume, it's good to see you!"

Guillaume stepped back. His stomach swooped unsteadily and he wished that he had not drunk so deeply from the leather wine bottle that had been passing from hand to hand around the circle of gamblers. "What sort of trouble?"

"I'd rather talk to de Perella and Pierre-Roger first. Do you know where they are?"

Guillaume scowled. His father still seemed to think of him as a child who had no business in the world of men. "I'm a senior knight, you know," he said, resentment in his voice. "I'll be in on anything you tell them."

"As you were in on Avignonet," Raoul said coldly as they walked toward the hall. "Rai of Toulouse came to me and told me that you were involved in the murders, and what was going to happen as a consequence. That's why I'm here."

Guillaume's square chin jutted. "I'm not sorry we killed those inquisitors. Given the opportunity, I'd do it again without remorse." His brow suddenly cleared. "You saw Count Rai. Did he say anything about sending us more troops?"

"Just take me to Perella," his father said wearily.

Guillaume gave a one-shouldered shrug, as if he did not care, and lengthened his stride.

Ramon de Perella and his nephew and coorganizer of Montségur's defenses, Pierre-Roger of Mirepoix, were talking in the hall over a late repast of bread and the local cured donkey sausage. Raoul was greeted warmly but with an underlying anxiety and was furnished with a chair, a portion of the meal, and a cup of wine. Uninvited but not rebuffed apart from a single sharp glance from Perella, Guillaume drew up a stool and sat down, too.

"What brings you to Montségur?" asked the commander. "Must be more than twenty years since last you were here. A family visit perchance?" The look in his deep-set eyes was cynical as it flickered between father and son.

"In part. Mainly I came to bring you a warning."

"Indeed?"

"An army is gathering in Carcassonne under Hugh d'Arcis—a thousand men at least, with the sole object of destroying Montségur and everyone in it."

"Rubbish!" Guillaume jerked to his feet, a jolt of fear rippling through his gut.

Pierre-Roger wiped the grease from his lips on the back of his hand and lifted his cup. "For the sake of your pride, I would not have put it as baldly as your son, Lord Raoul, but think, how often have we heard this kind of rumor before?"

"This is no rumor, but the truth!" Raoul snapped. "Do you think I would have ridden all this way for the sake of a rumor!" His gaze cut bitterly to Guillaume. "Or perhaps you do!"

Guillaume looked down at his fingernails, his color heightening. It was on the tip of his tongue to apologize, but somehow he could not quite release the words.

"I came because Count Rai himself gave me the warning, knowing that I have family and friends here," Raoul continued.

"Count Rai?" Perella's own cup stopped halfway to his mouth. "He would never permit such a thing. If this army marches, he will come immediately to our aid!"

"He won't." There was certainty in Raoul's voice. "He's angry at being excommunicated for Avignonet, which was none of his doing. He wants to be buried in consecrated ground when his time arrives, not left to molder in his coffin in a corridor like his father. He needs to ingratiate himself with the French. They suspect him of plotting against the Crown, and he doesn't want another army ravaging what lands and dignity are left to him. You, all of you, are to be the sacrifice—a symbol of southern resistance that's not going to cost too much to yield up. It'll satisfy the French king and remove the problem of the Cathars from Rai's attempts at reconciliation with the church. Now do you see?"

Perella and Pierre-Roger looked at each other with the beginnings of dismay.

"Papa, tell me it isn't true!" Guillaume said huskily. "Rai will keep faith."

"You're not a child anymore; I can't make your nightmares go away!" Raoul said tersely. "Especially not those of your own making. How can Rai ignore something of the magnitude of Avignonet? Already that inquisitor is a martyr of saintly proportions. His canonization sings in the corridors of Rome. Cut off one head and a thousand more grow to replace it." He put his face in his hands for a moment and then rubbed it wearily. "If your mother will come, I want to take her away before the army arrives—and two others if they can be persuaded."

De Perella said slowly, "If this is true, we will need to make arrangements for all the money and books to be taken out to safety."

"We can hold out!" Guillaume objected. "We've fought off all intruders before!"

De Perella looked at his nephew and Guillaume. "Let the valuables be removed to a secure place as a precaution," he said, and bared his stained, war-stallion teeth. "Then let the hordes of Beelzebub come, and let them die."

* * *

"I cannot leave," Bridget said when Raoul spoke to her in the infirmary some time later. "Not while Matthias still lives and the others need me more than I need to go. I know that Chretien feels the same way, but I thank you for your offer. Magda at least must depart with you."

"I'm as safe here as anywhere for the moment!" Magda objected. "I won't leave you!" She and Claire had been tending a cauldron of simmering water and herbs, but now she put her ladle aside and came to join the conversation.

"Daughter, you must," Bridget said in a voice slow with fatigue. "You have a sacred duty."

"The people need me here." Magda raised her chin stubbornly, her spine stiff. She stood a slender head and shoulders above her mother. "I am the one who goes among them while you tend Uncle Matthias. If I leave, they will feel just as betrayed as if you had gone yourself."

"That's as may be, but you still have your life before you, and it would be senseless for it to end here on this mountain."

"I could stay and help you awhile longer in the infirmary— help you build up a stock of remedies for when I am gone," Magda suggested.

"It is too dangerous now!" Bridget said, but Magda saw that she was weakening.

Raoul stepped into the silence of the unequal duel and made sure of the outcome. "There are no pressing claims of home or conscience to hold me back," he said slowly. "Everything that has ever meant anything to me in life is here at Montségur. My wife . . . my family. If you are all bent upon self-destruction, this is the last opportunity for me to be with you. I can take Magda wherever she wants to go when I leave. If she desires, she can live with me at Montvallant."

Magda felt an overflowing gratitude toward Raoul. "Thank you," she said, with a smile for him that acknowledged all that was known but unspoken between them. "But someone else is coming to take me away from Montségur."

"Who?" Bridget looked at her sharply.

Magda drew a deep breath. "Dominic. I want to wait for him."

It was the first time she had spoken his name before anyone except her mother and Chretien. Claire, whose presence at the cauldron of herbs had been overlooked in the contest of wills between mother and daughter, gasped at the mention of the name and spun round, scalding liquid dripping unheeded down the front of her Cathar robe.

"Who is Dominic?" Raoul questioned tautly.

Magda's eyes flickered from him to Claire. "Guillaume's half brother. I met him a long time ago in Toulouse when we were children, and again not long after the treaty of Meaux. He traveled the hills with myself and Uncle Chretien and learned our ways—he saved us from the Inquisition at cost to his own liberty. . . . For a long time I thought he was dead, but last night I learned that he still lives, and that he is coming for me."

Claire's face was bloodless, her eyes enormous. "It is impossible," she whispered. "It cannot be."

Bridget looked at Magda and nodded, a slow smile softening her face. "So you found him, my daughter?"

"In Gascony. Suddenly the wall was not there anymore."

"I know him," Raoul said, his eyes upon his quivering wife. "He once rescued Guillaume from rotting in the cells at the Châteaux Narbonnais, and after that he stayed for a while at Montvallant and I grew to know and like him against all my determination to hate him for the sins of his father. I heard that he had been imprisoned and tried for heresy; the rumor was even put about that he had died, but I never really believed it. To me, when I met him, he seemed a balanced and intelligent young man . . . more balanced than Guillaume, I sometimes think."

Claire staggered. Raoul quickly crossed the room and supported her, a comforting arm around her shoulders. "Dominic." She said the word haltingly as if it were in a foreign language, and her eyes were haunted with all the terrors, griefs, and guilts of the past thirty years. "God forgive me and show me the Light, for I have lost my way."

"Hush, love, hush," Raoul murmured, hugging her, his lips upon the mingled silver and chestnut hair of her crown.

"It is part of the pattern," Magda said. "De Montfort persecuted us, but his son has redressed that wrong. It is like two curves joining to make a perfect circle. Black and white, light and dark. One cannot be whole without the other . . . and I have been incomplete for so long."

"So have I," sobbed Claire softly. "So have I."

CHAPTER FORTY-THREE

"*IN NOMINE PATRIS et Filii et Spiritus Sancti, amen,*" Friar Bernard prayed, welcoming the discomfort of the hard ground upon his callused knees. The hair shirt beneath his habit irritated his skin, which was already chafed raw, weeping in the places of constant friction. A tight cord bound the undergarment to his body, digging into his waist, creating exquisite pain. *See how I suffer for thee, O Lord.* He had taken a vow not to remove the hair shirt until Montségur had fallen and every last Cathar had been destroyed, and for every day that they remained in possession of the summit, he had himself publicly flogged by one of the younger friars in his entourage.

The Cathars were evil, *evil*. To think of the doctrines that they preached made him weep and grind his teeth with rage and shame. They said that the Resurrection was a lie, that the idea that the spilled blood of Christ had bought redemption for mankind was the product of a dark, corrupt mind.

The Cathars all deserved to go to hell. They were so close and yet so unattainable, locked within their fortress two thousand feet above the encamped and still-arriving army. Were they kneeling and worshiping, too? Practicing their vile rites? Smearing filth upon the God whom he loved and so devoutly served? Bernard could not bear the thought; it filled his head with madness. Biting his lip until it bled, he prostrated himself before the altar in his tent and began to pray with renewed fervor. Behind his lids flickered the image of the Cathars burning in the flames of hell. And cool in the snow, the Virgin Mary mocked him with her heretic smile.

The mountain stream was as clear as liquid glass, and even in the heat of early summer, it was cold with the taste of meltwater. Dominic scooped a palmful, drank, and cupped his hands over his face. Beside him the horses dipped their muzzles and sucked up the water with thirsty pleasure. Half a day's ride was all that separated him and Simon from the army amassed at the foot of Montségur. Tonight they had made camp among the mountains a little to the west so that in the morning they could ride in fresh to the crusader assembly. It lacked an hour to dusk, but they had preparations to make for the morrow, and a good night's rest would not go amiss, for they had been riding hard.

To Simon, it had been as much pleasure as urgency that had led him to push their pace, easing out the creases of indulgent living, shedding surplus flesh. Dominic would have enjoyed it, too, had it not been for the nightmares that haunted him every time he fell asleep. Friar Bernard would chase him up and down crags, across fields and through towns, his fanatic's eyes alight, reflecting the gleam of a long knife in his hand. He would catch up with Dominic in a dark alley that ended in a blind wall, and Dominic would awaken sweating and terrified, his arms raised to protect himself. Dreams involving Magda were just as bad. They made him groan and toss for an entirely different reason, but the torment brought no release. Either Friar Bernard would appear with his knife at a moment close but not close enough to culmination, or Simon would nudge him hard in the ribs and complain about the noise he was making.

Dominic filled his waterskin and stood up, breathing deeply, inhaling the scent of pine needles and enjoying the slanting warmth of the late sun. Simon's mount threw up its dripping muzzle, ears pricked toward the trees, and nickered. Dominic quickly secured his grip on the leading rein that held the horses all together, his heart racing. The mountains were rife with wolves, of both the four- and two-legged variety. Something was approaching the stream through the dense forest on the other side. Simon's horse whinnied. There was a loud answering neigh. Dominic rested his free hand cautiously on his dagger hilt as a knight leading a glossy roan destrier emerged from the trees. His tawny surcoat was appliquéd with black chevronels, which were echoed on the shield hanging from the saddle, and he wore a sword on his left hip with the casual ease of long familiarity.

Slackening the reins, the man let his mount drink, and looked directly across the stream at Dominic. "God's greeting," he said, without the slightest hint of surprise.

Dominic stood utterly still, all thought and motion arrested. "Lord Raoul?"

The creases deepened around the other man's azure-blue eyes. "I was not sure that you would recognize me. I see that I've come as something of a shock." He crouched to drink, and the sunlight glinted upon the gold hairs threading the gray.

Dominic released the breath he had been holding. "What are you doing here?"

"Looking for you and playing escort to a certain young woman who told me where to seek."

"Magda!" Dominic's chest tightened and suddenly it was difficult to breathe except in shallow bursts. "Magda is with you?"

Raoul glanced briefly over his shoulder. "Not far away. There's a Templar knight traveling with us, too—Magda's cousin."

"And you are looking for me?"

"And your half brother."

"How did you . . . ?"

"We'll come to your campfire tonight?" Raoul shook the water from his fingers and stood up.

Dominic sought to muster his reeling wits, but with limited success. There was nothing beyond the thump of his heart reacting to the moment. "You'll be more than welcome," he heard himself say in the stilted voice of a stranger. "We killed a hare this morning and we have bread and olives if you don't want meat. . . . We were on our way to Montségur."

"I know," Raoul said gently, "and I believe you will still have to go there, but we can talk about that later. I'll go and fetch Luke and Magda before it grows dark."

Dominic returned to the camp in a daze, the thought of Magda a blinding light in his mind, obliterating all other considerations. He answered Simon's questions in monosyllabic grunts as the latter expertly cleaned the hare and set it to roast on a spit.

"A Templar, eh?" Simon mused. "I've heard it said more than once that their methods of worship would not stand up to scrutiny by the Inquisition."

"The Templars make their own rules and alliances," Dominic said distantly, his eyes upon the forest beyond their campfire. "Within the outer ring of ordinary brethren, there's an inner, secret core."

"How do you know that?"

"I once overheard Guzman and Bernard discussing it. They were angry because their people could not search the preceptories."

"Their suspicions appear to have been borne out."

Dominic shrugged. "To our advantage," he said.

Simon pursed his lips thoughtfully. "And this Raoul de Montvallant. You say he is your mother's husband? Very saintly of him not to hate your guts."

"He would have done if I'd grown up here and usurped his lands, but I saved his son from the Inquisition, and as men, we like each other well enough."

"How's he connected with your Magda?"

"I don't know." Simon's relentless quest for information was irritating him, and he deliberately walked away to help the squire hobble the horses.

A mouthwatering, smoky aroma of roasting meat soon filled the air. The sky darkened into dusk, the orange border of sunset smudging into an indigo hem. Dominic paced to the edge of the camp, impatience trembling through him. He felt as if the first layer of his skin had been peeled away, exposing his nerves to the cool, fragrant night air. Every sound, every scent, every brushing touch of breeze and insect, was magnified almost to the level of pain. *As a lily among brambles, so is my love among maidens.* So said the erotic and beautiful Song of Solomon, and he endorsed every word.

He heard the snort of a horse and saw a glimmer through the trees—a Templar's white surcoat, perhaps. A man spoke, a woman answered softly, and he realized that it was her gown that gleamed, for the Templar wore a dark cloak over his own robes.

"They are here," he said over his shoulder to Simon, and went forward to meet them.

Time slowed down as he greeted Raoul and was introduced to the Templar Luke de Béziers, a powerfully built man in his late prime. He must have made the correct responses but was not conscious of his lips moving, every fiber of his being concentrated upon the woman who had been sitting pillion on Raoul's stallion and was now lifted down by him.

Her hair was woven with wildwood flowers like a bride and rippled to her hips, heavy as ripe corn. A plain white woolen robe clung to her supple figure, relieved only by a cord of braided scarlet silk at her waist and the flash of an enameled medallion at her throat. Dominic stared, transfixed, her beauty filling him up.

"Dominic," she breathed, and was at his side, her hand linking through his, her eyes shining. He felt the tingle of the connection, the quickening of already quickened blood. Uncaring of the two men, he gasped, pulled her against him, and covered her mouth with his, feeling whole again for the first time since his capture by the Inquisition. The Templar smiled. Raoul's expression was wistful. There was no thunder in the mild air tonight, but nevertheless he felt the tension.

"I told Raoul and cousin Luke we would find you here," she said when at last they surfaced from the embrace, both of them breathing hard. "I have been so worried, so lonely. There is terrible danger."

"We've come to take you to safety." He pressed his palm against hers, felt the response of her fingers playing against his like needles in the blood. The delicate lines of her face, the gleam of her collarbone, the swift rise and fall of her breasts. *You are all fair, my love; there is no flaw in you.*

"And this must be your brother Simon coming now?" she murmured. "He has a life force so much like your father's."

"What?" Dominic turned fully round to regard his advancing half brother. The glimmer surrounding Simon was like the mountain stream—pure and strongly flowing with bands of indigo and green and blue at its margins. "It is nothing like my father's!" he protested.

"No, I mean like your father's might have once been— strong and idealistic. He gets what he wants, sometimes to his own detriment. Yours is not dissimilar." Her voice struck a more intimate chord and her fingers stroked his. Dominic responded with the ball of his thumb.

"Simon," he said, "I want you to meet Magda."

Over a meal of bread and wine, olives, and roast hare for those whose diet permitted meat, Magda and Dominic brought each other abreast of everything that had happened to them during their years of separation, years of wilderness, as Dominic saw in hindsight. It was time also to reappraise each other, measure the changes that experience and maturity had wrought, their attraction kept within discreet bounds by the presence of the others at the campfire. It was a sweet agony to touch and be touched, to lean shoulder to shoulder, and know that what they craved was only just out of reach, captured in a net of propriety. Tension was as tightly wound as the rope on a primed trebuchet. It was almost inevitable that when Magda announced she could not go to Gascony yet, Dominic should explode.

"Then God's grave, why have you come!" He sprang to his feet, his whole body taut and quivering like an overstrung lute. "I broke myself for you once; what more do you want!" Propriety was violated by the outburst. Suddenly Simon and the other two men might as well not have existed.

Magda stared up at him, her eyes glistening. "I want your help. Not just for myself, but for all of Montségur."

Dominic clenched his fists and turned his back, seeking the control not to seize and shake her, and it was Simon who answered. "You must know that it is impossible," he said coldly. "We came out of obligation to you and to Dominic's mother, not to die for a host of heretics."

"They are not heretics!" Magda answered him passionately. "They follow God's law more diligently than most of your priests!" Her white teeth snarled on the final word, and she drew a deep breath to steady herself. When she spoke again, it was to Dominic. She could feel his hurt, his anger, the undercurrents of love and lust, flashing and interlacing like a necklace in two colors of gold. "I did not mean that you should fight for us," she said in a gentler tone. "It is grief enough and cause of much dispute among our elders that we have soldiers to protect us at all."

Dominic turned stiffly. "Then what do you want?"

"There are certain items at Montségur that have to be taken away to safety."

"Such as?" Simon leaned slightly forward.

Magda focused on him, on the curiosity and acquisitiveness in his nature. "Books, money, treasure . . . the Grail cup." And she felt him bite. A glance revealed that Dominic was studying her with warily narrowed eyes.

"I thought," said Simon, a slight catch in his voice betraying his eagerness, "that the Cathars lived by the code that it is easier for a camel to pass through the eye of a needle than it is for a rich man to enter through the gates of heaven."

"The treasure has been bequeathed to us by wealthy people who have either become Perfecti and given all their possessions away, or by believers who want to ease their consciences or support us. You have such folk in your own church by the thousand, do you not? Our money is used to buy food and essentials for the community. We do not care about it."

"But you pay the soldiers?" Simon responded swiftly. "Feeding the hand that holds the sword. Is that not as bad as holding the sword yourselves?"

Magda sighed. "Indeed it is," she disarmed him, "but what else are we to do? Even if we did not pay them, most of the men are so committed to preserving the community at Montségur that they would fight without wages, and if we took away their weapons, they would use their bare hands."

"That is so," Raoul confirmed. "My own son is numbered among them, and I know for a certainty that money is not the reason that keeps him there. His hatred is as dark as the love of the Perfecti is light—like the other side of a coin." His expression hardened. "I'm not a theologian or politician. All I want is to see those I care for safe." He glanced at Magda.

Simon sucked a piece of bone out from between his teeth and said thoughtfully, "So what happens to the treasure once it's out of Montségur?"

"Oh, for God's sake, Simon!" Dominic snapped as he caught the drift of his brother's thinking. "I know you're short of funds, but aren't you being a little too obvious?"

Simon shrugged uncomfortably, but did not take his eyes from Magda.

"The gold has never meant that much to us," she said calmly. "You are welcome to a share in it if you will undertake to remove it to a place of safety. The money will go to our communities in Lombardy, and some of the books. The remainder I will bring with me."

"And the Grail?"

Magda looked directly at Simon. "You have read the tales of King Arthur," she said. "You may search forever and a day and never realize that all the time it lies beneath your nose. As to its symbol, that belongs to the Templars." She touched Luke lightly on the knee and smiled.

Simon frowned. She could see that he did not understand and was therefore ill at ease and more than a little hostile. "These books, are they heresies?" he asked abruptly.

"It won't damn your soul to read them, but they might change the way you look at the world," Magda answered. "Mostly they are Gospels translated from old scrolls and codexes by a man of learning in our community. They are teachings that have long been struck from the Roman version of the Bible, or never included in the first place."

Simon chewed his lip. "If I were a good son of the church in whose service my father was killed, I would have no more ado with any of this," he said. "I would ride away, find the nearest church, and immediately confess and do penance." His hazel glance went broodingly to Dominic. "But on the other side of the balance, my father left a debt that has gone unpaid for long enough. So be it, I will help." He spoke slowly, as if the words were being dragged out of some depth in himself that it surprised him to find. "You'll need an escape route and safe escort. Where are you planning to go?"

"England," Dominic said. "Your lands and power will give us security, and my own interests are there."

Simon considered, then nodded. "My jurisdiction only runs from Gascony. You'll still have to escape from Montségur and across the South." He frowned at Magda. "Why can't you come with us now as Dominic wants?"

"There is still a book to be completed, and they need me there, more than ever now. There are secret paths known only to the local people, and even with an army of a thousand men at his disposal, Hugh d'Arcis cannot surround the entire mountain. How do you think we came out?"

"What I suggest," said the Templar, who had been silent thus far, "is that Earl Simon organizes a safe route between Gascony and England, and that you"—a look at Dominic—"join the besieging troops and arrange the travel between Montségur and Gascony. I have contacts among the crusaders and can move relatively easily between both camps, so I can act as a message bearer. Raoul can be trusted to get Magda and the treasure out to you at a prearranged time, and the other women if they will come, although I doubt it."

Dominic stared beyond the campfire into the distance while he thought, and after a short time, capitulated with a sigh. "It is not how I would have wanted it to happen, but it seems sound enough to me. Simon?"

His brother nodded, too, a gleam in his eyes now that the thing was set in motion. Like his father, he excelled at planning and strategy, and to be requested to undertake this task, with its element of mystery and risk, was a temptation that had quickly become impossible to refuse.

"It is settled, then." Luke de Béziers raised his cup in salutation. Everyone drank. Magda put her empty cup down, regarded Dominic across the red firelight, and rising to her feet, walked away into the darkness. Dominic did not immediately follow her. He would look a fool if she had just gone to empty her bladder, and besides, he felt oddly nervous, as if it were his first time, and he had more than half a mind to run in the opposite direction.

After several minutes had passed, Simon nudged him. "You'd better make sure she hasn't been eaten by a wolf," he said, with more than a hint of tongue in cheek. "Not afraid of the dark, are you, Dom? Shall I go instead?"

Luke de Béziers was smiling. Raoul, expression knowing and sad, reached again for the wineskin. Standing up, Dominic scowled at Simon. "I always thought I was the family bastard," he said.

Simon grinned.

Magda was waiting for him near the stream, her arms embracing her knees, her body a pleasing symmetrical curve. The water tumbled and chuckled over the stones, and the grass on either side was lush and soft. He hesitated for a moment before he sat down beside her. Every nerve in his body was vibrantly aware of hers to a level verging on pain. He wanted to fuse with her in the white heat of physical release and yet he hesitated, constrained by her mystery.

"Will it seem strange living with me when all your life you have lived among Cathars?" he asked.

Magda turned her head and smiled. "Do you mean because I will be a baron's wife, or because you are a man with a man's needs?"

He plucked at the grass. "Both, I suppose."

She tossed back her hair and regarded the sky. "I have lived among soldiers and their wives for my entire life, so the first part will be simple enough. I shall found a convent in the name of the Magdalene with the money I bring from Montségur, and it shall be a sanctuary for the persecuted, whatever their need. As to you being a man . . ." Here she paused and laughed softly. "I do admit that although I know much of men's hearts and minds, their bodies are a mystery, and you left me with a taste to know more." She leaned toward him.

Dominic touched her hair. It felt like silk against his fingers. It was going to be hard to see her return to the dangers of Montségur, even harder to settle down in the enemy camp and make a pretense of being a crusader, attacking what he had come to preserve while arranging a route to Gascony.

Her breasts rose and fell swiftly beneath the simple white gown, and he sensed her tension. He heard the sound of his own shaken breathing and the rapid thud of his heart, driving the blood through his body. Tenderly he plucked loose a flower from her hair and moved closer, breath against her ear, her throat, upon her lips. The seal of a kiss, her lips parting. *Your lips distill nectar, my bride.* The feather touch of fingertips upon skin, the delicate unplucking of laces, yielding up new areas of discovery. Velvet breasts clefted with shadow and crowned by taut nipples. *Behold, you are beautiful, my love, behold, you are beautiful!* Cool, satin textures over which to glide palm and tongue. Smooth thighs, the inside skin softer than rose petals, and the heart of the rose itself, the mystery, the Grail. *A garden locked is my sister, my bride.*

Magda wrapped herself around him, making small, soft sounds as the pleasure grew within her, congesting her loins. *Let my beloved come to his garden and eat its choicest fruits.* Her spine arched to receive the first swollen thrust. He filled her and the pain was like scarlet fire. He murmured reassurances against her throat. A fine coating of sweat clung to his body, making his spine slippery beneath her fingers. His mouth covered hers, the kiss moving in rhythm with the motion of their bodies. Give and take and give. Magda opened her eyes to see the gleam of her lover's, the wheeling of the stars over their heads and the deep infinity of the sky. *Make haste, my beloved, and be like a gazelle or a young stag upon the mountain of spices.* She raised her hand to push a strand of hair from her eyes and he captured it in his, meshing their fingers. The flames consumed her, the stars turned; his fingers gripped upon hers, tightening and tightening as the tension rose, and she gripped in return, unable to gasp or cry out because his mouth was on hers. He made a sound in his throat and plunged and the scarlet fire became ripples of white heat, flashing through her body, engulfing and transfiguring her. She and Dominic were the fire. And through the burn of fulfillment, their hands remained joined, each imprinted on the other, nor did they disengage as the white light faded to the merest glimmer. *Set me as a seal upon your heart, as a seal upon your arm; for love is strong as death.*

CHAPTER FORTY-FOUR

Montségur, Autumn 1243

THREE WEEKS AFTER returning to Montségur, Magda knew for certain that she was pregnant. Pleasure and apprehension filled her in equal quantities. The journey to safety would not be easy. By the time they reached England, she calculated that she would be entering her final three months.

She kept the news to herself—although she was aware of her mother's sharp scrutiny—and went about her duties as normal. The besieging army at the foot of their rock had swollen in number, and now, at night, their campfires could be seen as yellow suppurations among the trees. The sense of danger was frequently suffocating. Wisps of fear, like thin, black smoke, trickled over Montségur's battlements and infected its occupants. The sanctuary had been defiled. Magda discovered that for all Montségur had been her home from birth, she would be glad to leave.

One of Raoul's men had gashed himself while cutting wood for their fires. Magda attended him, laying her hands upon the wound to stem the bleeding, then stitching it closed and smearing it with a honey salve. Raoul watched her at work, an odd, tender expression on his face.

"You are as gifted as your mother," he murmured.

"I owe my skills to her teaching." Magda replaced her equipment in her satchel and smiled at the soldier. "Rest easy for the remainder of the day, and tomorrow you will scarcely know that you have been wounded."

He smiled his thanks in return. "I scarcely know it now, Madonna."

"Perhaps you should rest easy, too," Raoul said with concern. "You look pale, and I do not like those dark shadows beneath your eyes."

"There will be time enough for rest later." Magda slung the strap of her satchel over her shoulder and stood up. The sudden change of position caused her to stagger; her vision swirled and darkened, and if Raoul had not caught her, she would have fallen. For a moment she hung between consciousness and oblivion. Nausea churned in the pit of her stomach and cold sweat broke out on her body. She heard Raoul call out for help.

"It is nothing," she mumbled, her lips barely forming the words. "I am all right."

More arms supported her and lowered her to the ground. "Don't just stand there like a fool," said the voice of Claire de Montvallant, "fetch a cup of sweet wine."

"I'm all right," Magda repeated, "I just stood up too quickly."

"It will not harm you to sit still for a moment," Claire said. "You take far too much on yourself, and pay no heed to those who tell you to slow down, even your own mother." She reached up, took the cup that Raoul handed to her, and set it against Magda's lips. "Drink. I am playing the healer now."

Obediently Magda sipped the wine. It was a Gascon brew, sweet and strong, and it warmed her veins, dispelling the sweat and nausea. Her body craved the sweetness, and before she knew it, she had finished the entire cup. "Now I truly won't be able to stand up," she said ruefully.

"I'll carry you back to your pallet in your mother's room, and you can lie down for a while."

"No, I cannot, I . . ."

Stooping, Raoul lifted her in his arms. "When you reach my years and experience, you realize that there is no such word as 'cannot,' " he told her, as he set off.

Bridget was on her way out of the tiny room she shared with Magda, but when Raoul appeared, she stepped aside to let him enter, and then she followed him.

Magda had recovered from feeling faint, but the potency of

the wine was having its effect on her now and her head was whirling. Raoul laid her down on the bed and told Bridget what had happened.

Bridget set her hand upon Magda's forehead. "Lie still, daughter," she murmured.

"Mama, it was nothing. I stood up too quickly."

"Nothing, was it?"

Magda colored beneath her mother's all-seeing scrutiny. "There is nothing the matter," she persisted, and there was a thread of fear in the undercurrent of her voice.

"And nothing that cannot wait for an afternoon of rest," Bridget said. "Besides, with a cup of Gascon wine inside you, your healing skills will be impaired, to say the least. Close your eyes and I will wake you in a while."

Magda struggled, but her eyelids were leaden, and the bed had never seemed so comfortable. Her mother's palm upon her forehead was soothing and cool. There would be no visions, it promised, only the peace of dreamless sleep.

Bridget stayed until Magda slept, then quietly left the room. Raoul was waiting just outside the door. "I wish she had not returned when you took her out to meet Dominic," she sighed. "She should have gone with him then. It would not have mattered about the rest of us."

"It would have mattered to her," Raoul said. "By the same token, I need not have come from Montvallant and volunteered to stay here. Nor yourself . . . You are not a Cathar."

"But Montségur is my home." She gave him a tired smile and lightly touched his cheek. "I suppose we all have our reasons, however foolish. I am glad that you have come."

"There was nothing left for me at Montvallant but the dust of memories, and not all of them happy. I used to think Claire mad when she said it was the spirit that mattered, all else was dross, but now I have a better understanding. I can take the soil of Montvallant, of my life, and scatter it to the wind." He kissed her fingers as she withdrew them from his cheek, and went slowly down the twisting stone stairs to the bailey.

Claire was waiting for him, her brown eyes anxious as she took her turn at grinding ears of grain into course flour, using a small hand quern. When she saw Raoul, she gave the task to another Cathar woman at her side, and dusting her hands on her grown, hurried over to him.

"How is she?"

"She's resting now, and seems to be all right." He grimaced, and glanced around the compound. A bitter wind was blowing, and gray clouds were boiling up across the mountains to the south, promising heavy rain. "Bridget is worried about her." He drew Claire into the lee of the wall and positioned himself to shelter her from the wind.

"Yes, I know." Claire pursed her lips and contemplated him for a moment. Then she said, "I believe that Magda is with child. If you ask me why, I would have to say it is a woman's instinct. It is not only her work and worrying about the soldiers without our walls that have put dark shadows beneath her eyes. It will be a difficult journey for her when the time comes."

"You do not know for sure."

"I have a very strong suspicion." She looked up at him, her expression an ambivalent mingling of pleasure and apprehension. "If she is to bear a baby, then it will be my grandchild. As a Cathar, and as Simon de Montfort's victim, I could wish it otherwise, but as myself, in my heart, I am pleased for her. She has desired this for so long. I can only wish her peace and joy, and a safe journey to her new life."

"It will be my grandchild, too," Raoul confessed softly, and braced himself for Claire's response. They had known each other for so long, had lived and loved and come to a parting of the ways. If anything, the parting had deepened their bond, but he had never told her about the night he had spent with Bridget, and the child that had come of their union.

"That, too, I had strongly suspected," Claire said in a gentle voice, then smiled. "You need not look so anxious. Once, I admit, I might have been eaten up by jealousy, but if I look back now, I can see the reasons—some yours and some mine—for Magda's existence."

"How . . . how did you come to suspect? Did Bridget say anything?"

"No, Bridget has never spoken of Magda to me, nor do I expect her to. We each respect the other's private thoughts. I watched Magda grow up, and sometimes she reminded me of you, but it was not until Guillaume came to Montségur that I saw the true resemblance. When they stand side by side, it is clear for all to see that they are brother and sister." Her smile, although sad, deepened. "I love Magda as if she were my own daughter."

Autumn tightened its hold on the fortress, the bitter mountain winds and sleeting rain making life uncomfortable for both besieger and besieged alike. Hugh D'Arcis, commander of the crusader camp, increased the wages and extended the periods of leave in the valley that he gave to his troops, but he held those on duty to a rigid discipline. No one was allowed to go home until Montségur was a deserted heap of rubble.

Within the fortress, firewood and provisions were meticulously rationed in the hopes of conserving them until the spring. On foggy days, foraging parties managed to creep out of Montségur, avoid the soldiers, and obtain provisions in the valley. Occasionally the sympathetic villagers would find ways of reaching the castle with supplies, but they were only a trickle, and the danger was terrible.

Magda's pregnancy continued to sap her strength and her vitality. Even ordinary healing tasks left her exhausted. Her body rejected food, even the smell of it made her nauseated, and the soothing possets brewed by her mother were the most that she was able to keep down. People watched her and worried, but there was nothing they could do for her except pray, and leave her to rest. They protected her as best they could, but they could not protect her from the nightmares.

On his narrow pallet, Friar Bernard twisted and writhed, beset by the torments of the damned that made the sores from his hair shirt and the stripes from his latest flogging seem no more than the caress of a lover's fingers. The pain was exquisite and he sucked it into himself, knowing that when it reached its crescendo, he must surely explode into a thousand particles and become one with his Savior. Was this how Christ had suffered on the cross? Oh, to feel some of the pain and know that it linked him with the God he so devoutly served.

He was climbing the rock of Montségur barefoot like a penitent, a cross of human ash drawn upon his forehead. The stones of the mountainside cut his feet and he felt the blood running between his toes, even as Christ's blood had run on the cross. The pain in his chest as he climbed was as cruel as the thrust of a lance, but he knew that when he reached the fortress at the summit, he would find his prize.

There were guards on the walls, but he had God's protection and they did not see him walk past them, nor did they see the bloody footprints that marked his trail through the castle. The heretics were sleeping, crowded together like corpses in a charnel house, and his heart cramped with savage joy to see the level of squalor in which they dwelt. A host of them were praying in the hall, their backs stooped to make one huge monster, each individual forming a cobbled black scale.

A little to one side, a soldier was studying the beast, a bearded soldier with the cross of truth embroidering his breast. Bernard tried to gain his attention and order him to strike at the foulsome creature, but the knight neither heard nor saw the frantic signals, and with gut-lurching shock, Bernard realized that the knight was one of the heretics, too.

Raising his arm, Bernard prepared to call down anathema upon the entire hell-spawn gathering, but his motion was prevented by a white-hot pain that stabbed like thorns through his limbs, arresting all motion. Even his feet ceased to bleed. A dazzling brightness encircled him, separating him from the Cathars, obscuring his vision and lifting him up. He was borne upon it, his agony so intense that it was beautiful. He floated through the roof and found himself upon the battlements. It was not the direction he had intended to take and he struggled against the strands of energy meshing him fast. He was propelled rapidly to the edge of the crenellations and catapulted powerfully outward and upward like a stone from a wound trebuchet.

The light exploded around him in myriad rainbow spangles that gradually winked out and vanished, leaving him to wade through a filthy black murk that filled his eyes and nose and mouth, clogging and suffocating. He struggled to reach the surface, but the morass stretched in all directions and he had neither the strength nor the breath to free himself.

"Jesus Christ, help me!" he croaked with his dying breath, and woke up choking to discover that his blanket was smothering his face and twisted tightly around his body. His heart pounded so hard that he thought it would leave his body. He took huge gulps of air and felt the humiliating discomfort of urine on his thighs.

When finally he gained sufficient control of his shaking hands, he kindled the small clay oil lamp at his bedside and sat up. His starved lungs were deprived again as he ceased breathing and stared at his feet, at the mottling of bruises and the dried blood that was caked between his toes.

Magda's eyes flung wide, and she awoke panting and sweat-drenched on her pallet. The dark terror had been so close. She had touched it, and it was so full of destruction that even its very center was black. Casting it forth from Montségur had stretched her abilities to the full.

She sat up, pushed her hair out of her eyes, and reached for the cup of wine at the side of the pallet to rinse the taste of fear from her mouth. Her hands were trembling, her stomach churning, and there was a pain lower down, dull and crushing.

"No," she denied, and pressed her hand across her abdomen protectively. "Oh, by the Light, please, no! Mama, help me!" The wine spilled over her lap, flooding her linen shift with a red stain even as the sudden gush of blood from between her thighs reddened the mattress.

CHAPTER FORTY-FIVE

DOMINIC HUNCHED INTO the squirrel-fur lining of his cloak and, with his knife, slit the seal on the package that the messenger had just handed to him. Simon's seal and Simon's neat, decisive writing. No scribe had been allowed anywhere near this.

> *Simon de Montfort, Earl of Leicester, high Steward of England, to his dearest brother Dominic, greetings.*
> *Herein enclosed is the list of contacts and places you asked me to obtain in respect of succor on your pilgrimage.*
> *Written at Portsmouth, this first day of October, year of our Lord twelve hundred and forty-three.*

That was it—succinct, to the point, nothing to incriminate either himself or Dominic should the letter be intercepted. A second sheet of parchment detailed the places where they would be welcomed and no questions asked. Dominic fished in his pouch and presented the messenger with a coin.

"No reply," he said, and rolling up the parchments, tucked them down between hauberk and gambeson. The man bowed and returned to his horse. Eyes half-closed against the stinging wind, Dominic watched the messenger pick his way carefully back down the mountain toward the main camp at its foot, then turned to look at the nearer edifice of the fortress towering over his head. Gray stone, gray sky, gray hopes of holding out. And ultimately, ash, too, was gray.

"Shall I load 'er up, then, my lord?" asked Jules, the belligerent little sergeant in charge of the morning shift manning the enormous trebuchet. Hugh d'Arcis had had it dragged up the mountain in pieces and assembled within range of Montségur's outerworks. "Cold 'un today," he added, blowing on his hands. "Could do wi' a good bonfire to warm us up." Cheerfully he spat. "Ever smelled heretics roasting?"

"I could keep warm all winter long on the amount of hot air that comes out of your mouth!" Dominic retorted witheringly. "Yes, load her up. They'll be firing at us soon enough."

"Right away, my lord!"

Another soldier brought him a cup of wine and a flat loaf sliced half-open and filled with pungent goat's cheese. Dominic did not feel much like eating, but he took the food and bit unconcernedly as if his mind were on the mundane and not on the escape that was so close now, just awaiting word from Magda. His own part was fulfilled. He thought of her and his stomach somersaulted with love and fear. How slowly the time was passing, and how quickly they were making progress with this damned trebuchet. A couple of times he had managed to commit minor sabotage, but dared not try again too soon for fear of raising suspicions and a corresponding level of security. Hugh d'Arcis was a cautious, hard-bitten commander who would relieve Dominic of his post in an instant rather than house so much as a single doubt. Thus far, Dominic congratulated himself sourly, he had not set a foot wrong.

Avoiding Friar Bernard in the camp below had been the most difficult of his problems. The man was everywhere, needing only a scythe in his hand to make him the image of the Grim Reaper. Dominic had circumvented recognition by letting his beard and hair grow unchecked—it offered protection against the mountain cold, too—and by keeping to the background as much as possible. The command of this trebuchet post had been an ideal opportunity to escape up the mountain away from discovery, but it had its price.

The sound of the counterweight slamming down, the ricochet of stone on stone. His gut reacted first as it always did with a sudden contraction like the jolt of the trebuchet as the wedge was yanked out of the windlass. Then the memories would whip into his skull and crash through barriers more than twenty years old to reach and pierce the small boy within. He knew the destruction of which a trebuchet was capable, could only pray that Magda, Bridget, and his mother were not tending the wounded anywhere near the outer defenses that were now so vulnerable to crusader attack. He tried not to think of that, but every time they launched another stone, he flinched, and every time the garrison above retorted, he remembered his father. Oh Christ, this was mad, and he would go mad soon if he could not escape with Magda.

Thump. "Stone!" bellowed Jules, and they all scuttered for cover like rabbits. Crash. Pebbles bounced away into the trees. Soldiers ran to retrieve the rock that had been hurled at them and prepared to reload it into their own trebuchet. One of them chalked a crude sketch on the boulder—a Cathar tied to a stake. Dominic watched, a groove of muscle tightening in his jaw. As they cranked the windlass he looked away and saw

Luke de Béziers riding along the track toward him. Abandoning the trebuchet, Dominic went quickly to meet him.

"I've had the details from Simon," he announced as the Templar dismounted. "Tell Magda. We can leave as soon as she's ready."

Luke sighed heavily and began to unstrap a bundle from his crupper. "That might not be for a long time."

"Why? What's wrong?"

Luke paused, his hands on the buckle, and looked along the furred shoulder of his cloak. "Did you know that Magda was with child?"

Dominic's mouth was suddenly dry. There was no joy in Luke's expression. "No, I didn't."

"She's been taking too much on herself—tending the injured, keeping the hysterical ones calm, balancing the evil surrounding us with her own spirit. It has drained her white. We have tried our best to shield her, but in the end to no avail."

Dominic thought that his heart had stopped beating, but it could not be so because he was still alive, because it hurt to breathe, and the wind was drying his open eyes, forcing him to blink. "What has happened to her?" he dragged out. "God's sweet pity, tell me!"

"I'm sorry, Dominic," Luke said. "She started bleeding last night. Bridget couldn't stop it and she lost the child." His callused hand pressed upon Dominic's taut shoulder. "There is great sadness among all the community."

Thump, bellow, crash. The noises rang hollowly inside Dominic's skull. Behind him he heard the men of the trebuchet team discussing in obscene detail what they would do to the Cathar women before they were burned. Heat stung his eyes and he clenched his fists, digging his nails into his palms while he brought his rage under control. "Will she be all right?"

"In time perhaps. There is no one more skilled in the healing arts than Bridget."

Dominic examined the Templar's face. It was indomitable and compassionate, and beneath the lined composure there lurked a gnawing anxiety. Fear hooked jagged claws into Dominic's gut at what went unsaid. What if Magda died? Or if she was too weak to travel when the final assault came? Darkness encroached upon him, the sense of being trapped and helpless. The thump of the trebuchet's counterweight was like a fist smashing him into the earth.

"I cannot do this anymore." He swallowed with revulsion. "I have to see her, Luke; take me into Montségur."

Luke regarded him with a perplexed and heavy stare. "You and I and Raoul are the bridge between Montségur and the world over which any survivors are to cross. You have to endure." And then his face changed. "Company from the camp below," he warned softly. "Hugh d'Arcis, no less."

Dominic turned to look and knew as it began to drizzle that his misery was complete. From all sides, thoughts and feelings clamored for his attention and had to be denied as he projected himself into the role of competent, pragmatic battle commander.

"I'll give you these books later," Luke murmured, restrapping the bundle to his crupper and swinging into the saddle. "And I'll see what I can do about smuggling you into Montségur." Leaning down, he slapped Dominic's rigid shoulder. "Courage, lad, you'll come through all right."

Body braced as if to bear a terrible weight, Dominic left the Templar and walked across to the commander in chief of the crusading army.

Hugh d'Arcis sat astride his tall brown horse and studied the work in progress and then, thoughtfully, the young man at his stirrup whose wooden expression gave little away. D'Arcis was reminded of Dominic's father, whom he had known and admired. A man after his own heart. Finding the heart of his son was more of a challenge. What kind of fire did Dominic le Couchefeu conceal?

"Good work so far." D'Arcis nodded. "But I think we would make more progress if we moved the stone thrower a couple of degrees to the left. We have to knock out the trebuchets on their outer works if we're to get any closer."

"Yes, my lord."

A wooden voice, too, d'Arcis noticed, and looking more closely, saw the lack of color in Dominic's face and the rigors that shook him beneath his cloak. "Caught a chill?" he inquired. "Or don't you like my proposal?"

"Something I ate," Dominic said quickly. "I'm all right."

The last thing he needed was to be sent back down the mountain.

D'Arcis grunted. "Not losing your stomach for the task?" he asked shrewdly.

"No, my lord." Dominic fought down the panic that jolted through him at his commander's astuteness. "Just sick of waiting. Day in, day out, it gets to you."

"Aye, they're determined, all right," d'Arcis said with grudging respect. "You could almost admire them if they weren't so tainted with heresy."

Within the fullness of his beard, Dominic tightened his lips and did not reply.

"There'll be some more soldiers coming up to you later this week—Basque mountain men." D'Arcis turned his horse. "They'll be stationed at your post, but they have their own commander and instructions."

"Yes, my lord."

The horse took three strides and d'Arcis drew rein and looked round. "Is that Templar knight a friend of yours?"

Once again Dominic was jolted. His commander missed precious little. Never tell a lie, he thought, mind racing. "We met a few months ago when we were both hunting in the mountains," he said with an indifferent lift of his shoulders. "He seeks me out sometimes in the way of an acquaintance."

"Has he said anything strange to you?"

Dominic prayed that the look he gave d'Arcis would pass for bewilderment. "My lord?"

"Rumor has it that he's a heretic spy, that his father is a leading Cathar."

Dominic continued to stare as if the notion were so shocking that it had robbed him of speech.

"Don't be seen in his company," d'Arcis advised. "It will sully your own reputation, and I don't want to dismiss a good man." He dug in his heels and the Ardennes swung into its heavy stride.

A mist was descending over the mountain, obscuring everything. Dominic felt a similar fog reaching gray tentacles of frustration and despair into his soul, as if all the evil forces of the world were gathering to strangle the light.

* * *

A bowl of broth in her hands, Claire tiptoed into the curtained-off section of the hall where Magda was being tended. At the bedside, Bridget was watching her daughter's pale, scarcely breathing form with a troubled gaze. Magda had lost so much blood that her body had been brought to the threshold of death. Bridget had done all she could. Now it was in the hands of fate.

"I have brought you some soup," Claire said. "How is she?"

Bridget raised her eyes. "No better, no worse. The bleeding has stopped and there is no fever, but her spirit is wandering the realm between this life and the next, and I cannot reach her. If only I were not so tired." She pressed the palm of her hand upon her aching forehead.

"We are all praying for her."

Bridget forced an exhausted smile. "I know. I have felt your love and been comforted." Taking the bowl of broth, she half-heartedly sipped.

Claire knew that Bridget bore a burden of grief at the moment. Matthias had died three nights ago. It had not been unexpected and it had been a golden release for his soul to escape the pain-riddled, contorted old body, but they all mourned the loss of his wisdom.

"Shall I sit with her awhile?"

"Would you?" Gratefully and with immense gentleness, Bridget disengaged her hand from Magda's. "Hold her hand, talk to her, don't let her slip away." After a final, lingering look, Bridget went slowly out into the hall.

Claire smoothed the bedclothes around her patient and rearranged the heavy blond braid. Magda's skin was alabaster-pale except for the blue-tinged eye hollows and the lips, which were tinted the merest pink. The rise and fall of her breasts barely stirred the coverlet. When she took Magda's fingers, Claire felt their iciness strike through her own warm, tanned skin. The pulse was a faint throb, barely enough to keep a shadow alive. With her free hand, she fumbled open her copy of the Gospels and started to read aloud. Magda remained cold and unresponsive, and once it seemed to Claire that her pulse faltered. Quickly she put the book down and leaned over the young woman.

"Stay." She squeezed Magda's cold fingers. "You must

stay!" Her thoughts scurried, seeking to forge a link between the two of them, something that would hold Magda to life. "I know you must be in pain and I know how much you grieve for your child. She would have been mine, too . . . my grand-daughter." Tears filled Claire's eyes and she brushed them away on the back of her hand. She had been present at the end of Magda's traumatic premature labor, had seen the baby, its hands perfectly formed and as tiny and delicate as daisy petals. A child of the Light returned to her source even before she had drawn breath.

"I lost my child, too," she said, not just holding, but strok-ing the frozen hand in hers. "The pain never goes away. I saw him once or twice at the wet nurse's breast. They bound up my own breasts to stop my milk and they separated us. I wanted him so badly and at the same time I was so afraid that I would hate him, that I was driven almost to madness." She stared in-tently at the pale face upon the pillows, searching its stillness for a response. "What is he like that you should want him above the other men you could have chosen?"

Magda made no answer, but Claire sensed that she was lis-tening and that she had gained at least a little space of time. And time for Montségur was running out faster than grains of sand through a punctured sack. They still had enough food stockpiled to hold out for months to come, and the winter rains had started to fill up the dangerously low water tanks, but the sheer doggedness of the crusaders was wearing them down. The trebuchet that had been erected near the summit slammed rocks at their outerworks day in, day out, and sometimes through the night. Conditions were crowded, with no place to sleep in peace even during the brief lulls in enemy activity. Nor did the crusading troops show any signs of leaving for the winter months as had been the case in previous campaigns. D'Arcis, it seemed, had the support and determination to see this siege through to its grim conclusion.

Claire pressed Magda's hand. They could not let him snuff out the light. He might destroy the lamp, but the precious flame must be preserved and found a new setting in which to shine. She could feel it guttering beneath her fingers. "Don't leave us," she implored Magda. "You must not give up!"

In the hall she heard the sound of prayers being led by

Bishop Bertrand Marty and Chretien de Béziers. A baby belonging to one of the solders' women wailed fractiously, and the sound sawed through the curtains and into Claire's heart like a dull knife. She wondered if Magda could hear it.

Male voices approached the curtain. She recognized Raoul's baritone and Luke's rumble, but the third one eluded her even while it held a familiar note—deep with a husky edge. The curtain was drawn aside. Briefly she glimpsed the cramped squalor of the hall and the backs of the other Perfecti bowed in prayer, and then her view was blocked by a tall young man whose black hair and beard framed rugged features. She did not know him, but his looks evoked such memories that the world dissolved around her and she became a terrified girl sprawled in the rushes of her own solar, her raptor's weight grinding her thighs apart.

She stumbled to her feet and, in blind panic, spread her arms, shielding Magda. "You cannot come in here!" she cried desperately.

He ignored her and, in true Montfort tradition, pushed past her as if she did not exist in order to fulfill his own need.

"Let him." Raoul grasped her sleeve and pulled her to one side. "He hasn't got long and he is taking a great risk being here at all."

For a moment Claire tried to shake herself free of Raoul's grip, but then she capitulated and turned her face in to the comforting breadth of his shoulder.

Dominic knelt at Magda's side. She had the same translucent stillness that he remembered seeing on the face of Alais de Montfort lying in state in her open coffin on the eve of her funeral, a memory that had stayed with him down the years because most of the dead bodies he had seen had been mutilated by war, and she had seemed in contrast as pure as unflawed glass. The similarity between Alais and Magda was terrifying.

They had told him that she had lost too much blood, that everything possible had been done to keep her alive, but that it still might not be enough. They told him that the child had been a girl. The words had echoed meaninglessly inside his head. Now, linked to what he saw with his eyes, he understood, and he refused to accept. Grasping her cold right hand, he pushed his fingers through the spaces between hers, weaving the link as it had been woven before in the act of creation.

"Magda, I'm here. Can you hear me? Can you feel me? Remember, remember this? You're not leaving me, I won't let you. I need you. We all need you!"

The twin notes of determination and anguish in the man's voice caused Claire to lift her head from Raoul's shoulder. She stared at the hard brown hand pushed against Magda's, the black hair bent against the shining blond braid, and sensed the pulsing strength of the life force within him. *Her son.* The thought hit her with more power than it had ever done before. Perhaps he looked like Simon de Montfort, perhaps he had the latter's driving strength of will, but the direction was different. It was the memory that haunted her, not the man. But how to separate one from the other? Leaving Raoul, she knelt opposite him at the bedside, and taking Magda's other hand, added her own prayers to the passion of his.

It was cold and dark and there was weakness, blood, and pain. Magda felt these things and avoided them. Why should she return to such discomfort when before her rippled a field of glowing rainbow light, alive with the memory of how it had been not to have a body? Unfettered, harmonious joy. At the other side of the field was a doorway, and she knew that once she had passed through its portal, nothing of her present mortal existence would remain except the uninhabited husk of her body on a different plane.

Uncertain, she hesitated, lingering near the pain, aware that something was incomplete and without it, she could not progress. Voices vibrated along the fragile silver thread connecting her spirit to her body. One owned a deeper resonance that struck so strong a chord that the rainbow field shimmered around her and merged into one bright light. Again and again the cry rang across the levels, and she could not help but respond to it. Here was the part that was incomplete. Energy flowed through her, illuminating the silver cord down which she must return to the solid particles of her earthly form, and she was drawn irresistibly back toward it. *Set me as a seal upon your heart, for love is stronger than death.*

She felt the uncomfortable jarring sensation of soul merging with body, the heaviness and pain. With a tremendous effort she forced open her eyelids and saw the hall at Montségur and Dominic leaning over her, his face wet and his hand tightly laced through hers, binding her to life with his will. She breathed his name, the slightest thread of sound.

"Oh, my love!" he said hoarsely, and drew her tightly against him. The embrace was all-encompassing; the strength of his body flowed into hers and the light of the other world receded, leaving only a crystal residue of heightened awareness.

She touched his face, her heart overflowing with love and grief. "You should not be here; it is far too dangerous!" she whispered weakly. "But I am glad, so glad."

"Hush, it's all right."

She held on to him for a long time, drawing on the comfort of his presence and the radiance of his life force until she knew that for his own safety, she had to let him go. "You cannot stay any longer," she murmured, holding his face in her hands and looking into his eyes. "It is not safe."

"It is you that matters; I do not care about myself."

"Then for my sake, go."

Dominic started to shake his head, but when he would have spoken, she pressed her fingers across his lips. "As soon as I'm recovered, we'll leave, I promise you."

His eyes never left her face as he kissed her fingers and slowly stood up. Her color had returned and her breathing was robust and regular. It was he who felt drained, but then he had given unstintingly of his own energy to bring her back from the brink of death. "Do not keep me waiting," he said with a smile in which there was more anxiety than lightness. "I love you." Stooping, he kissed her on the lips, and went to the curtain, glancing back once and lingeringly over his shoulder.

The other woman who had knelt with him at Magda's side was regarding him with agitation, as if she wanted to speak to him but was afraid to do so. Before the moment could become drawn out, she lowered her bright brown gaze and went to fuss around Magda. Too preoccupied to linger on the incident, Dominic went out into the hall, where the Cathars were still praying.

In low tones he told Raoul about the detail of Basque climbers that were to be sent up the mountain. "D'Arcis has a plan up his sleeve. Be on your guard against any attempt to scale the walls. We're moving the trebuchet in the morning—eastward. I'll try and hinder matters as much as I can, but I have to be careful. D'Arcis has a keen eye." He looked darkly at Luke. "We were seen and remarked upon yesterday morning. D'Arcis is suspicious of you. I dare not make contact again for a while at least."

"I thought this might happen," Luke said impatiently. "All right, we'll just have to take great care."

Raoul said curiously to Dominic, "How did you manage to escape your men tonight?"

"I told them that I had a tryst. My chief sergeant thinks that I'm whoring at the foot of the mountain." Dominic grimaced. Some lies sullied the mouth with their telling. "It's a good excuse to be sluggish in the morning, too."

He followed Luke from the hall and down a dark stone corridor that led through the bowels of the castle to a small postern doorway at the rear of a storage cave. The Cathar woman who had attended the sickroom was waiting by the iron-bound postern door, and as they approached her, Dominic saw that she was shaking like an autumn leaf in a storm wind. Nevertheless, as the two men drew level, the hand she set upon Dominic's arm to detain him was resolute. Luke, after one assessing glance, moved discreetly away into the depths of the storeroom, murmuring something patently fabricated about having lost his cloak pin.

"Lady?" The hairs stood up stiffly upon Dominic's nape, for there was a strange expression in her burning brown eyes.

She studied his face intently by the flickering light of the torch in the wall bracket and slowly shook her head. "You look so much like *him*," she whispered.

"Like who?" He heard the hollow ring of his own voice and became aware of how cold it was down here, and dark, the shadows only just held at bay by the fickle light of the torch.

"Like . . . like your father."

He had to lean toward her to catch her words as her whisper sank to little more than the pressure of ordinary breath. "He was older and grayer, more heavily set." Her hand left his sleeve, and although her eyes remained fixed on him, it seemed to Dominic that she was looking through him at something dark and unpleasant.

"You are my mother," he said, and wondered why he had not realized it earlier in the sickroom. Even now, with that realization upon him, he did not recognize the cry of blood, only the cry itself.

"I am the one who gave you birth; that much is true." Her slight frame was shaking. "But I never had the opportunity to be more than that, nor do I know if it would have been within me. All I can say is that I was so badly wounded by what was done to me, for a long time I wounded those around me, too, so that I would have companionship in my suffering. It was not until I came to Montségur that I truly began to heal and find peace." Swallowing, she steadied the quiver in her voice. "I can feel that you mean us nothing but good. . . ."

"But you cannot see it while you still see my father?"

She stared up at him intently, the years knife-carved into her face rather than pleated in gentle folds of experience. "There is a dark abyss within me that stops the person I am, becoming the person I want to be. All it takes is a leap of faith, but I am frightened that I will not leap far enough and fall into the abyss and that *he* will be waiting for me."

"I think that everyone has such a place within themselves," Dominic answered, knowing that he would not have to feign exhaustion when he returned to his men. He had never felt so drained or unsure of himself. "I for one cannot see a black friar without breaking out in a cold sweat of terror. I am afraid of failure, I am afraid that one day the hunger within me will consume me as it consumed my father. When I reached out to Magda, half of it was terror for myself. What would I become without her?" Shrugging, he took a backward step. Revealing his deeper levels to this woman who had every claim on him and no claim was definitely setting one foot over the abyss.

"I have to go," he said curtly.

She nodded and took her hand from his arm. "I'm glad to have met you. You have haunted me for a long time."

He smiled at her bleakly. "As you have haunted me. I wish it could have been different."

Her lips were tightly compressed, withholding emotion, and

it was obvious to him as she murmured, "Walk in the Light," before turning away, that she, too, had one foot over the abyss.

CHAPTER FORTY-SIX

THE JANUARY NIGHT was brittle with cold, no cloud cover to protect the mountaintop from the freezing, pure light of the stars. Fuel supplies were low in the fortress, and only the essential watch fires burned on the heights. The ordinary people huddled together for warmth, and the Perfecti, like the rock, endured. Dying from cold was easier than dying in the fire, and of death itself, the Perfecti were not afraid.

Magda practiced the discipline that Bridget had taught her for generating body heat, and as the warmth surged through her in pleasant, tingling waves, was able to unclench herself.

"Two more nights and you'll be gone," said Raoul. He was fumbling to buckle on his sword belt, his hands made clumsy by the cold. With a pang she noticed that his hair was thinner, almost white, and his finger joints knotted. When had he grown old? All their strength was being sucked away by the greedy, devouring thing down the mountain. And her love stood in its very maw.

She came to help him attach his sword to his belt. "A part of me will always remain here, and a part of you . . . of everyone in Montségur, will live in me forever," she said with quiet but passionate certainty.

He cleared his throat twice before he spoke, and even then, his voice was husky. "More than you know." He brushed his callused knuckles gently across her cheek.

"But I do know," she gave back steadily, her eyes clear and

filled with knowledge. "There is nothing you could tell me that would come as a surprise."

A sad smile deepened the grooves between nostril and mouth corner. "You are Bridget's daughter. It could be no other way."

He left to check the sentries on night watch, and sighing deeply, Magda began to take stock of the items that she was bringing with her on her journey to a new life. Her portion was not great, for they were of a necessity traveling light. She had custody of the most important books, the knowledge that was her birthright, money to pay their way, to pay Dominic's brother, and to found her convent. She also had the cup that was to be given to Luke.

Tracing the engraved spear pattern on the cup's shining surface with her forefinger, she placed her other hand lightly over her womb. Despite the fact that she had almost died at the time of her miscarriage, she had suffered no lasting harm. The time would ripen again even as season followed season, as fallow was plowed and sown and harvested. She still mourned her lost baby, snatched untimely from her by the insidious darkness outside their walls. As her child had died, she had felt the force of the hatred growing and swelling. Daily it sucked against their barriers, seeking a way inside. Sometimes she could almost see it lurking in the shadow of the walls, waiting.

A sound of self-irritation escaped her lips. Even now it attacked, sowing doubt in the hope of reaping despair. Magda set her jaw and narrowed her brilliant eyes, concentrating her mind. The shadows surrounding the torchlight became less thick and the flame itself leaped in the sconce. She would not yield.

Raoul paced the wall walk and talked to the soldiers on duty. The air was so cold that it was like breathing broken glass. Beneath his mouflon-lined boots the wooden boards were crunchy with rime and the tiled roofs of the bailey sheds far below glittered like the encrustations on an archbishop's robes. A powdering of snow had fallen earlier in the day and might do so again if this crystal weather broke. He glanced skyward and prayed that there would not be any severe falls for the next week at least in order to give Magda and Dominic sufficient time to escape.

Peering over the battlements, he could see the crusaders' campfires ringing the mountain at regular intervals like a hundred malevolent golden eyes. The slopes themselves were peppered with outposts, one of them Dominic's, and a beacon of hope among all the other portents of destruction. He walked on and tried not to think of the odds stacked against them, comforting himself with the thought that thus far Dominic had made a nonsense of all such odds and that amidst the confusion there was a pattern if only he had the vision to discern it. The sons of Simon de Montfort had been chosen as the guardians of the light that their father had fought to extinguish.

Blowing on his hands, Raoul went to inspect the eastern barbican, which commanded the outerworks of their defenses. It stood on a steep escarpment, attached to the main fortress by a narrow ledge of stone with horrifying sheer drops on either side.

Guillaume was in command of the barbican guards tonight, and he greeted his father with a sarcastic grin of delight and offered him a drink from his flask of strengthened wine. The breath that swirled from him in a white vapor smelled strongly of the brew, but his balance was steady and his speech gave no hint of being slurred.

Raoul declined the proffered skin. "Are you not being a little careless? A man needs his wits about him to take night duty on this wall."

"I do have my wits," Guillaume retorted. His grin did not falter and he lightly punched his father's arm with his free fist. "I heard you coming a mile away. If I had wanted, I could have had this skin concealed under my cloak, and you none the wiser."

"You cannot conceal your breath," Raoul said with an arched brow, and continued along the wall walk. Grimacing at his father's broad back, Guillaume took another defiant swig and followed him.

Two guards were leaning against the stonework, faces hidden in shadow, voices low and intent.

"God's life!" Raoul snarled. "Is this what you call being on duty? I've seen housewives in a marketplace better prepared than this! You two, pick up your spears and . . ." His gaze fell upon the coils of rope gleaming in the starlight, upon the flash of a grapnel biting the edge of the wall. He clawed for his sword, his gut dissolving as he recognized the terrible danger that stalked here. Every soldier of Montségur's garrison was known to him by face if not by name, and these held neither in his memory. Steel shimmered in their hands, the cold glitter reflected in their eyes. Behind Raoul, Guillaume swore and threw down the wineskin to draw his own weapon.

"Go!" Raoul snapped without taking his gaze from the two men as one sidled to his left and one to his right. "Raise the alarm. Run, damn your hide. Do as you're told for once in your life!"

Guillaume ran. The clash of sword upon sword vibrated through his skull, throbbed down into his gut, and twisted his loins with sick guilt. He was brought up short on the edge of the open high stone corridor by another intruder. Near the man's feet a barbican guard lay in a widening puddle of blood.

Guillaume refused to believe that this was happening, that they were being attacked by stealth in the middle of the night and that if the attack succeeded, the blame would be his for complacence and lack of attention to detail. "No!" he roared, and leaped at the enemy soldier.

The ground underfoot was treacherous, slippery with rime, and Guillaume skidded. In trying to save himself he lost his sword over the edge of the chasm. His opponent's long knife sliced into his body, but Guillaume's unsteady momentum turned the blade aside from all vital points. He stumbled against the soldier, and the impact of his weight brought them both down, Guillaume on top, thrusting his enemy's shoulder against a bulge of rock beyond which there was nothing but the darkness of space. A knee butted his groin. The dagger flashed toward his throat. Guillaume caught the wrist in midmotion and locked and twisted, his forearm and biceps straining. Blood ran down his side. He felt its hot burn in the freezing midnight cold. His arm was tiring and he knew that in a moment he was going to lose his grip. "No!" he sobbed again, and with gritted teeth, made a final effort.

The dagger clattered sideways. His opponent struggled, trying to buck him off, but Guillaume refused to be moved. He struck with his fist, felt his knuckles split upon teeth, struck again, heedless of the pain. The other man choked on blood. Guillaume wrestled his own knife from his sheath and struck a third time, and a fourth, and a fifth. The final time the point grated on rock and the soldier beneath him ceased to writhe. Weeping with effort and shock, Guillaume pulled his dagger free. The blade clung to its flesh-and-cartilage sheath, and it was almost more of an effort than his suddenly weak and shaking body could accomplish. Braced on all fours, he vomited up the wine that he had so profligately consumed.

The barbican was silent. All sounds of struggle had ceased and it was with a dreadful awareness that he was already too late that Guillaume staggered toward the main fortress to raise the alarm.

Raoul's cheek was pressed into the slippery white frosting of the wall walk boards. The hand that was trapped beneath his body was warm with blood; the other one gripped the planks, caught there in spasm. No strength remained within him to move it, his life draining away through the wound in his chest, which had been slashed open along the line of the old battle scar from Muret. He would already have been dead, but the severe cold had reduced the flow of blood to a thin trickle. Death encroached slowly, circling him like a stalking beast.

He had sold his life dearly. Three Basques stiffened in the starlight beside him, already claimed. It had made no difference to the final outcome. The barbican was lost to the defenders, and with it, the last hope for Montségur. He closed his eyes, too weary to keep them open, and besides, there was nothing to see; the stars had gone out.

Someone rolled him over. "Dead," he heard the rough Basque voice grunt.

"Throw him to the kites. There's no need for Christian decency toward a heretic!" growled a companion.

"Seems a pity to waste good armor. Come on, help me get this off him."

They stripped him of his hauberk, dagger, and gambeson, acquisitive as magpies. "What's this around his neck?"

"It's one of their evil talismans; throw it away!" The voice was rapid with alarm.

"Might be valuable, might bring me luck. You're just wishing you saw it first!" The Basque mercenary tugged at the cord of the dove and chalice medallion.

Raoul tried to thrust away the groping hand. At first his limbs did not answer his command, and then suddenly, as if a prison door had opened, it was easy . . . too easy. He stood up, feeling as light as thistledown. The Basques crouched over something on the ground, a broken chrysalis that looked strangely familiar. Grunting with effort, they carried it between them to the wall. Heaving it up, they toppled it into the chasm below and leaned over the stone, looking down. A slight thud echoed up, followed by silence. In curiosity Raoul would have pursued the sound into the darkness, but he was prevented by a rippling barrier of light, shimmering with a rainbow brilliance that reached out to absorb him. It was only then, with a feeling of detachment already of the spirit, that he realized this time he truly had crossed the divide between life and death.

Within his tent, Dominic restlessly checked that everything was prepared for the journey—traveling rations, blankets, thick cloaks, waterskins. He gnawed viciously on his thumbnail, his nerves taut, and wished that they had left the previous week when some of the books and treasure had been smuggled out over the side in baskets attached to ropes. That cargo was now safe in the caves of Ornolac, awaiting collection. Raoul's task and his own was going to be made that much more difficult now that the eastern barbican was crusader-occupied by some of Hugh d'Arcis's best troops. The trebuchet had been dismantled in order that it could be dragged to the summit and lodged in the barbican, where any stone fired was almost bound to score a direct hit.

Dominic sat down cross-legged on his pallet and breathed deeply in and out, emptying his mind, seeking calm, but before he had even found the thread of a shallow tranquillity, a young soldier burst into the tent, his expression frantic with excitement and fear. "Lord Dominic, come quickly. Jules and a Basque are killing each other!"

Dominic was more than tempted to tell the lad to let them get on with it, but the pretense had to be maintained. "All right, I'm coming," he said, adding irritably, "Next time, wait outside and crave admittance before you fling in on me like that." Without enthusiasm, he unfolded his limbs and picked up his sword.

"Yes, my lord." The youth lowered his eyes and stood aside.

The crowd of soldiers encircling the combatants parted rather sheepishly for Dominic. Stiff-backed, with an expression of cold disapproval, he shouldered through them to the brawl. Jules and the Basque were circling each other warily, weapons at the ready as each sought an opening in the other's defense. Both were bleeding from superficial wounds, and neither of them displayed any inclination to back down.

Dominic strode between them, his own blade raised. "Put up your weapons!" he said icily. "You know the penalty for brawling."

"It weren't me as started it!" Jules protested in a voice high-pitched with indignant rage. "I won the necklace fair and square. You can check the dice yourself, my lord; they aren't loaded!"

"Bastard, you cheated!" the Basque spat, and lunged, only to be brought up short by Dominic's sword.

"Drop your weapons!" Dominic said huskily, beginning to feel the flickering of rage himself. How easy it would be to let go and give vent to all the tension pent up within him in an explosion of violence that would leave his men cowering in terror. And because it was too easy, he kept a grim rein on his control.

He could tell from their raised voices and exaggerated gestures that both soldiers had been drinking. These disputes always followed the same monotonous course. Wine, dice, hot words, spilled blood. Even the penalties, ranging from public flogging to death on the gibbet, did not readily deter the men from brawling.

Jules sighed heavily, rolled his eyes, and slung his sword on the ground. Eyes venomous, the Basque dropped his own weapon. "He stole from me," he reiterated stubbornly as Dominic gestured and the crowd began dispersing. Jules immediately and furiously started to protest his own side of the matter again.

"Silence!" Dominic growled, his eyes no less dangerous

than his voice. "Precisely what are you fighting over? Show me." He held out his hand.

Jules briefly met his commander's hard, gray-green stare, felt it begin to draw his guts out through his body, and fumbled in the purse at his waist. "This, my lord, it's mine. I won it fair and square!"

"Liar!" spat the Basque as he started to lunge, and was again halted by Dominic's naked blade. Without relaxing his hand, Dominic looked at the talisman that Jules had so reluctantly handed to him. It was a disk of enameled silver dangling from a grubby cord of plaited red silk, the design that of a cup, or chalice, and rising out of it, a dove in flight. Dominic went cold.

"Where did you get this?" he demanded of the Basque.

The mercenary, misliking the granite intensity of Dominic's stare and the angle of his wrist bracing the sword, answered him with more cooperation than the encounter had first promised. "I took it from a dead Cathar on the east barbican, my lord."

"A dead Cathar?"

"Yes, my lord. A knight, he was—fought like one possessed, but we got him in the end. I took that for a momento. He had a good hauberk, too, but me and Gaston sold that and split the money."

Dominic's throat closed. He knew by this token that Raoul must be dead. It had been his task to inspect the sentinels, make sure they were at their posts. What now was he to do? His fist closed over the token until the edges bit into the flesh of his palm. "You should not have gambled with the thing if you set such store by it," he said harshly. "A dead heretic's token, perhaps even tainted with blasphemy. I think it best that neither of you have it. If I don't mention this to the priest when he takes the next mass, you will count yourselves fortunate, as you will count yourselves fortunate to receive ten stripes of the lash apiece and keep your necks unstretched!"

That was the facade, the crisp, controlled anger of a commanding officer rebuking squabbling children, but once he had seen the punishment administered and spoken to the Basque's commanding officer, Dominic sat down on the pallet in his tent and put his face in his hands.

* * *

Guillaume lay on his mattress, his face buried in his folded arms and angled away from the world toward the wall.

"Papa?" His small daughter patted his shoulder. "Papa, please don't cry anymore."

Her gentle touch was a barb, not balm, in Guillaume's wound. "I'm not crying," he croaked, and raised his head to show her dry but red-rimmed eyes. There were no tears left in him. "Look, doucette, just leave me alone. Go and find your mother."

The child sucked her soft, pink underlip. "Bridget sent me to find you, Papa; she wants to speak to you." She continued to pat his shoulder.

Slowly Guillaume sat up and rubbed his hands over his bristly face. He felt dreadful. The flesh wounds of his encounter on the east barbican were sore but healing well—bearable pain. It was the turmoil within that unmanned him, and he could not dull his ache with wine. The very thought of a brimming cup of cool, red poison made him sweat with longing and nausea.

Sancha perched herself on the edge of his pallet, huge brown eyes fixed on his face with anxious adoration. Trustingly she leaned her head upon his muscular arm. He had betrayed that trust in drink and carelessness, and now the enemy had access by trebuchet to every vulnerable part of Montségur. Seizing his daughter, he clutched her so tightly to his chest that she cried out in sudden fear and struggled. Above her dark curls, the downward curve of Guillaume's mouth was grimly set. There had to be a way out for her and Constanza. He dared not believe that he had caused their deaths, too.

Bridget was in the tiny room used for the storage and preparation of the medicinal herbs and roots that were used to ease the plight of the sick and wounded. Magda, Claire, and Chretien de Béziers were present, too.

"Have I been brought here to be judged?" Guillaume demanded belligerently.

"I think that you have judged yourself already," Chretien answered in his deep, resonant voice, to which his advancing years had brought the slightest hint of a quaver. "Nothing would be gained by such a confrontation."

"Then what do you want?"

"Your help," said Bridget.

Beneath her steady gray gaze, Guillaume removed his hands from his hips, where they had been braced. His eyebrows rose to meet the ragged line of his fringe. "You want *my* help?" he said incredulously. "After what happened to the east barbican?" He looked at his mother, and she looked back at him with such compassion and grief in her eyes that he could not bear it.

"Perhaps because of that," Bridget answered. "You won't take the crusaders for granted again, and you are hurting so badly that unless you make reparations, you will destroy yourself with recrimination. . . . You must understand that no one in this room blames you."

"How generous of you to desire to set my mind in order and grant me your absolution!" Guillaume spat bitterly, and turned his back, but he did not walk out. The tears that he had thought wrung dry at their source were suddenly hot behind his lids. He pinched the bridge of his nose and squeezed his eyes tightly shut, but knew that his breathing was giving him away. "What do you want me to do?" he asked in a choked voice, not turning around.

Behind him there was a long pause before Chretien cleared his throat. "Were you aware that your father was planning to leave Montségur?"

"No." Guillaume's voice sank to a whisper. "No, I wasn't. He said nothing to me, but then he wouldn't. He did not trust me, you see. Fickle and wine-wild. I proved him right, didn't I?" The last word rose to a wrenched-out sob.

"Stop it!" Magda hastened quickly to his side and, taking his arm, drew him farther into the room. "You must not poison your life with this bitterness and remorse! It was his choice to stay with us at Montségur. He could have left long ago, and no one would have prevented him or thought less of him for doing so. And he did not tell you because he was sworn to secrecy." With was only half-true, but not for the world would she have exposed the other half to Guillaume.

Guillaume shook his head and wiped his eyes on the side of his hand, but he remained silent and his body became less rigid.

"He was going to take me out of the postern and down to

meet Dominic," she continued. "If there was trouble, he and Luke de Béziers were going to deal with it while we made our escape. All the plans have been laid, routes, everything."

"Dominic?" Guillaume's brown eyes were suddenly wider than his small daughter's. He gaped at Magda. "You mean my half brother? Dominic? Dominic is here?"

She nodded. "Among the crusaders. We have been soul mates for a long time, and more recently lovers. It was our child that I miscarried."

Guillaume stared at her in astonishment. He had often wondered which man of the Montségur community she had taken to her bed, but never in his wildest imaginings had he contemplated what she was telling him now. Her and Dominic? Jesu!

"I'm so afraid that he'll be discovered; he's taking a very great risk. Luke has been his contact, but it's not safe anymore. Hugh d'Arcis watches Luke too closely, and so tight is the security around us that he cannot move in and out of Montségur like he used to."

Guillaume pushed his hands through his hair and wondered how these things could have existed beneath his nose without his knowledge. Perhaps the drink had rendered him blind to all save his own hatreds, or perhaps because he was so volatile and fickle, they had been at pains to conceal their secrets from him. Flinching from the investigation of such fraught implications, he said quickly to Magda, "Why should your escape be so important?" He saw the look that passed between the group and flinched again. "All right, don't tell me," he said wearily. "I know I don't deserve your trust. What do you want me to do?"

Bridget considered him. He had looked inside himself and been horrified at what he had found. That was always the hardest part. Some men and women never came to it, preferring to live shallowly for fear of what lay in the depths, until one day the shallows evaporated and they died of thirst. "No," she said in a firm, quiet voice. "You have a right to know why you are being asked to risk your life."

Guillaume watched Ramon de Perella knuckle his eyes in a gesture of unutterable weariness, and then sigh heavily and look around the group of knights who formed his inner council of war. "We cannot go on," he said. "Either we negotiate now for surrender terms while we still have a sting in our tail, or we negotiate in a month's time when we have nothing left to make it worth their while listening."

"No!" His nephew Pierre-Roger slammed his huge fist down on the trestle like a mallet. "We won't give them so much as an inch of ground unless they die taking it!"

"We are the ones who are dying," de Perella responded heavily. "Now that they have possession of the barbican, they can kill us at will. I have suffered torments even thinking of surrender. I once swore to turn the mountains red with the blood of those who dared to trespass on this holy mountain, but even I can see that to go on is to prolong our pain."

His nephew jerked to his feet and stalked the confines of the room, jaw grinding. "I cannot believe that you are advocating this!"

Two weeks ago, Guillaume would have leaped to his feet and taken Pierre-Roger's side in a fury. Now, tempered by grief and guilt and the weight of a dreadful responsibility, he remained seated and rode out his first instinctive denial.

"There are secrets here that the Dominicans must never lay their hands upon," he spoke out, adding his weight to Perella's, "but the net has been drawn so tight that it has become impossible for any arrangements to be made. Negotiations would give us that opportunity."

Pierre-Roger exhaled contemptuously, but his pacing stopped.

"Secrets?" Perella looked up. "Connected with the mystic women?"

"Yes, sir. My father was supposed to escort Magda to a contact on the mountain, but after what happened at the east barbican—"

"And we all know whose fault that was!" Pierre-Roger flashed nastily.

Guillaume's jaw clenched, but his tone remained level. "You can say nothing that I have not already said to myself."

"Don't be too sure!"

"Peace!" de Perella growled. "Recriminations are a waste of breath. Blame Guillaume and you might as well blame yourself for Avignonet in the first place! To open negotiations will be to open a channel to the world."

"And what of the Cathars?" Pierre-Roger flung. "You know what Hugh d'Arcis will do to them!"

"Will it alter anything if we hold out for another month, two at the most? This way at least, some of us will keep our lives." He thrust his head forward to emphasize his words. "I see no harm in suing for discussion, Pierre. We can always reject the terms if they prove impossible to swallow."

"I'm choking already!" his nephew sneered.

"Then chew it over properly! There's more at stake here than your pride!"

It was very quiet in the moments after Pierre-Roger slammed out of the room—not that there was anywhere to go to vent his temper. All space and safety had shrunk to a cramped corner of the ward where the shadow of the trebuchet did not reach.

"He'll see the sense of it when he's had time to cool," de Perella said uneasily, as if he did not quite believe his own words. "He has to." He stretched his lips at Guillaume in poor imitation of a smile. "How do you feel about conducting negotiations as my chief adjutant?"

The dove-and-chalice medallion suspended before him, Dominic concentrated until his eyes started to smart and he was forced to blink, breaking the moment. There was nothing, not even the vibration of a feeling. The fortress shunned him, permitting him no access to Magda. Upon the token, the dove seemed to palpate, an illusion caused by staring for too long. He turned it over and studied the obverse, which bore the symbol of a cauldron holding a quenched spear, and wondered again what it meant. The knowledge, like his grasp of Magda herself, hung just out of reach, encircled by danger. So near, so far away.

Dominic replaced the red cord around his neck and regarded his surroundings with loathing. The guardroom of the east barbican was more comfortable by far than a tent, but he hated the very feel of the stones. Raoul had died here, and so had the Cathars' hopes. A trebuchet crowned the battlements and spat stone destruction at the trapped Cathars. And he, too, was trapped.

A fist struck the guardroom door. Dominic tucked the medallion down inside his hauberk. "Come," he shouted brusquely, and rose to his feet.

The door creaked open and Jules stood on the threshold. His recent whipping and Dominic's bad temper had both failed to make a dent in his cocky, garrulous nature. "My lord, the heretics have sent someone out under a banner of truce," he announced, ferret eyes gleaming. "They must be getting desperate, eh?"

Dominic's heart quickened. Abandoning his brooding, he shouldered past the little sergeant without a reply and ran up to the battlements. After the briefest look, he snapped a command at the men on duty and hurtled back down the twisting stairs.

Guillaume was barely recognizable. The glow of young manhood was less than a memory in a face that was all bone and cavernous hollows. He was thin almost to the point of emaciation, pared down to raw, burning spirit. Suffering and hardship were imprinted all too clearly, and so was a terrible grief.

"I bear authorization from Ramon de Perella and Pierre-Roger of Mirepoix to negotiate a truce with Hugh d'Arcis," Guillaume said formally for the benefit of the men gathered around Dominic, listening, but his eyes told a different, more personal story.

Dominic lifted his brow. The unspoken message passed between them, and he swung to the shamelessly inquisitive crowd of soldiers and squires. "Have you no work?" he snapped, eyes narrow and dangerous. "Those who haven't, wait my pleasure and I'll soon find you some!" The spectators vanished as rapidly as mist in sunshine. "Holy God, Guillaume," he muttered, "what's been happening up there! I've been worried sick! Magda should be long gone by now!"

"How do you expect that to happen when your soldiers are all over the barbican?" Guillaume's lips drew back from his teeth. "Nothing moves without that their eyes see it!"

"They are not my soldiers!" Dominic retorted in a voice no less abrasive. "I warned your father to be on his guard for just such an assault. I do what I can, full knowing that it is not enough, but I dare not attach suspicion to myself if the escape channel is to be kept open."

"What use is an escape channel if we cannot reach it!"

"I assume that's why you're here now?" Taking Guillaume's arm, he drew him toward the guardroom. "Come on, we might as well flay each other in comfort."

Guillaume's weathered skin took on a deeper hue at the remark. Gritting his teeth, he followed Dominic into the barbican's guardroom, where only a month earlier he himself had sat in comfort, a flagon within easy reach of his hand—too easy.

The warmth of a brazier beckoned him to hold out his hands and experience the luxury of heat. Since late January there had been no fuel except for cooking and the heating of water to clean wounds. Feeling like a traitor, but unable to stop himself, he reveled in the warmth. The sound of wine trickling from a flagon to a cup made him swallow nauseously, his mouth filling with saliva.

"I don't want any," he said rapidly to Dominic, terrified that he would be unable to resist once the cup was in his hands. "Since . . . since my father died, I've forsworn all drink except water."

Dominic gave him a look that was so sharp, so perceptive, Guillaume lowered and half-turned his head. "I was in command of this barbican on the night he died," he said so quietly that Dominic had to strain to hear. "It was all my fault that we were taken by surprise."

Dominic did not speak. Guillaume risked a glance, but his brother's face was blank of expression. "Aren't you going to condemn me?" he challenged.

"I'm walking too narrow a ledge myself to lose my balance casting stones at others." Dominic opened one hand in a wry gesture and took a short swallow of wine. "What we have to do is get Magda to safety before this place falls, because when it does, there'll be no quarter given."

"I know." An aching anxiety filled Guillaume's chest. "I'm not only here for Magda, I'm here to negotiate for others whose lives might be saved if we surrender now. I have a woman and child in the fortress, neither of them Cathar, and it's the same for many other fighting men. There is no reason why the church cannot let them go free. While there's a truce for negotiation, you and Magda can escape."

"As I remember you back in Toulouse, you're hardly the material of which diplomats are made," Dominic observed dryly.

Guillaume grimaced. "I've changed since then. It alters you irrevocably when you reach thirty years old and see a rip in the fabric of your dreams for every one of those years. Suddenly you're threadbare to the world. . . . I want my daughter to live."

"I can understand that," Dominic said, and took another hard swallow of the wine. Then he set it out of his reach.

Guillaume remembered suddenly that Dominic's daughter had never even had the chance of life. "Jesu, I'm sorry," he said.

Dominic made a small gesture of negation. "Why should you apologize for my loss? We're here for a purpose other than commiserating with each other. Stick to business; it's far safer."

Guillaume stiffened at Dominic's tone, and all contrition vanished from his eyes, which narrowed coldly. "Business," he repeated, jaw tight. "Bridget has a scheme set for the eve of the spring equinox if I can drag out the negotiations that long."

"The sooner the better, I would have thought," Dominic said with a frown.

"No, at the equinox, the natural power is easier to harness and transform. Bridget no longer has the strength to conjure a storm out of nothing." He watched Dominic closely for signs of incredulity, but his half brother betrayed by not so much as a flicker what he thought of such a remark.

"So where do we go from here?" Dominic reached again for the goblet, but only to tip the wine out into the rushes. "To the One Light," he said softly, and looked at Guillaume.

CHAPTER FORTY-SEVEN

FRIAR BERNARD STARED at the fish head on his trencher, and it stared back at him out of sightless, candle-white eyes. Rags of flesh still adhered to its backbone. He stretched out his forefinger and touched the delicate, sharp tracery. How beautiful, how stark and mortal, and how blasphemous of the Cathars to believe that a human soul could be reborn into the body of a fish. Only man had a soul, and when he died, it either entered heaven's bliss, or suffered in hell. The Cathars were going to hell, every last one of them on that mountaintop. He was not going to permit a single one to recant.

"Is the fish troubling your digestion?" inquired Hugh d'Arcis with concern in his voice.

"No, my lord, the fish is excellent." Bernard pressed his fingertip into one of the stiff, needle-sharp bones until it punctured his skin. A tiny red jewel, vein-dark, glistened. *I will make you fishers of men.* "I was frowning over your decision to allow any recanting Cathars to survive along with the men and women of the garrison."

"The siege has gone on far too long already," said d'Arcis with badly concealed irritation. "This way, the staunch Cathars will die at the stake and we will obtain the fortress without having to exert any more time or expense. Once Montségur is in our hands, the heretics will never be able to use it again for a base. I tell you, Friar Bernard, and you have seen it in the camp yourself, I cannot hold my men in the field much longer; they want to go home."

Bernard's pale upper lip curled away from his stained teeth.

"The Cathars are concealing things from you. I know, I have seen. The ordinary heretics, yes, they will go willingly into the flames for their cursed beliefs, but there are, sheltered among them, people whose blasphemy is even greater than theirs. The Cathars will do everything within their power to help them escape and proliferate."

"What power?" d'Arcis scoffed. "They're trapped in there like lobsters in a basket!"

"Baskets can be used for escape as well as imprisonment—that breach of security the other night, for example." Some Cathars had escaped from the fortress with laden packs. A sentry had heard a sound and, glancing up, had seen the end of a rope snaking up the sheer wall into darkness. Although the alarm had been raised immediately and the mountainside thoroughly searched, the escapees had got clean away.

D'Arcis's face grew dusky. "Since then, security has been tightened to a stranglehold. Nothing will get past now," he said dourly.

The friar was far from mollified. "They do have power, I tell you, of a diabolic nature. I myself have experienced it at first hand."

D'Arcis looked at him with hard, pragmatic eyes. "That is for you to challenge, Friar," he grated. "My own concern is military."

"Then you should look to their negotiator. He's not to be trusted. Probably he spied out all our strengths and weaknesses before he went back into the fortress." He wiped the smear of blood from his finger onto his trencher and watched the bread absorb it the way his tongue absorbed a holy wafter. The truce ended at dawn tomorrow, two weeks from its commencement, and Montségur was honor-bound to open its gates. Tomorrow when the fires were lit and the heretics committed to the flames, he would remove his hair shirt and rejoice.

Unconcerned, d'Arcis selected a mussel from a dish in front of him. "I would expect any soldier worth his salt to do as much."

"And would you expect him to have aid from among your own troops?"

D'Arcis scooped the mussel from its shell, paused, and

looked gravely at the friar. "That is a most serious accusation. I trust you can substantiate it?"

"Do you really believe that these breaches of security are just carelessness? You must look at the men closest to the walls."

"I do not need a meddling priest to tell me my business! I've vetted all my commanders and found none of them wanting." D'Arcis pushed the shellfish into his mouth and ground it between his molars as if it were a substitute for his table guest.

Bernard's obsidian eyes narrowed. "I have the victory of our Lord Jesus Christ at heart."

D'Arcis pushed the dish of mussels aside and signaled his squires to begin clearing the board. "I know that you do," he answered wearily. "So do I, but let me be the best judge of my men." He started to rise. "If it will ease your zeal," he murmured, "I'll send up the mountain to the barbican watch and tell Dominic to be on the lookout for anything out of the ordinary tonight."

"Dominic, you said?" Bernard, who had been about to rise himself, sat back in his chair, his eyes upon the fish skeleton that the squires had yet to remove.

D'Arcis shrugged. "I believe he was named after the founder of your order by the Countess de Montfort herself. He's the bastard son of old Count Simon—God's athlete, as he used to be known." He smiled into his beard. "I hazard Dominic's athletics are considerably more secular where the fair sex is concerned." His brow contracted at the look on Bernard's face. "What's wrong?"

"I know all about Dominic FitzSimon," said Bernard in a soft, chill voice. "I was his tutor in Toulouse. If you have vetted all your commanders, then you will know he is a heretic of the first order, branded with the left-handedness of the Devil."

"Oh, come now!" D'Arcis laughed uneasily. "I've known several left-handers in my time, one of them a priest. You can't hold that against a man!"

"He was arraigned for heresy and banished from the Languedoc. The only reason he did not burn was because of his family connections." Bernard continued as if d'Arcis had not spoken. "His mother is one of the Cathar Perfecti locked in that fortress, his mistress another, and the envoy who came to negotiate terms with you, Guillaume de Montvallant, is none other than his half brother."

Hugh d'Arcis crimsoned and swelled. "I don't believe you!" he throttled out, but they were only words. He did believe him, he simply did not want to.

"Now I see the link," Bernard murmured. "It eluded me before. I must have seen him again and again, and not recognized him. I should have known." He pressed his fist to the center of his forehead. "It will be tonight; I feel it here, a gathering of the power."

The crimson fury had left Hugh d'Arcis, replaced by a far deadlier white tension. "I'll put out an immediate order for Dominic's arrest," he said grimly, and strode to the tent flap, sick inside as he remembered small, inexplicable incidents— the trebuchet constantly developing niggling faults, equipment breaking or being stolen, the occasion he had caught Dominic conversing with that Templar knight.

When d'Arcis and Friar Bernard had sat down to dine, it had been a clear, mild spring evening, but a wind was now beginning to ruffle the tent canvases and gust through the campfires. When he looked up at the sky, the stars were rapidly becoming swallowed in cloud.

"It comes," said the friar in a doom-laden voice. "Armageddon, the final battle."

The hackles rose along d'Arcis's spine and he discovered that it was Friar Bernard of whom he was afraid, not the Cathars upon their rock.

On the battlements, facing eastward to the place of sunrise, Bridget sat within the pentacle drawn of salt, her gray-streaked hair cloaking her naked back. Her body, weakened by fasting and privation, had lost all suppleness and tone, but the inner glow remained, flickering around her like a living entity more animated than the flesh containing it. Tonight was the equinox, tonight the power of nature was open to be harnessed, and they had never had more need of it than now.

Bridget closed her eyes and concentrated. She was the conduit through which the life force would flow to its destination. Her body trembled with the strength of the forces within and without. Even in her prime she would have struggled to control such power, and now, as it started to build, she knew that this summoning would end in the death of her earthly body.

Throughout her life she had glimpsed this night in brief visions no longer than the blink of an eye, or the flicker of a single bolt of lightning. It was a sacrifice that she was now ready to make; for Magda, for all the women who had gone before, and all who were to come and wear the inheritance of their royal name. There was sadness, but no grief. She had made her farewells steadily, without tears, and Magda had trimmed her own responses to fit her mother's. It was a parting of the ways, not an irrevocable sundering.

Across Montségur's battlements, the lightning ripped the sky like a glimpse of the world beyond, and the clouds boiled like steam billowing from the ancient Celt cauldron of life.

Resembling an ancient goddess, the huge trebuchet on the eastern wall was both the destroyer and the giver of life, the key to freedom. Dominic eyed the grotesque siege machine with loathing and a glimmer of satisfaction for what he was about to do. From early childhood, one of these had been a part of him. He could not remember a time when the thud of the counterweight and the creak of the capstan had not lived in his dreams and haunted his waking mind should he give it rein to wander. . . . His father crushed to a bloody pulp, men and women screaming. Friar Bernard's willow switch.

For a fortnight the trebuchet had stood a silent sentinel on the walls, muzzled by the two weeks of truce that had been granted to the Cathars in order for them to mull over the terms of the surrender and review their lives. Tonight the machine would be silenced forever, but not before it had performed one last service.

He had dismissed the men on watch to their meal in the guardroom below. While the truce was in operation, vigilance was not as strict upon the trebuchet and no one had complained or even thought his action strange, for he had made this the routine for the past four nights.

After a final glance around, Dominic set his foot on the winch, his hand on a beam, and pulled himself lightly onto the main body of the weapon. Reaching beneath his cloak, he carefully unfastened from the belt at his waist one of a dozen small clay eggs and placed it with meticulous care against a niche where two beams joined. The egg contained Greek fire—a dark liquid with spectacular burning properties, easy to ignite, almost impossible to put out. Methodically he climbed about the trebuchet, removing the other vessels from his belt and arranging them to suit his ultimate purpose—one on the capstan, another in the leather bag that held the stones, two on the ground supports, others on the superstructure. All his concentration was encompassed by the small, volatile shells of clay that one careless move or slip of the fingers would cause to explode in a ball of searing, unquenchable flame.

When he had completed the task, Dominic jumped down from the trebuchet and spared a moment to puff out his cheeks in relief and wipe his hands on his cloak. Wind riffled through his hair and he glanced briefly skyward. A cloudy night sky was rapidly absorbing the star-twinkled dusk. He turned to the barrels of pitch lined up neatly against the battlement wall. Two of these he rolled along to the trebuchet, positioned them on their sides, and then knocked out the bungs. A third one he broached, and tilted so as to pour a shining, glutinous trail from trebuchet to stair head. He was breathing hard now with effort, but through the exertion and nausea of nervousness surged a glorious exhilaration. The trebuchet had haunted his life for too long. Let it go in sacrifice.

"Benedicte," he saluted mockingly, and plucking a wall torch from its bracket, touched the flaring tip to the edge of the trail he had laid. Then, as yellow daggers stabbed up from the pitch, he ran.

"Fire!" he bellowed, flinging open the guardroom door. "Don't just sit there like sheep; the trebuchet's burning! Organize a bucket chain. I'll raise more help!"

Above him as he sprinted into the night, the roar of the flames was clearly audible as they were fanned by the rising wind, and upon the battlements, the first flickers of lightning dazzled the sky. Keeping to the shadows, moving as rapidly as a snake through the undergrowth, Dominic hastened toward Montségur's west wall.

* * *

Magda clung to the rope that was slowly being paid out over the sheer west drop of the fortress, and felt as vulnerable as a fly upon a wall, ripe for the swatting. Surely the guards would see her and Guillaume in the jagged flashes of lightning and cry the alarm; or the other thing, the black night walker, would sense the breach in Montségur's defenses and come on swift, silent feet to destroy them.

Fear gnawed at the edge of Magda's composure like a rat gnawing at the rope from which she was suspended in a flimsy leather harness. She must not fear. To fear was to give the darkness a wound on which to feast.

"Not far now," whispered Guillaume from beside her.

She could not see his face, but knew from his voice that he spoke as much for his own comfort as hers. The leather bit into her thighs, the rope swung, grazing her against the walls, and the wind howled like a demon unchained, whipping her hair across her face, battering at her. She thought that she heard Guillaume cursing, but could not be sure as all thoughts and words were carried away by the violence of the elements. The ropes securing herself and Guillaume lurched alarmingly as those who were lowering them, weakened by lack of food and exhaustion, struggled to hold them steady and did not succeed. Biting her lip, Magda tried not to think of the drop below, concentrated all her will instead on the image of Dominic waiting for her.

The lightning tore across the battlements like a charging bull, reached the barbican, and stabbed at the walls. In a lull of wind she heard Guillaume's growl of triumph as flames soared skyward from the barbican's summit, illuminating the trebuchet in a giant praying mantis of fire, attended by a bee swarm of molten sparks. They heard the boom of pitch barrels exploding and hugged it to their hearts, the exultation warming their wind-frozen bodies.

Suddenly there were loose stones and tufts of wiry grass beneath their feet. Guillaume, being the heavier, was marginally the first to land, and kicked himself free of the harness. A shape scudded through the darkness and he groped for his sword, then relaxed as he saw that it was Dominic.

"Good bonfire." Guillaume nodded at the barbican, his remark flippant to conceal his fear.

"It'll keep them occupied for a while." Dominic's reply was curt, all his attention for Magda, who was tangled up in her harness and struggling to rise. He helped her out of it and drew her to her feet and briefly against him. She fitted into the contours of his body as if there had never been any danger or heartache or parting, or perhaps because of it and against all the odds. Dominic spared time for a swift hug, a hard but rapid kiss, and set her free. "Give me your pack," he said. The wind whipped around them from all directions as if fighting with itself, and the lightning formed jagged stairways across the sky.

Rubbing the back of her neck to ease the muscles that the straps of her pack and the descent had tightened, Magda looked up at the rearing walls of the fortress, her cheekbones catching the purity of the brilliant light. She could feel her mother, but there was no space for benediction or a final farewell. She felt Bridget's struggle to hold the power of the lightning and would instinctively have tried to help her, but Dominic barred her way.

"Come now, quickly!" He tugged at her hand.

Her gaze was brought down to his fingers meshed through hers, forging the link to the future. She scrambled after him, the men's garments she wore feeling strange, but also a blessing. No skirts hampered her legs as she ran with him through the darkness.

"Torches," Guillaume warned, "spreading out below us, look!"

They paused to stare down the mountain at the bobbing dots of light advancing on them through the trees.

"Down here!" Dominic's voice was raw with urgency. "Hurry!"

Stones turned beneath their feet and rattled away down the mountainside. Magda skidded and slipped and clung tightly to the strength of Dominic's hand. If only she could stop for a moment to gain her breath and find the submerged sixth sense that would permit her to walk these slopes as if they were steeped in noontide sunshine. The illusion of the latter was briefly granted by a vicious bolt of lightning, pink and blue, that sizzled into the rocks close to the path and sent a small avalanche bouncing away into the trees below.

Dominic urged them onward and downward. They passed a

deserted picket post—Dominic had earlier dismissed the soldier from his duty—and entered the shelter of the pines. Here they paused for a moment to recover their breath, every sense straining. The easy part was over. Now all they had to do was rendezvous with Luke and the horses and slip between the campfires ringing the hill.

Magda's hand tightened in Dominic's. "There is a blackness stalking us," she whispered, staring along the dark trail they had to take. "It knows we are here, and it is very strong."

The first drops of rain spattered at them, sharp as needles and icy-cold. "We are stronger." Dominic held up their joined hands. "Stronger than death." He squeezed. She looked into his eyes and squeezed in return.

They started to pick their way down the slope, following goat trails through the trees, concentrating on keeping on their feet. The sudden flight of an owl from a low branch gave them all a flash of terror. Far more frightening, however, was the moment when the wind died down and they heard the baying of dogs.

"Fine night for a hunt," Guillaume muttered to cover the twist of his stomach as campfire tales of the black hounds of Satan were suddenly not improbable. Too close for comfort, as were the seeking torches. Behind them, the burning trebuchet was still in its death throes, the walls of the barbican illuminated in a weird red light upon which the lightning fed so that the sky burned and rippled like a vast, bronze sheet.

"It isn't far to the horses now," Dominic reassured. He had heard the bravado in Guillaume's voice and knew how close his brother was to the edge of panic, because Dominic himself was closer than he wished to be.

They hastened downward and the path widened. On either side of it were pale tree stumps where the pines had been felled and dragged down the mountain to build stockades and shelters for the besieging troops, and more sinisterly, a compound filled with faggots and brushwood for the purpose of destroying the unrepentant Cathars in the manner decreed.

An abandoned hut stood on the edge of a clearing. Below to the left were more cut trees, but the track to the right was still cloaked in thick forest. Beside the hut, one that Guillaume knew from a long-ago day of innocence and which Magda had known all her life, horsehide gleamed like blackened metal and Luke was waiting, holding the bridles of four restless coursers.

No words were exchanged. In rapid silence they strapped their packs to the saddles and began mounting up. Just as Dominic cupped his palms to boost Magda into the saddle, the first dog bounded into the clearing. Guillaume cried a warning and drew his sword, but even as he raised it, Magda screamed at him to stop.

"If you kill the dog, it will lead them straight to us as surely as if you let it live!" Leaving the horse, she stepped in front of Guillaume, one hand extended, forefinger pointing. The hound, a huge black alaunt, stopped abruptly as if it had struck an invisible wall, and staggered. Soft growls rumbled from deep in its throat. Magda kept her forefinger directed at the center of its skull, and beneath her breath, chanted softly to herself. To the men it sounded like a spell, but it was merely a device to concentrate the power of her mind and make the hound do her will above the will of those who had sent it to track them down.

As the rain started to seethe around them, the creature whined, and tail between its legs, ears flat to its broad skull, slunk sideways and backward, cringing. In a moment the clearing was empty. Magda slowly lowered her arm, then raised it again to press her palm across her forehead. With so much blackness surrounding them, every projection of her life force was so difficult, like rolling a boulder uphill.

"I'm all right," she answered Dominic's anxious query as she returned to her mount. "They will lose our trail from here. No dog will go beyond this point—they will feel the other one's terror and the rain will wash our scent away and make us difficult to see."

Their horses, dark-colored to blend with the night shadows, disappeared into the trees, and when, a few moments later, a group of searchers reached the old Cathar hut in the clearing, the dogs reacted with such terror that their handlers became terrified, too, and without so much as a perfunctory search for tracks and much signing of the cross, they hurried on toward the beacon of fire crowning the mountain.

Panting from his climb and soaked to the skin, Friar Bernard stared with venom-filled eyes at the trebuchet that still burned to defy the rain, and then at the soldiers who had been detailed to search the mountain. All of them were assembled now, close to the summit, and none of them had anything to report, apart from the men who had come up through the clearing and experienced such anxiety that they were convinced the old hut was haunted.

"Fools, they have slipped through!" Bernard said scathingly, eyes flaying the soldiers where they stood. "You did not look hard enough or take enough care. Why should the dogs be afraid unless one of the heretics had cursed them?"

The soldiers shuffled their feet and looked at their muddy boots. If there were curses afoot, they had no intention of putting themselves in jeopardy.

"They have to be stopped; don't you understand?" He turned to Hugh d'Arcis, who was standing to one side, grimly regarding the remains of his trebuchet. "We must set out after them, tonight, immediately. Give me five of your best men, my lord."

D'Arcis chewed his lip and considered. Tomorrow Montségur surrendered. He had to oversee that, not only as a matter of duty, but as a matter of triumph and revenge. He could not lead the pursuit himself as he would have wished. "Yes, take them," he said curtly.

Friar Bernard inclined his head, although there was nothing of respect in his manner, and hunching down into his voluminous black cloak, departed for the camp at the foot of the mountain.

CHAPTER FORTY-EIGHT

OVERHEAD THE STORM was so loud that it drowned out all other sound and feeling. Walking through Montségur, Claire felt it vibrate through her body until she herself was the thunder pursuing the tail of the lightning. She hoped that Magda and Guillaume were safely away from Montségur by now. The beacon in the east barbican was a testament to Dominic's determination, a funeral pyre to mark Raoul's passing. She thought of him, and of her sons, united by a common bond, and found within her a well of ungrieving sadness like the last autumn leaf on a threadbare tree.

Tomorrow the women and children of the garrison would walk out of the gates to the prospect of freedom. So would the Cathars, except that the door to their freedom was fashioned of fire. How long did it take to burn to death? Would she have time to know and scream? It was the false God who was putting such thoughts into her head, urging her to recant, to be free of pain at the peril of her soul. But he would not win. She was too strong!

The women of the garrison were huddled together in a corner of the hall. Sancha, undisturbed by the storm, was sound asleep in Constanza's arms. Constanza herself had been weeping. Although her relationship with Guillaume had been shallow, he had provided well for her and the child, and she had not wanted to lose him. Claire moved on. There would be time for Sancha and Constanza later; for the moment, she was seeking Bridget.

As she gained the battlements, another terrific stab of lightning struck the walls. The thunder this time sent her cowering against a merlon, her hands over her ears. The echoes rolled around the sky, growled and died away to an eerie silence, broken only by the thud of the rain. Heart pounding, Claire regained her feet and went unsteadily along the wall walk to the small platform built on the eastern tower wall to which Bridget had so often gone to view the sunrise and gather her strength.

She was there now, lying on her side within a pentacle of salt. Claire approached, her hands to her mouth. She knew that Bridget was dead, but even so, after she had mastered her first shock, she crouched to make sure and found her still warm, as if the heartbeat had only just ceased.

The wind keened across the battlements, and within the rain there were chips of ice that struck like stones and froze Claire through her threadbare cloak and gown. Vision blurred by tears, she composed the body as best she could and tried to tell herself that it was but a shell; the vital spark, like the lightning itself, had dissipated into infinity.

She became aware of another living presence and, turning, saw Chretien staring at Bridget's body with a great sadness in his dark eyes. "She is with the One Light," he said, a tremor in his rich voice. "I only wish that her parting from this life could have been easier." He laid a comforting hand on Claire's shoulder, and wordlessly she leaned against him like a sapling clinging to the support of an older, stronger tree. They stood like that for a long time. The rain ceased to fall and the sky took on a paler hue behind the mountains to the east. At last there came the sound of the main gate creaking open in surrender to the crusaders and the priests.

Hugh d'Arcis clasped his hands behind his back and examined the two groups of humanity standing in the castle ward. There was not a great deal to choose between them in terms of shabby, gaunt exhaustion. It was difficult at first glance to determine hardened heretic from stray Catholic sheep. The slightly larger group consisted of the men, women, and children of the garrison force who had been led into blasphemous ways but could yet be redeemed by reeducation and penance. A woman near the front of the line was eyeing his soldiers with bold and sultry eyes. On her shoulder a little girl with black, curly hair stared solemnly at the crusaders and sucked her thumb.

The other group faced him not with resignation and fear as he had half-expected, but with a burning certainty that outstripped all ordinary belief, their faces aglow with what he would have sworn was a residue of last night's lightning. For these Perfecti there was not even the glimmer of a doubt. Some of them even held out their wrists for the manacles that the soldiers were roughly clamping upon them.

Their possessions had been stripped from them and thrown into a small heap in the middle of the ward—mostly copies of the Gospels in the vernacular, but the Inquisition would need to examine them before they were burned. There were a few paltry necklaces and bracelets—the Cathars had no belief in adornment, and most had been taken from recent converts who still had sentimental ties with their past. Despite the rumors of fabulous treasure that had abounded throughout the crusader camp during the winter, there was nothing worth plundering.

Leaving the soldiers at their task, d'Arcis wandered through the fortress that had taken him nine months to reduce to surrender, deserted now apart from the captives in the bailey. His footsteps rang hollowly on stone and wooden plank. He paused at a cauldron of gruel, moved on past cramped sleeping quarters of rank straw. The fortnight's truce had permitted the Cathars rations and a degree of decency that they did not deserve. His trust had been abused, hence the manacles. Let them be dragged down the mountainside to their deaths like the gutterdregs they were.

He mounted the wall walk and paced along the battlements. The morning air was sharp after the previous night's cataclysmic storm, but it was scented and soft with spring now as the world turned toward the sun.

Tomorrow they would begin the task of slighting Montségur's great walls, tearing them down until what was left could not pose a threat. Strange how the edifice was oriented to make the most of the sun. It dazzled in his eyes as he reached the end of the wall walk and arrived at the small platform where a woman's body lay. She was middle-aged and thin to the point of being emaciated, but the bone structure of her face was quite beautiful, and her face wore a look of peace. He felt an odd qualm of tender pity, but that was replaced by revulsion as he saw the shape of a pentacle lightning-scorched into the wood. Crossing himself, he backed away and hurried down the stairs onto the main wall walk. That body, too, would have to burn, the sooner the better.

Claire stumbled over the rough stones of the steep descent. She could feel the ground through the worn sides of her sandals, every footstep keen with the pain of contact, of knowing that these were the last steps she would ever take, that her view of the mountains, blue in the spring haze and dark with pines, was her final one of this world. She wanted to stop, to take a moment for farewell, but the guards, in their haste to have the thing over and done and no Cathars to trouble their consciences, hustled them forward with sticks and horsewhips and the flat of sword blades as if their captives were animals being herded to the slaughter.

At her side, Chretien stumbled and fell. Claire stooped to help him, but was dragged brutally away by a young soldier. "Leave him, whore!" he spat in a voice that still grated with adolescence. His eyes were filled with fear. Fear of the inner self, she thought. Strip the covering to reveal the greatest terror of all. Repay hatred with love.

"May you walk in the Light," she said softly to him, and was struck across the face for her benediction. She reeled, clutching her cheek. Abruptly the young crusader jerked Chretien to his feet and shoved him so hard that he almost fell again. "Move!" he snarled at him, and rounded on Claire. "You, too, bitch!" His fingers bruised her arm as he flung her forward.

As they neared the foot of the mountain, the crusaders lined the path, jeering and spitting, running out of line to prod the Cathars with sticks. She saw the black cloaks of the Dominican friars, the gorgeous encrusted silks of a bishop, the blood-red robes of a papal envoy, the altar set up in the open air with its huge cross raised on high for all to see and adore. The stink of the army camp made the smell in Montségur during the last weeks of the siege seem like the sweetest perfume by comparison. Here were the stenches of worldly corruption that she had forgotten during her years on the mountain. Now the recognition flooded back with a taste like bile.

A stockade had been erected using felled, trimmed pines and it had been filled with faggots and brushwood over which priests were sprinkling holy water and soldiers were pouring pitch. Wooden steps led up to a walkway across the top of the stockade, and she saw a man in bishop's robes standing in the center of the walkway beside a crude wooden ladder that led down into the kindling. He waited for his victims, a cross held high before him.

Contempt and terror warred within Claire at this grotesque parody. It would have been too simple for them just to have a gate in the stockade and lead the Cathars in. No, they had to be bound in chains, dragged down the mountain and exhibited to the crusaders, spat upon, jostled and tormented, before mounting a stairway to be symbolically sent downward again to the fires of hell. Did these people not realize that hell was here? That what was coming was release, and that they had failed? No, she thought sadly, they realized nothing.

They were pushed forward, up the stairs to the ladder. When it came her turn to descend into the compound of faggots, pungent with the smell of cut wood and pine pitch, the bishop made the sign of the cross over her head. She looked him in the face and he averted his own gaze with the unease of secret fear. "You have failed," she told him aloud, and set her hands on the sides of the ladder and gladly went to join her fellow Cathars. When the last Perfecti stepped into the stockade, the ladder was drawn up to prevent anyone making a sudden dash for freedom. More than two hundred people stood waiting to die.

The bishop raised his crosier and started to speak, his words full of rhetoric, full of his own importance, of evil and delusion. Claire closed her inner ear and murmured her own simple prayer. She shut her eyes, too, so that she would not have to look upon the image of the cross as she prayed.

The smell of burning invaded her nostrils—not the general aroma of campfires, but the one she had been dreading. *For thine is the kingdom, the power and the glory, for ever and ever, amen ..."* Raising her lids, Claire watched the flames tongue upward above the level of the stockade amid resinous gouts of smoke. A few moments of pain and the waiting would be over. Another woman had told her to inhale the smoke; death would come quickly that way. She repeated the prayer again more loudly and powerfully, crying out for deliverance. And then the smoke snatched her breath and a sudden gust of fire caught the ragged hem of her gown, played with it briefly, and flashed up her body, consuming it. Her lungs filled with fire, her body became a torch. The first seconds of scorching agony were replaced with cool, flowing light that cleansed and smoothed and set a barrier between her and the fires of hatred and ignorance. Her body fell, was charred and twisted by the flames, but Claire de Montvallant was finally free.

CHAPTER FORTY-NINE

DOMINIC FINISHED RUBBING down the horses, threw blankets over their backs, and set about hobbling them for the night. At their tiny campfire, Guillaume busied himself gutting and skewering some trout, while Luke foraged for firewood.

The night was clear, the stars heavy and bright, but with a passive rather than illuminating glitter. Dominic glanced at them and resumed his task. Only this one more night and they would be across the Gascon border. Perhaps then the prickling sensation across his shoulder blades would cease. He had the strangest feeling that they were being followed, but all his checks from heights along the way, all the scrutiny of the other two men, had revealed nothing. Magda was aware of it, too, and he knew that she was not just feeding off his unease.

"Do you want some help?" She joined him even as he thought of her. It was often the way now, the merest spark of mind enough to alert each to the other. Competently she set about hobbling her gelding. The siege had left her painfully thin, but she had still proved capable of traveling at the pace he had set. She never complained, but he knew that he was pushing her hard. She would eat her rations when they stopped for the night, and then be sound asleep within minutes. He would have given her more time if he had been able, but a sense of urgency, of impending disaster, goaded him to travel hard and fast.

She removed the broad-brimmed pilgrim hat that in the daytime concealed her braid of shining hair. He longed to loosen it and feel it silky and cool between his fingers. When she stood up, he could not resist pulling her into his arms and kissing her. She laced her fingers behind his neck and responded with a mute, suppressed hunger the equal of his own. Dominic groaned softly and broke away. He knew that they could satisfy themselves here and now beside the horses. Guillaume and Luke would hardly interrupt them, but amid the stirrings of his body ran a thread of warning, a heightening of the sense of unease. He released her and, thrusting his hands into his belt to resist temptation, looked somberly at Magda. She returned his gaze, a question in her luminous gray eyes.

"When I was eighteen," he said slowly, seeking the words to explain what he felt, "I was impelled to bed with every woman who came my way, be they maiden or married, lady or serf; it did not matter." He shrugged uncomfortably. "I was still seeking the comfort of the breast, I suppose, because of my uncertain childhood."

"So now you are proving your maturity by abstaining?" Magda queried, with a half smile. "Surely you have no need with me?"

"No, it isn't that, you know it isn't. I passed that test a long time ago—with Chretien breathing down my neck," he added wryly.

"Then what?"

"I was a squire at the court of King Louis, and as usual, pulling forbidden fruit off every tree I could find and unashamedly devouring it. . . ." He looked at her sidelong. "One day I was caught with more than just my teeth in one particular apple by an irate husband. I have never forgotten that feeling—turning round and seeing a man wild with righteous fury standing over me with a drawn sword. It is with me now, as if something is just waiting for the moment I drop my guard to take revenge for my stealing what it considers theirs."

Magda shivered. "It is not just the legacy of your past," she said. "I have had similar feelings myself. I believe we were followed from Montségur."

"It is not over yet," Dominic said softly, and cast his eyes toward the blue distance of the mountains.

In a grave mood they returned to the fire and drew close to its welcoming warmth.

"We'll rest the horses for a couple of hours and cross into Gascony tonight," Dominic said to the others as they dined on the trout, flat wheat cakes, and raisins. "Does anyone object?"

As one, Luke and Guillaume shook their heads, and Dominic saw that they, too, were troubled.

Friar Bernard considered the glimmer of light that marked out the heretics' campfire. He could see the figures stretched out on the ground sleeping, the man on guard and the tethered horses. Close now, so close. Like a wolf, he lifted his nose to the wind and he touched the dagger in the sheath at his waist. It was a hunting weapon, a German poniard and full nine inches long. He had prayed over it and purified it in holy water and blessed its wickedly honed edges. Thus he knew that the heretic woman would die, and her knowledge with her. His strength was greater than hers, because his strength came from God. God had told him what he must do.

Unable to sleep, Dominic folded his blanket into a neat bundle for his saddle roll and came to crouch beside the fire where Guillaume was on watch.

"Surely not time already?"

Dominic shook his head. "I couldn't sleep, I'm too much on edge." Picking up a twig, he flicked it into the fire and watched the flames consume it. Then he glanced along the wolfskin collar of his cloak at his half brother. "What will you do now? After this is over, I mean?"

Guillaume moved his shoulders as if shifting a weight that chafed. "I cannot return to Montvallant. I will be branded an outlaw from Marseilles all the way to the cold Narrow Sea for this."

"You would be welcome to make your home on my English lands. French writ does not run there."

"I'd rather not be beholden to a de Montfort for my daily bread," Guillaume said. "Perhaps there might be justice in it somewhere, but I think I'd rather starve."

This time it was Dominic who remained silent, not trusting himself to speak. The bond of blood linking himself and Guillaume was more of a stumbling block than one to mount to a higher understanding.

"It wouldn't work, don't you see?"

"Clearly now," Dominic said coolly. But he knew it was the truth, and after a moment made a wry gesture of acceptance.

"Anyway," said Guillaume, cocking him a look, "I've more or less decided to go with Luke and take Templar vows."

Dominic started to speak, studied Guillaume, and changed his mind. Probably there were more Cathars and Cathar sympathizers among the Templars than there had ever been among the entire population of Montségur, and as Magda said, they were the guardians of the Grail. Not only that, but neither the pope nor the Dominican friars were able to touch them, for they wielded power and influence in all corners of the Christian world and beyond. He turned his mouth down at the corners and nodded slowly in approval.

Magda whimpered in her sleep and tossed, and Dominic turned his head, attention distracted. Guillaume rose and moved restlessly like a caged beast scenting freedom on the breeze.

"She's my half sister, did you know?" he said.

"I suspected it. Fair hair was a rarity in the South until the French came, and to see you together is to know without a doubt." Swept by a feeling of protective tenderness, Dominic stooped beside her.

"Yes," Guillaume muttered with a touch of malice. "You'd think looking at you and me that I was the northerner."

"Skin-deep," Dominic said, refusing to be drawn. "It's what lies in the heart that counts." And he received no satisfaction when he saw Guillaume flinch.

Magda's whimpers grew louder, becoming cries, and her arms and legs thrashed as if she were trying to kick off an assailant. Dominic murmured reassurances, but they were drowned out as she started to scream.

Dark shapes attacked like wolves out of the blackness. Guillaume drew his sword. Luke, roused by Magda's cries, had thrown off his blanket, his weapon already to hand. Dominic covered Magda with his own body to protect her and realized that this was the very position his mind had imagined, except that no lovemaking was involved, and that if he died, it would be for more than just a matter of seconds. Beneath him, Magda's eyes were dark pools of shock and fear.

"They have found us!" she gasped as sparks struck the night and blade met blade and rasped off. Guillaume lunged and was rewarded by a shriek of pain. His attacker staggered backward, tripped on a piece of kindling, and fell heavily into the fire. Smoke gushed in an engulfing, choking cloud and retching coughs came from the combatants.

Dominic hauled Magda to her feet and pulled her toward the horses as Guillaume covered their escape. As they ran, he dragged his own sword from its scabbard. A soldier came at them. Dominic parried, parried, and cut, pulled Magda onward. And then a black shape leaped out at them, body spread to form a black star, a silver gleam at its upper edge. Dominic felt a cold blow against his ribs and heard Magda scream. His nostrils were filled with the musty odor of wool and old incense. The blow, although deflected by his mail, caused him to stagger, and in that moment, Magda was wrenched from him. He saw the glint of steel raised on high and threw himself at her attacker with whiplash speed.

The three of them went down together. Again and again, driven by the assassin's superhuman strength, the razor-edged poniard flailed and struck, flailed and struck, the grip becoming slippery with blood as Dominic strove to disarm the man. At last he succeeded in grabbing the priest's wrist, but Magda screamed, "Let go of him!" in a voice so wild and imperative that against all instinct, he obeyed. He was not fast enough. The first jolt ripped through him as well as his enemy and hurled him backward in a moment of blinding agony.

There was light in his eyes, a blaze of rippling fire, but hotter than flame and colder than ice. Through it he could hear the other man screaming like a wounded rabbit, or perhaps it was he who screamed, or his father beneath the walls of Toulouse. How could a man with a crushed head scream?

The sounds diminished to a weak, hoarse crowing that Dominic could now distinguish as separate from his own harsh breathing. He opened his eyes, squinting because they were still light-dazzled. His hands were deeply gashed and pouring blood. His mail had saved him from worse damage than bruises and the odd pinprick wound. On the ground near him, Friar Bernard still moved weakly, eyes rolled up in blindness, blood frothing from his mouth, and a knife hilt protruding from the center of his breastbone.

"He stabbed himself in his own frenzy," Magda panted shakily. "I turned his own evil back upon himself."

Even as they stared at the priest in appalled horror, he ceased to breathe. The knife hilt trembled one last time and then was still. Magda looked at her blood-soaked gown and then at Dominic's lacerated hands and went convulsively into his arms. They kissed with shock and relief, this time neither of them fighting the wildness. Magda put her hands on his and concentrated until the golden strength flowed through her fingers into his. Her own body was scratched and sore, but the one plunging blow that might have killed her had been turned aside by the dove-and-chalice medallion.

"I felt him stalking us in my sleep," she gasped as they broke apart. "I tried to wake up and warn you, but at first I couldn't! He had me trapped!"

He started to smooth her hair and stopped, conscious of the state of his hands. They were still covered in blood, but it was no longer flooding out of the cuts and there was very little pain.

Guillaume ran up to them. "Jesu, how badly are you hurt?" he demanded. His gaze darted rapidly and with growing concern over Magda's saturated garments and the dark slashes on Dominic's hands. "Jesu!" he said again.

"It looks worse than it is," Magda said quickly to reassure him. "I'm not hurt above a scratch, and Dominic's hands will heal quickly enough. What about you?"

Guillaume pressed his palm to the stitch in his side, and leaned on his sword hilt, which no self-respecting knight would normally do. "Not a mark," he puffed, and suddenly grinned. "They'd been hanging around in an army camp for nine months and their edge was as dull as a rebated blade." He looked over his shoulder at the shambles around the campfire. "Too flabby and well fed to cause Luke and me any problems."

Luke, still gasping, did not possess the wind to disagree as slowly he wiped and sheathed his sword. All he knew was that Guillaume was going to make a formidable addition to the ranks of the Knights Templar.

Guillaume stooped to peer at the dead friar. "I know him," he said with a hint of surprise. "He's a papal inquisitor."

"Do you not remember him from Toulouse?" Dominic asked. "He was the friar who had you arrested outside the Château Narbonnais."

Guillaume shook his head. "They all look alike to me." He cleaned his sword blade on the black cloak.

"Not this one," Dominic said with soft intensity. "He has shadowed my life since I was born, and he'll shadow it still even though he is dead." He took Magda's arm. "We're not going to get any more sleep tonight. Let's ride for Gascony."

CHAPTER FIFTY

England, May 1245

IN A WILLOW basket beneath the apple trees in the garth, the baby opened and closed her fingers, trying to grasp the dappled light filtering through the leaves. By tradition, being only five months old, she ought still to have been swaddled, but Magda would have none of it. Her daughter would know what her hands were for from the very beginning; she would never be confined.

"Anyone would think she was talking to the trees," Dominic

said, sitting down beside his wife on the turf seat. The day was sufficiently warm for him to have discarded his tunic, and he wore only his shirt and hose. Here, in his own pleasance, he could be as casual as it suited him to be. Simon had recently left for the court again, trailing chests of rich garments piled upon staggering sumpter mules and flaunting banners and panoply to suit his station. Dominic much preferred to live a quiet existence on his own lands on the edge of the fens with his wife, his new daughter born at the winter solstice, and the fraternity of masons who shared the castle with them while they constructed Magda's convent.

"She *is* talking to the trees," Magda said. "She can see their life force; it's not just the sun dapples she's trying to hold."

Dominic set his arm across his wife's shoulder and played with the silky end of her braid. Throughout her pregnancy she had blossomed like a rose; indeed, she looked like one now—pink tinted with gold, and glowing with vitality. Bridget's birth had come in the depths of an iron-hard winter, but it had been smooth and easy, without complication, and the child herself was a source of constant delight. Dominic did not believe that he could ever be more content, these moments given clarity and a depth of feeling beyond expression by the trauma of what had gone before.

Magda leaned into his touch and watched the shadows of leaf and sunlight, the blending ripples of his aura and hers and the baby's. "What if I told you that I was descended from the Magdalene?"

Dominic shrugged. "Then she must have been very beautiful."

"Seriously . . ."

"It would make no difference to me were you to claim Hecate herself for your great-grandam. It is you I care for, not your ancestors."

"But they have bequeathed my bloodline some strange and dangerous gifts."

Dominic spread his hands. They bore the fading scars of a madman's dagger. "I'll admit to that, but I still say it matters not to me."

She held his gaze. "Not just the Magdalene. She was married to James, brother of the Christ, and her children were the grandchildren of the Virgin Mary. The bloodline continues with our daughter."

Involuntarily his eyes went to the gurgling infant. "You must have proof," he said, "or the priests would not have been so determined to silence you."

"Oh, yes." Magda nodded. "As you have seen yourself, I have the texts from Montségur. There is a copy of a Gospel written by the Magdalene herself. Her family were persecuted, so she and her children fled to southern Gaul. At first they were hounded for being Christians, and then, in later generations, as the power of the Roman church grew, for being heretics and proclaimers of blasphemy. A branch of the family fled across the Narrow Sea to Britain. My mother was the surviving member of that branch. As you can see," she said with a tender look at the baby, "the line usually runs to girls. Each generation is taught to use their gifts for good—for helping and healing." Her gray eyes grew somber. "And for that we are hunted down and branded as witches and whores." Bending, she raised her daughter out of the basket and kissed her soft, dark hair. "It has to be nurtured quietly, in this generation at least, and perhaps for a long time to come."

Dominic lifted on his forefinger the dove-and-chalice medallion she wore over her gown. "So you are the Grail," he mused. "Yes, I see that, the bearer of the holy blood, the cup of grace." He turned the medallion over. "And I am the spear?" His eyes glinted with wry humor. "I suppose that, too, is fitting."

Magda lowered her eyes, her skin suddenly a warmer pink at the intimate note in his voice.

"The bloodline is safe in my hands," he said as he laid the medallion gently back against her gown. "They have been scarred and mutilated enough to prove it, and I'm a part of it now, in flesh and blood and spirit." He held out his forefinger and his daughter curled her own small fist around it and gave him a beaming smile.

They sat on in the garden while the day mellowed around them and the sun changed its angle, creating around the three of them a golden nimbus of light.

AUTHOR'S NOTE

READERS OF MY novels often ask me how much of what I write is historical fact. I tell them to imagine that my book is a tapestry. The real events and people form the backdrop on which I weave the colors of my story using my own characters and imagination. So, how much of *Daughters of the Grail* is embroidery, and how much is historical truth?

During the twelfth and thirteenth centuries in Europe, there was a growing dissatisfaction with the established church. People thought that priests had become too corrupt and worldly. Religious sects whose aim was to "get back to basics" proliferated. Some, such as the Dominican movement, or the Franciscans, had the sanction of the Catholic Church. The pope understood that there was a place for reform, as long as it was under Rome's control. The Cathars did not conform to that philosophy; indeed, they rejected it outright and thus were viewed as heretics and a threat to order.

The Cathars were dualists. They believed in two deities. In very general terms, this meant that they worshiped a good God, benevolent and far removed from the lusts and turbulence of the world. They also believed that he had an evil counterpart—Rex Mundi—who presided over everything that was fleshly and materialistic. Rex Mundi, as his Latin title suggests, was "King of the World" and can be very roughly equated with the God of the Old Testament.

Cathars believed that each time a human infant was conceived, a pure spirit was dragged away from the realm of the good God and forced to enter the flesh of the child. Thus the spirit became trapped and gradually, because of the contamination of its earthly life, forgot its pure origins and became bogged down in the sins of the flesh. Only by living an exemplary life could the spirit return to its pure, unfettered origins. This involved for the Cathars the taking of strict, almost monastic vows. A commited Cathar was celibate, vegan in diet, and owned no possessions. At a time when a chronicler could say of a leading Catholic bishop that "his heart was a bank," the ordinary people were only too keen to look to the Cathars for their spiritual comfort.

The Catholic Church denounced the Cathars whose rituals were simple and whose methods of worship it viewed as downright blasphemous. Cathars, for example, worshiped wherever they gathered, not in a place especially consecrated for prayer. Women were allowed to become priests. They did not believe in baptism or marriage, and saw the idea of Christ suffering on the cross to redeem everyone's sins as both untrue and abhorrent. Their ideas were so different from those of the established Church that they were bound to come into conflict with its officials. But it was not until the Cathar movement began to gather enough devotees to threaten the power of Rome, that the pope decided to act.

The lords of what is today southern France were tolerant to Catharism. They had a more liberal outlook than their northern European counterparts, and allowed Cathars, Jews, and Moslems to flourish in their communities. Their culture and society still bore vestiges of the rule of the Roman Empire, and they spoke a different language from the North—Occitan. Through trading links with the Mediterranean and the East, they were a wealthy, cosmopolitan people. Theirs was the land of troubadours, culture, and courtly love. The rougher, northern lords coveted such a lifestyle for themselves.

It was almost inevitable that the South's wealth, allied to its religious tolerance, should bring its lords to grief. Pope Innocent III tried to bully them into purging their towns and villages of the Cathars. When rejected, he called a crusade that the warlords of northern Europe were only too delighted to join.

The soldier who led the crusaders to victory after victory over the southern armies was Simon de Montfort, a French baron who had a hunger for land and the fighting skills to take it. A superb and energetic general, he seized control of much of the Languedoc, dispossessing its existing ruling houses to do so.

He was killed in 1218 beneath the walls of Toulouse, and as mentioned in *Daughters of the Grail*, he was indeed struck a direct hit on the skull by a missile from a stone-throwing machine operated by a woman.

The atrocities of the Cathar war were also taken from history. The entire population of Béziers was massacred, a total of between ten and fifteen thousand men, women, and children, Cathar and Catholic alike. Geralda of Lavaur was thrown into a well and stoned to death. In other captured towns, Cathars were burned in the hundreds.

The final stand of Catharism in southern France took place at Montségur, a castle built upon a mountain in the Pyrenean foothills. Much has been written about the castle, the siege, and the mystery surrounding the Cathars. Rumors abound that they were in possession of a fabulous treasure. This has variously been interpreted as consisting of the treasure of the temple of Solomon, or perhaps priceless books full of esoteric and cabalistic lore. There is even a story that the Cathars were the guardians of the holy bloodline of Jesus Christ. Whatever the truth of such matters, the Catholic Church was determined that the Cathars of Montségur be exterminated.

Following a siege lasting nine months, the garrison surrendered. More than two hundred Cathars were led down the mountainside to a field, and there they were burned to death en masse.

A memorial stone stands there now. Fresh flowers and wreaths adorn its base. The people of the Languedoc still remember. I have climbed the mountain myself in the course of my research and have explored what remains of the walls. There is a stillness and silence about the place, a tranquility that belies its bloody past, and from its diminished battlements, the Pyrenees stretch beyond the eye's reach, their colors as chameleon as the moods of the sky.

Daughters is a work of fiction, but for those who want to know more about the Cathars and the Albigensian Crusade, as it came to be known, I include a brief bibliography of some of the books I found useful to me in the course of my research.

Elizabeth Chadwick, Nottingham, England 1995

BIBLIOGRAPHY

Baigent, Michael, Richard Leigh, and Henry Lincoln. *The Holy Blood and the Holy Grail.* Jonathan Cape, 1982.

Birks, Walter, and R. A. Gilbert. *The Treasure of Montségur.* Aquarian Press, 1987.

Christie-Murray, David. *A History of Heresy.* New English Library, 1976.

Foss, Michael. *Chivalry.* Michael Joseph, 1975.

Guirdham, Arthur. *The Cathars and Reincarnation.* C. W. Daniel, 1990.

Hallam, Elizabeth, ed. *Chronicles of the Crusades.* Weidenfeld & Nicolson, 1989.

Labarge, Margaret Wade. *Simon de Montfort.* Cedric Chivers, 1972.

Ladurie, Emmanuel le Roy. *Montaillou: Cathars and Catholics in a French Village 1294–1324.* Scolar, 1978.

Paul, Richard. "Heresy and Holy War in Languedoc." France Magazine, Spring 1990.

Riley-Smith, Jonathan. *The Atlas of the Crusades.* Guild Publishing, 1991.

Strayer, Joseph R. *The Albigensian Crusades.* Dial, 1971.

Sumption, Jonathan. *The Albigensian Crusade.* Faber, 1978.

Wakefield, W. L. *Heresy, Crusade and Inquisition in Southern France 1100–1250.* Allen & Unwin, 1974.

Walker, Barbara. *The Women's Dictionary of Symbols and Sacred Objects.* Harper & Row, 1988.

Walker, Benjamin. *Gnosticism: Its History and Influence.* Aquarian Press, 1983.

ELIZABETH CHADWICK

Published by Ballantine Books.
Available in your local bookstore.